FINAL CURTAIN

Books by R. T. Jordan

REMAINS TO BE SCENE

FINAL CURTAIN

Published by Kensington Publishing Corporation

FINAL CURTAIN

A Polly Pepper Mystery

R. T. Jordan

KENSINGTON BOOKS
www.kensingtonbooks.com

KENSINGTON BOOKS are published by

Kensington Publishing Corp.
850 Third Avenue
New York, NY 10022

All Kensington titles, imprints, and distributed lines are available at special quantity discounts for bulk purchases for sales promotion, premiums, fund-raising, educational, or institutional use.

Special book excerpts or customized printings can also be created to fit specific needs. For details, write or phone the office of the Kensington Special Sales Manager: Attn. Special Sales Department, Kensington Publishing Corp., 850 Third Avenue, New York, NY 10022. Phone: 1-800-221-2647.

Kensington and the K logo Reg. U.S. Pat. & TM Off.

Library of Congress Card Catalogue Number: 2007934398
ISBN-13: 978-0-7582-1282-5
ISBN-10: 0-7582-1282-8

First Printing: February 2008
10 9 8 7 6 5 4 3 2 1

Printed in the United States of America

For Patricia Elizabeth and Benjamin Pitman Jordan

Acknowledgments

Hooray for Hollywood? Hmm. Writing this novel took me on another of Mr. Toad's Wild Rides through this weird town in which I live and work. Fantasyland? Indeed!

My unlimited gratitude goes to Kensington Publishing's illustrious editor in chief, John Scognamiglio, who lets me take these far-fetched journeys in the first place.

For research I interviewed Karen Morrow, who provided fascinating stories about her career starring on Broadway and in national musical tours. Carole Cook and Tom Troupe were indispensable for their always hilarious behind-the-scenes-in-show-business anecdotes. Chris Gasti regaled me with tales of being on the road with Mitzi Gaynor (an authentic Polly Pepper!). Dinner table conversations in the homes of gracious hosts Jane A. Johnston, Jackie Joseph and David Lawrence, and Judy and Don Bustany are always a source for further fabrication in books.

Thanks also to my super-duper agent, Joelle Delbourgo (whom I *must* meet one day). My handy-dandy support team includes the ever-popular and hugely talented Kevin Howell, Julia Oliver, Pat Kavanagh, Cathy and Randy Wharton, Bob and Jakki Jordan, Gayle Willman, Andrew W.M. Beierle, Robin Blakely, Chris O'Brien, J. Randy Taraborrelli, Richard Klein, Gary Correa, Laura Levine, Carolyn See, Rick Copp, Marcela Landres, Steven Smith, Richard Ostlund and Don Mueller, and Karlyn Hayle. A special note of thanks to Mr. Billy Barnes, who gives the world the gift of music, and me the gift of clean laundry.

Forever and throughout eternity: Dame Muriel Pollia, Ph.D.

Television has brought back murder into the home—where it belongs.

Alfred Hitchcock

Chapter 1

"I'm just a Broadway Baby," television musical/comedy legend Polly Pepper began to sing in a strong, cheerful voice as she pressed the Off button on her cordless telephone and placed the handset on her concert grand piano. She performed an impromptu soft-shoe across the carpeted floor of the great room at Pepper Plantation, her Bel Air mansion. With a smile as wide as the Wal-Mart happy face on a price-busting day, Polly skipped and twirled and finished the song, belting out "... in a great ... big ... Broad-way ... show-oh." She held the last note for a long moment, long enough to grab the attention of her still-living-at-home adult son, Tim, who rushed into the room.

"Did I hear 'Broadway'? You got a show?"

"Yep!" Polly opened her arms and hugged the light of her life. "But I'm more of a Broadway *maybe*," she amended.

"Out-of-town tryout?" Tim pressed.

Polly nodded. "Sorta."

Polly's maid and best friend, Placenta, had also heard the commotion and rushed to her employer's side just in time to hear the words "Broadway" and "maybe." Her brown eyes locked with Polly's blue ones. "Let me guess. Your smart-ass agent J.J. booked your usual summer gig and says there's a *chance* this one may crawl into New York?"

Polly waited for Placenta's other accusatory shoe to drop.

"Sure. And there's a *chance* that Harry Connick Jr. will let me iron his underpants."

Polly made a face and whined, "For once in your life, try to practice positive thinking. Be happy for me. For you too. These summer tours pay your salary. Musical revivals are all the rage on Broadway, and J.J. says that he's heard through the grapevine that if this production is half as good as expected, I can end up on a billboard over Times Square!"

Tim folded his arms across his chest. "A revival? What moth-eaten show are they *dragging* out this season? *La Cage Au Folles?*"

"Getting warm," Polly said.

"*Hello, Dolly!? Mame?*"

"Bingo." Polly clapped her hands. "Four solid weeks in one of my all-time favorite roles! You're too young to remember, but I was a sensation as the Belle of Beekman Place when I played the Music Tent in Manassas."

"A quarter century ago," Placenta reminded her.

"The critics stumbled all over their typewriter keys to find superlatives to describe my performance," Polly countered.

"What's a typewriter?" Tim teased.

"And don't forget that split week in Little Rock. Audiences cried when I was suddenly widowed by John Davidson."

"Because they were stuck with you and Rita Moreno onstage for the rest of the night," Placenta said. "And where, pray tell, does New York fit into this improbable dream?"

Polly hesitated. "All I know is the new Sondheim show is apparently so depressing it's actually scaring away the Broadway tourist trade. They need a fun and familiar place-holder at the Palace Theatre until *Snakes on a Plane—The Musical* opens in February. The producers are looking at

Mame. Please, dear Lord, let me get to Broadway before God brings down the curtain on my life."

For reasons beyond her control, starring on The Great White Way eluded Polly. Over the years, four musicals had been written expressly for her, but they either closed in Boston or fell apart while in rehearsal.

Now, as Tim watched his mother's joy turn to self-doubt, he decided to act as if she were a Tony Award winner. "Another op'ning, another show . . ." he sang and faked a wild and crazy Steve Martin–esque tap dance over to the wine cooler.

"Hold your hats and hallelujah, Polly's gonna show it to you," Placenta sang a lyric from "Rose's Turn." "Broadway, here we come," she announced, helping to cheer the atmosphere. "By way of—"

"Em, Glendale," Polly reluctantly admitted. "We're at the Galaxy Theatre for the summer."

Tim and Placenta both stared at Polly.

Glendale, California, had only one thing to recommend it: Forest Lawn Cemetery, which boasted the remains of more stars than there were on the devil's rotisserie spit. After one had seen the celebrity homes in Beverly Hills, and found their favorite stars' names embedded on the Hollywood Boulevard Walk of Fame, the natural progression was to visit the plots and vaults where their famous bodies or ashes were dumped. Forest Lawn was a tranquil plot of acreage where, among the sweeping lawns and clusters of evergreen trees, headstones served as reminders that Clark Gable, Carole Lombard, Humphrey Bogart, Jimmy Stewart, and even Walt Disney—who everyone knew was collecting freezer burn somewhere in the bowels of Disneyland—all had expiration dates on their passports to earth. Otherwise, Glendale was the sort of town where the residents considered the Olive Garden fine dining.

"I know it's not Boston or Chicago, or San Francisco," Polly said. "But it's a job."

Despite the grim prospect of having to spend his summer shuttling Polly to and from work each day, Tim tried to sound enthusiastic. "You'll kill the audiences," he said as he pulled out a cold bottle of Veuve Clicquot from the cooler. "Placenta," he said, "call Wolfy and reserve our usual table. We need to celebrate." Tim was actually pleased for his mother, but was also delighted that he wouldn't have to spend the hottest part of the year sweltering in St. Louis, or Kansas City, where Polly usually toured during the summer.

Polly smiled as she once again began to feel that her career was on the upswing. "My personal psychic at Futuretense-dot-com recently e-mailed me and said that after all the dark shadows and negative energy that have stalked *moi* during the past few months—what with dead movie stars cluttering up my last film location—it's definitely time for a big shift in my planetary fortunes."

"Famous people die just like run-of-the-mill folk." Tim popped the cork from the champagne bottle. "This is Hollywood. Everyone knows a killer or two."

"But they're usually agents and personal publicists," Placenta said.

As Tim poured three flutes of champagne he added, "You've had your once-in-a-lifetime encounter with real-life blood and guts—if you don't count that week on your show working with Vicki Lawrence—and you lived to tell about it. The fact that you're now the main topic of conversation at every cocktail crush in town is publicity you could never afford to buy. The notoriety is money at the theater box office."

"I admit there were moments when tracking down the killer was actually fun," Polly said. "But it was scary too. Like Faye Dunaway's new face. Still, I've promised that I'd never interfere with police work again."

Polly was suddenly quiet as she considered her pledge to the new man in her life, Detective Randal Archer. After years of self-imposed exile from romance, Polly met Detective Archer during the investigation into the murder of television legend and her archrival, Sedra Stone.

Tim raised his glass and the trio simultaneously clinked their Waterford crystal flutes together. "To the legendary Polly Pepper and best Auntie Mame ever," he began. "As you descend on Glendale, may all the bodies you encounter be breathing . . . and holding tickets to see Polly Pepper live onstage!"

Polly gave her son a playful shove. "Slaughtering an audience is what I do best, dear. It's why I get the big bucks." She paused. "Although they certainly are tight with a dollar at the theater. J.J. said that with the exception of a piano and a couple of strings and percussion, the orchestra is canned. The sets are mere suggestions for the imagination. There's no budget for new costumes either. I'm stuck with Kathie Lee Gifford's stinky wardrobe from the road company of *The Vagina Monologues*."

Placenta took a long sip of her drink and asked, "Who else is in the cast?"

Polly furrowed her eyebrows as she tried to recall. "A couple of soap opera stars, I think. Never heard of 'em, but apparently they're dying to work with me."

"You can recall verbatim entire paragraphs from old reviews, but you can't remember what J.J. said about your cast just a few moments ago?" Tim complained. "For the role of the adult Patrick Dennis, please tell me it's Trent Dawson from *As the World Turns*! Or better yet, Don Diamont from *The Young and the Restless*! Ooh! Make that Paul Satterfield from *One Life to Live*! I think I'm going to love working in the theater again."

Polly and Placenta looked at each other and nodded, knowing that Tim would be in love before the first week of rehearsal was over.

Tim giggled. "It's about time that Andy Hardy found romance again, or at least a summer fling. You have a sexy police detective. I'll settle for a *Days of Our Lives* soap stud."

* * *

As had become her custom before leaving home to go to work, Polly Pepper stood in the center of the great room of her mansion and took a nostalgic look at the awards displayed on lighted glass shelves. "Lord, forget about keeping your eye on the sparrow. Keep 'em both open wide on my Emmys," she prayed, as a wave of separation anxiety washed over her.

It was late June, and Polly was heading out for what she euphemistically called her "mortgage tour." Although this time she was only going a few miles to Glendale, she generally traveled to regions of the country where, thanks to perennial rebroadcasts on local cable stations of her classic '80s television variety show, Polly Pepper was still a star.

Beyond the age to believably play a virginal singing nun-turned-nanny, and tired of working alongside smudgy and obnoxious little girls as moppet orphans, Polly would own the stage this year as Mame Dennis Burnside, one of theater's most enduring roles for a star of a certain age. She dismissed the denunciation of her few critics who, upon hearing that Polly Pepper had been cast in this classic, bellowed, "The role must be played by a great lady—like Angela Lansbury. Polly's a clown!"

But being a clown was what made Polly famous in the first place. No one made audiences laugh at everyday situations and the absurdities of life the way Polly Pepper did. Throngs of devoted fans would surely drop their barbecue briquettes on a hot summer's night and drive to the theater to see her cavorting onstage. At least that was the hope of the Glendale Civic Light Opera.

Polly looked at her wristwatch and sighed. In a few minutes Tim would honk the horn of Polly's Park Ward Rolls-Royce and whisk her over the hill to the theater. She squared her shoulders and blew a kiss to the room. "Be good while Mommy's away," she whispered, and closed the door behind her.

The drive from Bel Air to Glendale was hardly a whisk. In Southern California, every hour is rush hour, and when Tim finally found the theater the parking lot was full. He let his mother and Placenta out at the curb and he went in search of a space to park on the street. As Polly ascended the steps and walked into the forecourt of the old theater, she was reminded of being in an ancient Egyptian temple. "They don't make theaters like this one anymore," she said to Placenta, who walked slightly ahead of Polly and pulled open the entry door.

Entering the lobby, Polly stopped for a moment to look around and absorb the intoxicating scent and feeling that she always embraced when working in a theatrical shrine.

Polly's euphoria was abruptly shattered, however, when Gerold Goss, the theater's artistic director, appeared from the men's room. Upon suddenly seeing Polly, he began yelling. "You're four hours late! Just because you're the famous Polly Pepper doesn't give you the right to treat the rest of the cast with disrespect. Their time is just as valuable as yours!"

Polly was stunned. She looked at her wristwatch. "Honey, I'm five minutes *early*. It's only quarter to two!" she stuttered. "Everyone knows that I'm the most prompt star in Hollywood."

Gerold ground his teeth and the veins at his neck began to pulsate. "Rehearsal from *ten to two* does not mean *one-fifty*!"

Polly was mortified. "Ten to two. Ha!" she laughed. "I thought it meant starting at ten minutes to two."

"No one has your phone number!" Gerold growled. "Your agent wouldn't return my calls! It occurred to me that at your age you might be dead. Wishful thinking!"

"My *age*? I'm expressing my deep regret to you for the little misunderstanding, and promise that it will never happen again. But I'm a little concerned about your imperious attitude." She squared her shoulders. "Stars are people too. Sometimes we make mistakes. I'm sorry and I won't be tardy again. Mea culpa already!"

Polly turned to leave. "If you'll kindly direct me to the rehearsal room, I'd like to express my apologies to the director and the rest of the cast."

"They're all on the stage," Gerold yelled as Polly began to rush away. "You and other over-the-hill stars should be on your knees giving thanks for another chance to be in a show. I didn't even want you for this role. Now you act like a diva! There's no place in the theater for ego!" He turned and stormed away in the opposite direction. As he retreated, he nearly collided with Tim, who had just entered the theater lobby.

Polly was now in a panic and rushed for the double doors to the auditorium. "That damn J.J. gave us the wrong schedule," she called back to Tim, who, along with Placenta, was following at Polly's heels.

"Your mama's just been given thirty lashes from that schmo Gerold Goss," Placenta said. "Seems we were supposed to be here from ten this morning until two in the afternoon."

"I thought the call time was odd," Tim said, trying to catch up to his mother, who went barreling into the auditorium.

Polly rushed down the aisle and threw out her arms as she called out, "Everybody! Everybody! I'm mortified that I missed our first day! Please, please forgive me! I'm never ever late for anything, especially anything as important as work!" When she arrived at the stage, the entire cast stood to greet her. Now out of breath, Polly clutched her chest and walked up to Karen Richards, the director. "Ms. Richards," she panted, "this is a horrible way to begin our relationship. Please don't be harsh on me. You'll see that I'm the most professional artist with whom you'll ever work. I promise."

Karen smiled warmly and shook her head. "Not a problem, Miss Pepper. First of all, I'm your most ardent admirer." She reached out to shake Polly's hand. "In fact my college thesis was an examination of your amazing career. I even have the boxed DVD collector's edition of the first season of *The Polly Pepper Playhouse*. I'm dying for the next season to be released."

Polly exhaled a deep sigh of relief.

Karen continued. "You've played this role exactly three hundred and seventy-seven times over the years. All to rave reviews. You missed one little rehearsal today. I'm not at all concerned. Let me introduce you to your cast."

Karen knew precisely how to treat divas in order to induce mutual trust and respect. In Polly's case, however, Karen was a genuine fan. She had set out on her career path with the mission of one day working with Polly Pepper. This was her golden moment. "This is Emily Hutcherson, our Vera Charles and your 'bosom buddy,'" Karen said as she singled out Emily from the group.

Both actresses smiled and shook each other's hand. "Lovely to meet you, Emily," Polly said. "You know you really have the best role in the show."

"It's not the lead," Emily said through gritted teeth.

"No, it's not, honey." Polly returned Emily's frosty greeting.

Karen continued. "Marshall Nash is our Beauregard. Sharon Fletcher is Gloria Upson. Charlotte Bunch will be playing Agnes Gooch. Hiroaki Goldfarb is Ito. And here's little Ward Stewart, your adorable nephew Patrick." As Karen introduced the entire principle cast, Polly was overwhelmed by their graciousness. No one other than Emily Hutcherson seemed to mind that the star had nearly missed the entire first day. However, she again apologized to each of them for her untoward and totally out-of-character behavior.

Karen looked at her watch. "Okay, gang," she said.

"Thanks for a terrific first day." She glanced at Polly. "I'll see all of you back here tomorrow at *ten* A.M."

As the cast collected their cell phones and car keys, they each welcomed Polly again with handshakes. Part of Tim's job was to pay attention to the people his mother met in business and social situations. She was notorious for her inability to remember the names of anyone who wasn't a star. However, as Polly made small talk with her cast, Tim's peripheral vision picked up something interesting. Instantly his gaze was riveted to a muscled stud in a tank top leaning against the auditorium wall and who seemed to be intently observing all the action onstage. For Tim, the world instantly came to a freeze-frame stop. However, the planet abruptly began to spin again when director Karen Richards walked up the aisle, kissed the god, and left the theater with him linked in her arm. Tim's heart sank as deep as the *Titanic*.

When most of the other actors had left the stage, Sharon Fletcher, who was cast as bubblehead Gloria Upson, approached Polly. "Miss Pepper?" she said.

Polly looked up and smiled. "Please, dear, call me Polly. And you are . . . ?"

"We met a moment ago. I'm Sharon. Fletcher. I'm engaged to your nephew, Patrick, but of course I'm the wrong woman for him, and you'll get rid of me." She laughed.

A light dawned on Polly. "Didn't I see you on *Hygiene of the Stars*?"

Sharon blushed. "That's awfully sweet of you. I mean a great big star like you knowing about little ol' me and my unique flossing technique. I'm flattered. I just wanted to tell you how happy I am that I get to work on the same stage with you. Wait'll I e-mail my dad, who thinks you walk on water. Oh, I hope I'm not being sacrilegious! I just mean that he worships you. I do too, of course."

Polly was instantly captivated by the pretty, young actress. She assessed Sharon and instantly decided that her blond hair was natural, as were the two substantial breasts, which nested in her pink cashmere sweater. "Shelley," Polly said, "I feel terrible that I've never seen your daytime drama, *One Life*—"

"Weather," she corrected. "And it's Sharon."

Polly looked puzzled.

"*It's **Never** Fair Weather*," Tim translated for Polly, as he held out his hand to Sharon and gushed, "I'm Polly's son. Wow! I watch your show all the time. This is very cool. Where's your husband, Troy?" He looked around.

Sharon sniggered. "That's just on the show, silly. But Heart—the real name of the guy who plays Troy—is one of my best friends. He'll be around and I promise to introduce you," she said, as she looked Tim up and down.

Now it was Tim's turn to blush. "I'm not usually starstruck, but Troy, er, Heart is—"

"Tell me about it," Sharon interrupted. "Even I'm in awe of his looks. As a matter of fact, *he's* in awe too." She and Tim shared a laugh.

Polly chimed in. "Sharon, honey, if you're not booked for dinner this evening, why don't you come to our little place? You can fill me in on what I missed today. And give me a rundown on everybody else in the cast. I'm still feeling abominable for the screwup. It was my agent's fault."

"Ach! Agents! You can't work without 'em and you can't kill 'em. I was negotiated out of the role of Lois Lane when my brilliant agent insisted on more money than Warner Brothers was willing to pay. I should have had Kate Bosworth's agent. Oh, and I'd be absolutely thrilled to have dinner with you!"

Polly acted as though she were the grateful one. "Everyone seems so darn nice around here," she said. "Except Gerold Goss, of course."

"Oh, him," Sharon said with a shake of her head. "He

stormed in this morning and began cursing at poor Karen. What a temper! He backhanded a can of Coke on the table and sent it flying into Hiroaki's lap. Anyway, from the way Karen and Gerold were acting you'd think they were either lovers or mortal enemies. I figured one of them would murder the other. He's too weird."

Chapter 2

It didn't take more than one bottle of Moët for Polly, Placenta, and Sharon to become new best girlfriends. As Placenta served her famous salmon tortilla appetizer, and Tim kept the glasses filled, Polly the primetime TV legend and Sharon the daytime drama star found that they had much in common. Sharon described her brief marriage to an actor who had a fear of disappointing his fans—so he slept with all of them.

"I had a lousy starter marriage too," Polly sighed. "The second Mr. Pepper turned out to be a variation on the same ol' theme of the bluebird of happiness crapping in my wig."

"Third time's a charm," Sharon insisted, and raised her glass to Polly's future. "Just don't go looking for true love in L.A.," she added. "I have a theory. The San Andreas Fault shakes out all the quality men and leaves the losers behind. They end up working in show business."

While Polly laughed she also thought about her new relationship with Beverly Hills police detective Randal Archer. Polly reluctantly admitted to herself that she, Tim, and Placenta were far from successful in their quest of Olympic gold in the mating marathon.

Sharon raised her glass again. "Don't get me wrong

about the seismological activities separating the wheat from the chaff. There's a lot of good-looking rubbish in this town! And on a lonely night, I don't mind a little trash for company!"

Tim and Placenta both hailed, "Amen!" and clinked their glasses together. The unspoken consensus at Pepper Plantation was that having another bright woman in the house, especially one as down-to-earth as Sharon Fletcher, who had a bawdy sense of humor that matched Polly's, was a refreshing change from the sycophants who were afraid of saying something of which Polly might not approve.

Polly took another long sip of champagne and took an even longer look at her guest. "Dear, with your Nicole Kidman skin and Bambi-like eyelashes, not to mention your Pamela Anderson boobs, don't sit there and tell me you're not a magnet for the crème de la crème of eligible gazillionaires! The first time down the aisle you're allowed to marry for love. After that, one must go for all the perks that come with the package of being a trophy wife."

Sharon gave Polly a wink of her eye. "Trust me, I'm trawling. I can't do the soap diva thing forever. Susan Lucci I'm not! Did you see me in *People* magazine last month? I'm this close to reeling in that cute philanthropist who escorted me to the opening of the Mel Gibson wing of the Museum of Tolerance." Sharon raised her glass to herself and clinked champagne flutes with her hosts.

"Enough about my personal life," said Sharon. "You invited me here to rag about the rest of your cast. I'll say this much—watch out for your costar, Emily Hutcherson. When you didn't show up for rehearsal today, that gorilla Gerold Goss announced that Emily would replace you. The moment you came through the doors, she morphed from a beaming supernova to a woolly mammoth trapped in a glacier."

Polly sat in silence for a moment. As a certifiable legend, she wasn't used to having to watch her back around actors of lesser celebrity. "Thanks for the 411," Polly said. "What about the others? And what about our divine director? What's your take?"

Sharon held out her glass for another refill, and considered the question as Tim poured. "I Googled Karen. She's directed tons of rep and regional theater. Trained at Yale. Turned down *Steppenwolf* and the Geffen Playhouse to work in Glendale. Seems genuinely lovely. Strong but confident enough not to be mean. Of course this was only day one. By day two, everything could change. By the way, you'll undoubtedly see the hottest man on the planet hanging around the theater. He's Karen's boyfriend, Jamie. They're trying to keep a low profile but doing a terrible job of it."

"I caught their act this afternoon," Tim said.

"Oh, and the guy who plays your rich southern suitor, Beauregard—his name is Marshall Nash—he's a bit more conceited than the average aging thespian," Sharon continued. "He starred on that short-lived cable daytime drama, *Sins of the Father*, until he was written out by way of an altar boy uprising. Imagine drowning in a challis of Gallo red? Now he mostly does dinner theater in Maine. Decent singing voice—as he'll be the first to tell you." Sharon shook her head and added with incredulity, "But, Polly! You know everybody in the business. Surely you've worked with these people before!"

Polly waved a hand and sighed. "I know a million people, and have worked with a trillion more. But it seems that as I get older my professional circle shrinks. I used to be able to rattle off the names of every Emmy Award winner. Now I can't keep up with today's fifteen-minute celebrities. However, I do know Charlotte Bunch, our Agnes Gooch. She's a decent character actor. An obnoxious Chatty Cathy, but I can put up with her for a few weeks. She'll make an excellent Gooch."

Polly noticed that Sharon twisted her mouth. "What? Something about Charlotte?"

Sharon shrugged. "Oh, it's probably nothing."

"I've known Charlotte for years," Polly said. "We're not joined at the hip, but she's on my Christmas card list. I think."

"Well, it's like this." Sharon scooted over to be closer to Polly. "When it looked like you were going to be a no-show today, and after Gerold made his casting change announcement, Charlotte and Emily got into an argument over who should replace you as Mame. Emily thought that she was the logical choice for the role, and Charlotte disagreed, saying that because of being a regular on some sitcom ages ago, she herself was actually the more famous and therefore better marquee value."

Polly made a face. "Yeah, maybe she'd be swell as Miss Hannigan in a Jehovah's Witness Kingdom Hall production of *Annie in Armageddon*, but she's all wrong for the part of Mame. Funny, yes. Sings a little. Dances somewhat. But she has no grace, no sophistication. She's most famous for that Jack In The Box TV commercial. Remember? After the E. coli outbreak she played an irascible customer who orders the Biggie Burger with special sauce and barks, 'And hold the crap!'"

"That all-purpose phrase made her famous for a while," Placenta said.

"Charlotte doesn't have the ethereal quality that Angie Lansbury carries so effortlessly," Polly continued. "Nah. She's nuts if she thinks she'd be any good in the lead role."

Sharon drained what remained of her glass of champagne. "Just wanted you to be aware of the parade of loonies who await you tomorrow. And they're not all in the cast. I suppose you know that Gerold Goss didn't even want you in the show, but when the theater's subscribers were polled, you in *Mame* won out over Kathryn Crosby in *When Pigs Fly*, and Debby Boone in *Urinetown*."

Polly's jaw dropped and her eyes popped. "It was a toss-up between me and a dead legend's wife, and a wannabe legend's daughter? For crying out loud, who did that swine Gerold really want for his theater? Ruta Lee as Heidi?"

"Try Howie Mandell in *Hairspray*. But don't worry, Polly," Sharon cooed, "Karen is totally committed to you and the show. And speaking of our show, we've got an early morning call. I'd better drag my weary butt back home."

Polly and Tim saw Sharon to the door and watched her get into her car, a Mercedes SL 500 with vanity plates that read ME♥WNR. "Me Love Winter?" Polly tried to decipher the cryptic language. "Me Heart Want New Romance?"

"*Emmy* Winner," Tim said.

Polly gave her son a playful push. "Text-messaging has made you too smart." They watched as Sharon's car headed down the cobbled driveway to the twin iron gates at the edge of the estate, which slowly parted as she rolled past the electric eye sensor. As Sharon's car nosed out onto the street, she gave her horn a quick double toot and then disappeared down the canyon road.

Polly and Tim closed the front entry door, set the alarm system, and joined Placenta in the kitchen. In tandem, they went about the task of cleaning the dinner dishes and discussing Sharon. Without exception, they all adored their new friend and agreed that Polly would have at least one ally in the theater company. "It's important to know who your friends and enemies are right from the get-go," Polly said. "You two keep an eye on my cast for me. I'm never in the mood to be upstaged. By the by, do we know any rich eligible men—straight or gay, as long as they're loaded—to whom we can introduce Sharon?"

"She's got that wealthy philanthropist," Placenta reminded her.

"Shows he can't hang on to a buck. Imagine the insanity of giving it away?"

Eventually Polly folded her dish towel, laid it on the granite countertop, and announced that she was heading

off to bed. "I've got to go over my lines before beddy-bye.
I'm so excited about tomorrow." She left the kitchen and
headed for The Scarlett O'Hara Memorial Staircase, which
led to the second-floor landing of the mansion, and her
bedroom suite. From the distance she yelled back, "I'll kill
that albatross Gerold Goss if he publicly insults me again."

Chapter 3

Morning arrived at Pepper Plantation and to the shock and awe of Placenta, the mistress of the manor was awake at six thirty, seated in the kitchen, and ready to be served breakfast. "I couldn't sleep," Polly explained. "I'm too eager about going to work. Plus, I want to be extra early. No butter on the pancakes, please. I'll show that bombastic rat that I'm as reliable as rain on a weekend."

Presently, Tim staggered into the kitchen. Until his first cup of coffee he had the physical lethargy and verbal ability of a corpse. He too was not used to getting out of bed before the morning was half over. But when his mother was working and needed a chauffeur, Tim fought the impulse to complain. He reminded himself that Polly asked relatively little in exchange for his weekly allowance, a new car every year, a personal fitness trainer who made house calls, and charge accounts in Beverly Hills at Neiman's, Armani, Pierre Deux, and Bijan. Usually, by the time Placenta poured Tim a second cup of his favorite fresh-ground Ethiopian java, he was able to focus on the comic section of the newspaper and offer guttural responses to simple questions.

This morning, however, Tim wasn't given time for the paper, or for consuming more than one blueberry muffin to go with his allotted one cup of joe. Polly was in a hurry, and when the queen said to move his tushy, Tim did as instructed. He quickly showered and dressed and was waiting in the car when Polly and Placenta stepped into the vehicle at 7:45. The drive to Glendale took less time than expected and when they arrived at the theater, there were plenty of parking spaces in the section of the lot reserved for the cast and crew.

Polly looked at her wristwatch. "Not even half past eight!" Then she spotted a familiar car. "Talk about punctual, Sharon's already here." Polly pointed to the Mercedes with the vanity license plate. "These new kids have to advertise all of their accomplishments! Oh, hell, it's probably the only time she'll get an acting award, so why not boast? Goody," she added, looking at the reserved parking spots for the director and artistic director, "Karen and Gerold are here too. They can all witness how early I am."

Tim eased the Rolls into a space near the stage door entrance. For effect, in case anyone was watching, he slipped out of his seat and made a big deal about opening the rear passenger door for his mother and Placenta and formally ushering them out of the car. He stood at military attention, then made the motion of clicking the heels of his Nikes. He led the way to the artists' entrance to the theater and opened the door.

After a brief exchange of "good mornings" with old George the doorman, and signing in on the daily attendance roster, Polly and crew wended their way to the lavatory to check her makeup. A few minutes later they climbed the stairs leading to the stage wings. Calling out in her most theatrical and projected voice, Polly announced herself in advance, "Guess who's not only on time, but *extremely* early?" Her voice preceded her arrival onstage, but when she and her entourage stood together facing an empty house, she looked confused. "Where is everybody? Sharon? Karen? Gerold?" Polly asked.

As Polly, Tim, and Placenta roamed about the half-dark stage and then checked out the auditorium, they killed time by commenting on the need to reupholster the seats, splash a coat of paint on the proscenium, and shampoo the carpet along the aisles. "Ugh. Glendale," Polly said. Then, one by one, the other cast members began to trickle in.

Charlotte Bunch was first. She beamed when she saw Polly and hurried from the wings onto the stage to greet her old friend. "Isn't it too wonderful that we're doing a show together again?" Charlotte embraced Polly. "My short-term memory isn't what it used to be, but I clearly recall that week you invited me to be a guest on your show."

Polly smiled. "I remember too," she said, remembering the extremely low ratings of that particular program. "At the time you were doing guest-starring roles on *The Bob Newhart Show* and *Mannix*. Seems as though for a couple of seasons you were everywhere! *Johnny Carson, Merv Griffin, Dinah Shore, Rhoda.*"

Charlotte sighed. "I should have bought my apartment building when I had some dough. You were smart to buy that big ol' place in Bel Air. Bet you couldn't touch it now. I saw Pepper Plantation in *Architectural Digest* a few years ago. My God, you probably paid pennies by today's standards! I especially loved your Emmy room."

"It is rather impressive, isn't it?" Polly beamed. "It's been a lovely home in which to raise my family," she said, knowing that Charlotte had never married and never had children.

Charlotte's face turned a slight shade of green as she looked over at Tim.

By ten o'clock most of the cast had assembled onstage. While everyone waited for the director and ingénue to walk through the door, they all made small talk among each other. Polly feigned interest in Beauregard's lengthy list of stage and television credits, which he reeled off like a waiter explaining the house specials for the evening.

Polly plastered a fake smile to her lips as Emily Hutcherson sidled up to her. In a warmer greeting than the day before, she announced that she was writing her memoirs and would Polly please consider offering a blurb for the book jacket. "And risk committing career suicide? I'd love to," Polly said.

"I haven't exactly started the book yet," Emily said. "But all my friends tell me I absolutely have to put pen to paper and share the funny showbiz stories with which I regale my guests at dinner parties."

Polly smiled, predicting that Emily would never take the time to write a book.

Another half hour passed and Polly was still tapping her foot on the wooden stage waiting for director Karen Richards and daytime drama diva Sharon. "Were you all as pissed at me yesterday?" she chuckled.

"Coming over the hill this morning, the traffic was wretched," Charlotte said, explaining the probable cause for the absentees.

"Sharon's here. Somewhere," Polly said. "Her car's in the lot, next to Karen's."

"I have that space," Emily said.

"It was there when I arrived," Polly said. "Something's not right. Has anyone seen the beast, Gerold? His car was in the lot too. Perhaps he's giving Sharon and Karen one of his excoriating lectures in his office. We don't have time for his games. Someone call Karen's cell and find out how long they're going to be."

Tim, who along with Placenta was seated in the audience trying to stay out of the way, volunteered to place the call. "I've already programmed all of your numbers." He flipped open his phone and pushed the address book key. He scrolled down to Karen's number and pushed the Talk button. In less than a moment he simultaneously heard ringing in his earpiece and a personalized ring tone of "Popular" coming from behind the stage curtain. The instant that the ringing stopped in his own phone, so too did the hit song from

Wicked coming from behind the curtain, as an automated voice message announced that Karen Richards was not available. *Beep.*

With a strange feeling in the pit of his stomach, Tim flipped his phone closed.

"The acoustics in this place are wonderful," Polly said. "Tim, dear, push Redial."

When Tim redialed Karen's number, the same music wafted from backstage and the entire cast huddled together. Tim and Placenta joined them onstage as Polly began to lead the way into the wings.

Dark and grim, the ancient backstage area was eerie with its vaulted height and cavernous depth. There were creepy vibrations in old theaters, and the Galaxy was no exception. Ghosts were everywhere. The only illumination backstage was ambient light that filtered in from the auditorium. Polly felt a sense of trepidation as she moved into the abyss. With the exception of the echo produced by each footstep on the concrete slab floor, the backstage area was deathly quiet. Polly looked at Tim. "Call Karen's cell again, hon."

Tim flipped open his phone and redialed. "Popular" ricocheted throughout the vast backstage area. En masse, the curious cast followed Polly toward the ring tone. Then, just as the music ended and the automated voice message system engaged, Emily Hutcherson tripped over a thick electrical cable and fell—facedown onto a sandbag. "Holy Mother of Christ!" she screamed.

At the same time, Tim found the light switch panel and turned on all the overhead spots. Emily screamed even louder as she realized that her face wasn't resting against a sandbag but rather a body.

The body of director Karen Richards.

Polly rushed to Emily's side and held out her hand to help the actress back onto her feet. But Polly was more interested in taking a closer look at Karen. Immediately she noticed that blood had pooled on the floor around the back of Karen's head. Her unseeing eyes were staring up at the fly space above the proscenium.

As the rest of the shocked and confused cast stood almost as lifeless as Karen lying on the floor, Placenta had the wherewithal to call 911.

Although the paramedics arrived in a matter of minutes, it was too late. Karen was a goner the instant her brain began to seep through the crack in her head. The police followed quickly behind the EMTs and dutifully began taking pictures of the death scene, and questioning the cast. When an officer asked Polly if she had seen anything unusual, she explained that it was what she didn't see that might be more important.

An officious-looking detective in a gray suit overheard her remark. "And who are you?" the brusque bully of a policeman asked as he walked over to Polly. He looked down his nose at the star.

"She's Polly Pepper, and if you don't know that you should be clutching the halter of a guide dog," Tim snapped, as he elbowed his way through the assembled cast. "She's the star of this show, and a living legend for that matter. And who are *you*?"

"I'll ask the questions," the detective responded, and then turned to Polly. He softened his approach. "I'm sorry, Miss Pepper, I didn't recognize you. I used to be a big fan. When I was a kid, I mean. Let me rephrase that. I don't have time to watch television or keep up with Hollywood news anymore."

Polly smiled warmly and held out her hand. "Of course you don't. There are some jobs that people think are more important than showbiz. It's a pleasure to meet you. Detective . . . ?"

"Collins. Wayne Collins."

"Detective Collins, this is my son, Tim, and our maid, Placenta." Polly pointed to each and then began introducing the rest of the assembled cast. "And as you may know we're putting on a stage musical. That's our darling director behind the tape barrier." She pointed to Karen. "She's unexpectedly turned up brutally murdered."

"Murder hasn't been established," Detective Collins quickly pointed out.

"If it looks like a duck, and no longer quacks," Polly scoffed.

"What were you saying about something you *didn't* see being potentially important?" Detective Collins continued.

Polly explained that although the other cast members claimed that actress Sharon Fletcher had never arrived for the morning rehearsal, she had definitely been at the theater that morning. "Tim and Placenta and I saw her car in the lot. Along with the body. I mean Karen Richards. Our obnoxious artistic director, Gerold Goss's car was here too, but none of them ever showed up for rehearsal. Karen obviously had a good excuse."

"Which one of you actually found the body?" The detective's tone was at once curious and accusatory.

"We all did, the entire cast. All at the same time."

In that moment Gerold Goss blustered onto the stage demanding to know what was going on and why he had to identify himself before being allowed past a guard at the door to his own theater. He looked at Polly. "Now what have you done?"

"The police are here because someone let Karen have their Emmy Award—buried in her pretty head," she said matter-of-factly.

Detective Collins interrupted. "We haven't established the scenario."

Polly folded her arms across her chest and pointed to the scene of the crime. "Body. Emmy. Blood. Scenario established." She turned back to Gerold. "Where were you when her lights went out? So to speak."

Gerold put his hands on the back of a folding chair to steady himself. "What happened?" he asked in a small voice as he sat down. "Who did this to Karen? Was it robbery?"

Polly placed her hand on his meaty shoulder. "Robbery? No," she said.

Again Detective Collins stepped in to explain that motive had not been established. Polly again faced the man. "How many hoods do you know who run around with sacred acting awards, let alone leave them at the scene, when they commit robberies?"

"Nothing in Hollywood surprises me anymore," the detective said.

"This is hard for all of us to accept," Polly sighed, returning her attention to Gerold. "We're now a show without a director, a ship without a captain. Did you see anyone suspicious hanging around the theater this morning?"

Detective Collins reiterated, "I'll ask the questions." He waited a beat and then said, "Did you see anything out of the ordinary here this morning?"

Gerold looked confused. "I just got here."

"Your car was parked in the lot when we arrived at *eight twenty-five*." Polly enunciated the time as clearly as if she were doing speech exercises: *How. Now. Brown. Cow.*

"Yeah, I drove in at around eight, then went for my daily walk. Cardio. I never actually came into the theater," Gerold said.

"Any alibis?" Detective Collins asked.

Again Gerold shrugged. "A lot of people walk. But if you're asking whether or not I ran into anyone who can vouch for me being at the corner of Brand and Main at the time of Karen's murder, the answer is no. I hope that the fact that my car was here doesn't make me a suspect. Do I need an attorney?"

Detective Collins waved away Gerold's fears. "Just don't leave town until we figure this whole thing out." He returned his attention to Polly. "You mentioned a cast member who was missing." He consulted his notebook. "A Sharon Fletcher?"

Chapter 4

When Detective Collins arrived at Sharon Fletcher's house in the upscale Los Feliz area of Los Angeles, he introduced himself through an intercom. Sharon buzzed him through the front gate. She was dressed in her flannel pajamas and a silk bathrobe, her nose and eyes red. Her famous hairstyle had mutated from the two-hundred-dollar coif that thousands of women around the country tried to copy, into a reasonable facsimile of the wig that Bette Davis wore in *Whatever Happened to Baby Jane?* She clutched a fistful of Kleenex and sniffled a lot. "I'm not well enough to talk now," she said and tried to close the door.

Detective Collins wedged his foot between the door and its frame. "This is important, Miss Fletcher. I won't take long." Sharon heaved a sigh of resentment but stepped aside, held the door open, and led him into the sunken living room. "I'm afraid I have some sad news," he said. "A crime was committed at the Galaxy Theatre this morning. The director of the show, Ms. Karen Richards, is . . . dead."

Sharon looked at the detective with horror. "That's not true. She was . . . We were just . . ." Sharon let out a small wail of grief.

"I need to ask you a few questions. Just routine stuff."
Collins withdrew his notebook.

Sharon nodded her head.

"You didn't show up for rehearsals today. Where were
you from approximately eight to eight thirty this morning?"

"Here. I was sick as a dog all night. I knew I wouldn't
make it to rehearsal, so I called Karen. She told me to stay
home. She didn't want me spreading germs among the
other cast members. I can't believe that she's dead."
Sharon sneezed and blew her nose.

Detective Collins nodded his head. "What time did you
two talk?"

Sharon thought for a moment. "I was awake half the
night, but I waited until I thought it was a reasonable hour
to call. Around seven, I guess."

Again, Detective Collins nodded. "Did you call from
your cell phone or the landline?"

"Um, the cell."

"Mind if I see your phone? I'd like to get your call history. Just routine. We need to establish the exact time of
the call so we can get a better idea of precisely when Ms.
Richards died."

Sharon shrugged her shoulders. "Oh, sorry. I called
from the phone beside my bed. The cold medicine, plus the
news of Karen's death . . . I'm not thinking clearly."

Detective Collins nodded again. "If it's all the same to
you, may I see the cell phone anyway? With your permission, we'd like to look at your phone log."

"Don't you need a warrant or something?"

"If we have to, but we're hoping you can help us out."

Sharon reluctantly left the living room to retrieve her
mobile phone. She sneezed again and wandered into her
bedroom. A few moments later she returned with her purse
in hand. "It's not here. I always keep it in my purse. I tend

to easily misplace it, so I make a point of always putting it in this particular compartment." She showed Detective Collins the interior space of her bag with a zippered pocket, which was empty. "I must have left it at Pepper Plantation— that's the home of our star Polly Pepper. I had dinner there last night."

The detective sighed. "Is there any other place you might have left it? Think hard, because it's not at Pepper Plantation."

Sharon gave the detective a long quizzical stare. "If you know it's not at Pepper Plantation, then you know exactly where my cell phone is. So why don't *you* tell *me*?"

"Just take a guess, ma'am. Where were you this morning between eight and eight thirty?"

"What's going on? I've already told you that I was here in bed, sick with this cold. So I made a mistake when I said I used my cell. That doesn't make me a killer."

"What makes you think that Ms. Richards was killed?" Collins asked.

Sharon swallowed hard. "I just presumed . . ."

"At the moment, Ms. Fletcher, your cell is in a plastic bag down at the crime lab," Collins said. "It's evidence in this case."

"Evidence?" Sharon said.

"Miss Fletcher, your cell phone was found next to the body of Ms. Richards. I believe that you did speak with the deceased this morning at seven. In the outgoing log of *her* cell, there was a call to your cell number. But it appears that you were also at the theatre around the time of her death. Eyewitnesses place you there at around eight twenty-five."

"Wait a minute!" Sharon begged. "The fact that my cell phone was at the theater means nothing! I must have left it there yesterday."

"We also have another bit of evidence, Miss Fletcher."

Sharon slumped into her chair. "My Emmy," she said.

"It has blood all over it," Collins said. "When the lab results come back, I'm confident that it will match the victim's blood type. Miss Fletcher," Detective Collins said, "I'm placing you under arrest for the murder of Karen Richards."

Chapter 5

Gossip in Hollywood travels faster than an Internet search for "Dead wives of Robert Blake." Polly and Tim and Placenta were stunned when they received a text message on Tim's cell phone from the precocious little kid with the role of young Patrick in the show. They read the news of the arrest of Sharon Fletcher and collectively gasped in disbelief. The fact that Sharon was a soap star made the arrest the main headline for every media outlet around the globe. From *E.T.* to *Anderson Cooper 360* to the *Huffington Post,* the story was big news, and gave Polly Pepper and the Galaxy Theatre's forthcoming production of *Mame* more publicity than Tour de France cyclists shooting up with prohibited testosterone. The notoriety made Gerold Goss equal parts ecstatic and smug. The day after Sharon Fletcher's arrest, Gerold called for a full cast meeting—in lieu of a much-needed rehearsal.

Polly and her cast, minus the accused murderer, assembled onstage at 9:00 A.M. While waiting for their artistic director to arrive, each visited the site where Karen's body had been discovered. They all clucked clichés about the good dying young, and the theater having lost a shining beacon. Finally at nine fifteen, a stern and self-satisfied-looking Gerold Goss waddled onto the stage holding a black leather notebook. He took Karen's reserved seat at the head of the long reading table.

Silence filled the theater as the imposing Goss, wearing an extra-large Hawaiian shirt that did nothing to conceal his girth, and revealed thick hairy arms and tufts of dark fur climbing from his chest up to his throat, silently stared into the eyes of each cast member. After a particularly long look at Polly he announced, "What's done is done. There's no time to waste on the past. Our show opens in ten days and I'm taking over as director. It's time to get comfortable with being uncomfortable!" He cleared his throat. "I'm making a few casting changes."

The assembled group began to murmur. Gerold continued. "I'm not the callow and spineless Karen Richards. I didn't agree with a number of her casting choices and now I have the authority to mold my cast into a Broadway-caliber production of *Mame*."

Polly raised her hand and before being granted the floor she said, "With all due respect, Mr. Goss, I haven't kept up with second-tier directors, so I don't know your credits."

The cast made a feeble attempt to stifle giggles.

"I'm sure you're a very talented man," Polly continued. "But which musicals have you directed? *South Pacific*? *Cabaret*? *Rent*? Karen had enormous successes at Yale Rep, Goodspeed, the Guthrie, and Williamstown. For the record, would you enlighten us with your CV?"

Gerold Goss gave Polly a hard look. "Everyone needs a debut."

"Ah." Polly nodded. "How lovely for you to be embarking on such a grand and arduous adventure. However, I've starred in several productions of *Mame*, and without impeccable direction it's nearly impossible to properly follow the great Jerry Herman's vision for his masterpiece. I must have a strong director who has gads of experience in musical theater. James Lapine, Susan Stroman, Tommy Tune. Any of them would be acceptable to me."

Gerold's heavy fist slammed onto the table and echoed out from the stage and into the auditorium, causing the startled cast to jump. "How's that for strong! Miss Pepper, check your contract. The days of you having director and cast approval are long gone. Patti LuPone you're not! If I'm unacceptable to you, then you're unacceptable to me. However, as much as I'd like to say good-bye to you, the theater has already invested far too much coin advertising your appearance in this show. And while I'm loath to admit it, based on your name value, the box office is actually doing brisk business."

Polly smiled with self-satisfaction.

"Still, if you feel that we can't work together, by all means return to your Pepper Plantation," Gerold said. "But I assure you that by the time you reach the monogrammed gates, a team of attorneys will be waiting for you. The breach-of-contract lawsuit should keep you out of any other work for a very long time."

All eyes turned to Polly Pepper, who swallowed hard and stared into Gerold's black beady eyes. "As a matter of fact, I've only worked with two directors during my career who were of much use. I'm usually expected to simply speak my lines, sing a little, and use my celebrity to draw audiences. I can do it again, without anyone's help or support from you."

Gerold was silent for a long brooding moment, and then opened his notebook. "Moving on. With Sharon Fletcher in the slammer for murdering Karen Richards, she'll be replaced by Mag Ryan."

"Now, that's actually a brilliant idea," Polly said. "Everyone loves Meg Ryan! We're old friends. She'll be sensational!"

Gerold shook his head. "I said *Mag* Ryan. Not *Meg*."

"Who the hell is *Mag* Ryan and why can't she get her own name?"

The cast sniggered.

"I don't expect you to know her work. She's relatively new. But she personifies the Gloria Upson character, which she'll be playing."

Then, not looking up to face the rest of the cast, Gerold turned the page of his notebook and said, "Charlotte and Hiroaki? Nothing personal, but I'll messenger your final paychecks to your homes."

"We're fired?" Hiroaki said.

"'Replaced' is how the trades will report it," Gerold said. "We're going in a different direction with these characters."

"The characters are what they are and always have been. What do you mean by 'going in a different direction'?" Hiroaki asked.

"I don't really think you want to fire me," Charlotte said in a calm voice. "I suggest you give your decision a little more thought . . . considering, um . . . everything."

Gerold was quiet until Hiroaki interrupted his thoughts. "I've already learned my lines," the actor complained. "I need this show for my Equity insurance!"

"Don't look at me as the bad guy." Gerold tried to sound contrite. "The decision to replace you was made the first day of rehearsal. Karen was supposed to tell you yesterday morning. Her death doesn't change anything."

"Karen Richards cast me. She knew I was perfect for the role," Hiroaki whispered.

Everyone around the reading table was aghast. With as much dignity as they could each muster, Hiroaki Goldfarb and Charlotte Bunch rose from their folding chairs. Charlotte blew a kiss to her now former cast members, and she and Hiroaki began to walk off the stage. "Things aren't always as they appear," she said, looking back at her colleagues.

"This *appears* to suck," Hiroaki spat.

"I'll call you," Polly yelled out as they disappeared into the wings.

Chapter 6

During the drive back to Pepper Plantation, Polly steamed in silence. When Tim finally turned the car onto the estate grounds and parked under the front portico, Polly got out and climbed the two steps up to the front door. She pushed the keypad to disarm the alarm system and opened the door. Tim and Placenta followed behind as Polly made straight for the great room and the wine cooler.

As she withdrew a bottle of Krug and handed it to Tim to open Polly exclaimed, "I loathe bullies! Gerold Goss is the adult male version of Mandy Montevecci, my personal bête noire from Hollywood High. For no reason whatsoever she hated my guts from the moment I walked on campus. After I became famous I tracked her down, mainly to rub her nose in my success, but I also wanted to find out why she treated me so poorly all through school. You know what she told me? She said she didn't know why she hated me, but that she just did. Then she said that she hated my show too."

"But she must have watched it to make that judgment," Tim said.

"Gerold has the same problem as Mandy," Polly continued. "He hates that I'm popular and talented and he's a big fat garbage bag. Those who *can*, do. Those who *can't*, diet on Ding Dongs and Twinkies and become small-time regional theater directors or critics!"

Tim poured three flutes of champagne and handed one each to his mother and Placenta. He raised his own to theirs. "Gerold never said one word that suggested how sorry he is about Karen's death, or that we should think positive thoughts for Sharon. It's weird that he didn't declare a moment of silence, or insist that Sharon was innocent until proved guilty. Even if it's true that she was responsible for Karen's death, you're supposed to pretend to hold out hope that the real killer will be found. Even O.J. promised to track himself down."

"Everybody grieves in his own way," Polly said. "But you're right that he should have at least suggested that we support Sharon. I mean, just because her car was at the scene of the crime around the time of Karen's death, and that her Emmy was the murder weapon, and her cell phone was discovered beside the body, and that Sharon and Karen's phone logs show that they were in communication with each other that morning, despite the fact that Sharon lied about being at the theater, doesn't mean that she's guilty. We've got to hear her side of the story."

Polly stood up and walked to the cordless telephone that was resting in its charging station on a chrome and glass desk by the bay window. She picked up the handset and pushed the numbers on the keypad to connect with her paramour, Detective Randy Archer of the Beverly Hills Police Department. In almost an instant, Polly seductively cooed, "Hey, you." In a childlike voice she said, "Are we still on for Friday night?" She chuckled. "Ooooh, you're too naughty. Say that again."

Tim and Placenta looked at each other and smiled as they eavesdropped on what was obviously lovers' podgy-woo chatter. After years of watching Polly's lack of interest in dating, they were happy to see that she was finally realizing that just because she was a woman of a certain age, that didn't mean she wasn't still alluring and able to take a handsome lover.

Polly continued her conversation but cleverly steered it in a different direction. "You've obviously heard the horrible news about my director's death. Would you do me a terribly big favor? I need to check on Sharon Fletcher, the girl who's been arrested for Karen's murder."

Polly stopped and listened for a moment. "I promise, I'm *not* getting involved with the crime investigation. I swear! I just want to see how Sharon's doing in that horrible jail cell." She appeared to listen a moment longer, then added, "Scout's honor, I won't interfere one teensy bit. But if you could get me in to see Sharon, I'd be awfully grateful. How grateful?" Polly paused and whispered something into the phone and then sniggered. "You're good when you're bad. Is today too soon? Brilliant. Yes, of course I remember where the jail is. I've spent rather a lot of time there over the past few months. Thank you, Precious Buns." Then she hung up the phone.

"Let's go!" Polly slugged back the rest of her flute of champagne before walking out of the great room. "We're off to visit Sharon."

Sharon Fletcher's physical appearance was what one would expect from a guest of any jail. She was disheveled. Gone was her makeup, which had hidden a freckled nose. Her lacquered nails were clipped and stripped of polish. Her shoulder-length hair was no longer L'Oreal "I'm worth it" silky smooth, but rather Brillo pad "I'm a wreck, and don't I show it?" In other words, she looked like a troll doll on suicide watch.

Polly was momentarily taken aback by Sharon's unflattering new look. "We can't touch or hug," Polly finally said, "so please accept this." She blew a kiss to Sharon, who forced a smile and would have returned the gesture if her hands weren't shackled by a pair of cuffs and chained to her chair. "My dear," Polly began, "I don't believe for one instant that you killed Karen Richards. But why did you tell all those lies to the police? I personally saw your car at the theater."

Sharon bowed her head. After a long moment of silence she said, "All my life, whenever I thought I might be in trouble, the first thing I do is try to cover my butt. That was my natural reflex when the police showed up. I figured that no one would have believed me if I'd admitted to being at the theater apparently moments before Karen was killed. So I played dumb and pretended to have a cold and said that I'd been sick in bed all day."

"What about the fact that the police found your Emmy with Karen's blood all over it, and your cell phone next to the body?" Polly asked. "It had your fingerprints and Karen's all over it."

Sharon began to explain. "I was mad at Gerold Goss and threw my phone at him. It bounced off his big grizzly bear body and Karen must have picked it up after I stormed out of the theater."

Polly did a double take. "Gerold Goss was in the theatre? You saw him?"

"It's hard to miss a man who looks like Pavarotti's fatter twin brother."

Polly heaved a deep sigh. "But Gerold said he was . . ." She stopped herself. "Let's go back to the beginning. Tell me what happened and why you were at the theater so early in the first place."

"I received a call from Karen at seven," Sharon began. "She asked if I could come to the theater before the rest of the cast arrived because there was something personal she wanted to discuss with me. She said it wasn't good news but that she wanted to talk to me about it in person. With all the animosity between her and Gerold, I thought maybe she was quitting and wanted me to be the first to know. It never dawned on me that I was getting fired."

Polly blanched. "Why were you being let go? You and I are the only real names in the cast."

"Don't be naive," Sharon scoffed. "It's the oldest reason in the book. The horny artistic director wants his little Lolita to have the role. Someone helped me that way once. I guess it's payback time."

"But you've got an Emmy! Or at least you did until the police got hold of it," Polly said. "What does Bambi or Barbie or Beebee have that you don't?"

Sharon stared at Polly as though she were an idiot. "She's young, and Gerold's not. Need I say more? I don't know how my Emmy ended up with Karen's blood all over it. I don't ever want that thing back in my house. I could never look at it again without thinking of this horrible nightmare."

Polly looked as perplexed as Tim and Placenta. "How the hell did your Emmy find its way to the theater in the first place? I have a house full of those precious darlings and I won't even let my own mother have one to display in her assisted living home, let alone take them out for show-and-tell."

"That's exactly what it was doing at the theater," Sharon said. "Charlotte Bunch coaxed me into bringing it in. You can ask her. On the first day of rehearsal, she said that she'd watched the Daytime Emmy Awards and was thrilled to know a winner. She said she'd never in a million years have one of her own, and asked if I'd bring mine in and let her hold it. I agreed. I wrapped it in a towel the night before and placed it on the hall table by the front door, next to my car keys so I wouldn't forget it. On the way out to see Karen I grabbed the keys and the Emmy and off I went. Karen was interested in the Emmy too, so I let her hold it before wrapping it back up."

"More fingerprints," Polly said.

"After the argument I left the theater and forgot to take the award with me."

"You argued with Karen about being terminated?"

"No, Gerold. That detestable SOB," Sharon said. "Karen was just about to tell me that I was being let go when Gerold walked in with his jailbait, Mag Ryan—imagine that name! He asked what was I doing there. He'd apparently instructed Karen to take care of the ugly firing business the day before. When he figured things out he made fun of Karen for not being man enough to tell me that I'd been replaced. Naturally, I was shocked. That's when I threw my cell phone at him. I was upset, but not enough to kill anyone. I swear it! I left the stage, went to the ladies' room, and cried my eyes out. I didn't want to run into any of the kids in the show, so I ran out of the theater and drove home. I sobbed all the way."

Polly cooed in understanding. "Charlotte and Hiroaki got the boot from Gerold this morning. They're being replaced, just as you said."

"How did they take the news—for the second time?" Sharon asked.

"No tantrums or disgruntled employee threats."

"I never thought that my neck would be on the chopping block," Sharon said. "Guess none of us are indispensable. Except you, Polly."

"Trust me, dear. If Gerold could get rid of me, he would," Polly said. "He'd love for me to quit. But I'm here for the run of the show. I've worked with some of the most angry men on the planet, like Jerry Robbins—who at least had talent. Gerold's a mere pimple on the butt of life for me. And an amateur at that!"

Polly sighed. "Who else had motive to clobber the director?"

Sharon shrugged her shoulders. "She was too divine. I can't imagine Karen having any enemies."

"Except Gerold Goss! There was no love lost between those two."

Sharon thought for a moment. "Gerold's got a mean streak a mile long, but do you think he'd actually kill someone? People are more apt to want to kill him."

Polly shook her head in confusion. "I swear, if I live to be a thousand, I'll never understand human nature. But don't worry, sweetums, we won't let you fry in the chair without a battle."

Sharon's facial expression instantly changed from hope to fear.

Placenta said, "Don't scare the poor kid any more than she is already. This is a lethal injection state."

Chapter 7

"What's wrong with this picture?" Polly said to Placenta as Tim drove the Rolls along Santa Monica Boulevard in Beverly Hills, heading home. "Who's lying? Sharon says she quarreled with Gerold, but Gerold swears he wasn't in the theater—although we saw his car in the parking lot."

Tim glanced at his mother and Placenta in the rearview mirror. "You heard Sharon. Whenever she thinks she's in hot water, she tries to cover her hiney. In other words, she's a liar."

"Human nature," Polly tut-tutted. "How many times have I given an interview and had to call Lindsay or Christina or Barbra and insist that I was quoted out of context? It's called 'The Blame Game.'"

Placenta harrumphed. "I vote for Gerold being the super-sized Fib Monster."

"Yeah, I don't buy Shamu strolling the streets of Glendale for exercise at eight in the morning," Polly said. "The only activity that man gets is reaching for Little Debbie—and I don't mean the snack cakes. We need more personal info about that Yeti—and Sharon too. Turn right at Sunset, hon," she instructed Tim. "Let's pay an unexpected visit to dear ol' Charlotte Bunch."

The Beverly Hills stretch of Sunset Boulevard was wide and bordered on both sides by tall palm trees and immense neo-Renaissance-style mansions of unimaginable expense. Estate after ostentatious estate, the grandeur became so commonplace that after a while one hardly noticed the homes. As Tim chauffeured his mother and Placenta east toward Hollywood, he entered Charlotte Bunch's address into the car's GPS and followed the voice directions. After forty-five minutes the voice chip finally announced, "You have reached your destination."

Tim double-parked the Rolls on Gardner Street, opposite a two-story, four-unit apartment building with a sign on the front wall that announced TUSCANY VILLAS. LUXURY ONE-BEDROOM APARTMENTS. VACANCY.

Polly frowned. "Luxury? Maybe compared to a cave in Afghanistan."

The building was a disaster, with curb appeal that only a demolition contractor would appreciate. The stucco was probably white at one time, but was now Purina Puppy Chow beige with layers of dirt and smog that had filtered through the air and settled on the paint. The balcony decks on the second level were slanted and looked unsafe to hold even a Hibachi grill. One unit was decorated with a string of Christmas lights around the front door, and a paint-on-velvet portrait of the Virgin Mary, which was hung like a holiday wreath—in July. "God, this could almost be the apartment I grew up in," Polly said. "Except that ours had Elvis on velvet."

Placenta shook her head. "We should have called first. Charlotte's going to be embarrassed when she opens the door and finds the rich and famous Polly Pepper standing on her cracked concrete front step."

"We don't have time for social etiquette," Polly snapped as she opened the car door.

Tim complained that the parking situation looked bleak. "Even if I find a place, it wouldn't be wise to leave a Rolls-Royce unattended in this neighborhood."

"That's why we have insurance. Park it in that driveway." Polly pointed to a narrow lane between Charlotte's building and the even more squalid apartment units next door. "If someone needs access they'll honk."

"Or shoot," Placenta warned.

Tim rolled his eyes and followed his mother's instructions.

The trio approached apartment number 1. At the pockmarked door a hand-printed label above the doorbell read C. BUNCH. Polly looked at Tim and Placenta with a "Here goes" expression and then pushed the button. After a moment the door flew open and a Siamese cat raced outside. Charlotte, who was wearing jeans and a sweatshirt, yelled, "Let the coyotes make a meal of you. D'ya think I care?" Now, standing before Polly, she plastered a wide smile on her face.

"As I live and breathe!" Charlotte cried. "It's Polly Pepper! For heaven's sake you are as sweet as your image— coming to check up on me after that nasty bit of business this morning." She leaned in to hug Polly. "Please come in!" Tim and Placenta followed.

"You're not opening your wrists in the tub, I see," Polly said as she moved past Charlotte and into the apartment. "It only *seems* like the end of the world, hon. You'll get a better job."

The interior of the building—at least Charlotte's unit— was the polar opposite of the exterior. Charlotte's small apartment was clean, although extremely cluttered, and boasted calming cream-colored walls and dated cottage cheese ceilings. The furniture wasn't new, but it was well crafted and heirloom quality. A Persian rug accented the floor, and framed, autographed eight-by-ten black-and-white pictures of famous Hollywood stars were neatly arranged on tables throughout the living room. Polly and her entourage were impressed and each said as much to Charlotte as she offered them a drink.

"Maybe a teensy flute of champagne," Polly suggested.

Charlotte laughed. "Safeway-brand red table wine is about as good as it gets in this house. I can get a whole case for the cost of a bottle of the brand of champagne that the *National Peeper* says you suck down night after night."

Polly tittered. "As long as the wine isn't poured from a box!"

"You haven't lived until you've enjoyed Chateau Walgreen's!" Charlotte peeled with more laughter. "The twelve-thirty P.M. reserve vintage is *très extraordinaire!*"

"With a screw-on cap and expiration date on the label?" Polly joked.

"A skull and crossbones, too! Right next to the surgeon general's warnings about side effects from prolonged exposure to the fumes!"

Polly could only hope that she was kidding.

"Sit, sit, sit," Charlotte insisted as she turned off the television, which was showing an old movie on TCM. She moved into the kitchen—which was actually part of the large open room, divided from the living space by a bar counter—and brought out wineglasses from a cupboard. When she reached for a bottle, Polly gave a silent sigh of relief to see that it required a corkscrew.

"Haven't got any brie and crackers or hors d'oeuvreez," Charlotte apologized. "But this is actually a good bottle that I've saved for a special occasion. And what could be more special than a visit from TV's greatest star ever? Oh, listen to me, I'm sounding like a fan. Which of course *I am!*"

Polly smiled. "I'll bet you say that to MTM and Carole B. too. But please keep stroking—said the bishop to the nun—'cause I never get such attention at home!"

Charlotte regained her composure. "This wine came from Maureen Stapleton's cellar. Most of what I have comes from dead celebrity estate sales. The old-timers are dropping off so fast, there are one or two such sales almost every month. I can hardly keep up."

As Charlotte handed the drinks to her guests, Polly wondered which dead star once owned the sofa on which she was seated, and who, she asked herself, previously sipped from the glass she now held in her hand? As if reading Polly's thoughts, Charlotte pointed to the sofa and said, "Shelley Winters. Feel the dent where she sat?" She then lifted her glass and tapped the nail of her index finger against the side and made a *ping* sound. "Richard Dawson." She frowned. "No, that can't be right. I think he's still with us. Oh, I know, June Allyson. See what I mean? It's impossible to keep up!"

"After the day we've had, this is just what the doctor ordered, eh?" Polly raised her glass to Charlotte. "I still can't believe that no-talent maniac Gerold Goss canned you and Hiroaki. Hands down, you would have stolen the show. Even from me!"

Charlotte smiled. "No way. You're the star! You're the living legend that audiences want to see. I'm just a supporting player. Although I do have some good lines, don't I?" Charlotte spoke with an air of self-assurance. "By the way, I've been *unfired*, or whatever the word is for getting my job back."

Polly's eyes widened in astonishment. "You're your own replacement! Splendid! I suspected you were bargaining with Gerold this morning when you told him he'd be wise to reconsider his decision to terminate your services."

"I don't think I ever said that." Charlotte's brow furrowed. "I think Gerold knew that with the show opening in only ten days, and Sally Struthers in Cleveland with *Damn Yankees* all summer, he would be hard-pressed to find another Gooch on such short notice. Another drinky?" Charlotte took Polly's near-empty glass from her hand and walked back into the kitchen area.

Polly spoke up to be heard on the other side of the room. "It's dreadful that Sharon Fletcher, a beautiful young soap star with everything in the world going for her, would beat the living crap out of our dear Karen . . . with her bleeping Emmy no less! Usually nothing in Hollywood is original. However, I have to give her kudos for a novel way to kill the messenger."

Tim and Placenta each sat up a little straighter. "If you ask me, it was premeditated," Polly said. "Sharon knew she was being dumped and wanted to get even. I'll bet she thought it would be poetic to use an acting award as her weapon of choice."

"God knows a cheap-o Tony wouldn't have made more than a dent in the poor woman's skull," Charlotte agreed as she returned Polly's glass to her guest.

Taking another long sip of wine, Polly swallowed and asked if Charlotte agreed that Sharon probably knew in advance that she was being booted out of the company.

Charlotte turned to Tim and Placenta. "More wine for you two?"

"She couldn't have avoided the rumors," Polly said.

"Rumors?" Charlotte asked innocently.

"Hell, when my agent called to say I'd booked this job he insisted that I watch my back. He warned that it was common knowledge that Gerold Goss had plans for his girlfriend to be cast in this show, which could ruin our chances of getting to Broadway. But what better part for her to play than the character who is practically her real-life counterpart? Or so I've heard." Polly shook her head. "And who is this little wannabe anyway? Where does she come from? Where has she worked?"

"Other than on her back?" Placenta said.

"Is she Equity or SAG?" Polly continued. "Is she listed on IMDB?"

"Mag Something-or-other," Charlotte said. "She has a Valley Girl accent. Uses a lot of words like 'cool' and 'rad' and 'awesome.'"

"Brava!" Polly raised her wineglass, impressed with Charlotte's performance. "You should be Meryl Streep's dialect coach!"

"It's why I became an actor." Charlotte beamed. "Can you guess who this is?" She then told an old chicken joke in a voice that was dead-on Polly Pepper. Then, a cappella, she launched into the song "Let Your Fingers Do the *Talking*," special musical material from Polly's 1980 Emmy Award–winning one-hundredth-year musical birthday television celebration of Helen Keller: "Lady *Signs* the Blues" (in which Polly had starred with Ray Charles, Stevie Wonder, and Diane Schuur).

Polly, Tim, and Placenta applauded wildly. "Where did you learn to do that?" Polly said, still laughing at Charlotte's caricature of her.

Charlotte shrugged her shoulders. "I can't help impersonating people. This talent used to get me into trouble when I was a kid. One day I tricked my mother into thinking she was talking on the phone to Ed McMahon. Using his voice I told her that the Prize Patrol had taken a wrong turn and couldn't find our house. After Mother gave directions, the poor thing waited all day and all night for Ed to arrive with a big cardboard check, champagne, and a bouquet of flowers and balloons. Of course he never did come to the house. Mom even called *The Tonight Show* to try and reach Ed. I know better now, but at the time I didn't think it was cruel. I just wanted a big laugh." Charlotte sighed.

Without prompting, the hostess volunteered that during the first rehearsal for *Mame*, director Karen Richards had taken issue with her Irish brogue. "Lovely woman, but don't tell me how to speak my lines with an accent, Irish or French or German or Russian. I excel in all of them," Charlotte said. "Hell, Marlene Dietrich is living up here." She pointed to her temple. "I'm not usually so adamant about anything. But don't tell me that I should practice with a dialect tape!"

"God only knows why directors cast us if they're not going to let us do what we are hired to do!" Polly said. "What did Karen say?"

Charlotte took another sip of wine. "Karen let it pass. After all, I'm not usually a tantrum-throwing Michael Richards. I was about to apologize when you came in and rushed the stage. Now I feel guilty that I never had an opportunity to tell her that I was sorry for acting like an amateur."

Polly shook her head. "I'm positive that she didn't give it another thought. Her bio says she directed Kelly Ripa in *Ain't Misbehavin'*. Surely in your worst moments your fits couldn't compare to her rumored legendary flare-ups."

Charlotte put a hand on Polly's shoulder and sighed. "I wish that I could be more like you. Everybody in the business adores Polly Pepper. She never makes a fuss. Never makes a false move, publicity-wise. No scandals. How do you do it?"

"Champagne," Polly deadpanned. "There's nothing like inebriation to make you forget what you've done. Kidding of course," she quickly added. "But speaking of problems, Sharon Fletcher has a big one. I'm all for stringing her up, but Tim and Placenta over there have their doubts about her guilt."

Tim and Placenta glanced at each other. "These nonprofessionals don't know what a dog-eat-dog business we're in," Polly said. "You and I both know that some people in this town will do anything—including bludgeon a director to death—to secure a role. Stranger things have happened.

It goes further back than Fatty Arbuckle and the famous Coke bottle! However, I do agree that there are a few unanswered questions, like why would Sharon be summoned to the theater so early in the morning? Okay, so she was going to be fired, and perhaps Karen wanted to spare her the embarrassment of being given the news in front of others. Or she didn't want to give her the news over the phone. Still, Tim and Placenta seem to think that doesn't make sense. Go figure. What do you think?"

Charlotte looked at Tim and Placenta as if they were morons. "Anyone who has watched Sharon Fletcher's soap opera knows that she's capable of murder. She killed a couple of ex-lovers and a maid who forgot to clean the lint tray in the clothes dryer. Kinda like Naomi Campbell without the anger management classes. She's a real-life phony baloney, for sure. I don't buy her off-camera sweet-as-pie act one teensy bit."

Placenta nodded. "Only the Lord knows what's in Sharon's heart. But before I judge the girl as guilty, I need to see some hard facts, not just circumstantial evidence."

"I'm the last one to cast aspersions," Charlotte said, "but I think a jury would have an easy time convicting Sharon. She had motive, means, and opportunity. She was disgruntled over being fired. The blood all over her Emmy was Karen's. She was alone in the theater with Karen. It seems like a slam-dunk case for the district attorney."

"Absolutely! I couldn't agree more," Polly said. "Don't forget that she lied to the police and that her fingerprints and Karen's were the only ones found on the bloodied Emmy. And I'll testify that her car was in the theater parking lot at the approximate time of the murder. But so was Gerold's. Do you buy his alibi? Out walking?"

"No reason not to."

"On that lovely note . . ." Polly rose from Shelley Winters's sofa. "We both need our rest so we'll be in top form for Gerold tomorrow."

As Polly and her posse said good-bye to Charlotte, she gushed about having a lovely evening and that the next time they got together it would be for a dinner at Pepper Plantation. Charlotte was thrilled with anticipation and accepted for any night that Polly found convenient. "Let's check our calendars and discuss a date tomorrow," Polly suggested as she stepped out into the cool evening air and walked down the sidewalk. As she waved back at Charlotte she said sotto voce to Tim and Placenta, "The wine tasted like Listerine."

Settled into the car and cruising down Fountain Avenue toward LaCienega Boulevard, Polly said, "Let's recap. Likes dead celebrity possessions. Quick to convict Sharon. Admits to having a temper. Somehow got her old job back."

Placenta added, "Sally Struthers isn't in Cleveland. I was in line with her at Gelson's Market yesterday. She was buying up all the Entenmann's cheese Danish rings."

"Add liar to Charlotte's resume," Polly said.

Chapter 8

The world of regional theater was a distant universe, far away from the mundane bore of an insurance company office or auto parts warehouse. However, regardless of where one worked, there was one common denominator: sex. In every show, on the first day of rehearsal, the cast and chorus sized each other up and soon partners were paired up for friendships and sexual trysts that seldom ran beyond the end of the production. Girl dancers two-stepped with boy dancers. Boy dancers do-si-doed with other boy dancers. An ingénue might fancy the older star who was on television when she was a kid. The female lead might take a chorus boy for her temporary lover. There were as many backstage sex scenarios as there were worldwide productions of *Mama Mia*.

Polly had seen the entire spectrum and combinations during her years in television and touring in summer stock. She had witnessed wives arriving from out of town with the kids to join their actor husbands on the road for the summer, missing by moments the actor's boyfriend or girlfriend scurrying out of the hotel room. She'd overheard actors on their dressing room phone lying, "Honey, we're working really hard. If you visit right now, I don't know when I'd get to see you." In the meantime, a new para-mour in the dressing room was doing God only knows what to satisfy the actor.

A star of Polly's stature was particularly vulnerable to someone paying romantic attention to her and she could succumb in a nanosecond. Therefore, when they traveled, Tim felt it incumbent upon himself to assess the members of the theater company and decide who in the show might be particularly stupid enough to try to latch on to his mother. Thankfully, this time out her daydreams were not about a muscled twenty-something dancer with a prodi-gious hokeypokey; her thoughts were preoccupied with police detective Randy Archer.

It was already warm and smoggy in Glendale when Polly, Tim, and Placenta arrived at the theater at eight thirty the following morning. Tim parked the Rolls near the stage entrance and no one in the car missed seeing that Gerold's Jaguar was in the lot too. "I wonder if he's out walking off his Häagen-Dazs today," Polly said. "I'll wager that his happy hands are getting their exercise on Mag Ryan."

Placenta scoffed, "In that case, there ought to be a portable heart defibrillator backstage. I'd love to give that ape a jolt of seventeen hundred volts."

The trio stepped from the car and walked through the doorway marked ENTRÉE DES ARTISTES. They whispered good morning to George, the half-sleeping old man sup-posedly guarding the door, and Tim signed them in on the visitor log. Then they made their way down the hall to-ward the stage wings.

In her trademarked yodel, Polly called out ahead as she approached the stage. "I'm hee-er!" she announced. As Polly predicted, Gerold and his young girlfriend were already at the reading table when she walked under the proscenium. He was giving her a shoulder massage. Mag looked up. "Is that her?" she said.

The kid wasn't subtle, or quiet for that matter, and the acoustics amplified her voice. Gerold simply cast a steely look at Polly, who beamed a bright smile back at him and headed straight for Mag. "Indeed, it is I," she said in an exaggerated theatrical voice. "I'm *the* Polly Pepper. You must be the immeasurably talented Mag!"

The young girl blushed and cast her eyes to the floor.

"There's no place for modesty in the theater," Polly gently reprimanded. "I've heard gads about you, and surely Gerold has told you tons about me. All lies of course."

"Cool," Mag said. "I mean that you've heard of me . . . and all." She flipped her long hair over her shoulder. "I've heard of you too."

Polly held out her hand to shake Mag's. "*Enchanté.*" Polly assessed the young actress and smiled. "I can tell that you're going to be memorable as Gloria. If there's any teensy thing that I can do for you, I trust that you'll feel completely comfortable about calling on me."

Mag smiled. "This is totally rad. It's like, you know, so awesome that you're in my show. Like you used to be a totally big star, and all. Way cool."

"Way," Polly deadpanned. "*Your* show will be most amusing. I have a sixth sense about all things related to masks of comedy and tragedy. Instead of 'I see dead people,' I see 'stars on the rise.'" Polly thought for a moment. "As a matter of fact, I've begun to see dead people a lot lately too. But that's another story."

Gerold interrupted with a gruff rebuke of Polly for bringing guests to the rehearsal.

"Good morning to you too, Gerold," Polly said. She squared her shoulders and offered him the same hard look she used on her agent J.J. when he tried to convince her that an endorsement for Gerber's new line of pureed liver and onions for seniors would do wonders to increase her public visibility. "Our director has been murdered. A maniac is on the loose, and the killer may well be someone connected with the theater . . . perhaps from our very own cast. Are you going to spend big bucks for a security detail? Not just for me, but for the entire cast? If so, I want a posse of no-neck wannabe rappers with loads of tattoos and ostentatious bling to escort me to and from the theater each day and night." Gerold stared at his shoes.

"I thought so," Polly said. "Then you won't mind that my entourage will be at my side every day until the end of the run of this show. If you have any complaints, take them up with Actors' Equity and my agent. But I don't think you want J.J. coming down here to play referee."

Gerold heaved a deep sigh. "Is this how you're going to start off? The 'maniac' who killed Karen is behind bars, thanks to the fast work of the police, and Sharon's sloppy commission of the crime."

"You know that the killer isn't Sharon Fletcher."

Mag blanched.

Just as Gerold opened his mouth, a happy voice issued from the wings. "*Buenos dias,* amigos!" It was Charlotte Bunch heading onto the stage, followed by the actors playing Beauregard Jackson Pickett Burnside and Vera Charles. Hearing the tale-end of the conversation, Charlotte asked, "Our little murderess isn't guilty after all?" Her tone was equal parts excitement, skepticism, and disappointment. "Gerold's ready to say who did the evil deed?"

"No! Nobody!" Gerold spat. "Not nobody," he corrected himself. "Sharon, of course. There's nothing to suggest otherwise. End of subject. Where the hell are the others?" He looked at his watch, then looked around the stage and auditorium for his cast. Everyone had quietly assembled.

By the time the company had their first break, the tension between Polly and Gerold had softened. In fact, everyone in the principal cast was getting along well. The table reading was going smoothly, and Polly discovered that

Mag wasn't untalented. Her line readings were thoughtful and she had a flare for comedy. Unless she suddenly developed stage fright, she was not going to be an embarrassment to the production, as Polly had feared. When Gerold called, "Fifteen!" and left for the bathroom, Polly pounced on the opportunity to sidle up to Mag and pour out her charm.

"You're doing well, my dear!" Polly cooed, taking a seat at the table beside the young actress. "It's taken me this long to refine my perfect comedy timing. You're a natural. You must have studied Doria Cook's performance from the movie."

Mag smiled awkwardly and Polly knew that she had never heard of Doria Cook. Nor, Polly surmised, had Mag seen what was affectionately known as *LucyMame*—the Warner Bros. musical debacle that screwed Angela Lansbury out of the film version of her Broadway triumph in the title role. That film practically sank the unsinkable Jerry Herman musical, and it tarnished the otherwise sparkling career of Hollywood legend Lucille Ball. As one reviewer said at the time of the film's release in 1974, "Lucy wanted to make *Mame* in the worst way—and that's what she did."

Polly rambled on. "Never mind, Mag. You're doing a lovely job on your own. I imagine that Gerold's a marvelous help at home. What I would have given to live with my director on that stupid indy I made in Mexico, *It Oozed Through the Crack*—the better to get extracurricular coaching. Gerold's probably much better than stiff ol' Karen would have been. Poor Karen. What a shame. Dead at such a tender age. Perhaps the publicity from her shocking demise will pay off at the box office. Does Gerold like to walk? Does he often stroll through Glendale early in the morning? Does he have another alibi?"

Mag asked in a low voice, "Does everybody know that

I'm 'the girlfriend'? Do they think I got this role just because Gerold and I have feelings for each other?"

Polly put her arm around Mag. "Does a smart young
woman such as you give a rat's ass that her colleagues are
tittering under their Max Factor mask-of-comedy faces?
We know that it doesn't matter how we get our big breaks.
The important thing is to have the talent to back up the
opportunity when he, er, it, comes along. You've got loads
of talent. But don't let your relationship with Gerold get in
the way of you becoming part of the company. It's important that you spend time with the rest of us. Get to know
the chorus kids and stage hands. Have your meals with us.
Spend your off hours with members of the company. It'll
be good for dispelling all the rumors and for us to learn all
about you."

Mag looked nervous. "Rumors?"

"The usual. That you're using Gerold for career strategy, and that you and he lied to the police."

Mag swallowed hard. "Why can't people mind their
own business? Everybody makes mistakes."

"Gerold or the nosey cast?" Polly suggested that the kid
playing Little Patrick in the show claimed he saw Gerold
in the theater early the morning of the murder. "Which
contradicts Gerold's insistence that he was taking a long
walk."

"Damn kids, as my father used to say," Mag pouted. "If
Gerold hears this, he'll drag that little monkey out of
the show. He gets way cranky whenever the subject of the
murder—especially the police investigation—comes up. He's,
like, in my face twenty-four-seven if I ask about the girl who
murdered Karen. I swear, sometimes he's a totally gnarly
drag."

"You know how actors love to chat. Backstage gossip is
de rigueur, especially when you're sleeping with the leading man or the director or the producer, or all of the

above. But almost everybody sleeps with those who can help advance their careers."

Mag involuntarily smiled. "I'm not trying to be a star, or anything. I just want to do good work."

Polly forced a smile and patted Mag on the shoulder. "That's all any of us want for ourselves. As well as fame and fortune. But doing our best isn't always enough. We have to be our own cheerleaders. We have to push and fight and do whatever it takes for the right people to notice us. It's a killer business, and I think it's even harder for young people like you who are just starting out. You have to be willing to do anything, and I mean anything, to get ahead."

"I'm willing," Mag said in earnest. "I'm totally focused. What else do I have to do?"

Polly nodded. "Do you take acting lessons? Elocution? Dance? Singing? Are you immersed in the works of Mamet, Strinberg, and Cole Porter? Do you have a five-year plan? Do you even know who Ethel Merman is? Did you kill Karen Richards for a job?"

Mag quickly stood up. "That's a terrible thing to ask. Is that one of the rumors circulating among the cast? Gerold's not going to like it when he hears that people are talking this way behind his back. Duck and cover is what you and everybody else should do. Gerold warned me about you. I was almost ready to tell him that he's an idiot, but now . . . ."

Polly shrugged. "But he *is* an idiot, dear. He's like my manicurist who thinks that Ann Coulter is a messenger from the one and only true *Republican* God. Leave it to Coulter to have a partisan creator, and to Gerold for wrongly thinking that Sharon Fletcher killed Karen Richards. It's true that there appears to be lots of silly stuff like . . . evidence . . . against her, but all of that can be explained. I won't believe in Sharon's guilt until she confesses. Even then . . . Let me ask just one dumb question. Where was

Gerold during the time of the murder? Walking off the Ben & Jerry's from the night before? Enjoying an intermission with you? Throwing Emmys as though they were horse-shoes?"

"I'm way insulted, Miss Pepper. Like I'm totally stalled by your insinuation."

"It's just that a man with his, shall we say, girth would have been perspiring heavily in the heat of the morning if he'd been walking for two hours. He didn't have one bead of sweat when he arrived at the theater."

Polly reeled herself in. "I apologize, dear. I have a nasty habit of saying whatever comes into my mind. Thoughts just tumble past my lips."

"Then it obviously crossed your mind that I had some-thing to do with Karen's death," Mag shot back. "I didn't even know the woman."

Mag turned on her heel and walked off the stage. When she eventually returned, she was beside Gerold and speaking in a voice too low for anyone to hear. Every few seconds they glanced at Polly with threatening eyes.

Chapter 9

A s the publicity campaign for *Mame* ramped into high
gear, the streetlamp poles in Glendale were hung with
banners depicting the famous Hirschfeld caricature of
Polly from her infamous musical flop, *Erma La Douche*.
That show never made it past the savage critics in Chicago.
They had lambasted the star for her attempt to reinvent
her goody-goody image in a Las Vegas extravaganza–style
show about a blithe Parisian prostitute. Equally excoriated
were the lascivious choreography and the mundane songs.
(However, rap artist Vel-Vee-Ta recorded the show's most
memorable songs: "Romeo in Juliet" and "Tits a Wonderful Life.") Under the headline FOUL PLAY, the *Sun Times*
critic wrote of the musical, "The cacophony is as monotonous and incessant as the screeching of a baby on an air-
plane." Polly's sights on Broadway were diverted back to
Bel Air.

The backers of the show lost their investments, and the
producers lost any chance of seducing funds from their
wealthy friends for future projects. All were ruined, except
Polly of course, who survived the disaster because the
John Q. Public had more pressing priorities in their lives
than to ferret out theater reviews of a stage musical. Other

than the audiences who squirmed in their seats through the half dozen performances of the show in the Windy City, few people even knew that Polly was on the road desperate to get to Broadway.

Remembering Chicago, Polly said, "God, that banner brings back memories of my recurring nightmare during the show's short run. The one where I morph into Anita Bryant while singing 'Oklahomo!'" Although Polly complained, she loved the attention. She hadn't known this sensation since before the cancellation of her legendary musical variety television series in the 1980s. Although that show, *The Polly Pepper Playhouse*, had run for more than a decade, and earned her a dozen Emmy Awards as well as a worldwide legion of fans, none of Polly's subsequent projects ever lived up to the freak success of that classic sketch comedy and music program.

When anxiety descended on Polly Pepper, there was only one thing to lift her spirits—besides a Xanax and champagne chaser. "Let's have a party!" she said to Tim, as he parked the car in the theater lot. Throwing a big social soiree was Polly's antidote for everything from low quarterly earnings in her stock portfolio to higher than believable White House approval polls.

Everyone who had ever been to a party at Pepper Plantation agreed that Polly was unrivaled as a hostess and that her son, Tim, was a champion in the art of creating high-end Hollywood shindigs. Just as an invitation to Elton John's Oscar night party used to be *the* most sought-after social ticket in town, everyone wanted to receive a call to a Polly Pepper blowout. But after the success of his last big bash, Tim knew he'd have a tough time topping his *Immigration Reform* theme. For that affair, which was given in honor of the Mexican consulate who had written a gushy fan letter to Polly, Tim had outdone himself. The dress code mandated that guests wear (without first washing) the sweat-stained work clothes of their gardeners, maids, mechanics, handymen, or plumbers. On the other hand the valets and catering staff wore Dior evening gowns and Hugo Boss tuxedos.

The character reversal playacting probably didn't change any political minds, but the guests whooped it up mimicking the various foreign accents of their "domestic engineers" and addressing each other with names and epithets that if used on their real employees would have them being sued for unlawful workplace harassment. Still, Polly felt she had performed a social service by reminding her friends that their so-called menials were an important part of the fabric of their cushy lives.

"The party that I have in mind is just for the cast and chorus kids," Polly added, sensing Tim's unspoken reluctance to tackle a big affair.

Tim sighed and shook his head. "You hardly know these people."

"All the more reason for a party," Polly declared. "Relax. Make it a simple theme." She thought for a moment. "How about a cell phone swap? Everybody tosses their phone into a bowl, and then blindfolded they reach in as if they're drawing a prize. Like the old car key games of the swinging sixties!"

"Ooh! Then everyone dials their own number and they go home with the person who answers their line!" Tim laughed with excitement. "But you're not entertaining Charlie Sheen. Sophistication is clearly the guide for this event. These people all have you pigeonholed as a legend, and they'll expect nothing less than high style. Waiters with crudités on silver trays. A champagne fountain. The usual. Trust me, business attire and a string quartet and a giant ice sculpture of your initials will make them remember the night forever."

"Boring," Polly complained. "You know that I always hate to see my PP drip!"

Placenta nudged Tim. "We'll have that cell phone party the next time your mother goes . . ."

As the trio approached the stage door entrance, Polly suddenly stopped. She sniffed the air, as if she were a deer sensing a nearby hunter. She looked around the parking lot. "Hmm. Notice anything unusual?"

Tim and Placenta followed her gaze. After a long moment Tim said, "Um, isn't that Hiroaki Goldfarb over there? In the Honda Civic?"

"Bingo!" Polly said.

Placenta squinted. "You can't tell it's Hiroaki."

"Don't say 'Because they all look alike,'" Polly demanded.

"I'm just saying I can't identify who's in the car from this distance," Placenta insisted. "All I can see is that the car is black and it's obviously been in an accident. Look at that front end. Anyway, he doesn't drive. He doesn't have a job here either. So it's not him."

Polly shrugged and quickly turned away. As she led the way through the theater entrance she said, "I read somewhere that criminals return to the scene of their crime. Hiroaki had a motive to kill Karen!"

"Arsonists return to the scene of their fires," Placenta corrected.

Tim quickly pointed out that Hiroaki had taken the city bus to the theater the day of the murder and, in fact, had arrived just before the call time.

"Or so he says," Placenta added. "Did the police ask to see his bus ticket?"

"No ticky," Polly said. "I noticed that he carries a monthly pass. It's in a plastic sleeve on a lariat that he wears around his neck. That doesn't prove that he actually rides the bus, or that he didn't take an early one as he did the day he was first fired," she continued. "Hmm. I'm beginning to think we have to pay a visit to Mr. Hiroaki Goldfarb."

"What the hell kind of name is that?" Placenta said. "I

never heard of a Japanese Jew. And I'm not a racist! I'm an *observer* of cultural phenomena."

Polly was exhausted when rehearsals ended for the day. But she proposed they drive to Reseda.

"Hiroaki will never believe that you were 'in the neighborhood,'" Tim sassed his mother.

"I've always wanted to see how the Northridge Quake improved Reseda by flattening the place," Polly said. "I can say that I'm researching a new role and need to find out why the hell anyone would purposely chose to live over a major fault line."

Tim gave her a baleful look.

"Okay, so I'll call him first. Speed-dial and hand me the phone." Polly let out a deep sigh of dissatisfaction, accepted the phone, and after a brief exchange with Hiroaki, the car was gliding toward the Ventura Freeway.

When Tim finally saw the Sherman Way off-ramp he signaled a right-hand turn and rolled down to the surface street. Following directions from his Magellan, Tim passed dozens of gas stations and strip malls before being guided by the sultry voice in the GPS to Pacific Gardens Terrace. "We're nowhere near the Pacific, I don't see a single garden, and the only terraces are on those awful faux Spanish-style apartment buildings," Tim said, cringing.

"It's a darling little bedroom community," Polly said facetiously. "I may be in the market for some cheap income property. But I have to wonder what people do here."

"They plot their escape," Placenta said. "Now, in which building do you suppose Hiroaki resides?"

"That one," Tim said and pointed to the shabbiest three-story structure on the block. "He's in unit 303."

"The penthouse!" Polly trilled.

Tim found a parking spot not far from the apartment building and the trio stepped out of the car. "We'll make the visit as brief as possible," Polly promised.

When they were at the front entrance, Tim's eyes scrolled down a list of residents behind a glass-encased directory. "Goldfarb, H.," he said triumphantly. "Code 303." He pressed the numbers on the keypad and in a moment, Hiroaki's baritone voice was on the intercom.

"Sweetie, it's Polly and company. Can we come up for a teensy while?"

"I'll meet you at the elevator," Hiroaki said before pressing the buzzer to let his visitors in.

Tim pulled the handle and held the door open for his mother and Placenta and immediately wanted to wash his hands. When they were in the so-called lobby, which was a musty-scented tiled room with gold-veined smoked mirror squares on the walls, the threesome looked at each other as if they'd stepped into a condemned tenement. "The lobby is usually the nicest part of a building," Tim said. Then he pushed the cracked button for the elevator.

When the car arrived, Tim stepped in first to make sure it was suitable for his mother. It wasn't. The walls were covered in plywood that had been scarred and defaced with graffiti. "All clear," he said and ushered Polly and Placenta into the wooden box. "Don't touch anything or you're liable to catch Ebola," he cautioned as he pushed the button for the third floor. After an inordinately slow ride, the car came to an abrupt halt and the door slid open. As promised, Hiroaki was waiting to greet them.

"Follow me," Hiroaki said without further salutation. Polly and her troupe accompanied the actor down a long corridor. They passed a warren of doors leading to other apartments, all of which, Polly suspected, were cookie cutouts of the others. After several right turns, they arrived at number 303. Hiroaki unlocked the door and his guests followed him inside.

Polly's heart sank. She couldn't imagine anyone living in such a small and dingy apartment. Not only was it poorly lighted and cluttered, but the place reeked of cat urine and mildew. As if reading Polly's thoughts, Hiroaki explained that the pipes had burst last month and the landlord hadn't replaced the carpeting. "Meet Miss Lana Turner," he said, picking up an old gray cat from the sofa. "I'll put her in the bedroom so you'll have a place to sit."

The moment Hiroaki turned his back and walked down the short hallway to his bedroom, Polly, Tim, and Placenta gave each other the same look of despair. They quickly surveyed the place and saw an entire wall of autographed eight-by-ten black-and-white pictures of celebrities staring back at them from within cheap drugstore frames. "Just like Charlotte's collection," Polly said.

Several movie posters were taped to cinder block walls, and a small television occupied a corner. The kitchen, which was part of the room, as it had been at Charlotte's apartment, was a repository for newspapers, magazines, books, and a sink full of unwashed dishes. The trio stood in the center of the room, awaiting the return of their host.

Presently, Hiroaki was back and leaned into Polly for a hug. He then shook hands with Tim and Placenta and suggested that they take a seat on the sofa, which was covered with an afghan blanket and enough cat hair to weave into a rug. "How about a glass of water?" Hiroaki said.

After seeing the state of the kitchen, the three guests simultaneously replied, "No!" Polly added that they only planned to stay a moment; that they just wanted to check up on Hiroaki to make sure he wasn't too upset about losing his role in *Mame*.

"Of course I'm upset," Hiroaki spat. "No employment, no insurance! I'm screwed unless I can get eighty hours of work between now and October thirty-first. Karen understood how important this gig was to me, financially. But that son of a bitch Gerold Goss cares nothing about my situation. I'm surprised someone didn't kill *him* instead!"

Polly blanched. "Speaking of death and killing and murder, and all that fun stuff, who do you suppose opened dear Karen's head? Everyone in the company seemed to adore her."

Hiroaki was silent for a long moment. Then he stood up and moved over to the kitchen counter. He picked up a glass tumbler out of the sink, turned on the tap, and rinsed it out. Then he opened the freezer and withdrew a bottle of gin. "Would you like one?" he asked, holding the half-full bottle for Polly and her family to see.

Again there was a simultaneous burst of "No, thanks!" from the trio.

Hiroaki poured three fingers into the tumbler and took a small sip. "Who opened Karen's head?" he repeated Polly's question. "I think that the police are right to be looking at the cast for the killer. However, I doubt that it's the soap opera girl. She was quiet and reserved. Of course, isn't that what they usually say about ax murderers and psychopaths with a basement full of dismembered bodies?"

"So you don't think that Sharon is guilty?" Polly asked.

Hiroaki shrugged. "It's not for me to say. But there are others who should be considered."

"I'm all ears," Polly cooed to Hiroaki. "Do tell Polly all the dishy backstage naughtiness!"

Hiroaki smiled and took another sip of his drink. "Well, if I were investigating this case, I'd ask Charlotte Bunch where she was at the time of the murder."

"They already have. She was en route home after being fired by Karen—just like you."

"Then ask Miss Bunch if she carried a grudge against Karen for humiliating her."

Polly and the others perked up.

"It wasn't Karen's fault that Charlotte felt slighted," Hiroaki continued. "You know how sensitive actors can be. It was during the read-through that first morning. Charlotte prides herself on being the Meryl Streep of community theater, you know, the accents and all. Well, Karen interrupted Charlotte several times and politely suggested that her Irish brogue could be a wee bit more authentic. Charlotte was mortified, even though Karen was directing her in the classiest way imaginable. That afternoon, as we left the theater together, she was seething and said that no one was going to tell her how to do an authentic accent of any kind—especially Irish—as she had the entire cast of *Riverdance* holed up in her head. She was going to confront Karen with this fact first thing the next morning."

"Did she?"

"I didn't see her until we were all gathered waiting for Karen to show up."

Polly was curious. "Charlotte let a little thing like a director doing her job of trying to guide her performance upset her? I thought she was more professional than that!"

"Charlotte's a lot of things, including a good actor," Hiroaki said. "But she's hardly one to accept the slightest criticism, constructive or otherwise, without feeling insulted."

"How did she feel about getting the ax?" Polly asked. "I hear that you both knew that you were on Gerold's short list of cast members to be replaced."

Hiroaki rolled his eyes. "Where do these rumors come from? Why does everybody think we knew that we were being replaced? I didn't know. I'm always afraid that I will be canned from a job, but this one was different."

"So you didn't have an inkling that your days in *Mame* were numbered?"

"I signed on to do this musical and thought it would be a breeze. I've played Ito in a dozen productions of *Mame*. I'm like the token Asian whenever there's a production of *South Pacific*, or *The King and I*, or *Flower Drum Song*. I'm Pat Morita, George Takei, and Sab Shimono rolled into one. So I didn't think I'd be fired from this production."

Polly nodded. "Dear Hiroaki, please know that I will

personally keep my eyes peeled and my ears cocked for any forthcoming production of *Pacific Overtures*. Perhaps Disney will do a stage version of *Mulan*."

Hiroaki took another sip from his glass and rose to escort his guests to the door, but as his hand reached for the knob he was interrupted by one last comment from Polly.

"Lord knows your alibi is airtight. Taking the city bus all the time, I'll bet you run into the same people day in and day out. At least the drivers. By the way, how long does it take you to get from here to the theater? It must be hours!"

"Yes, hours," Hiroaki said vaguely. "But it's not so bad. I get a lot of reading done. It's tough not having a car, but with the cost of insurance and gas, there's no way I can afford such a luxury."

"By the way, you have a twin running around giving you a bad reputation for taste in automobiles. We saw him this morning in a battered old Honda. Watch out for identity theft, dear."

Polly patted Hiroaki on the cheek. "Things are bound to turn around for you. But if they don't, well, there's a reason for everything. Keep bugging your commercial agent to send you out for Panda Express commercials!" Polly made a kissy-kissy sound and walked out through the doorway. "We'll find our way back to the elevator. Give Constance Bennett a tickle for me."

"Lana Turner."

"Whatever."

Polly, Tim, and Placenta were silent as they retraced their steps to the elevator and while they were riding down to the lobby. However, once outside, they began to whisper to each other. Polly said, "So pathetic!"

"The poor man is in dire straits," Placenta lamented.

"I mean his choice of gin!" Polly corrected. "Send him some Stolly tomorrow," she said, looking at her maid-slash-secretary-slash-Welcome Wagon. "Gerold couldn't be more mean to deprive Hiroaki of his ability to earn a living and to qualify for his Actors' Equity health insurance!"

Tim added, "From now on, Mother, I'll be a good boy and do whatever you tell me, as long as I can live at Pepper Plantation forever. And I swear, we're never having cats!"

Placenta suddenly stopped a few yards from the Rolls. She looked at a car as if experiencing déjà vu. "Um, er. Honda. Black. Smashed in grill. Where have we seen this before?"

The others looked at the car, and then looked at each other. Then they looked back at Hiroaki's apartment building.

Chapter 10

En route back to Pepper Plantation, Polly looked at her watch and cried out, "For heaven's sake, we're missing Lush Hour! Open the fizz!"

Placenta reached into the car's custom-made wine cooler and withdrew a bottle of Veuve. As she stripped off the foil covering the cork, and twisted away the wire bonnet, Polly withdrew two champagne flutes from the mahogany glass holder and held them out for Placenta to fill. "Watch the speed, sweetie," she cautioned Tim. "We don't need any of Reseda's so-called finest to want a tour of a Rolls-Royce. They bag Willie Nelson on his bus all the time." Just as Placenta popped the cork, Polly's cell phone rang.

Polly looked at the caller ID and smiled. She flipped open the phone and cooed, "I'm breaking the law even as we speak. Would you like to arrest me?"

Tim looked into the rearview mirror and caught Placenta rolling her eyes.

"What does the California Penal Code suggest as appropriate punishment for having an open container of alcohol in a moving vehicle?" She smiled as she listened to her paramour. "Sounds like fun. Not to worry, Timmy's my designated driver. Placenta is actually the guilty party—she opened the bottle. I'm just trying to unwind. It's been a day of work, work, and more work. This weary legend needs a release."

Polly listened for a moment and then giggled. "Is that what arresting officers do to celebrities with blood alcohol levels above .08?" She giggled again, then changed the subject. "You'll be very proud of me, Mr. Policeman. Of course you are already. I mean I'm being very good about not interfering with the case of who killed my brilliant and delightful young stage director."

Placenta and Tim both laughed loudly enough for Polly to have to cover the cell phone's mouthpiece with her hand. She gave them a look that warned not to contradict her.

"Even though I know it's not Sharon Fletcher, everyone agrees that the killer is probably someone in the cast, or more than likely one who was once part of the cast. The rumors are flying! Charlotte Bunch thinks Hiroaki Gold-farb may have had a hand in the deed, and Hiroaki thinks that perhaps Charlotte should be fingered. It's all too interesting and I'm having the time of my life working on the show and dishing about death in between scenes."

She stopped smiling and swallowed hard. "I promised that I wouldn't interfere and I'm not, dear. I swear it. I'm just . . . making small talk—"

She listened again and nodded her head in agreement. "I realize that, and you're a doll to be concerned, but I—" Again she was interrupted. "But what if Sharon's *not* guilty? Sweetums, I just can't sit by and let the poor thing rot in a Beverly Hills jail cell. I'm not about to—" Polly pursed her lips in frustration. "Let's talk about something more fun, shall we? Did you know that Brad and Angelina sleep in a bed of Vaseline each night to keep their skin looking fresh and supple? Oh, and we're giving a cast party next week and you'll be there too."

Polly paused for a long moment. "Excuse me? Not unless I stop what? Um, Randy, darling, I'm Polly Pepper. I don't accept ultimatums, I give them. And by the way, most people listen to me as if I have something important to say. I swung the last mayoral election because I endorsed that adorable Hispanic hombre who I'm told will probably be our next governor. Let's chat later, shall we? Like the day after Prince Charles gets his fanny on the throne of England! The highway patrol? You wouldn't dare!" Polly quickly slapped the phone shut. She was stone silent.

"The honeymoon's over," Placenta said.

"He's just concerned for Polly's safety," Tim said. "I think it's very sweet that he cares so much."

"He's a control freak," Polly pouted.

"Like minds attract," Placenta reminded her.

Polly gave her a look. "Bad combination, two headstrong Tauruses. Cops are all alike. They think they hold all the cards just because they wear a badge and look sexy in a uniform. Well, no one tells Polly Pepper to mind her own business!"

"I'm with Timmy," Placenta said.

"You're both ganging up on me!" Polly protested.

"Archer cares for you," Placenta continued. "He doesn't want to see you get into trouble or worse, get yourself hurt. He's the first man in years to stand up to you. I rather like that."

Polly considered what her maid had said. "Yeah, I sort of like that too. But what am I supposed to do? I won't be pushed around, and someone has to help prove Sharon's innocence."

"Sharon could well be the killer," Tim said over his shoulder. "No one likes to think that their friends are capable of such a horror, but people often disappoint. Heck, Phil Spector was always nice to you. Bobby Blake could be charming, and he's still on your Christmas card list. The evidence against Sharon is pretty irrefutable. If I were on a jury I'd have a hard time finding reasonable doubt."

Polly shook her head in annoyance. "I know, I know. Why on earth do I always have to play the do-gooder? I should have simply sent Sharon flowers and a good-luck note. But no, I had to be drawn in, and to believe someone who has made a career out of make believe. Face it, actors are liars."

Placenta refilled Polly's champagne flute and topped off her own glass. "You're gullible all right, but with the exception of the schmucks you married, your intuition about people is generally spot-on."

Polly looked at Placenta and smiled. "It's a gift. Like my comic timing. So screw Detective Archer! I'm on a crusade to help Sharon. And if she's really guilty and it wrecks my chances for a relationship with Randy, I'll murder the bitch myself."

By the time Tim rolled the car under the front portico and parked, the trio was exhausted from a long day. "It's Lean Cuisine night," Placenta said as she yawned and stepped out of the car. Polly slipped out from her side of the vehicle and added, "I'm not hungry. Just open a bottle of Krug Grand Cuvée and maybe a bag of Chex Mix. And a couple of Advils, please."

As Tim pushed the numbers on the keypad of the alarm system he said, "You're right about actors being liars. Not you of course," he conceded. "But already we've caught Charlotte and Hiroaki in untruths."

Tim gallantly stood to the side as Polly and Placenta entered their home. Then he stepped in and closed the door behind him. He reset the alarm system and followed the others toward the kitchen.

"We don't know for sure who is lying or if they all are," Polly defended her fellow thespians. "But before rehearsals tomorrow, we're running over to the Beverly Hills jail for another chat with Sharon. If she's guilty and I have to beat a confession out of her, I'll do just that! Depending on what she has to say for herself, we'll tackle Gerold at the theater."

The distance to the Beverly Hills jail was a relatively short drive from Stone Canyon Road in Bel Air. It was only seven thirty in the morning, and the day shift at the station hadn't arrived. Still, Polly worked her charms on the handsome BHPD officers and was allowed into Sharon's cell.

Sharon was half asleep when Polly and her entourage showed up in front of the iron bars with a police escort. Her face was creased with wrinkles from sleeping on her pillow and her hair looked wind-tousled. "Girl, you need an emergency visit from José Eber!" Polly tsk-tsked Sharon's sorry state of appearance. Then she turned to the policeman. "Is it too much to ask that you keep your celebrity guests camera ready? How would you like it if people saw you looking like Kate Moss auditioning for a lead in *Planet of the Apes*? Would you please let me in to the animal cage?" Polly turned back to Sharon. "Honey, we've got to talk serious business."

When the guard had locked Polly and her clan into the cell with Sharon and stepped out of earshot, Polly sat down beside the inmate. "Have a breath mint," she said, opening her Marc Jacobs clutch and withdrawing a Mentos. "Now, here's the deal. You're guilty until proven innocent. At least that's the way the cookie crumbles in the media. And at the moment, there's not one shred of support for your virtue. Give me something to work with. Tell me all the things that you kept from the police. And make it quick, 'cause I've got to get my roots done before rehearsal."

Sharon sat on the edge of her bed and bowed her head. Her mussed hair fell in her face. "I've told you and the police and my attorney everything," Sharon whispered. "For the hundredth time, here's the instant replay. Karen calls me and asks that I come to the theater early. I arrive at eight-oh-five. I bring my Emmy 'cause Charlotte asked to see it. Karen holds the statuette and pretends to make a speech, 'I want to thank my boyfriend, Jamie,' yada, yada. Both of them bow to each other. Gerold walks in with his Twinkie. He's shocked that I'm there and says that he had ordered Karen to fire me the day before. I get upset and throw my cell phone at him. It bounces off his big fat body and Karen catches it. I storm out of the theater and drive away crying like an idiot. I spend the morning sobbing until the police arrive and arrest me for murder. End of story."

Polly nodded her head. "But why did you lie to the police about calling in sick and pretending to have a cold?"

"Because I didn't want anyone to know that I'd been among the last to see Karen alive."

"But Gerold and his Cupie Doll would have vouched for your innocence," Polly insisted.

"Have you seen either of them come forth yet?"

"You made matters a million times worse by not coming forward in the first place," Polly said.

"What's happened is exactly what I thought would happen," Sharon sniffled. "And Gerold hasn't said one word in my defense. If you ask me, he killed Karen."

"Wait a minute," she said. "You just said that Karen bowed to her boyfriend, Jamie. You never mentioned that Jamie was there. No one else has either. Why tell me now?"

Sharon gave Polly a blank look. "I've told this same timeline to everyone. I'm sure I mentioned Jamie. Those two were inseparable. I'm sure it's in the police records."

Tim said, "I would have remembered if you had said that Karen's lover was there."

Sharon blinked as though she couldn't comprehend

leaving out any detail of that morning. "I'm sure I mentioned it. Jamie's a sweet and sexy guy."

Polly thought back to the morning of the murder. She clearly recalled Jamie coming in from stage left loaded down with cardboard trays of Starbucks coffees and brown bags of apple fritters and crumb cakes. It was after nine o'clock and he'd offered as an explanation for his tardiness that the line for double banana coconut Frappuccinos was around the block. "You're sure Jamie was there?"

"They were joined at the hip. They came to the theater together the first day, and left in Karen's car. Must have done the same the morning that Karen was killed. Charlotte, the backstage gossipmonger, said they were living together. They were certainly an odd couple. She a Plain Jane. He a gym-built Adonis."

Polly looked at Tim. "Hon, did you see Jamie with Karen?"

"Who could miss them?" Tim replied. "He's probably the hottest thing I've ever seen and Karen was definitely not in his league."

Polly slapped her knees and stood up. Tim and Placenta followed her. "It's late, my dear," Polly said to Sharon and brushed hair out of the young actress's face. "We're rehearsing that freaking Moon Lady number today. If I don't get killed straddling that fake crescent, it'll be a small miracle."

"How's the show coming along?" Sharon asked with envy in her voice.

"Delightful. That is if you don't mind a screaming director, a brat with an ego the size of a wharf rat playing Little Patrick, and a Gooch who drives everyone nuts mimicking the rest of the cast. Oh, and by the way, you're lucky you're not playing Gloria. The so-called actor they hired to be your fiancé, the grown-up Patrick, is a toad. And that's being nice."

Sharon chuckled unconsciously. "Gerold's main squeeze

has my role, and he obviously wouldn't want anyone attractive kissing her. Shows you how dumb I am," she said wistfully. "I thought they were having difficulty casting the role of Patrick because they couldn't find a decent boy singer. Gerold planned to give his whining trophy doll my role all along and had to find a stomach-turner to whom she could play opposite. But Gerold had to go through Karen, who told me that she planned to appeal to the producers if Gerold tried to make any more casting changes."

As Polly hustled out of the jail cell she called back to Sharon, "Shall I send José over to touch up your roots too?"

Chapter 11

"Timmy, sweetie, step on it," Polly pleaded. "And hand me the phone."

Tim passed the cell phone to his mother in the backseat. Polly handed it to Placenta. "Call José and tell him I have a serious case of something."

"The usual?"

"*Infectiouschronicosis*. It always works. Just ladle it on extra thick. Make sure he gets the picture that the symptoms make for a not-so-pretty sight. Combine bird flu with hemorrhoids, a fever, and everything running all at once. Rather than José and my roots, we need to visit Jamie before rehearsals. Timmy, darling, can't you please make this chariot fly any faster?"

As Polly's car eased onto Woodlawn Terrace in Sherman Oaks, it slowed to a crawl as Tim and his passengers searched for Karen's house number. "Twenty-five forty-one. There it is," Polly said, pointing toward a one-story ranch-style house on a street of gardener-manicured lawns. "And look who's having a party," she said, heaving a thumb toward the open garage. Jamie was inside and appeared to be entertaining someone. As Tim pulled the Rolls into the driveway and parked behind a silver BMW, he said, "The widower has excellent taste."

"Let's see what these two cohorts have to say for themselves," Polly said as she opened the car door.

The sight of a Rolls-Royce occupying the space behind his car made Jamie and his friend walk out of the garage to see who was visiting so early in the morning. When he saw Polly Pepper, Jamie smiled broadly and swiftly walked to her side.

Polly opened her arms. "Darling boy, I would have come sooner, but I'd heard that you were in seclusion. I wanted to respect your privacy. You've been through the most god-awful trauma. Is there anything at all that I can do for you?"

Jamie held on to Polly for a long moment before they released each other.

Polly looked up at the other young man who had come to stand beside Jamie. "How do you do?" she said, holding out her hand and smiling up into the green eyes of a six-foot-four-inch soap-star-handsome man. "I'm Polly Pepper."

"Of course you are," he said as he shook Polly's hand. His army camouflage shorts revealed muscular legs with a dusting of blond hairs. A tight T-shirt advertised a packed chest, and biceps that, should Polly try, she would not be able to put both of her hands around. "I'm Steve."

Polly turned to her mascots to introduce them. She was perturbed to see that Tim's and Placenta's jaws had dropped at the sight of Steve. "This is my family, as embarrassing as it is to admit," she said, giving Tim a nudge with her elbow to his ribs. "My son, Tim, and our maid and dear friend, Placenta." She looked at Jamie. "What are you boys up to and can we be any help?"

Without asking, Polly made a beeline for the garage before anyone could stop her. She wanted to see if Jamie and Steve were perhaps destroying important documents that would implicate one of them in the murder of Karen Richards.

"Cleaning out my former life," Jamie said, as he and Steve followed Polly, who was now peeking into boxes and opening cabinet doors. "I've been instructed by Karen's mother's attorney that I have three days to vacate the premises. My home! Karen's home. I keep forgetting." Jamie sighed. "In two weeks, after the show opened, we were planning to find a house of our own together. Steve here is with the estate. He's to watch my every move to make sure that I don't take anything that isn't encrypted with my DNA." He looked at Steve. "He's actually been very supportive. Considering."

Polly was peeved. "Considering what? Considering that you've just lost the most important person in your life? Considering that with the blink of an eye your entire future was irrevocably changed? That some harridan of a mother wants to deprive you of what little you have and that your inalienable civil rights aren't recognized? That's some lousy consideration!" She reminded herself of why she had come to visit Jamie in the first place. "Honey, can we talk? Privately?" She looked at Steve. "I promise not to purloin so much as a Kleenex." She then turned to Tim and Placenta. "Keep Atlas amused for a few ticks."

Jamie nodded toward the house. "Come on in. Coffee's on." Polly followed behind him up a flagstone path to the front door.

"Charming home," Polly said when she entered the house and had an opportunity to admire the décor. As they moved from the foyer through a hallway that divided a large sitting room to the left and a formal dining room to the right and then opened into a combination great room and kitchen, Polly could sense that the house was once filled with joy. Now it was as dull and dead as Karen. Even the morning sunshine filtering in from the French doors that led to the backyard swimming pool failed to brighten the rooms.

"Yeah, we both loved the place. Her mother never bothered to visit. She didn't approve of her daughter working in the theater. But she knows exactly how much money she can get for the place. And a team of appraisers from Sotheby's has already started tagging the furniture and art. I'd say she's been keeping an eye on the booming L.A. real estate market just in case her daughter happened to die intestate, which she did." Jamie sighed. "I don't blame her. At least she'll have something from Karen. Even if it's just a couple of million dollars."

"And what do you get from Karen's death, besides heartache?"

Jamie picked up the carafe from a Braun coffeemaker and poured into two mugs. "Cream? Sugar?"

"Yes, please."

When Jamie placed the mugs on the table and motioned for Polly to be seated he said, "I get the most valuable asset that Karen had."

Polly took a sip from her coffee mug and focused her eyes on Jamie.

"I get the legacy of all that she taught me about life and about the theater. Intangible things can't be lost or stolen or ordered by a court to be returned to an estate. No one can take away my memories of Karen."

Polly almost choked on a sip of coffee. She wanted to roll her eyes and beg for an encore so that Tim and Placenta could enjoy a laugh. Instead, Polly reached across the table and placed a hand on Jamie's. "Why did you lie to the police?"

Jamie flinched and Polly did too. They simultaneously withdrew their hands from each other's. "Um, er, what do you mean? I never lied to the police, or to anyone. Why would you say that?"

Polly offered a wan smile. "I had a lovely conversation with Sharon Fletcher. She tells me that you were present with Karen when that no-neck monster Gerold fired her.

An argument between Karen and Gerold ensued and you were there to witness the whole ordeal. But you claim you were at Starbucks at the time. It simply doesn't add up . . . the timeline, I mean. One moment you're in the same room as Sharon and Karen and Gerold, and then poof, you've gone to collect coffee for the cast. I don't think so, dear."

Jamie sat back in his chair and looked defeated. "I wasn't there when Karen died. I swear it. When things heated up between Sharon and Gerold, Karen tried to protect me by sending Mag and me up to the office for her bottle of Xanax. By the time we got back Sharon was gone and so were Karen and Gerold. When you discovered her body backstage, that was the first time I'd seen her since about eight fifteen."

Polly touched Jamie's hand again. "You were as in love with Karen as she was with you?"

Jamie nodded.

"Then why would you leave her alone if there was even a hint of trouble that might place her in an unsafe situation?"

"I trusted Karen. If she wanted me to leave, it was so that I wouldn't see the tough business side of her personality. I never for a moment thought that anything bad could possibly happen to her, especially not in the theater. Not in the place she loved best. How was I to know? But of course I feel guilty now. If only I'd hung around a few minutes longer . . ." Jamie began to weep.

Polly stood up and looked around. She saw a box of Kleenex on the granite bar countertop and brought it over to the table. "Forget my promise to that inordinately unattractive space alien outside."

Jamie chuckled as he wiped his eyes and dabbed at his running nose. "Did you really think that I could have anything to do with the death of such a beautiful and talented woman as Karen Richards?"

Beautiful? Polly thought to herself.

"I'm not a perfect person, and I've made some bad judgments in my life, but I'd found the woman of my dreams and I wouldn't do anything to jeopardize that."

Polly sat down again and leaned forward on the table. She looked deep into Jamie's eyes. "Do you think Sharon killed Karen?"

Jamie shrugged. "I don't want to believe it, but Sharon's Emmy Award was the murder weapon, and Gerold and I and Mag were there when she was fired. She was naturally angry, so she has a motive. If she didn't do it, I don't know who else would have. Gerold? His girlfriend? Charlotte or Hiroaki? Maybe."

Polly sighed. "But ol' Gerold and his little tart claim that they didn't see anyone else before Karen's death."

"There was Charlotte and Hiroaki."

"Together? When did you see them?" Polly asked.

"Eight-oh-five."

"It's all so complicated," Polly whined.

"Some things are more obvious than others. Do you want a cup of coffee—to go?"

"I've had my fill, thanks." Polly rose from her chair at the table. "By the by, now that you're being evicted from your home, where are you going to live?"

"I've got a roommate thing in West Hollywood," Jamie said. "I always land in clover."

"A handsome boy like you always does," Polly said and gave Jamie another hug. "Please come to dinner at the Plantation one night this week. I know that you and Tim would get along well, and I want to know more about Karen. She had such a great reputation for creativity. Check your schedule and we'll call you later," Polly added as she followed Jamie back through the house and out the front doorway.

Once outside, she was not surprised to see Tim and Placenta both engaged in conversation with muscle-bound

Steve. Tim was especially flagrant as he flattered Steve with admiring questions about his tattoos, and asked for pointers on what vitamin supplements he should take after working out at the gym. Sotto voce to Jamie, Polly said, "Ignore Tim. He's been a virgin for nearly a month."

Jamie sniggered. "Steve's a stunner all right. He could make a man forget his grief."

Chapter 12

"That was quite a show back there," Polly said once her car was out of sight of Karen's house.

"A-men!" Placenta agreed. "When God decides He wants to punish His children, He makes a specimen like Steve so we all hate ourselves."

Polly snorted, "I'm talking about Jamie! He's either the most sentimental young fool, or he's a hell of an actor. By the way, I'm utterly mortified by the way you both behaved around that U.S. Marine Corp poster boy." Polly mimicked Tim panting like a dog. "'Show me your tattoos.'" Then she imitated Placenta demurely asking, "'How do you keep your teeth so white?' You both had better find boyfriends ASAP."

"What do you think we were trying to do?" Placenta said.

"As I was saying," Polly continued, "the performance that Jamie put on for me was a doozy." Now she mimicked Jamie exalting the merits of Karen. "However, he still won't admit that he lied about being present at his girlfriend's last gasp."

Tim divided his attention between the road and watching his mother in the rearview mirror. "I take it that he didn't come right out and say he was a Menendez brother," Tim said.

"Not in so many words. But his alibi and sorry story about being at Starbucks at the time of the crime has as many holes in it as Bonnie and Clyde. But I've got a plan."

Placenta and Tim were listening intently as Polly reached into her suit jacket and withdrew an eight-by-ten black-and-white head shot of Jamie that she had carefully hidden under her arm. "When our boy was weeping over the loss of his great love—or the loss of his house—I snatched this, which was lying beside a box of Kleenex." She held up the picture for all to see.

"So Jamie's an actor, eh?" Placenta said as she took the glossy from Polly's hands. She turned the picture over and began to read his credits listed on the reverse side. "*Les Miz*. Of course. *A Chorus Line*. Natch. *Annie, Fiddler, Rent*. Not bad," she said, sounding slightly impressed. "Get this—seven productions of *Mame*! In every production he had the role of adult Patrick."

Polly pondered the situation for a moment. "What's wrong with this picture?"

"It's at least five years old?" Placenta said.

"Not the eight-by-ten!" Polly snapped. "The *big* picture. Here's an actor, living with the director of a show that he's done a gazillion times. Why isn't he in this production?"

"Probably burned out from doing the same part over and over," Tim suggested. "I mean, how many times can a guy sing 'My Best Girl' to his old lady aunt?"

Polly took back the picture and studied the head shot. She read his other theater credits. "Perhaps the director found him hot in bed, but too limp onstage. That could be a motive for murder."

"People have killed for less," Placenta said.

"Sharon said they couldn't cast that role for the longest time," Polly said. "Perhaps Jamie was expecting that they'd eventually see that the right actor for the part was in their midst. When Karen ultimately said no, Jamie went ballistic and bashed her head in. Just a thought."

"So, what's this plan you said you have?" Placenta asked.

"It's brilliant. I was trying to think of a way to refute Jamie's story about being at Starbucks. The best way to get to the truth would be to ask the baristas who were on duty. When I saw his head shot it instantly occurred to me that armed with my charm and celebrity and his photo, it would be easy to get someone to swear that Jamie was in the store on Tuesday morning. Or not. Aren't I the most clever star in Hollywood?" Polly beamed.

"Not so clever, if you're late for rehearsals," Tim said. "We don't have time to run around showing mug shots today."

Polly heaved a sigh. She leaned forward toward the driver's seat. "Hand me the phone," she said and once again forced it into Placenta's hands. "Gerold. You know the drill. *Infectiouschronicosis.* But tell him I'll drag myself onto the stage ASAP, ethical star that I am. That should buy us a couple of hours. Hell, I know the show backward and forward anyway."

Placenta shook her head as she speed-dialed Gerold. "Mr. Goss?" she said when he answered his cell phone. "This is Placenta calling for Miss Polly Pepper. It's not pretty. . . ."

The long line at the counter inside the Starbucks store on Brand Avenue across the street from the Galaxy Theatre was crowded with office workers desperate for their first infusion of caffeine of the day. Tables scattered about the room were filled with wannabe writers at their notebook computers and unemployed or self-employed people killing time. When Polly and her crew walked into the shop they were in line for only a moment before she was recognized.

"You're that lady on the banners!" said a man who was wearing the uniform of a gas station mechanic. In a louder voice he said, "I seen youse on the tay-vay."

Suddenly everyone in the store was staring at Polly. Even those who were too young to remember her career understood that someone famous was in the café. Once she had been pointed out, the older customers instantly recognized Polly and began telling her about particular episodes of her old show that they remembered most fondly. Polly was delighted for an opportunity to play the humble legend, and she did so with ease and mastery. "Stars are people too," she giggled. "We have to have our java just the same as any ordinary garden variety mortal."

Suddenly a voice called from the front of the line, "Miss Pepper, I'll help you over here." A tall woman behind the counter waved her over.

"No, these lovely people were here first," she said, and was immediately accosted by the entire line insisting that she go before anyone else. Polly forced a blush. "I'll wager that La Streisand isn't treated this well! You really don't mind? I am rather in a hurry to get to a rehearsal. Oh, I'm starring in *Mame* at the Galaxy. Please do come and see me! I guarantee I'll be fabulous in the show! I've done the role dozens of times, so I won't disappoint you. As if I could.

"You're a doll," Polly said when she reached the barista who was wearing a green smock and holding a paper cup and a black Sharpie in her hands. "So many options! I'm an old-fashioned plain black coffee girl, and I don't want to tie up the line, so I'll make it simple. A grande toffee nut latte ristrato. Extra whipped cream and heavy on the crunchy caramel sprinkles. Better make *three* of the same. Oh, and have you ever seen this man?" She held up a copy of Jamie's eight-by-ten.

The line only got longer and a bit of complaining began among the growing crowd as Polly monopolized the four

baristas who were trying to simultaneously fill her complicated coffee order and answer her questions about the
man in the picture. After five minutes of grilling the workers and getting only blank stares when she asked them to
think back to Tuesday morning and to identify Jamie from
the hundreds of customers they had served, Polly gave up
in frustration.

Tim handed the cashier a twenty-dollar bill and picked
up the coffee order. As they left the now restless line of pa-
trons and headed for the exit door, Polly called out,
"Don't forget to come and see me at the Galaxy. We open
on the fifteenth!" By now, the novelty of seeing Polly in
person had worn off, and the crowd merely mumbled
words that she couldn't understand.

"That was a complete waste," Tim said when they were
once again settled in the car. "We got nothing! Not even
freebee coffees!"

Polly took a sip from her cup. "On the contrary, we got
what I hoped for."

"You're happy with nothing?" Placenta said. "Talk
about the benefits of low expectations."

"Don't you see? This proves that Jamie wasn't at Starbucks when he said he was!"

"It only proves that no one remembers seeing him,"
Tim interrupted. "For heaven's sake, look at the picture.
It's been retouched to the nth degree! And it's possible that
the baristas we talked to weren't even on duty when Jamie
was there."

"Oh, damn!" Placenta said. "Look." Polly and Tim followed the direction where Placenta pointed. "There's another Starbucks over there! And over there! And there!
Holy moly, they've taken over the planet. Maybe Jamie
didn't go to the Starbucks we visited. We'll have to go to
every one in order to refute his story. My bladder can't
take it!"

Polly was crestfallen. "This could take days! We need an

answer now! Get a move on. We'll start with the one across the street."

At ten minutes to four Polly and her pose arrived at the theater and walked through the artists' entrance. Tim signed in for the trio and then caught up with his mother and Placenta just as they entered the stage wings. While Polly walked straight onto the stage, Tim and Placenta veered to the right and walked down several steps that led from the stage to the auditorium. They sat in seats several rows back and watched as Gerold excoriated Polly for what he called her unprofessional conduct.

"Miss Pepper has deigned to grace us with her internationally renowned presence. Shall we all give her a warm round of applause? I think not! That would simply encourage her inappropriate behavior."

Polly pursed her lips and looked bored. "Dear Gerold, don't be monotonous," she said and sat down at the reading table.

Stilted sniggers of approval from several of the other cast members made Gerold turn beet red with simmering rage. "I'll see you in my office after the rehearsal."

"Alone? With you? We should be chaperoned." The others at the table giggled with pride. "Really, dear, I'd love to have a tête-à-tête with you, but I have another engagement this evening. Call my agent, J.J. He'll relay your message. If he thinks it merits my attention." She opened up her play script. "Now, which scene are we rehearsing?"

Chapter 13

At six o'clock Gerold closed his copy of the script. "Thanks to a certain so-called legend, we're behind schedule. Therefore, tomorrow, and for the remainder of the week, Miss Polly Pepper will be spending her days at the Ginger Rogers Dance Studio blocking the dance numbers with the chorus and our choreographer." Gerold opened his folio and handed Polly a sheaf of papers. "This is your agenda for the next five days—including Saturday. Dance lessons. Vocal coach. Costume fittings. When you return to us on Monday, we're going into full rehearsal. Know your lines and choreography!"

Although it was common for stage productions to have dance and vocal rehearsals in rented studios scattered around Los Angeles, Polly was aware that the Galaxy Theatre had its own network of studios in the basement of the old building. She suspected that Gerold was sending her off-site to prevent her from collecting more gossip about Karen's murder. "I'll miss all of you," Polly said to the cast. "What will I do without Charlotte's hourly game of 'Guess the Dead Star's Voice'? And I'm bonding so well with my Beauregard and Vera and Little Patrick and Ito and Mr. Babcock." After a week of daily interaction with these actors she still didn't have their real names committed to memory. "Be sure to text me with any juicy dish!"

As Polly stood to leave the stage, she called out, "Everybody! Save the date! I'm hosting a lovely party a week from Saturday. I'll fax you all with directions. Business attire, please!"

A collective hum of excitement and anticipation immediately ricocheted back to Polly, who smiled and waved good-bye to her associates. Mag sidled up to her and whispered, "Gerold says we're busy that night. But we're not. I'm desperate to see your house! Invite him personally. Please?"

"Of course, dear." Polly smiled and collected her script and purse. As Tim and Placenta were marching up the steps to meet her on the stage, Polly spied Gerold retreating up the auditorium aisle, presumably headed to his office. She looked at Mag and said, "I'll ask him now." Then she turned to her family. "Give me a sec. I'll meet you at the car." Polly walked down the stage steps and followed Gerold, who had already disappeared through the double doors and into the lobby. By the time Polly arrived in the cavernous lobby, she had lost Gerold. Not knowing exactly where his office was located, she made an educated guess.

The Galaxy Theatre boasted two massive carpeted grand staircases on either side of the lobby. Ascending the stairs, you could easily pretend you were in a European palace. Polly found herself on the staircase playacting that she was Queen Elizabeth going up to her bedroom suite at Buckingham Palace. When she reached the second-floor landing she looked to her left. The balcony seemed only to lead to doors for entrance into the mezzanine. However, signs on the wall in front of her indicated that restrooms were located straight ahead. Polly supposed that perhaps the general offices were also along this corridor, and she continued along the carpeted passageway.

From the distance, Polly heard a door close. She smiled to herself, proud that her instinct for directions had not failed her. She walked past the men's room, then the ladies' room and found herself proceeding with the stealth of a cat creeping along toward a bird. As she continued she noticed that the overhead lighting fixtures were illuminated only up to a point, and soon she was engulfed in a dark maw. She stepped cautiously as she proceeded, still searching for the room from which the sound of a closing door had echoed down the hall. Arriving at an intersection of corridors, she looked to the left and saw only complete blackness. She looked to the right and could see a strip of light wedged under a door in the otherwise black distance. Polly reached out her right hand to find the wall, and using it as a guide, she continued down the hall toward the light. Soon she could hear muted voices. One voice was unmistakable; it belonged to Gerold Goss.

Polly saw another sliver of light from under a door that was only a few feet in front of her. She quickly realized that the voices she heard were coming from this room. As she got closer, she cocked her ear to try and distinguish who else was with Gerold. Were there more than two people in the room? Could Gerold be yelling at Mag? No, although the voice was much softer than Gerold's, Polly could tell it was a male voice. And then she heard her own name spoken by Gerold—"That damned Polly Pepper!" he spat. The other voice said, "It's too late. She's bound to know."

Polly swallowed hard. "Know what?" she wanted to say aloud. Instead she stood outside the office with her head nearly resting against the door. Still, it was difficult to make out all that was being said. Once again she heard her name mentioned. *Is that Jamie's voice?* she asked herself. The voice then yelled, "You promised me! You're going back on your word. The police would love to hear my revised statement. The truth!"

Gerold laughed in a tone of contempt. "I'm a witness! Say a word about this to anyone and it's bye-bye, career! Of course, where they'd send you, you'd have lots of boyfriends to take your mind off showbiz. Now get out of my face."

Polly backed up and in her haste, brushed against an aluminum trash can and tipped it over. The sound of metal on the carpet was a soft thud, but loud enough to startle her. She quickly ran toward the weak light at the end of the corridor. The door to the office had opened behind her and she could tell she was under hot pursuit. Turning at the corner, Polly could see the staircase ahead of her but knew that she'd never make it down the long flight of steps without being seen. She made a snap decision to hide in the ladies' room.

When she opened the door she found the light switch and turned it off. With only a flash of memory of the layout of the room she made her way as quickly as possible to the stall at the end.

As Polly crouched on the toilet seat in the darkness, her heart beat loudly enough to be heard in the otherwise silent room. Her breathing was labored and she swallowed hard. Then her worst fear came to pass. She heard the sound of squeaking hinges as the bathroom door was slowly opened. Footsteps moved furtively and echoed on the tile. They stopped midway into the room.

For a few moments, there was no sound at all, but Polly could sense the vibration of someone else in the room. Cowering on the toilet seat, she felt her legs becoming sore and then going numb. In the darkness her sensory depravation was bringing on vertigo. But she concentrated on not moving a muscle. Suddenly the room was flooded with light as the intruder flipped the switch and blasted the room with fluorescent incandescence. The door opened again and Gerold's voice said, "I got her. It was one of the cleaning ladies. She doesn't speak English."

"What was she doing and why did she run?" the other voice asked.

"The hell if know! I said she doesn't speak English! *Comprendo*? Now get out of here and don't let me see your ugly face again."

In a moment, the lights were turned off and the men were gone. Polly waited a long moment before she plucked her cell phone from her clutch purse and dialed Tim's number. "Don't ask any questions," she whispered when Tim answered. "Just pull the car out of the parking lot as quickly as possible. Don't let Gerold or anyone see that my car is still here. Pick me up at the Starbucks directly across the street. I'll be there as soon as I can. But if I'm not out in ten minutes, call Randy and tell him I'm in trouble."

Polly didn't wait for a response and flipped the cell phone lid closed. In a moment she felt safe enough to slip out of the bathroom and make her way down to the lobby. In the distance she could hear a vacuum cleaner moving over the carpet. She also heard a few voices speaking in Spanish. From listening to Berlitz CDs to learn to speak to Hector, her gardener, Polly picked up a few phrases. "Fat ass!" She could understand the words of one woman. "The man is loco!" She translated another's sentence. Then she slipped down the stairs and out the front door.

It was early evening and still bright outside. When she reached the crosswalk, Polly looked around with intense paranoia, afraid that she would run into Gerold or Jamie. When the light turned green, she sprinted across the street and found Tim and Placenta. "Move it!" she yelled before she was inside the car. She didn't speak for the remainder of the drive home.

The gates to the Pepper Plantation estate parted and Tim eased the Rolls down the cobblestone lane. From the distance Polly could see another vehicle in their drive park.

"What's he doing here?" she asked, perturbed by finding Detective Archer leaning against his Honda Accord.

"I made an executive decision," Tim said. "When you called and said to notify Randy if you weren't out in ten minutes, I decided to call him anyway. You're getting yourself into deep doo-doo and I don't want you to be the next corpse someone stumbles over!"

Polly was in a snit. "I can certainly take care of myself, thank you very much."

"You're our responsibility," Placenta blasted Polly. "If you're going to go around doing crazy, dangerous things on your own, be prepared to have us bring out the collar and leash!"

The trio stepped out of the car and Randy met them at the front steps. "Polly, I need to have a word with you, please."

Tim pressed the alarm system keypad and opened the door for his mother and Placenta. "Come on in, Randy."

Polly ignored her beau until she arrived at the great room. There she plopped herself onto the sofa and waited for Placenta to bring a glass of champagne.

"Polly—" Detective Archer began.

"Wait until Placenta brings reinforcements, dear. I've just had the most god-awful experience and I'm in desperate need of nourishment."

Presently, Placenta arrived with an open bottle of Dom in an ice bucket and four champagne flutes. Tim poured. Polly drank.

After a few silent moments and her glass practically empty, Polly heaved a heavy sigh and looked first at Tim, then Placenta, then Detective Archer. "Okay. I know you're all going to give me hell, especially you, Randy, but I couldn't help what happened. It wasn't my fault, and I'm probably going to end up dead."

Tim and Placenta both gasped.

"What exactly happened?" Randy asked.

"Mag asked me to personally invite Gerold to our party," Polly began. "I figured he was probably in his office, so I went looking for him. When I got there, I overheard him yelling at someone and he mentioned my name. Then that someone said I knew something that I shouldn't—and don't. It appears that they think I know who killed Karen Richards. Then two men chased me. I was damn lucky to escape."

Detective Archer stood up and pushed his hands into his pants pockets. "Polly!" he said sternly. "This is exactly why I warned you about meddling in police business. Dozens of people get killed in this town every day, and for doing little more than taking a parking space that someone else was waiting for. Here you are, snooping around and asking questions of people who love to gossip and may be telling everyone else that you're curious about finding Karen's real killer, and this just gets you into danger. If you want to jeopardize our relationship by getting killed, you're being selfish. Helping Sharon is admirable, and I'm all for being loyal to friends. But while you're snooping around on her behalf, you're obviously making someone nervous. If Sharon isn't the killer and you get too close to the truth, whoever whacked Karen would have no hesitation sending you to the same fate."

"You're more upset than I am." Polly reached out to have Randy take her hand in his. "I didn't mean to find myself in hot water. And I certainly would never deliberately give you cause to be concerned for me. You're sweet to be mean about this."

"Not mean," Randy said in a calmer voice. "Protective. It's what I do. Would you please not pursue this mission of playing amateur sleuth?"

Polly nodded her head. "I can try. But sometimes I find myself immersed in a situation and I honestly don't know how I got there. Like the time I found myself in Sylmar making *The Can Opener*, that dreadful low-budget feature about a Cybill Shepherd clone and her penchant for giving enemas to stray cats. Tonight I was trapped in the ladies' room with a homicidal maniac bursting through the door with an ax, like Jack Nicholson in *The Shining*."

"An ax?" Tim cried out.

Polly shrugged her shoulders. "An ax, a gun, or a rope. Who knows? It was dark."

"So you never actually saw an ax," Placenta said.

"I said I was hiding in a lavatory stall. I don't have X-ray vision."

"But someone did follow you, right?" Tim asked.

"Of course!" Polly was indignant. "I'm fairly sure that it was Jamie. I'm thinking that someone from Starbucks tipped him off that we've been asking about his alibi."

Detective Archer shouted, "That's exactly what I'm talking about! You've watched too many detective shows on television. You think you know how to conduct an investigation."

Polly held out her glass for a refill. "How hard can it be? One has only to ask a lot of questions," she said, and was then quiet for a long moment. "Okay. You win. I don't know what I'm doing and could find myself dead waiting in Purgatory's Greenroom for an audience with St. Peter. But I refuse to believe that Sharon is guilty of murder. I won't believe it until she confesses. As a matter of fact, the very idea that someone thinks I know the truth means that Sharon is really innocent!"

Chapter 14

The alarm clock in Polly's boudoir buzzed at 6:00 A.M. Soon thereafter, Randy quietly closed the bedroom door behind him. With his shirt halfway buttoned and the tales untucked, and his ruddy face in need of a shave, he crept down the long corridor to the Scarlett O'Hara Memorial Staircase. As he descended to the main level of the house he looked around, baffled about how to leave the palatial residence without setting off the security alarm system. The last thing he wanted to do was to summon the Bel Air Patrol. But if he returned to Polly's bed to ask for the security code he'd inevitably end up crawling back under the sheets beside her.

"'To *service* and protect,' eh?" Placenta's voice came out of nowhere and startled Randy as he stepped off the stairs and into the cavernous living room of the still dark house.

"Jeez, Placenta! Give a guy some warning before you pounce on him! And it's "to *serve* and protect.' That's the official motto."

"Mmmm." Placenta offered with a wry grin. "Coffee's on. I'll make breakfast."

Archer hadn't bothered to eat the night before and he

was hungover from too much champagne and a long stretch of making love to Polly. Although he was due at his station at eight, his body needed fuel if he were to survive the morning. The aroma of freshly brewed coffee was all the incentive he needed to follow Placenta to her domain.

"Have a seat at the island," Placenta said, pulling out a bar stool for Archer to sit on. She poured two mugs of coffee and set one on the granite countertop before her guest. "Milk and sugar are there." She pointed to a silver tray on which a small ceramic cow filled with milk stood next to a small barnyard rooster, the back of which was hollowed out to hold sugar cubes. "Egg whites? Toast? Blueberry pancakes? Your choice."

"Real blueberries?"

"Comin' right up." Placenta opened the refrigerator and withdrew a carton of premixed pancake mix. She supposed the blueberries were probably processed or genetically engineered, but like a can of Pringles potato chips, who cared if they were real potatoes, or if the blueberries were bits of laboratory-made nuggets containing artificial flavoring and purple dye number 12? "You and Polly have patched things up?" Placenta said, although the answer was obvious. "After that row you guys had the other day, we thought things may have cooled down."

Randy nodded. "She realized that she has to be rational. I'm trying to keep her from getting hurt."

"Rational? Polly?" Placenta sniffed. "You're dating the wrong legend if you want common sense and analytical reasoning in your woman. Don't get me wrong. Polly's as bright as a *Jeopardy!* winner, but she doesn't live in the real world. No one in Hollywood does. At least not the ones who have made it big the way she has. Her image is that of a totally down-to-earth star—and she is—but heaven forbid Polly ever has to use an ATM card at a grocery checkout. She's used to having me and Tim, or anyone else she can find, do the mundane things that everyone else on the planet does as a matter of course every day. Do you know that Polly's never learned to fill her gas tank? Nor has she ever had to wait for a table at Spago. So maybe you can understand her frustration when she was told by you to keep her nose out of this case. She's not used to anybody, including big-time directors, telling her what to do."

"I'm sort of the same way. I mean, I pump my own gas of course, but I don't like having anyone tell me what to do either. Especially when I'm told to do something that I intuitively know isn't right."

"That's Polly," Placenta said. "She has a sixth sense about people and in this case, she's sure that Sharon Fletcher is innocent of murdering Karen Richards. Do her a big favor, will you?"

"Anything."

"Find out what the police are doing about evidence to corroborate Sharon's claim that she wasn't in the theater at the time of Karen's death. Have they done background checks on all the cast members, the tech crew, and especially Jamie Livingston? Find out if there's anything unusual about these people—other than the fact that they're actors."

Placenta heated the griddle and opened the container of batter. "The woman often gets things mixed up because she doesn't pay attention to what people have to say—unless they're saying something about her. But according to what she revealed last night, Gerold and Jamie *were* talking about her. So I believe that she's onto something.

"I had terrible dreams last night about Polly being attacked in the theater—and it wasn't by the opening night critics," Placenta continued. "I couldn't see who the assailant was, but Polly kept trying to yell for help and no sound came from her voice. We all thought she had just forgotten her lines and that the chase scene was in the script of whatever play she was doing. Now that I think of it, the simple interpretation of the dream is that Polly's try-ing to tell us something, but no one is listening."

Placenta looked at Randy. "I'm glad the nightmare didn't cause me to check on her during the night to see if she needed protection. I'd have likely had worse nightmares had I stumbled onto whatever you two were up to."

Randy smirked. "She and I both should have had pro-tection last night."

Placenta dropped her spatula on the floor for effect and slapped her hands over her ears. "TMI!" she squealed. "I don't need details, please! Just drink your coffee and spare me the visuals!" Placenta cackled. "At least someone in this crazy house is getting a little nookie."

When Polly eventually came down to breakfast at eight o'clock, Tim and Placenta were waiting to take her to the Ginger Rogers Dance Studio in North Hollywood. "I can't dance today," she moaned. "I'm exhausted. Randy and I—"

"What time did he finally leave?" Tim asked. "You two were still swilling champagne when I hit the sack after Jon Stewart."

Polly glanced at Placenta, who gave her a knowing look.

"Eat your pancakes, drink your coffee, and get dressed," Placenta ordered. "I hear that Tatanya Morgan is a choreo-grapher who throws fits that would make Jerome Robbins pee in his BVDs, and we would not be starting on the right foot by being late."

En route to the dance studio, Placenta teased Polly. "Must be mating season." She smirked. "I could hear the bucks mounting doe out in the garden."

Tim complained, "If we start having deer problems again, Hector'll have a fit. They thrive on his plants!"

Polly glared at Placenta, who simply sniggered and then pretended to be interested in the traffic as they turned off

Sunset Boulevard and climbed serpentine Laurel Canyon and on down through Studio City to North Hollywood.

North Hollywood was in the San Fernando Valley of Southern California, over the hill from the more famous Hollywood. It was a city with a multicultural mix of mostly blue-collar workers, and where the billboard signage in Spanish beat English two to one. The dance studio and rehearsal hall was in a less desirable part of an already undesirable low-rent city. "I always forget how much I loathe the Valley," Polly scoffed as they arrived at the studio. "It's so flat! The buildings all look alike. How many Pay-Day Advance stores does a city really need? Park up front, hon," she said to Tim.

Tim reluctantly parked the Rolls in a space that boasted a large sign that declared RESERVED FOR GINGER. "I suppose she won't be needing it."

As the trio stepped from the car, Tim popped the trunk latch from a button on his key fob and reached inside for Polly's Capezio dance bag. The zippered pockets and flaps of the well-worn bag contained everything from tap shoes to pointe ballet slippers, leg warmers, leotards, towels, makeup, and bottled water. Tim slipped the strap over his shoulder and began to follow his mother and Placenta up the steps to the rehearsal halls.

As he turned and pointed the key fob at the car to transmit the lock signal, he noticed a black Honda slowly pulling up and parking on the street outside the dance studio lot. The car looked like the same one they had seen with Hiroaki behind the wheel, and outside Hiroaki's Reseda apartment. As furtively as possible Tim whispered to Placenta, "Try not to look like you're looking, but over there, the car with the smashed front. Isn't that . . . ?"

"Yep," she said to Tim. "Let's get your mama inside quickly."

Once inside the old one-story building, they stopped at the reception window and asked for Tatanya Morgan's room. "I'll catch up with you guys during lunch break," Tim said, handing over Polly's dance bag to Placenta and sending them in search of room number 4 and the nefarious Tony Award–winning choreographer. The walls along the corridors boasted dark paneling decorated with movie posters from not only the fabled career of the studio's late owner, but old movie posters from many MGM, Paramount, Warner Bros., and Republic Pictures films. "She has as much junk on the walls as we do at home," Polly said, thinking that perhaps it was time to redecorate the upstairs landing of Pepper Plantation.

Tim cautiously peeked out of the screen door and saw that the black Honda was no longer parked beside the building. He stepped out on the porch for a better view. Still, he didn't see Hiroaki or the car. He shrugged his shoulders and moved back to the Rolls to steal a nap while his mother was working her butt off under the dictatorial reign of Stalinist Tatanya.

When he arrived at the vehicle and unlocked the door, he noticed a white envelope pressed to the glass under the driver's-side windshield wiper blade. He removed the envelope and slipped into the car. He yawned, desperate to close his eyes for twenty or thirty minutes. But the envelope, which was addressed to MISS POLLY PEPPER. PERSONAL AND CONFIDENTIAL, intrigued him. He looked around afraid that whoever left the envelope could be watching him. He dared not open it while in plain view of possible voyeurs.

Tim stepped out of the car and headed back into the dance studio. He nervously searched for rehearsal room number 4. When he found the thick double doors, behind which he could hear the title song from *Mame* blasting through a sound system, he hesitated a moment, but then slowly opened the door wide enough to peek inside. First he spotted his mother. She looked like someone wanting to be put out of her misery by a firing squad. Tatanya the Terrible was yelling loud enough to be heard over the blare of the famous Donald Pippin musical arrangements. Tim scanned the room of ballet bars, folding chairs, and mirrored walls and finally spotted Placenta, who looked concerned for Polly, who was being verbally beaten up. He caught Placenta's eye and motioned for her to meet him in the hallway.

Soon Placenta exited from another set of doors down the hall and came to Tim's side. "Tatanya makes Caligula look like a Miss Congeniality winner. It's taking all of my efforts not to pummel the witch. What's up?"

Tim held up the envelope.

"So?"

"So, this was on the windshield of the car."

"It's addressed to Miss Polly Pepper. Give it to her at lunchtime," Placenta said.

"It could be a fan letter, but it could also be related to the case. Hiroaki's car was gone when I went out again, so I'm thinking that he left this for her."

"Or Century 21 is advertising new homes in North Hollywood and an underpaid delivery boy slipped it onto the car like a parking ticket."

Placenta sighed and grabbed the envelope out of Tim's hand. "As Polly's maid and personal assistant, I can open and read her fan mail." She slipped her forefinger under the sealed flap and tore the envelope open. She withdrew a sheet of paper and in an irritated tone began to read aloud: " 'Dear Snoop Sister. If you want Sharon F. to beat this charge, and your show to go on as scheduled . . .' " Placenta's manner instantly changed as she continued to read but now with a far slower and more sober enunciation. " '. . . come to West Hollywood Park tonight at eleven sharp. Bring one of your Emmy Awards and leave it in a brown paper bag under the water fountain outside the park's restrooms. In exchange, information about Karen's killer will be forthcoming.' "

Tim and Placenta both looked at each other with fear in

their eyes. "Of course, it's not signed," Placenta said. She looked at the letter again. "There's a postscript. 'P.S. Come alone, and don't mention this letter to anyone. Or else . . .'"

"First off, Polly would never let one of her cherished Emmy Awards out of the house, let alone give it away in exchange for information that could save Sharon Fletcher's life," Tim said.

"Your mama's a friend indeed to a friend in need, but her Emmys are her most prized possessions. Giving one to a stranger just for life-and-death information is almost the ultimate price to pay."

"Merely holding one without asking permission is an invitation to getting one's hand slapped," Tim added. "I propose that we not say a word about this to Polly and call Randy."

"But the letter clearly states that no one else is to know!"

"It said that Polly wasn't to tell anyone. She doesn't even know the letter exists, so technically she's not responsible. Go back inside and keep an eye on Polly. Make sure she doesn't accidentally on purpose fracture Tatanya's instep. I'll call Randy."

Chapter 15

Tim found a quiet place in the men's dressing area of the dance studio and speed-dialed Detective Archer's cell phone number. In a moment he was connected with voice mail and left a message begging for an immediate callback. Tim sat on a long bench surrounded by metal lockers. He waited impatiently for Randy to return his call.

After a half hour, Tim placed another call and again had to speak to an automated voice mail system. "This is really important, Randy," Tim said. "Polly could be in deep trouble. Please call me!" He left his phone number in case Detective Archer hadn't entered it into his speed dial. More time passed and soon Polly was on her lunch break and morosely walking down the corridor. She looked as though she were dragging an invisible bag of bricks.

"Kinda tough, isn't she?" Tim said when his mother passed by en route to the ladies' dressing area. "But she's a rising star in Broadway choreography circles. This show's lucky to have her."

"I'll be lucky if I live to dance on her grave," Polly barked. "Run along to the kennel and bring me back an angry pit bull. Or take me to lunch."

Just then, Tim's cell phone rang. He looked at the caller

ID and flipped open the lid. "Personal," he said to Polly. "Go and change. I'll meet you in the lobby."

Polly shuffled on toward her locker.

"Randy?" Tim said. "Polly's received an extortion letter. What do we do?" He listened for a moment. "Nope. No money. An Emmy. She hasn't seen the letter. Placenta opened it. Well, it wasn't sent by the United States Postal Service, so what's the crime? You're splitting hairs. I'm bringing it to your office after I take Polly to lunch."

Returning to the dance studio at 5:00 P.M., Tim met Polly and Placenta on the front steps of the building. Polly was so exhausted she could hardly walk. Helping Placenta ease his mother into the car, and then settling in himself, Tim proceeded to drive back to Bel Air.

Although Polly was used to hard work, and generally enjoyed physical activity, she was angry with both Gerold Goss and Tatanya. "This is not the original Onna White choreography that I've danced to a thousand times," Polly said with a voice that sounded as worn out as she felt. "I'd say they're trying to sabotage me and my performance in the show."

Polly put her head back against the brown leather seat and closed her eyes. She whispered, "Wake me when my bath is drawn." And then she was asleep.

After a long moment to make certain that Polly was indeed unconscious, Tim whispered to Placenta, "Archer has a plan."

Placenta, who was nearly as tired as Polly, perked up. "He saw the letter?"

"It's going to take our help—naturally—and Polly might lose an Emmy in the process, but he actually had an interesting idea. Remember Lauren Gaul? The stand-in from Polly's last picture?"

Placenta yawned. "Sure. We saw her on *CSI* recently. Looks like her career has picked up since all the fuss about two dead stars on Polly's movie set. She's acting now, instead of just being a prop for the DOP. What's she got to do with this plan?"

"Archer and I contacted her this afternoon. She's going to stand in for Polly at West Hollywood Park tonight. We're taking one of Mom's Emmy Awards, placing it in a Gelson's paper sack, and loaning her the Rolls for the evening. She'll make the connection."

Placenta was intrigued by the strategy. "Is she willing to face a killer?"

"She sounded excited and sees this as an adventure. Plus, she claimed that Polly was the only star who ever thanked her for doing the boring work of standing in for her on set. Said she'd do anything to help Polly out. The fact that I promised to pay her two thousand dollars was sort of a good incentive too."

Placenta held out her hands, palms facing the ceiling. "Let's see, rent for a month, and maybe a new pony, or knife through my heart? Hmm. Tough choice. Is she nuts?"

"Archer's men will be stationed at various points around the park. He'll do his best to not let anything happen to Lauren. The important thing is that Polly won't be there! In fact, she shouldn't even know what's going on. Now we just have to think of a way to smuggle an Emmy out of the house, and figure out an excuse for Archer to borrow the Rolls."

"I'll put your mama to bed early tonight, which I don't think will be a problem. Maybe you should hit as many potholes as you can to keep her awake now, so she'll be out like a light as soon as she steps out of her bath." Placenta paused. "Is the threat for real?"

"It's authentic all right. Randy's very concerned. He thinks that whoever sent the letter might be the killer. If what Polly overheard at the theater is true, then someone thinks she knows too much about the case, and believes it's time to take her out of the equation." Tim was quiet for a long moment. "Placenta, I'm really scared."

Placenta leaned forward and patted Tim on the shoulder. "Your mama's lucky. Detective Archer won't let anything happen to her. He's got a vested interest. If you haven't already guessed, he didn't go home last night. After you hit the hay, they did too. Although I imagine they had more fun than you or I did."

"What's wrong with us that we're not canoodling with our own variations on Mr. Right? We're both marriage material!"

Placenta softly sang a lyric to a Carly Simon song. "Now the river doesn't seem to stop here anymore."

Tim sighed. "I'm only twenty-seven and already the river has turned into a trickle. I'm wading in mucky tributaries!"

"I'm stuck in a dried lake bed!" Placenta said. "The last man I dated had sex problems. His wife didn't want him having any with me!"

"Archer says that Polly is the best thing to happen to him in years, so I'm completely confident that he'll take every precaution to keep her safe."

Placenta leaned forward again and whispered, "Did you tell Archer that we saw Hiroaki's car and that he's probably the one who delivered the letter?"

"Yeah, I described the car. Archer ran a DMV check for Hiroaki Goldfarb. He's not licensed to drive a car. So it probably wasn't him that Polly saw at the theater. And it's just a coincidence that we saw a similar car outside his apartment building. As for the Honda we spotted this morning, it could belong to anyone, but not to Hiroaki. There's no vehicle registered to him."

"Honey, this is Los Angeles," Placenta said. "Nothing here is ever exactly as it seems. Just as not everyone who drives a Mercedes is solvent, not everyone follows the law. Half the motorists don't even stop for red lights, let alone renew their licenses or registrations. And don't think that everyone is insured either."

* * *

Like a pet that after a long drive in a car seems to know when it's almost home, Polly perked up as Tim drove on to serpentine Stone Canyon Road. "Siestas are underrated in this country," she said. "After forty winks I feel almost as good as new. I think I'll phone Randy and see if he's up for a night on the town to celebrate my getting through this horrid day."

Tim and Placenta exchanged eye contact through the rearview mirror. "I really think you should rest, Mother," Tim quickly countered.

Placenta hastily added, "Another hard day tomorrow, you know. You need to conserve your strength. You'll have a lovely bath, then we'll all sit down to whatever you'd like me to order from Wolfgang."

As the gates to Pepper Plantation parted, and Tim drove down the long cobblestone way, Polly sighed in resignation. "I certainly hope that Tatanya twat is happy with the way she's paving her way to an eternity in hell for mistreating stars."

"Ever since Randy came into the picture, I thought that you were feeling like a younger woman," Placenta interrupted.

"If you must know, my girlish insouciance isn't because of Randy or any man. It's because I'm preparing for my Broadway debut!"

"Absolutely!" Tim said. "And if you're going to take *Mame* back to The Great White Way, you'd better get plenty of sleep so you can handle the new choreography as well as all the other physical demands of eight shows a week. Placenta's right. When we get into the house, you're heading for the Jacuzzi. Then a light repast, a bottle of Schramsberg of course, then off to bed—alone."

Tim parked the car and they stepped out into the warm evening and headed for the steps to the house.

Once inside Pepper Plantation, per his routine, Tim

placed the car keys and his cell phone in a colorful cloisonné dish on the marble tabletop by the front door. "I'm
parched," he lied. "While Placenta draws your bath, I'll
get us both started on Lush Hour. In the meantime, why
don't you put your feet up and rest until we're ready." Tim
moved off toward the kitchen, while Placenta climbed the
Scarlett O'Hara Memorial Staircase, en route to the mas-
ter bedroom suite.

Polly heaved a sigh as she looked at herself from various
angles in the mirror that hung in the foyer over the table.
"Randy must like wrinkles," she whispered to herself and
felt a tinge of sadness. "Time to see Dr. Fix-It about the
eyes." She touched the skin under her jaw with her finger-
tips and lightly pulled it back a few centimeters toward her
ears. "*Knifestyles of the rich and famous*. Oh, but how far
to go? What if anything went wrong with the lift? I will
not allow myself to look like post-op Nanette!"

The ring tone from Tim's cell phone blared out a techno
version of Weezer's "Only in Dreams." Polly called out to
Tim, "Phone's ringing!" She looked at the caller ID and
recognized Detective Archer's number. Without thinking,
she flipped open the phone and sparkled, "Did you forget
my number, you sexy thing, you?"

Suddenly her smile faded. "Who shall I say is calling?
Lauren Gaul?" Polly's smile returned as she recognized the
name and voice of her stand-in from the still unreleased
teen musical comedy that they'd filmed several months back.
"When, dear, are we ever going to get together again? I
don't want to be one of those Hollywood types who make
empty promises to do lunch."

Polly knitted her eyebrows. "Tonight's actually a little
too soon. But . . . if Tim said so, then I guess we'll see you.
Around eleven? Lovely. Ta!"

Polly shook her head, flipped the phone closed, and
made her way down the long corridor to the kitchen.
When she arrived in the cavernous room full of modern

appliances and custom cabinets, Tim was popping the champagne cork and setting the bottle into a bucket of crushed ice. "Dear, your phone rang," she said, handing the cell to Tim. "I wouldn't have answered it but I must have misread the caller ID. I was certain it was Randy's number. Instead, it was Lauren Gaul."

Tim froze. "Um, Lauren Gaul?"

"She left a message for you. Said she'd be here at eleven. Tonight." Polly blinked her eyes. "Why is she coming to the Plantation? And why so late? Please don't tell me you're going straight and she's your new love. Not that there's anything wrong with being a straight man . . . I'd love you just the same, and I'm sure that Lauren would make a wonderful daughter-in-law. But a mother wants to be as proud of her son as possible, and I'd hate to have my friends know that you're not gay. Of course I'll support you, no matter what."

"Lauren's just dropping by for . . . um, to give me . . . to borrow . . . er, to discuss plans for a party that she wants me to do with her. Yeah, a party," Tim blurted. "We're making plans. You know, themes, and food ideas and entertainment. Just business stuff. There's no need for you to stay up to greet her. You need your rest after an exhausting day today. You'll see Lauren again soon."

Polly gave her son a quizzical look. "Are you sure there's nothing going on between you two? You're acting rather strange."

"Strange? Nope. Nothing's going on, except planning another party, of course." He lifted the tray on which the champagne ice bucket, bottle, and glasses rested. "Let's get you into the tub."

Polly grabbed Tim's arm. "Lauren was calling from Randy's office phone. I'm sure of it. She's very pretty, and a lot closer to his age than I am."

"What are you thinking, that Randy may be seeing Lauren? Trust me, he's not!"

"You can't be sure," Polly pouted. "Randy and I haven't known each other very long. Maybe he started an affair with Lauren during that god-awful time when he was investigating the deaths on our last movie location. What if—"

"Don't be silly. I know for a fact that Lauren's not seeing Randy. My impression is that Randy's a one-woman man. My gaydar may be shot to hell, but I still recognize a man of character. He's not the type to cheat."

"Should I confront Randy about this?"

"No! I mean guys don't want to have to explain themselves. Do you want to place Randy in a position of feeling that he has to reveal his every move to you? Anyway, your theory is nuts. There's nothing to suggest that Randy and Lauren are seeing each other in any capacity other than professional. The only evidence you have is that she used his phone."

"Well, why would she even be in his office?"

"Maybe Randy's finalizing the crime report on your last murdered misfits, Sedra Stone and Trixie Wilder."

Polly sighed. "I'm simply afraid that the difference in our ages could mess things up. Heck, even if this relationship . . . if you can call that . . . only lasts a few weeks or a month, I'm having a dandy time." Polly yawned. "I'd better not have anything to drink if I'm going to be sober when Lauren arrives."

Tim set the silver tray down on the kitchen island and poured a glass of champagne. He handed it to Polly and said, "Drink up. You're taking a bath, then going directly to bed. As Placenta said, you've got a tough day tomorrow. You'll see more of Lauren as her party plans come together."

Chapter 16

At eleven o'clock, the intercom to the estate gates chimed. Tim answered and spoke to Detective Archer, who had arrived with Lauren, then buzzed them onto the property. In a few minutes Tim and Placenta and their guests were seated in the great room nervously talking about the night's plans. Placenta had raided Polly's closet and secreted out a Bob Mackie dress and wig for Lauren to wear. The rest was up to Lauren and Randy.

"The West Hollywood Police Department has been staking out the park since late this afternoon," Randy said to help ease everyone's concerns. "This whole letter thing, demanding an Emmy Award, is probably a crank, but we won't take any chances. Lauren'll be safe, and so will Polly's Award. She'll never know it left the house."

Placenta looked at her watch and suggested that Lauren change into her costume. She escorted her to the guest powder room. "I'll guard the door," she said. "If you need anything just call out."

Tim turned to Randy. "Other than Sedra Stone who, since her cremation is now just dust in the wind, Polly's never had any enemies. I can't understand why all of a sudden she's being threatened."

"Friend to friend, is there something about this case that Polly's not telling me? I need to know everything."

"I think she's got you up to speed. She's talked to Sharon, you know that. She's also interviewed a couple of the members of the cast, and she sort of interrogated the dead director's boyfriend, Jamie. After half overhearing what Jamie and Gerold Goss had to say the other night, as well as not being able to corroborate Jamie's alibi, I think she's focusing on him as Karen's killer."

"Polly never mentioned that she'd been in contact with Jamie," Randy said. "I don't want her to see him again. Understand?"

Tim looked confused. "What's up?"

"He's a person of interest."

"Like a suspect?"

"Everyone's a suspect," Randy said. Suddenly, they were startled to see Polly standing in the doorway with Placenta. After a thin moment, Randy and Tim realized that it wasn't Polly Pepper after all. Rather, it was Lauren Gaul in disguise.

"Amazing!" Tim said.

"Could have fooled me," Randy said.

Placenta added, "This is one dress that Polly would notice missing, so please return it without any blood or bullet holes."

"Not to worry." Randy looked at his watch. "We'll be back as soon as possible. I just need the keys to the Rolls and we're on our way."

"They're by the front door," Tim said. "Please, no blood on the leather upholstery either. Keep me informed, okay? Call every half hour. I'll be up all night if I have to be." Then he led the detective and the decoy out of the great room and into the corridor leading to the foyer. As they passed through the sunken living room with its grand staircase they were suddenly stopped in their tracks by the sound of Polly's voice.

"Don't mind me," Polly pouted. "I was suddenly wide awake and decided to come down for a glass of champagne and a Xanax. Looks like I've interrupted a party— in my own home. I wish that someone had thought to invite me. Randy, dear, your date looks familiar."

Randy walked over to Polly to embrace her, but she stiffened and backed away. "I'll explain everything later. Right now, we've got to go. Just trust me, please?"

"That's all I've ever done," Polly said. "Shame on me." Then she turned and headed back up the staircase. "Placenta! The wine cooler in my bedroom is empty!"

Detective Archer looked at Tim. "Damn! Say something to her for me. She's obviously got the wrong impression."

"As a matter of fact, this just supports her big fear. Polly answered Lauren's call earlier because she saw your number on the caller ID. She thinks you and Lauren are having an affair."

"She's crazy! Okay, look, I'll deal with this later. Right now, we've gotta hustle! Oh, damn! The Emmy!"

Tim smacked his forehead as he raced back to the great room to select one of Polly's trophies for Lauren to take with her to the drop-off site. He reached for the one that Polly received for a guest-starring role on an episode of *China Beach*. When he returned to the foyer, Placenta had a Gelson's shopping bag ready and together they lovingly laid the Emmy inside the paper sack.

"Okay, we're off," Randy said as Tim handed him the keys. He opened the door, stepped outside, and walked Lauren to the Rolls and handed her the key. "Think you'll be okay driving this big ol' thing?"

"No sweat," Lauren said. "A car's a car. Just give me a moment to adjust the seat. I'll see you back here after I drop off the loot. Keep an eye on me."

Detective Archer returned to his car and followed Lauren as she drove off the estate.

*   *   *

Polly, dressed in her silk monogrammed robe, wandered down the stairs and into the great room. "I'm ready for that champagne now, please," she said to Placenta with an edge to her voice. "In fact, I'm ready for a short explanation for what's going on behind my back. I watched from my window and Lauren drove away in *my* car. I know what grand theft auto is. What's even more bizarre is that Randy drove off in his own car. I suppose there's actually a logical explanation to all of this."

Placenta opened a bottle of Moët and poured three flutes full. She handed one to Polly and Tim and took one for herself. "Drink up. You'll need the fortification. Tim has something to tell you."

The trio drained their glasses and Placenta refilled each.

"Mom," Tim began, "you've said yourself over and over that in this town seldom is anything as it appears to be. Earlier you jumped to the conclusion that just because Lauren Gaul called from Randy's cell phone that they were having an affair. Now you find the two of them together. To top it off, Lauren drives away in your Rolls. All circumstantial evidence—like Sharon Fletcher's. So, which do you want first, the good news or the bad news?"

"The truth would be lovely," Polly said, draining her second glass of champagne. "What the hell is going on, and why do I seem to be the only one who's out of the loop?"

Placenta looked at Tim. "Give Polly the letter."

"What letter?" Polly asked.

"It's with the Beverly Hills Police Department. But I've made a copy." Tim reached into his shirt pocket and withdrew a quadruple-folded sheet of paper. "We should have given this to you earlier, but Randy wanted to spare you any concern." He handed the paper to his mother.

"This is what's called 'sparing me'?" She unfolded the page and began to read silently. Suddenly she shouted, "An Emmy? Never! I almost beat Mary Tyler Moore for the most wins. I'm not giving one of my babies up to some two-bit psychotic killer."

"Even if it means saving Sharon Fletcher's life?" Placenta said.

Polly thought for a moment. "You're mean to put it that way." She patted her bosom and sighed. "Which one did you sacrifice?"

China Beach, Tim said. "But we'll get it back, and someday you'll be able to regale dinner party guests with the amazing history of that particular trophy and how it helped solve a crime. Otherwise, what do you make of the letter?"

"You thought that I'd be upset by a letter?" Polly asked. "Hell, I've read about a gazillion fan letters over the years. Most were in praise of me of course, and the show too. But there were a few that had to be sent to the police for investigation. I had my own stalker once."

Tim gave his mother a mortified look. "When? You never mentioned having a stalker."

"I was saving it for my autobiography. He was actually divine. They say you're nobody until you have your very own shadow. I got a ton of expensive baubles from him. He's now in Folsom. Each week for months, on the night we taped the show there'd be a box from Tiffany or Cartier or some such store, in my dressing room. His card was simply signed 'Your ardent admirer, Joe.' Then the well suddenly dried up. Shortly after the presents stopped coming I was summoned to appear before the grand jury in the case of Wilson versus Fay Wray, Julia Child, and Janet Leigh. That bastard Joe Wilson was two-timing me. He was simultaneously sending gifts to King Kong's lover, that wine-slurping French chef, and the *Psycho* lady. I thought I'd nabbed a rich fan, and he turned out to be no more than a Beverly Hills mailman who stole from the rich on his daily route and gave to his favorite divas. I'd inadvertently accepted stolen property and had to give it all back! What I'm saying is, most fan mail has an agenda.

They want to get either an autographed picture or, better still, a piece of correspondence that they can show to their friends and brag about knowing a world-renowned star."

Polly read the letter once again. "I'm bereft. I may never see that beautiful statuette again. And all because you two haven't learned to read between the lines of a fan letter!"

Just then, Tim's cell phone rang. He looked at the caller ID. "It's Randy."

Polly grabbed the phone from her son's hand and flipped it open. "Turn the car around, and bring back my personal property, or I'll call the police! I know that you are the police. You're splitting hairs. You had no right to commandeer my Rolls and make off with my prized possession."

Polly slumped in defeat. "The Emmy's gone. Whoever's behind this farce didn't keep his end of the bargain. No exchange of information? I see. I could have told you so. Now some freak-o fan has a bit of Hollywood television history sitting on their coffee table. Mad? Ha! Why would I be mad?" Polly closed the cell phone and handed it over to Tim.

"What about Lauren?" Placenta said. "Is she all right?"

Polly shrugged. "Pour me another glass."

Tim sidled up next to his mother on the sofa. "Trust Randy. He's a good cop. He has your best interests at heart. Wait'll he gets back and gives you the details before you decide to ruin a good relationship."

Polly waved away Tim's explanation. "I'm sure he did the best he could. If it's at all possible, he'll get my property back ... eventually. Still, I don't know if I can go on seeing someone who isn't comfortable enough with me to be up front and honest. I'd have given him full permission to do whatever he felt was best. But to enlist the help of you two, and not even consider that I might be as eager as anyone to ferret out the killer, well, I'm just at a loss for what to think."

Tim put a hand on his mother's arm. "We should have been more discreet."

"More loyal!"

"I take full responsibility," Placenta said. "If I'd just handed you your mail instead of taking it upon myself to play secretary . . ."

Polly picked up the letter. "What did you two see in this message that made you so concerned?"

"For one, they called you a 'Snoop Sister,'" Tim said.

"That's so derogatory!" Polly agreed.

"For another, they threaten that your show won't go on unless you follow their stupid demands and hand over an Emmy," Placenta added. "I'd say extortion is a fairly reasonable excuse to get the police involved."

Polly stared off into the distance. "The letter referred to me as 'sister.' Only another woman would think of me as 'sister.' And why would the price for information about Karen be something as specific as an Emmy Award? Why not a million dollars? Or the new boxed collection of *The Polly Pepper Playhouse,* season two?"

Tim and Placenta both stared at Polly.

"Charlotte Bunch was awfully keen to have Sharon bring in her Emmy Award for show-and-tell," Tim said. "She's sort of Emmy-crazy, and would love to get her mitts on one of those awards, even if she didn't earn it."

"No," Polly said. "I'm thinking that Angela Lansbury has gone nuts and decided to steal an award that she rightfully should have received for every year of her *Murder, She Wrote* series."

Chapter 17

"It got a little scary when a man who lives in a cardboard box a few yards from the restrooms thought I was Carol Burnett," Lauren said, with a soft chuckle. "I sort of made a big deal that I was the legendary television icon Polly Pepper, for the benefit of whoever was making the pickup. I wanted them to know that I was there, or rather that you were there, just as instructed. I guess it worked because after I explained to the poor homeless man who I was, er, who Polly Pepper was . . . is . . . when I turned around the bag was gone. Now I realize that the grungy fellow must have been part of the operation. I mean, the snobs in WeHo don't allow homeless people in their town! He certainly succeeded in distracting me. How could I have been so stupid?"

Polly nodded her head in agreement. Then she turned to Randy. "I suppose it's too much to hope that you caught the thief on surveillance tape."

Randy hung his head. "I'll check tomorrow, but I've heard that the West Hollywood Police Department's budget cuts have eliminated video surveillance."

"And how many of your men, out of the legions assigned to watch me, er, Lauren, saw anything out of the ordinary?"

"At the very moment that Lauren walked into the park, we got a call to break up a fight at Rage, just up the street. I wasn't leaving Lauren alone for anything, but the other guys had to hustle. I was distracted for a moment. And that's when they swooped in for the kill . . . so to speak."

Polly rolled her eyes. "And he might very well have killed me, er, Lauren. You're obviously not a father, otherwise you'd know you can't take your eyes off a child for even the briefest of moments, otherwise they could wind up with a plastic bag over their head, or fall out of a penthouse window."

"I've disappointed you, and that's the worst thing about this whole mess," Randy said.

"No, the worst thing is that I'm out one Emmy! I promised to leave them to Debbie Reynolds' Hollywood Museum upon proof of my demise."

"Speaking of death," Placenta said, "no one was hurt tonight, and what we should really be talking about is how grateful we are for this miracle." She turned to Polly. "Now, change the subject and tell Randy your latest hypothesis."

All eyes turned to Polly as she readjusted herself on the sofa. She held out her champagne glass and waited for someone to fill it. After a long pause she finally said, "It's the same subject—my Emmy! But I've come to the conclusion that Charlotte Bunch is your man."

Randy nodded his head. "Could be. What specifically makes you peg her?"

"It's this letter," she said, waving the paper in Randy's face. The salutation. I'm referred to as 'Snoop *Sister*,' which sounds rather like I'm part of a category, or an alliance, to which the letter writer also belongs. Just a guess. Plus, Charlotte gets goofy about Emmys. Remember, Sharon said that Charlotte had specifically asked her to bring her statuette to the theater because she wanted to see a real one. And the person who promised information about the case was willing to exchange information for an Emmy. Anyone else would have insisted on a suitcase full of gems or my *For New Kate* gold record."

Everyone in the room simultaneously nodded.

Placenta said, "But what about Gerold and Jamie? You heard them plotting against you in the theater last night."

Tim interrupted. "There isn't necessarily a connection between Charlotte and Gerold and Jamie. It's possible that Charlotte has information about Karen's death independent of the other two."

"Which brings up an interesting point," Polly said. "Perhaps more than one person knows what happened to Karen. On *Matlock*, silent witnesses often came out of the woodwork after danger had passed, or when there was something for them to gain by passing on information."

"Six major suspects in this case," Lauren said. "That's a fairly good number."

"That's one too many," Polly corrected, counting on her fingers. "Charlotte. Jamie. Gerold. Mag. Hiroaki."

"And Sharon," Randy said.

"Nope! Not Sharon," Polly insisted. "I refuse to believe that she had anything to do with Karen's death. Even with her bloodstained Emmy, she's innocent. And if you can't help me prove it, then I'll . . ."

Randy gave Polly a hard look.

Polly huffed. "I'll sign you up for dance classes with Tatanya Morgan. Believe me, you'll regret not helping me."

Polly realized she had to report to Tatanya at the dance studio in only a few hours. She looked at Placenta. "Any rooms available at the inn?"

"As a matter of fact, the Cleopatra Jones Suite has fresh sheets. But the Englebert Humperdinck Room and the Donny Osmond Suite are a mess, and of course the Natalie Wood water bed needs a refill." She smiled evilly.

Tim and Randy looked at each other and simultaneously froze.

"We've got dozens of other guest rooms," Tim said.

"I'm not that tired after all," Randy said. "It's not that far to my apartment."

Polly, Placenta, and Lauren each exchanged looks of amusement.

Tim caught Polly's smirk and realized they were teasing. "It's not that I have anything against sharing a bed with straight policemen," Tim said. "On the contrary . . ."

"No, of course not. Me either," Randy said, trying to be as politically correct as possible. "It's just that I snore and thrash around a lot. I end up monopolizing the whole bed."

"Not a problem. It's a king," Tim said. "I roll around a lot myself."

Polly stood up and declared, "It's settled. You boys will have a sleepover. You can tell ghost stories with a flashlight under the sheets."

Randy gave in. He was too tired to try to find alternate arrangements. He followed Placenta, Lauren, Tim, and Polly up the staircase. When they reached the second-floor landing, Randy leaned over to Polly and whispered, "Can't I please crash with you for the night?"

Polly smiled weakly. "I'm exhausted. And I haven't totally forgiven you for losing my Emmy. Plus, I look abominable. We'll talk in the morning. Timmy can be just as much fun. You'll see." Polly gave a wide smile and said good night to all.

As Placenta escorted Lauren to her room, Tim guided Randy to his own. When the two men reached their suite, Randy said, "What do you sleep in?"

"The bed, of course," Tim replied.

"No. I mean . . . ?"

Tim laughed slyly. "What about you?"

"Generally, um, um . . ."

"Generally, um, me too," Tim said, removing his shirt and tossing it onto the love seat beneath the window. "Top or bottom?" Tim smiled as a flustered Randy made an audible swallow. Then Tim opened a drawer in his highboy and withdrew a pair of silk pajamas and tossed them at Randy. "Take both."

"What about you?"

"I'll brush in the guest bathroom," Tim sniggered and began undressing, the sight of which caused Randy to turn and walk to the bathroom. "Fresh toothbrushes are in the top vanity drawer," Tim called out.

By the time Tim returned and slipped out of his bathrobe and into another pair of pajamas, Randy was pretending to be sound asleep.

"Go away! Let me die in peace," Polly complained when Placenta woke her at 7:00 A.M. "I'm too tired and too hungover to dance today."

"You can't call in sick," Placenta demanded. "Polly Pepper doesn't let choreographers push her around. Now rise and shine and take a shower. Coffee's on but you're not getting a cup until you come downstairs. Now get your famous fanny in gear!"

Polly groaned and slowly pushed the bedsheets and comforter away with her feet. She dangled one arm over the side of the mattress and tried to recall what had happened the night before to make her so exhausted. She knew that she'd gone to bed at an early hour and . . .

"My Emmy," she softly cried out as she raised herself into a sitting position with her legs over the side of the bed. She hung her head in both pain and sadness. "Why go on living if just anyone can come along and take your hard-earned status symbols of success? I'll be damned if I'll sit by and wait for the Beverly Hills Police Department to do the jobs for which I pay my outrageously high taxes."

With new resolve, Polly stood up and dragged herself to

the bathroom. By seven thirty she was dressed and entering the kitchen. Tim and Lauren were seated at the breakfast table and being served crepes Lucerne, fresh-squeezed
grapefruit juice, melon balls, English muffins, and black
coffee. "Morning, all," Polly called, pretending to be as
bright and energized as Ellen DeGeneres when an especially exciting movie star guest was scheduled to appear
on her program. "Did we all sleep well? Placenta, coffee,
please, and a BM. Pronto."

"Like a log," Lauren said, enjoying the lavish array of
food set before her.

Tim wasn't nearly as awake as the others. The most he
could manage was a monosyllabic "Ugh."

Placenta set a Bloody Mary and a mug of coffee before
Polly and surreptitiously laid two Advil tables on a napkin
beside Polly's plate. Polly looked up at her maid and
formed the words *thank you* with her lips. Placenta nodded and went back to the stove to retrieve more crepes.

Polly looked around. "Where's the other one?"

"The other one what?" Placenta countered.

"There was another man in the house last night. His
name is Mud."

"You mean Tim's roommate?" Placenta teased. "He got
up and out early to try and make amends for letting your
Emmy slip through his fingers."

"I always wake up alone," Tim said.

"Guess it's true that there's no such thing as a completely straight man." Placenta elbowed Tim as she passed
by with a plate of English muffins.

Polly furtively popped the Advil into her mouth and
chased them with a long pull from her virgin Bloody Mary.
"I owe the *National Peeper* a scoop on the latest gossip. A
story about the Beverly Hills party planner and his cadre
of LAPD sex slaves should satisfy them until Jennifer An-
niston gets engaged and dumped again."

Placenta slapped the back of Tim's head, and took

Polly's empty Bloody Mary glass. "We're late," she said. "Brush your teeth and get in the car." She looked at Lauren. "Feel free to hang out here all day long, if you like. Use the pool. It's supposed to be a scorcher."

Lauren smiled and thanked Placenta and Polly and Tim, but insisted that she had a million things to do and would leave at the same time as the rest of the family when they drove off the estate.

After another grueling day at the hands of Torquemada, Polly lethargically dragged herself out of the dance studio and into her waiting Rolls. "When Jerry Herman sees what Gerold Goss is allowing this woman to do to his masterpiece he'll have a bigger cow than when Lucille Ball stomped all over the movie version of *Mame*," Polly said. "We'll never make it to Broadway once the critics get a look at the techno trash that she's come up with."

From the driver's seat Tim said, "Speaking of trash, Gerold messengered this over from the theater."

"What is it?" Polly took a number 10 business envelope from Tim's hand.

"I don't read your mail anymore. For all I know it could be a letter bomb. Better that you open it than me or Placenta."

Polly leveraged her thumb under the envelope flap and ripped through the fold. She withdrew a note and read silently. "Well, this really sucks!" Polly handed the letter to Placenta.

"It's the rehearsal schedule," Polly said to Tim. "We're starting twelve-hour days on Saturday."

"So much for our party," Tim said.

"Change it to Monday, our day off," Polly said. "These kids today party all the time. For them, a night off from rehearsal just means a night without anything to do. No one will give up an opportunity to visit Pepper Plantation."

Tim heaved a heavy sigh. "At least Randy will be happy to hear of your extended rehearsal days. There's less time for you to get into trouble."

Polly yawned. "Nonsense. We all have twenty-four hours a day. The trouble we get into depends upon how we use those hours. In fact, we have another six left in this one. Take the Los Feliz exit and let's drop down to Hollywood and pay another visit to Charlotte Bunch. I think she may have something that belongs to me."

Chapter 18

As Tim parked the car across the street from Charlotte's dilapidated building on Gardner, he and Placenta were still complaining that they'd had just as long and hectic a day as Polly, and they wanted to go home. However, their grousing was met with Polly's reasoning that they should be doing all they could to help rescue her Emmy Award. "If either of you had endured the backstabbing competition that I did to get one of those babies, you'd know how much they mean to me. How would you like it if one of your siblings went missing?"

Placenta turned to Tim. "Shhh. Don't let the others know that one among their ranks isn't merely away being polished."

Tim looked in the rearview mirror and saw his mother's lack of mirth. "So, what's our excuse for unexpectedly popping by Charlotte's place this time?"

"Let's try the truth," Polly said. "I'll simply say that we want to personally make sure that she knows that we've changed our party to Monday night."

"The *truth* indeed," Placenta huffed. "Charlotte's not dumb enough to display stolen property as a centerpiece on her coffee table—next to the colon irrigation kit she bought at Betty Hutton's estate sale."

"Perhaps all that junk in her apartment is stolen. Anyway the truth is that I want to know what's going on at rehearsals."

Polly opened her door and stepped out of the car. Her entourage followed and in a moment they were once again standing at the door to Charlotte Bunch's one-bedroom apartment. Polly pressed the bell. "Charlotte, darling!" she called through the door. "It's Me. Polly. Pepper. Just dropped by to see how Gerold and company are treating you, and ask if you've seen the theater ghost."

The sound of someone moving about in the apartment could be clearly heard from outside, but no one answered the door. Polly looked at Tim. "She's running around trying to hide the evidence. Once we get in, you two distract her while I rescue my baby. Drag her out to the car and lock her in the truck if you have to." After a moment Polly once again rang the bell. "Charlotte, lamb, I've brought a bottle of bubbly from Mary Steenburgen's estate sale."

"There's nothing wrong with Mary," Tim said, hoping he was right about one of his favorite stars.

"We can use your Alexis Smith champagne flutes. We're not Jehovah's Witnesses. I Promise."

Tim flipped open his cell phone and scrolled down to Charlotte Bunch's number. He pressed SEND. In a moment, the trio could clearly hear the phone ringing inside the apartment, but it went unanswered. "She's ignoring you," Tim said. "All the more reason to think she's guilty of something. Can we please leave now? I'm hungry."

In that moment, Charlotte Bunch's cheerful voice called out from the sidewalk behind Polly. As the trio turned around in surprise, they found Charlotte coming through the chain-link fence gate, carrying a plastic bag of groceries from Von's in one hand, and another sack from The Liquor Locker in the other. "Perfect timing!" she announced.

Tim said, "Miss Bunch, how long have you been away?"

"Rehearsals went way over Equity rules, but of course Gerold won't report it and we won't see any overtime in our pay envelopes."

As Charlotte continued walking up the sidewalk with her apartment keys in hand, Polly gently touched her arm to steer her away from her route. "Don't panic. But I'm calling the police."

Charlotte laughed. "They can't do anything about Gerold breaking union contract rules. We're opening in mere days and nobody's ready."

"No!" Polly said impatiently. "I mean don't panic because there's someone in your apartment."

Charlotte's face drained of its color. "Are you sure?"

"Is there a back door to your place?" Tim said.

"There's only one way in or out, through the front door. Or a window, I suppose."

Tim put a finger to his lips to silence the others. Then he cautiously walked down the driveway and headed to the back of the building.

"Be careful of celebrity killers, Timmy!" Polly called out in a voice loud enough to cause the upstairs tenant to look out his window.

When Tim arrived in the alleyway behind Charlotte's building, he saw that indeed a window to her first-floor apartment was open. He dragged a trash can beneath the window and climbed onto the thick plastic bin. When he peeked inside, what he saw made him feel creepy.

Returning to the front of the building, he was already on the phone with Detective Archer. "Send backup right away," he said and hung up just as he reached the others. He looked at Charlotte. "The police are on their way. Let's sit in the car until they get here."

"I've got to see what they've done to my place," Charlotte insisted. With her key still in hand she plowed ahead toward the door.

Tim looked at his mother and in an ominous voice he said, "Be prepared."

Charlotte unlocked the dead bolt and slowly turned the doorknob. With adrenaline rushing through her body she gingerly pushed the door open and let her eyes make an advance tour of the room before she cautiously stepped inside. The apartment was quiet and it appeared that no one else was in the residence. She turned to Polly. "Wait here until I make sure that all is clear." Charlotte then closed the door on Polly's startled face.

Polly looked at Tim. "I can't believe she's making us wait outside."

"We shouldn't disturb the scene of a crime," Placenta said. "You're already on thin ice with Randy. If you leave so much as a submolecule of DNA, his meltdown will make Chernobyl look like a marshmallow roast."

Tim looked at his mother. "I've gotta tell you something about Charlotte's bedroom."

"A pigsty, right?"

"You know those banners that are on light posts all over Glendale?"

Polly shrugged her shoulders. "Yeah. Hirschfeld. *Erma La Douche.*"

"Charlotte's got six of 'em on her bedroom walls."

Polly smiled with self-satisfaction. "She and I go way back. She's proud to know a star like me."

"She's drawn mustaches and black eyes and devil's horns and forked tails on you!"

Placenta cackled.

Polly looked mortified. "I'm sure she simply rescued them from graffiti taggers. Nobody hates Polly Pepper enough to deface her image."

At that moment a single police patrol car arrived. Two officers stepped out of the vehicle and walked up to the building at a pace that made it clear they were uninterested in a simple burglary. "You guys called about something?"

Polly looked at the taller one and focused on his name badge. "Mr. Kasharian, 'or something' is not a reason for which I would ever interrupt your coffee break at Dunkin' Donuts."

"Mom?" Tim said. "Let's just tell the nice officers about the burglary, shall we?"

Officer Kasharian looked at Tim and their eyes met with a mutual agreement that each thought the other was nice to look at. "Where's the scene of the crime?"

"In there." Polly pointed to Charlotte's apartment. Just then, Charlotte opened the door.

"All clear," Charlotte called out before seeing that the police had arrived. Her disposition immediately turned to worry and she quickly explained that Polly Pepper had incorrectly thought that the apartment was under siege.

"Mind if we have a look around?" Officer Kasharian asked. Polly slinked past Charlotte and into the apartment. By the time anyone could react, Polly got a short head start on searching the premises. Despite hearing objections and warnings not to touch anything, Polly was already opening closets and looking behind furniture, searching for her Emmy. Then she reached the bedroom. "Mother of God!"

Charlotte walked to Polly's side. Together they looked up at the banners. "I got a little crazy when I heard that Karen was going to fire me," Charlotte said. "Nothing personal. Your face represented the whole show."

As the two actors stood side by side, Detective Archer arrived. "Time for another police report," Randy said to Polly and Charlotte. "By now you must be getting pretty used to giving official statements to the LAPD."

"If I was burgled the only thing that seems to be missing is my cat," Charlotte said. "You can see I've got a lot of stuff, so it'll take a while to inventory. But on the surface,

I'd say that the legendary Polly Pepper probably came along and scared away my poor Miss Maxine Andrews. I leave the bedroom window open in case her favorite Tom drops by. She has instructions not to let him in."

Polly considered this idea. It was possible, she thought, but it was more probable that her timing was just right and she'd actually saved Charlotte from coming home and unexpectedly interrupting a burglar.

As if reading Polly's thoughts, Charlotte said, "I probably owe my life to Polly Pepper! Perhaps she scared away a pervert! Who do you know at *Daily Variety* who can write this up? The publicity will be good."

"I suggest you concentrate on getting stories about *Mame* in the paper, not gossip about being at the center of another crime," Randy said.

Polly reluctantly agreed. Then, as she was about to summon Tim and Placenta and leave for home, she had an idea. "Honey, dear," she said to Charlotte, "you'd better stay at the Plantation tonight. I don't want you here alone. What if Ted Bundy returns?"

Chapter 19

Charlotte Bunch had only appeared as a regular on one long-running television sitcom and a classic commercial. As happens with thousands of actors who have enjoyed a modicum of success in supporting roles, they are popular during the run of a hit series but are seldom if ever heard from again after the network dumps the show. Charlotte was simply a footnote from television history. She now accepted any acting job that came along. Generally, the roles in which she was cast had only a line or two of dialogue, but they kept her SAG health insurance premiums paid up.

However, the way that she rattled on to Polly, Tim, and Placenta, describing her long career, one would have thought that she and Meryl Streep were constant competitors for every film that required a spot-on Dutch, Estonian, or Chechen accent. Indeed, her repertoire of foreign dialects, as well as impersonations of a hundred living and dead celebrities, was astounding. From Tallulah Bankhead to Ted Knight, Charlotte was the talented but completely overlooked female equivalent of Rich Little.

While seated in the great room of Pepper Plantation, waiting for dinner to arrive from Spago, Polly graciously allowed Charlotte to hold court. When Charlotte recalled the summons to London she received from Andrew Lloyd Webber to replace the actress who played Christine (the name of whom she couldn't recall) in *Phantom of the Opera*, Polly simply smiled and nodded her head. When Charlotte drew on her memory of auditioning for *Green Acres*, *The Beverly Hillbillies*, and *M*A*S*H*, her courteous audience never asked the logical question of what happened that she never actually appeared on those programs. Just as Charlotte began her story of being asked to entertain at a State Dinner in the Carter White House, the loud chime from the intercom at the main gate interrupted her.

"Food!" Polly exclaimed and made the sign of the cross. She then looked at Charlotte. "Excuse us for just a tick. We'll be back to hear all about Jimmy and Rosalynn and little Amy. Don't forget your impersonation of Henry Kissinger making love to Jill St. John. Help yourself to another glass of champers."

Charlotte did just that and when she was finally alone, she wandered around the room oohing and ahhing the many mementos that were on display from Polly's legendary career. She ran her fingers over the People's Choice Awards. She picked up the Grammy and squinted to read the inscription on the tarnished nameplate. "'For New Kate,'" she read aloud, and rolled her eyes, remembering the brouhaha that erupted from the Catholic Legion of Decency when Polly's song debuted at number ten on *Billboard Magazine's Top 100 Chart*.

Then she came to Polly's collection of Emmy Awards and her heart skipped a beat. She picked one up. She felt the weight of it and the cold metal. It was tarnished with age, and she wondered how anyone could let such a treasure fall to the ravages of oxidation. "Precious baby," she cooed to the woman with lightning bolt wings who was holding aloft what was presumably the universe. "Three nominations and I never got to take you home. I could have killed Elena Verdugo, Jean Stapleton, and Dinah Shore," Charlotte sighed. "I want you all to myself."

"Always a bridesmaid, eh?" Tim's voice startled Charlotte. "You were so great on your show, by the way. You really deserved to win the supporting actress Emmy."

Setting the trophy back on the glass bookshelf, Charlotte looked at Tim. "Them thar are the breaks, eh? Anyway, it was an honor just to be nominated by my peers. Is my nose growing?"

"Those awards don't really mean much. It's a popularity contest."

"Thanks a ton. So I'm a lousy actor *and* I'm not popular."

"You know what I mean. Polly sent me to escort you to the dining room. Shall we?" He held out his arm for Charlotte to take hold.

As Placenta set plates of risotto with bay scallops, sweet shrimp, and lobster before Charlotte and the rest of the family, Polly said that Wolfgang Puck had sent his best wishes to Charlotte.

"He docsn't even know I exist," Charlotte said.

"He does indeed. Said he'll never forget that episode of *Bay Watch*."

"I really should have been nominated for *that* role," Charlotte said. "I mean, how often does a woman of a certain age get to splash around in the Pacific with Billy Warlock? I'll tell you all a little story about that shoot."

Polly reluctantly set her cutlery down on her plate.

"After about the seventh take for our scene I was freezing in the water," Charlotte began. "Billy swam over and wrapped his arms around me. Great biceps, and such a delicious chest! Little did I know that David Hasselhoff had kept the cameras rolling, and when I noticed that Charming Billy was holding his swimming trunks in his hand, the shock that viewers saw on my face was authentic. It was exactly the shark attack expression that Mr. Hasselhoff had been trying to get from me all day."

Everyone at the table coughed a fake laugh.

"I touched Billy's wee-wee, and then I—"

"TMI!" Polly called out with a spirited laugh. "Sweetheart, you have a splendid memory for details. I'm sure that you and Billy were inseparable for the rest of the shoot, but I think I'll save that scenario for my own overactive imagination. But while we're on the subject of shock and awe, don't you agree that Karen's death was probably the result of a lovers spat between her and Jamie?"

Charlotte did a double take at the non sequitur, and then shook her head while scraping up the last of her risotto with her fork. She drew another long sip from her champagne flute and said, "Nah. I've never seen a girl more in love with a guy. He was always hanging on to her. They were inseparable. Watching those two made me wish I'd been born a lesbian. I would have had a better chance at finding a lasting relationship."

The room suddenly became quiet as everyone realized that Charlotte was not going to cooperate by providing much information. They finished their appetizers; then Placenta excused herself to clear the table in order to serve the main course. "Give me a hand, Tim," she said and picked up Charlotte's plate. Tim retrieved his and his mother's china and followed Placenta out of the dining room and into the kitchen.

Charlotte reached out and placed a hand on Polly's. "It was so good of you to invite me to spend the night," she said with an inebriated slur in her voice. "I would have been on pins and needles wondering if someone was going to break into my apartment and do me in."

"It was probably your cat we heard after all," Polly said. "One look at your place and a thief would know that you don't have a bean. Unless they thought they could fence an autographed picture of Bob Cummings. Or an Emmy Award."

Charlotte bit her lower lip as she looked into Polly's eyes. "If I had an Emmy I'd be mortified if it was stolen . . . from me." She paused. "There's something I didn't tell you . . . or the police. I found this in my dressing room." Charlotte reached into her blouse and withdrew a number-10-size business envelope. "It was addressed to you but I figured 'finders keepers.'" She handed the envelope to Polly as Tim and Placenta reentered the room with the main course of the dinner.

"Something tells me that I'm about to be not very hungry," Polly sang as Placenta set a plate of steamed Alaskan salmon and baby spring vegetables before her. "We have another letter. Courtesy of someone at the theater."

Tim and Placenta each took their seats and eagerly watched as Polly reached into the envelope and withdrew a sheet of paper. All eyes were locked on Polly as she silently read the letter. Her face wore a lack of expression that would have made a poker champion proud. Then she looked up and said, "There must be another Polly Pepper hanging around Hollywood, because this idiot seems to think I know more about who murdered Karen Richards than I do!"

Tim took the letter from his mother's hands and began to read aloud. "'Snoop Sister. Let's try again. You. Alone. An Emmy. The forecourt of the Chinese Theatre. Two A.M. tomorrow. Paper bag on Fred Astaire's footprints.'"

Tim looked up at his mother. "Forget it! You're not going. Placenta will sit on you. Randy won't let you do this either. That's final!"

Polly drained her champagne flute and waited for a refill. She was deep in thought as she took a long sip from her glass. "I don't want to risk losing another Emmy. And how the hell did this demon know it wasn't me who made the first drop?"

"What's going on?" Charlotte said. "Are you being blackmailed for something? What's up with having to use your Emmys as a bargaining chip?"

Tim quickly filled Charlotte in with the central facts of the situation. "Last night's *CSI* episode had a hair-raising scene that the writers must have ripped out of Polly's very own life and near-death experience. Did you watch it?"

Charlotte hesitantly half nodded her head as she took another sip from her champagne flute. "Sort of. I was dozing off."

Tim began recalling the episode for Charlotte. "You saw where Catherine and Brass were interviewing the lone survivor of the sequestered jury? Nobody's supposed to know what hotel they're in and yet one by one they end up falling from their terraces or drowning in their toilets."

Placenta and Polly both looked at Tim and nodded. Placenta looked at Charlotte and added, "Did you get to the part where the hostess in the hotel restaurant takes the private elevator up to one of the rooms? She carried a briefcase, so I thought she was going up to meet the manager. Instead I think she was a hired killer, but I dozed off myself. What happened next?"

Charlotte shrugged. "Beats me. That was where I hit the sack. I'll catch the rest of it in reruns. But surely Polly's experience wasn't nearly as traumatic as the *CSI* show. What exactly happened to you?"

Polly waved her hand. "What I'm curious to know is who in hell left this message for me."

"Damned if I know," Charlotte said. "But it backs up my theory that someone in the cast or crew is responsible for Karen's death. Whoever it was obviously knew that I'd be seeing you. They just didn't count on me opening your mail."

"It doesn't add up," said Placenta. "The letter instructs Polly to make a drop-off *tomorrow* night. The whole cast knows that Polly's in dance rehearsal for the rest of the week. If we hadn't stopped by your apartment, you wouldn't have seen her until Sunday. No one could have known that we'd be stopping by your apartment this evening."

Charlotte looked baffled. "I don't know what to say about anything anymore, except that our dinners are cold, the bottle of champers is empty, and you're about to be out two Emmys!"

Chapter 20

"I'm screwed!" Polly announced, as she guided Charlotte to the great room.

"Make it clear that you don't know anything about Karen's death and maybe whoever sent the letter will leave you alone."

"What? No! I mean, our show opens in eight days and I'm screwed because we haven't had a full-cast rehearsal! Gerold's shipped me off to that Gulag in North Hollywood with Stalin's more sinister sister. I'm not ready to face an audience."

"Let's do our own run-through. Here. Now."

Polly smiled. "We could. A test of how well we're doing."

"I'm still not off book with my own role, but if you've got a copy of the script I can do it along with all the other roles."

Polly skipped over to the telephone table and pushed the Talk button on the system's intercom. "It's showtime!" she announced. "Do the dishes tomorrow. Charlotte and I are about to perform *Mame*. Oh, and find my script."

Soon Tim and Placenta were moving the twin sofas to face the center of the great room, which was now a makeshift stage. Tim placed a CD of the Broadway cast album of *Mame* on the stereo carousel. He cranked up the volume of the famous overture, then settled down beside Placenta. They watched as Charlotte reentered the room as the character Agnes Gooch. She spoke the first lines of the play, telling her young charge, Patrick, as well as herself, not to be frightened in post-Katrina New Orleans, and that soon they'd be safe with his Auntie Mame.

"I still think that Jerry Herman and the estate of the authors will have a stroke when they find that Gerold has changed the location of the story from New York to New Orleans," Polly whined.

Then Charlotte began singing "St. Brigid," perfectly imitating Jane Connell from the original cast of the Broadway musical. Tim and Placenta applauded wildly.

Next, when Polly entered and sang "It's Today," composer Jerry Herman's celebration of life, Tim was instantly reminded of why his mother was a star. Even singing a cappella she was sensational. The voice wasn't all that good—it never was—but her acting was seductive.

Although Polly was without question the star, Charlotte made a positive impression. They were surprised by how well she moved from one character voice to another, without missing a beat. By the time they sang the finale together, it was clear to all that the show would be smooth sailing.

Taking their bows and accepting applause and flutes of champagne, Polly and Charlotte agreed that it was high time that they retire to their bedrooms. Morning would come too quickly, and their respective rehearsal schedules were becoming more and more arduous. Polly and Charlotte walked holding hands as they followed Placenta up The Scarlett O'Hara Memorial Staircase. On the second-floor landing, they hugged and went in opposite directions down the corridor.

Placenta showed Charlotte the amenities of her suite and reminded their guest that breakfast was at seven. They would leave for the theater by eight thirty.

In Polly's boudoir, Tim stretched out on the bed next to his mother and rested against the headboard. Placenta lay sideways across the comforter at the foot of the mattress and faced Polly. Polly pointed at her closed bedroom door and in a forced whisper said, "She knows more than she's letting on! What was all that cock-and-bull at dinner about watching *CSI*? It wasn't even on last night."

"I made up that entire scenario!" Tim said. "She pretended that she saw the program."

"And that latest letter from your so-called Snoop Sister just happened to be delivered to Charlotte's dressing room. Give me a break!" Placenta said.

Polly added, "All in favor of voting Charlotte the most likely to kill a director say aye!"

"Aye!" they all said in unison.

"Still, someone was in Charlotte's apartment when we dropped by this evening," Polly said. "We all heard the same noises."

"Her cat on speed?" Placenta said.

"An accomplice?" Tim suggested. "Someone working with Charlotte to hide the truth about Karen's killer. By the way, did either of you see a computer and printer in the apartment? The letters are both printed in the same font."

"There's so much junk in that place, it could have blended in with the stereo from Eve Arden and the dollhouse from Demi Moore," Polly said. "I guess someone's going to have to be late for dance class tomorrow. Tim, dear, you take Charlotte to the theater in the morning. Placenta and I will pay another visit to Chez Bunch."

Suddenly, the sound of the doorknob turning startled the trio and Tim jumped off the bed. "Who's there?" Tim demanded and automatically reached for the can of Raid that Polly kept by her bed for protection.

Charlotte's voice answered as she pushed open the door. "Polly?" she said in a weak voice. "Sorry to bother you, but I don't feel too well. Dizzy and sick to my stomach. Too much champagne and excitement, I guess."

Tim put down the can and approached Charlotte. He wrapped his arm around her shoulder and steered her back down the corridor. "I've got just the remedy. Let's get you back to bed, and I'll make my patented Alcoholics Anonymous Step Thirteen. A little sorbital. A pinch of sodium bicarbonate. A spoonful of mineral oil. All yucky stuff that'll make you want to die, thus taking your mind off the spinning room. A complete Betty Ford program in a six-ounce glass. By tomorrow, you'll feel as though you've been sober for a year."

"I'd settle for a new head," Charlotte moaned.

Soon Charlotte was settled into her bed, the awful taste of Tim's potion lingering on her tongue. As she hugged her pillow and settled in for sleep she said in a drowsy voice, "I've had a lovely evening. You're all so generous. So nice of you to take me to work in the morning."

Tim was stunned that Charlotte had heard at least that part of Polly's plan. "Sleep well," he said as Charlotte began to snore. He turned off the light, closed the door, and returned to Polly's suite.

"Open a new window, open a new day . . ." Charlotte sang as she waltzed down The Scarlett O'Hara Memorial Staircase and breezed into the kitchen where the household was in pow-wow about their respective agendas for the day. They abruptly ceased their conversation and pretended to chat about a dream that Polly had had during the night. Charlotte stood behind Tim's chair and kissed the top of his head. "Your magic elixir should be bottled and sold to the kids at the Viper Room. I feel like a new woman!"

"Did you sleep well, dear?" Polly asked.

"Thanks to Tim's voodoo."

"Speaking of the black arts, we'd better hustle you over to Gerold Goss, and me to Tsarina Tatanya," Polly said. "Tim will take you to the theater and pick you up this evening. Placenta will drive me to the Valley. Anything special you'd like for din-din?"

Charlotte shook her head. "Nah. You've got to get ready for your meeting with your Snoop Sister. I'll just be in the way. As a matter of fact, I'll be staying at my place this evening. I'm over my fear of Freddy Krueger hiding in the hamper." She turned to Tim. "As a matter of fact, just drop me at my place. I'll take my own car to the theater."

Tim looked at Polly, who shrugged. "If Jeffrey Dahmer's twisted twin is cleaning out your freezer, feel free to change your mind. *Mi casa, su casa*, et cetera."

Charlotte hugged Polly and Placenta. "This is like Neverland Ranch, only without all the case workers from Child Welfare Services. I've adored every minute here. See you at Sunday's rehearsal. Oh, and of course I'll be here for your big party on Monday!"

"Can't wait," Polly deadpanned. "Will you excuse us for a nanosecond?" she added. "Timmy gets huffy if I don't break the piggy bank for his weekly allowance. Back in a flash."

Polly walked out of the kitchen trailed by her son and maid. She continued blazing the trail until they were halfway across the mansion in the wardrobe room where many of Polly's old Bob Mackie costumes were displayed on mannequins. She turned to Tim. "She's going back to her apartment to hide or destroy evidence. I knew that she heard our plans. Here's what to do. Take the most congested route possible, or have a flat tire, or some other automotive disaster. Just don't scratch the paint on the car. I need at least a half hour in her place to search for my precious Emmy."

"Done," Tim said. "She can fake a voice. I can fake car trouble."

Placenta chided Tim. "The only thing you know or care about cars is how adorable the service station attendant is who pumps your gas and cleans the windshield."

Tim sniggered. "Thank God for the full-service island. But what if you get caught? I can't keep her away for too long. She'll call a cab or, worse, fix whatever I say is the matter with the car."

"Leave it to me," Polly said confidently. "Call me when you're getting close, and I'll call you when I've finished my search and rescue operation. Miss Bunch is so anxious to get back to her ordinary life that I'm convinced that she knows more about Karen's death than she's letting on."

"How do you plan to gain access to her place?"

Polly smiled and sang the lyrics to a Sondheim song. "Everybody ought to have a maid," she warbled, then turned to Placenta, who wiggled a key ring in front of Tim's face.

Chapter 21

"That was a waste of precious time!" Polly snapped when she reached Tim on his cell phone. "Placenta obviously pinched the wrong key from Charlotte's purse. We dug around her front door until a nosey neighbor in the next apartment came out and asked why we were shaking out the doormat and rearranging the flowerpots. The moron didn't recognize me! But he's bound to describe us to Charlotte. She'll know we were there."

Tim pretended to be speaking to an Auto Club operator. "I've been waiting for over an hour," he said while gritting his teeth and looking askance at Charlotte.

"Oh, heavens, you're not still faking car trouble, are you? Why on earth would you keep up the charade for so long?"

"Because your lovely *dispatcher* didn't *ring back* to say that the mechanic had completed *her* last job," Tim sniped.

"I'm having enough trouble remembering my dance numbers, I can't be responsible for recalling trivia. Oh, hell, there's Madame T. I don't want her to see me before our rehearsal. She'll drag me in early. Gotta go. See you at lunchtime."

"You say that this pricey car comes equipped with a self-repairing engine?" Tim said in a huff.

Polly had hung up, and Tim turned the car key while still pretending that he was on the line with AAA. The engine easily turned over. He looked at Charlotte and shrugged. "Guess it was just flooded, or something."

"Or something," Charlotte said with an icy tone to her voice.

"I'll be darned. That did the trick." Tim flipped his cell phone closed and signaled to enter traffic. "Sorry about the delay, Charlotte. You'll be late, but I'll explain everything to Gerold."

Charlotte sighed. "That won't be necessary. I'll call Gerold from the apartment. He understands trouble. Especially when Polly Pepper is involved."

"That's a little unkind, Charlotte. Lately, Mom's been a magnet for dead bodies, and now an insane person is on the loose who could very well be out to kill her. Frankly, I don't know what to do. If she doesn't comply with this lunatic's demand for another of her Emmys, Sharon could be convicted and get the death sentence. On the other hand, maybe Sharon's guilty and this nutcase is looting Polly's trophy room."

Charlotte's eyes expressed sympathy. "I didn't intend to be mean. But you have to admit, things between her and Gerold are about as pleasant as the relationship between Sir Paul and Heather. There's just no getting around the fact that they hate each other's guts."

"Gerold started it. Polly's a very easy person to get along with. I don't know why he despises her so. Mom's professional, she's cooperative, and she's going to be a huge draw in this show. So what if she was late that first day? Karen was understanding, but not Gerold. He's had it in for her even before she started."

As the Rolls moved east along Fountain Avenue, Charlotte was quiet for a long moment. Then, as Tim braked for a red light, Charlotte said, "The truth is that the animosity started because Gerold and Karen had opposing ideas about the casting. Gerold of course wanted his main squeeze in the scene-stealing role of Gloria Upson, while Karen wanted a real actress. Karen wanted your mother in the lead but Gerold wanted Candice Bergen. He didn't think that Polly was a big enough draw. The fact is he sort of blames your mother for Karen's murder."

"That's too ridiculous!" Tim said. "Mother wasn't anywhere near the theater when the crime occurred!"

Charlotte shrugged. "I think he feels that if he'd gotten his way with the casting in the first place, there wouldn't have been that ugly fight."

"Fight? Between Karen and Gerold? Did Gerold kill Karen?"

Charlotte rolled her eyes.

"I wouldn't be surprised if Gerold was the killer," Tim insisted. "Everyone else on the planet adored Karen. Except for you and Sharon and Hiroaki, that is."

Charlotte dismissed Tim's comment. "We were naturally upset about being replaced, but none of us were mad at Karen. Gerold is the one who went over Karen's head to get the producers to agree to replace us. They wouldn't let him touch your mother, though. The box office business was doing so well."

Tim turned onto Gardner Street, and Charlotte said, "I'm over there," while pointing to her apartment. When he pulled up to the curb Tim said, "Truth be told, I've been suspicious of Gerold from the start."

"I never said that Gerold had anything to do with Karen's death."

"Then who? You said there was a fight."

"I didn't say who was involved."

"Polly's on someone's hit list, and I'll wager it's the same person who killed Karen. Gerold is really the only logical candidate. Nobody else hates her as he does."

"Hollywood's a killer town, all right," Charlotte said. "People here will do just about anything for fame and fortune, and to cover their butts when they've done something that could cost them their careers."

"She's clueless about a lot of things, including who murdered Karen Richards. Sure, she's got her suspects—especially you and Hiroaki, but—"

"Why would I knock off my director?"

"Because you were canned."

"A show isn't worth the negative karma of taking another's life over a stage role. How could she think that I had anything to do with the murder?"

"For one thing, you've been lying about a few things."

"I don't consider embellishing my *Bay Watch* story a lie."

"You weren't really burgled yesterday."

"We've established that." Charlotte squared her shoulders and stared out of the windshield. "Vivien Leigh is a scaredy cat. She made a ruckus that you confused with a burglary."

"That's almost as absurd as David Caruso thinking he could leave TV for a career in feature films. I believe that someone *was* in your apartment. In fact, Detective Archer is pretty certain that he knows who it was."

"He doesn't know anything of the sort!" Charlotte pulled on the door handle, but Tim had locked all the doors. "Let me out!"

Tim unbuckled his seat restraint and turned to face Charlotte. "Do yourself a favor. Explain to me why you sent those letters. Polly won't press charges if you return the Emmy."

"I've got a rehearsal to get to," Charlotte growled. "If you don't open this door, I'm calling the police."

"Be my guest." Tim held out his cell phone. "I'm sure the West Hollywood Police Department will totally believe that you're being kept against your will in a Park Ward Rolls-Royce. And when they find out who I am, and who you used to be, they'll think you're just a batty old Norma Desmond starved for publicity. Now tell me why you sent those letters and why you want to hurt my mother."

"I don't want to hurt your mother!" Charlotte cried. "She's always been civil toward me. And I have no reason to want a stupid old Emmy Award! And the Snoop Sister letters are not from me!"

"You're not leaving this car until you come clean."

Charlotte pursed her lips and refused to speak. For the next minute she divided her time between glowering at Tim and making surly nonverbal noises.

"That's it." Tim started the engine again. "We're going back to Pepper Plantation. You can stay in the wine cellar until you come to your senses. You'll like the temperature, that is if you're a case of Chateau Coutet and you're used to a lovely forty-five degrees Fahrenheit. You'll be missed by Gerold and the cast, but I'll explain that you're down with Polly's favorite disease—*infectiouschronicosis*. She's used it often enough that the CDC actually has a warning out about international travel to Lapland where Polly claims she first contracted the symptoms. Like shingles, it recurs whenever she's under stress." Tim looked at Charlotte. "Yes, I can see the symptoms. Thankfully, there is a cure. The antidote is simple. Tell me everything you know about the murder of Karen Richards, and why Polly Pepper seems to be in the middle of it all, and I'll tell you how to cure this icky malady."

"If you take me back to Pepper Plantation I'll file kidnapping charges."

Tim laughed heartily. "Are you nuts? No judge would construe being Polly Pepper's guest at her luxurious estate as kidnapping. In fact, Detective Archer was there when you accepted Polly's invitation. It's likely they'd put you away for psychiatric evaluation for confusing abduction with hospitality. Perhaps the wine cellar is too good for you. Polly's wardrobe museum in the east wing might be a more suitable prison. You can spend your time trying on Bob Mackie dresses and wondering why you never became a star." Tim signaled a right turn and began to move into traffic.

"That hurt!" Charlotte said softly. "Okay. Stop the car. I'll tell you all that I know. It's not much, but it's all true. I swear it."

Tim reversed the Rolls and once again parked against the curb. He turned off the ignition and looked into Charlotte's eyes. He said, "Cough it up, old lady."

Polly was dripping with perspiration when she left the rehearsal room at noon and met Tim and Placenta in the hallway. "We'll have to do IHOP or Denny's," she said. "Dragon Lady wants me back at precisely one o'clock. I'm never going to get her damned choreography! The steps are nothing like what I've done in every past production of this show. On opening night, Jerry Herman's going to be as pissed off as Lauren Bacall was the night she didn't win the Oscar."

As the trio walked toward the changing room, Tim said, "I've got interesting news. Charlotte thinks she knows who killed Karen."

Polly and Placenta both stopped abruptly and looked at Tim.

"Who?"

"How?"

"What?"

"When?"

Polly said, "I suppose Charlotte just volunteered information because you played the Good Samaritan and drove her home. What gives?"

"Ha! I dragged the confession out of her. Like they do at Guantanamo, but without the waterboards or electrodes or that snarling Doberman-rottweiler Lynndie Englund."

"So what did she tell you?" Placenta eagerly asked. "It's Sharon, right?"

Polly gave Placenta a slight shove. "It's not Sharon. I've told you. It's Gerold. Or . . ." Polly thought for a long moment. "I can't concentrate with all this perspiration soaking my clothes. Let me change and I'll tell you who the killer is over luncheon."

"A shower won't help with this riddle." Tim smiled. "But change anyway, and then I'll fill you in on the results of my little interrogation this morning."

Finally seated in a booth at IHOP, Polly ordered iced teas for the trio. As soon as the waitress left to fetch their drink order, Polly turned to Tim. "Hand it over. What did that conniving Miss Nobody say? Who killed Karen?"

"You said you'd tell *us* who the killer is."

"It's not as simple as naming names," Polly backtracked. "First, I've gotta hear what Charlotte had to say."

"We don't have all day," Placenta reminded her; then she turned to Tim. "What's the bottom line?"

Tim grimaced. His well-rehearsed recounting of how he had expertly tortured Charlotte would go unheard. "Okay. Long story short . . ."

The smiling waitress returned to their table with her order pad. "Have ya'll decided what you'll have?"

"A large order of privacy, please," Placenta said.

Polly smiled up at the dumbfounded waitress and placed a hand on her arm. "Please forgive this indigent, dear. She's off her meds. I graciously picked her up off the street and offered a much-needed hot meal. Still, would you do me a favor and give me another five ticks to decide that I'll have something that looks like the yummy food I see on your TV ads?"

The waitress had recognized Polly the moment she

walked into the restaurant, and was thrilled to find that she was a sweet down-to-earth star. "You betcha!" she said, then disappeared from the dining room into the kitchen.

"There's no need to be mean to the help!" Polly chastised Placenta. Then she turned to Tim. "Yeah, yeah. Long story short. Make it shorter. I haven't got more than a few breaths in my body before the pancake girl comes back."

"Here's the thing," Tim began. "Charlotte's a sicko. She thinks that all signs point to Sharon, or Karen's boyfriend, Jamie."

"Not Mag?" Placenta said.

"What makes her think that Jamie is the killer?" Polly said, startled by the revelation. "From all I've heard, he and Karen were a pair of matching smooching bookends."

"Charlotte explained that Jamie badly wanted the role of Patrick Dennis, but that Karen didn't want to mix business with their personal life. When Charlotte arrived at the theater that morning, she overheard them arguing about the role. It actually makes perfect sense."

Polly said, "Karen was being sort of a jerk not casting Jamie. I mean, in this biz who one knows is how everybody gets jobs. It's tradition. Let's suppose it was Jamie who committed the murder. He still didn't get the part of Patrick. But Mag did get to play Gloria. And Charlotte was recast as Agnes."

"Charlotte also said that Jamie knows that you took his eight-by-ten. He surmises that you deduced that since he's an actor who's played the Patrick role as often as you've played Mame, you're bound to think it's suspicious that he wasn't cast in his own girlfriend's show."

"I am suspicious . . . now," Polly said.

With slight trepidation, the waitress returned. "Need more time?"

"Sweetheart," Polly said, pointing to an A-frame card on the table with a picture of a plate of Belgium waffles, "why don't you bring us each whatever that is. Oh, and we're sort of in a hurry to get back to rehearsals. I'm doing a production of *Mame,* you know, at the Galaxy Theatre down the street. I hope you'll come and see me. Tell your friends, and all your customers too. You're a dear. Oh, and waters all around, please. *Merci beaucoup.*"

"You're a carnival barker and a walking billboard rolled into one," Tim chided his mother.

"Lucy Ball once said to me, 'Half my job is acting. The other half is publicizing the work.'"

Placenta interrupted. "I still don't understand how Charlotte came to the conclusion that Jamie is the killer. Where's her evidence?"

"Frankly," Tim said, "she doesn't have any. It's just a hunch."

"If Jamie is the killer, I can handle him," Polly said.

"What if he's not the murderer? What if it's someone totally unexpected? You don't know what you're up against," Placenta said.

"I've got a plan," Polly whispered. "Although I'm loathe to risk another Emmy."

Chapter 22

"Are you sure that you wouldn't rather bunk with Timmy again tonight?" Polly teased her beau as she spoke with him over the cell phone en route back to Pepper Plantation. "Trust me, he doesn't give a lick about your webbed toes." Polly put her hand over the phone and chuckled. "He hates for anyone to know about his toes," she whispered to Tim and Placenta. "Say again?" she returned to Randy. "Tim and I both smell good? We both use the same citrus and ginger body splash. How close did you two get the other night? Lovely. And so metrosexual. No, sweetheart, that's not . . . Dear, we're just now at the gates, so I've gotta run. See you at eight. Cheers." She closed the phone and handed it back to her son just as the Pepper Plantation gates parted.

"Webbed toes?" Tim grimaced. "Is he part amphibian? Any sign of a tail or cloven hooves?"

"No, but I could knit an afghan rug with the hair on his chest." Polly felt a flutter of excitement at the thought of seeing Randy for dinner. "By the by, Randy said that he adored your satin sheets. He wants a set of his own. I'm not sure what concerns me the most, that he used the word 'adored' or that he suddenly craves satin."

When the trio entered the mansion they automatically drifted to the great room where Placenta opened a bottle of Bollinger. Polly and Tim plopped themselves down opposite each other on the twin Tahitian cotton sofas. They kicked off their shoes and rested their feet on the glass-top coffee table. Tim said, "Have you decided which poor Emmy will be sacrificed tonight?"

Polly knocked back her champagne and set the glass down, stood up, wandered over to the bookshelves, and lovingly touched each of her awards. "Eenie. Meenie. Minie. Mo." She picked up her fifth consecutive season win and held it to her bosom. "There's nothing worse than losing a loved one," she said with a cry in her voice.

"Especially if they're gold-plated," Placenta added. "I'm looking on the bright side. Less dusting for me."

Polly heaved a heavy sigh. "Forgive her, Father, for she knows not that with one more crack she'll be working for Candy Spelling." Polly brought the Emmy to the coffee table and carefully set it down on the glass. "I should have had all my babies equipped with microchip tracking devices, like domestic pets. If I survive this calamitous night, I assure you that every Emmy, People's Choice, and Mr. Blackwell's Worst Dressed award will be branded for identification."

Tim sat forward and looked at his mother. "I'd better hear that you're getting Randy involved in this latest ransom demand. Otherwise, I swear I'll call 911 and tell them everything."

Polly waved away her son's concern. "After dinner with Randy, I'll suggest a romantic stroll down Hollywood Boulevard. I'll accidentally on purpose wander over my star on the Walk of Fame, then we'll make a nostalgic stop at the Chinese Theatre and I can impress him with never-before-told anecdotes about some of my dead friends in the forecourt."

"Sounds dreamy," Tim teased. "What if the 'phantom'

sees you on the arm of a police detective? You're supposed to make the drop alone."

"I plan to ask Randy for a moment of solitude. I'll say that I need to meditate over Joan Crawford's pumps. I'll keep him within shouting distance, in case I get into trouble."

Placenta refilled Polly's champagne flute. "How do you propose explaining the brown paper bag stuffed with an Emmy? They're heavy suckers. Gentleman that your detective is, he's bound to insist on carrying the sack. He'll catch on soon enough."

Polly admitted that she hadn't thought that far ahead, but insisted that she would certainly be convincing with whatever ruse she decided to use on Randy. "Not that I enjoy subterfuge—at least not this early in a relationship. However, if I'm to help exonerate Sharon, this is what I have to do."

Tim reached for the bottle of Bollinger and added another splash to his mother's glass, as well as his own. He was silent for a moment, and then he made a decision that he knew would be rebuffed by his mother. "Despite your armed police escort, Placenta and I are shadowing you all evening." He quickly countered his mother's objections. "Ah-bub-bub!" He spoke and halted her protest with a "talk to the hand" gesture. "You'll never convince me to let you out of my sight . . . at least not until I know you're safely delivered to Randy's apartment. If anything happened to you, I'd spend the rest of my life wracked with pain for not having you put me back in your will. You're not leaving this planet until you disinherit that crazy Society for the Prevention of Unauthorized Kidney Harvesting in Unsuspecting Business Travelers."

Polly's response was less confrontational than either Tim or Placenta expected. In fact, she was suddenly contrite about not including her family in her potentially dangerous plans. "As long as you keep your distance," she said. "I don't want Randy to think I'm being chaperoned. I'd advise you both to wear a disguise." She turned to Tim. "If Jamie's behind this travesty, he'll recognize that adorable cleft in your chin a mile away. Of course, you could distract him by wearing your tightest jeans and a tank top. Hmm, not a bad idea. Never mind. Just stay as far away from me as possible. Randy won't let me be hurt."

Placenta said, "While you're at Fred Astaire's feet, Randy may be over by Norma Shearer's handprints. What if the place is jammed with Japanese tourists and he's so blinded by their flashbulbs that he can't keep an eye on you?"

"Trust me, I'm the one who's blinding him. He can't keep his eyes off of me, which is freaky while he's driving. Speaking of looking at me, it's getting late and I'd better hop in the tub and shave my legs. I'll be wearing my new Antoinette Catenacci."

"Wouldn't something a little less conspicuous be more appropriate for the occasion?" Tim said.

"This is my evening too! I'm not lowering my standards for some extortionist bum who thinks he can prey on a legend and totally disrupt my life. As a matter of fact, I have a mind to leave him a bag of bricks and let the police worry about Sharon."

"Do that," Tim said. "I'd better get gussied up myself. Now, what shall I wear? If I could find my old hair extensions I could be like Jim Caviezel in that Mel Gibson Jesus flick."

As Polly rose from her seat on the sofa, she turned to Tim. "Now who's calling attention to themselves? Don't forget our pact. You never upstage me in the looks department in public!"

"When we're together," Tim reminded his mother.

"Ever!" Polly scolded and left the room, taking her Emmy with her.

"Your mama's gotta be the showstopper, you know

that," Placenta said. "If you go out in public looking like a supersexy Christ, she won't get a shred of attention."

"That's rather the point. I want her to be as inconspicuous as possible. People are going to recognize her. That could make the situation even more dangerous. Okay. I'll just wear a pair of jeans and a T-shirt. I'll pretend to be a tourist."

Placenta nodded. She set her champagne flute down and stood up. "I'd better make sure your mama's got a fresh razor. Wouldn't want Randy's lips to get sandpapered from stubble under her pits."

The next hour galloped by as Placenta helped Polly bathe and dress, then sequestered herself in her own suite to prepare to accompany Tim for a night of undercover work. In the meantime, Tim laid out his wardrobe and completed his own ablutions just as the chimes from the front gate pealed throughout the house. "He's early!" Polly called out. "I still need an hour to do makeup. And no flapping your lips about our plans!"

Placenta flew down the stairs and when she reached the intercom she pushed the release button to open the gates. She quickly returned to the great room to clear away the evidence of Lush Hour. Just as she finished tossing the bottle into the trash compactor, and setting the glasses in the dishwasher, the doorbell rang. Placenta hustled out of the kitchen and down the main hallway to the foyer. "Coming," she called out. When she reached the door she set a smile on her lips, turned the knob, and pulled. In a flash her smile disappeared; two men were at the door and neither one was Detective Randal Archer. Her attempt to close the door was stopped by the large steel-toe work boot of one of the men, who then shoved the door open all the way, and pushed Placenta to the side.

Placenta lunged for the panic button on the alarm system but she was caught in midstride by the smaller of the two men. "No, you don't, sister," he said, and twisted Placenta's arm as he pulled her toward the sunken living room. "Shut up and don't try anything stupid," the larger and more menacing looking of the pair demanded.

"What do you want?" Placenta found her frightened voice.

The smaller man tightened his grip on Placenta. She had read somewhere that crime victims should never try to play to their attacker's humanity by acting obsequious or weak. She was as angry as she was petrified, but instinctively found the strength to castigate her assailants. "Get the hell off this property!" she yelled and was rewarded with a stiff backhand against the left side of her face.

The stone on the intruder's ring broke the skin of her cheek and she began to bleed. The two men dragged Placenta through the house and found the great room, where they shoved her to the floor. The smaller of the men withdrew a roll of duct tape from his army-surplus jacket and plastered a strip of tape across Placenta's mouth. While the larger man gingerly walked out of the room and stepped stealthily down the hall, Placenta's wrists were taped together behind her back. She was left on the floor as the thug hurried to catch up with his partner.

Back in the sunken living room, facing the Scarlett O'Hara Memorial Staircase, the men cautiously ascended one step at a time. On the second-floor landing they separated and set out in opposite directions.

Tim was admiring himself in the floor-to-ceiling bathroom mirror, giving his moussed hair another scrunch, when out of the corner of his eye he caught a shadow reflected in the mirror. He froze. Polly and Placenta would never enter his room unannounced, even if the door were left wide open. They'd call out in advance to give him time to address his modesty, if need be. For an instant he thought perhaps Detective Archer had come in. But again, polite visitors would broadcast their presence. In an instant, Tim's sixth sense told him to hide. But there was nowhere to go in his sleek modern bathroom. Even the shower stall was clear glass.

He stepped behind the door. In the space between the door frame he again saw the ominous shadow. And then he saw a face. His heart raced as though he'd just finished a marathon. A thousand thoughts coursed through his mind, including the location of his cell phone, which was on his bedside nightstand next to his wallet.

At the same time, the intruder saw Tim reflected in the mirrored wall of the bathroom. He withdrew a pistol from his jacket and stepped back from Tim's view.

Tim decided he had to face the enemy in order to get to his mother. His eyes scanned the bathroom for a weapon. There was nothing. Other than an electric toothbrush, a few scented candles, and bottles of various Dolce & Gabbana skin care products on the marble vanity, he kept his bathroom immaculate and uncluttered. He thought of quickly shutting the door and locking himself inside, but if Polly wasn't in jeopardy at this very instant she would be the second that he was seen as a coward and no longer a risk to the intruder.

In a moment of sheer terror, he removed his belt, which was a thick leather strap with a silver and turquoise buckle. It wasn't much of a weapon against a man with a gun, but Tim held the belt as if it were a whip and lashed at a spray bottle on the vanity. The bottle crashed into the sink and brought the intruder back into view.

It was Tim's plan to wait until the intruder stepped into the room, then shove the door as hard as possible to throw him off balance, thus giving Tim a moment to perhaps seize the gun—or be shot. Tim never got the opportunity. In an instant, the barrel of a gun was pushed through the space between the door and molding, and aimed directly at him.

"Move," was the word Tim heard. He stepped from behind the door with his hands up in the air. Instructed to put his hands behind his back, Tim was soon bound like Placenta, with silver duct tape around his wrists and across his mouth. All that he could think of was his mother's safety. As he was pushed down the corridor toward Polly's room, Tim didn't hear a sound coming from her suite, and he feared the worst.

Tim was being used as a human shield as they approached the double doors that led to Polly's bedroom. Then, just before entering, the gunman pulled him down to the floor and warned him not to move. Tim watched in horror as the assailant slowly moved into his mother's boudoir, his gun drawn, looking from side to side like a mercenary in guerrilla warfare.

Suddenly, he heard a scream of intense pain and agony. His attacker came running out of the room holding his hands to his face and crying in anguish. He tried to run down the corridor but tripped over Tim's legs, and crashed to the floor. He struggled to get up and once righted, raced for the stairway. Still screeching, the man was confused and disoriented and when he tried to navigate the first step of the staircase he tripped and tumbled head over heels to the floor below, where he came to a loud stop as his head met the limestone floor.

For a moment the house was eerily quiet. Tim's eyes were wide with fear as he raised himself to his feet and listened for any sign of activity in his mother's rooms. Then he heard her whisper, "We're being burgled. Send backup." He heard her hang up the phone as he stumbled into the room.

In the instant before she recognized that the lumbering man was Tim she quickly raised her can of Raid and held it out in front of her like an amulet to give protection from an evil spirit. When she realized it was her son bound and gagged, she rushed to his side and ripped the tape from his mouth.

Tim cried out in pain but knew it was nothing compared to what he might have felt had the attacker chosen to beat him, or worse. "Mom! Are you all right?"

As Polly cut Tim free with a pair of toenail scissors, she said, "Jesus, Joseph, and Mary! This man"—she pointed to a body lying facedown on her bathroom floor—"came into my room holding a gun—unannounced no less. I had to take drastic measures. I got him in the eyes with my spider spray. Anyway, while he was wailing like a little crybaby, I clobbered him with the Emmy—exactly like someone did to Karen. It was handy and I acted on instinct. Who knew these things made such great weapons!"

Polly and Tim hugged each other tightly. "Oh my God! My poor Placenta! Come! First lock the bathroom door so the asshole—if he's alive—can't get out," she said. Then hand in hand the two walked with trepidation down the staircase to the body on the first floor.

"This one fell so hard, he'll be lucky if he only has a broken neck," Tim said. "I think we can leave him. I doubt that he's going anywhere."

Tim led his mother through the house, still mindful that there might be other intruders. First, they checked the kitchen—there was no sign of Placenta or anyone else. When they finally reached the great room, they raced to Placenta's side. They could see that she'd been roughed up, but at least she was conscious. When she was released from her bonds, Placenta sobbed an apology. "I let them in. I thought it was Randy. I didn't bother to ask who was at the gate."

Polly and Tim both hugged Placenta. "It was a natural mistake," Tim said.

"They came around the same time that Randy was expected. You couldn't have known," Polly cooed. "Look what those animals did to you!" She helped Placenta over to the sofa and then ran to the bar for a cold bottle of champagne to place against Placenta's cheek.

"I think we'd all rather be drinking this stuff," Placenta said. "Bring three glasses and a cold damp towel."

"I'll never again threaten you with having to work for Candy Spelling!" Polly cried.

The trio was suddenly startled by the sound of the chimes from the front gates. Walking past the still unconscious intruder at the foot of the staircase, Tim went to the intercom by the front door. Reminded of what Placenta hadn't done, Tim now asked the visitor to identify himself. When he heard Randy's voice, he quickly pushed the entry button and returned to the great room. "Our knight in shining armor is here. If a bit late."

Chapter 23

As a team of police EMTs placed the two now-conscious Pepper Plantation intruders on rolling transfer stretchers and wheeled them out of the house, Polly, Tim, and Placenta formed a receiving line beside the waiting ambulances. "The next time you want an autograph, send ten dollars and a self-addressed stamped envelope," Polly said to the man whom she'd clobbered with her Emmy. For extra measure, she rapped the back of her hand against the bandages on his head. She looked at the smaller man. "As for you, pipsqueak, don't ever underestimate the strength of a legend."

Addressing Randy Archer, Polly proclaimed, "Take 'em away!" She gave a slight giggle. "I've always wanted to say that! Better yet, 'Off with their heads!' I once played a mean but somehow lovable queen on my show. Got to turn Jerry Lewis into a dog's behind, which is actually his natural state."

"But you digress, Mother." Tim ushered her and Placenta and Randy back inside the mansion.

While a team of police inspectors and forensic experts were dusting, scraping, photographing, and recovering bits of hair, fingerprints, blood samples, and wads of duct tape,

Polly and her family were busy relating the chronology of the evening's events to Randy. When they got to the part about Polly planning a clandestine rendezvous at the Chinese Theatre and her resolve to forfeit another Emmy for the sake of information leading to the clearing of Sharon's name, Randy became edgy. "I guess I make a rather good pawn. Good ol' Randy. He can be wrapped around Polly Pepper's little manicured finger."

"I simply didn't want to worry you any more than I had to, dear," Polly explained. "Don't tell me that your masculine ego is bruised because I was thinking only of your well-being. I was doing what I considered to be the right thing at the time. All right. You win. I was stupid and naive. If it makes you feel any better, I'm not going to show up at Fred Astaire's feet tonight or give away another Emmy just to help Sharon out of this jam she's gotten herself into. Sorry, Sharon," Polly said loudly, as if transmitting her thoughts out through the window, into the garden, and all the way to Sharon Fletcher's jail cell. "Although I have complete faith that you didn't kill Karen, all the necessary evidence to support my intuition will have to be revealed without any further support from *moi*."

Randy wasn't appeased by Polly's declaration, but he tried to show appreciation. "It's not that I don't value your help, Polly," he said, giving her a hug. "I admire how generous you are to actresses who somehow find themselves jailed for murders they didn't commit. But I don't like to see you in jeopardy." Randy gave her another tight hug. "In a few hours we'll have a complete biographical profile of who your uninvited guests were. Perhaps they'll lead us to Karen's killer. Presuming there's a connection."

"There is," Polly prophesized. "I feel it. Call it my Agatha Christie complex, but I have a sixth sense about these things. During the past week I've been stalked and stolen from and ransomed and lied to, and now it seems that I'm on a hit list, just like Ann Coulter. Odds are two to one that if I hadn't been on my knees behind the bed searching for the top to my Chanel bottle when that orangutan lumbered into my room, he would have seen me first and probably emptied his Saturday night special into my head! I was lucky too that my Emmy was at hand, and that he was distracted by his melting eyeballs. I suppose my bloodstained Emmy is joining Sharon's as crime evidence down at the Beverly Hills Police Station, eh?"

Randy nodded. "We'll take good care of Emmy. I promise." Almost bashfully, Randy looked down and mumbled, "I guess you're exhausted from all the excitement."

"You have a sixth sense too," Polly kidded.

"Then I suppose we should postpone our dinner and . . ."

Polly, still wearing her gorgeous, red Antoinette Catenacci dress, said, "Under the circumstances, since I've been brutally attacked by an army of murderous marauders in the sanctity of my very own twenty-seven-room Bel Air mansion from which, on a clear day I have a view of the Pacific—"

"Absolutely, I understand," Randy said.

"—I'd feel safer if I could be with you for the night." The two smiled at each other. "So let's wrap up this dreary official business and get down to monkey business." She blushed as crimson as her dress when she caught Tim's and Placenta's eyes.

Dinner was at Crustacean in Beverly Hills, and as Polly and Randy were sipping champagne and holding hands across the table, several of Polly's friends and colleagues dropped by to say hello and to get an up-close look at her beau. "Oh, don't stand on ceremony, dear," Chita said to Randy as he began to rise from his chair to greet the Broadway legend. She shook his hand, and then kissed the air beside Polly's check. After whispering a lascivious thought into Polly's ear about Randy and chuckling conspiratorially, Chita demanded a call first thing in the A.M. "Just the facts, ma'am," she teased.

As the Broadway diva departed she was replaced by Tony Bennett, who was elegantly dressed in an Armani blue blazer, gray slacks, and an impeccable red silk necktie. His perfect toupee too was exquisitely styled and taped firmly in place. He gallantly kissed Polly's hand and introduced himself to Randy. "We don't see enough of you," he said to Polly in his seductive voice. Before the dessert menu was presented, Polly and Randy had received Aretha Franklin, Cyndi Lauper, Diahann Carroll, and George Clooney.

Although Randy was heady from champagne and the reflected starlight from a galaxy of celebrities, he nevertheless remembered that he had to call the police station for an update on the identities of the men who had trespassed into Polly's home. "Do you mind?" he asked, holding out his cell phone.

As Randy spoke to a colleague at the Beverly Hills Police Station, Polly tried to read his body language. A nod of his head. A roll of his eyes. The knitting of eyebrows. All of Randy's mannerisms might have spoken volumes to a psychic, but Polly couldn't interpret the cryptic gesticulations. When Randy finally closed his cell phone he was silent for a long moment. Polly nudged his arm. "What gives?" He took a deep breath and sighed.

"What?" Polly asked.

"The good news is that we have positive identification."

"No bad news tonight, please," Polly begged.

"They're both actors."

"Oh, that *is* bad. Imagine, actors in Hollywood. There goes the neighborhood. Thespians come in and take all the really good jobs, like cater waiters, temporary office help, and tour guides at the Universal Studios Tour."

"That's not what I meant," Randy said, trying to get a word in.

"God knows that acting leads to aberrant behavior, most notably from divas, has-beens, and Australian Catholic alcoholics with too many children and a Christ complex."

Polly was quiet for a long moment. She asked, "But why would anyone want to break into my house? If they were auditioning for assholes of the year, they win those roles, hands down!" Polly caught herself swearing in public, an image-destroying practice that she tried to avoid at all costs. She looked around. "Excuse my unattractive language," she begged to anyone who might have overheard her.

"They aren't just any garden variety actors who work in storefront theaters on Melrose Avenue," Randy began.

"Don't tell me. Mr. Affectation, James Lipton, has interviewed them on *Inside the Actor's Studio*."

"Let me finish giving you the full report." Randy poured the dregs of a bottle of Dom into Polly's flute. "Another bottle?"

Polly shook her head. "When we get to your place."

"When you hear the rest of what I have to say, you may have a headache and need to go home."

"Don't keep me in suspense."

"Your two attackers are Jonathan Martin and Clem Collins. They have a lot in common with Sharon Fletcher."

"Other than being actors, what could those two Geico Neanderthals possibly have in common with chic Sharon?" Polly raised an eyebrow. "I don't see Sharon as the type to associate with lowbrows."

"For one thing, they share Sharon's address."

"She mentioned that she likes to fool around with trash," Polly recalled.

"For another, they've appeared on her daytime drama," Randy continued.

"I don't understand."

"They rent Sharon's guest house."

"She gives thieves a place to live and offers them parts on her show?"

"Bit roles. One liners every now and then."

Polly stared for a long moment into the stalks of bamboo growing in large cloisonné pots against the wall behind Randy's back. Then she smiled. "That solves the mystery of why anyone would want to harm poor defenseless me. It's obvious that Sharon must have talked about visiting Pepper Plantation and how large and elegant my Bel Air palace is. These two unemployed actor thugs decided to try to make a heist at my expense. That's the last time I invite a relative stranger over without first having Homeland Security do a complete background check and credit report on them and all of their friends. There! I've solved the puzzle, or at least part of it."

"What part?" Randy asked.

"The part about why they broke in—"

"They were let in," Randy reminded Polly. "There may be other reasons for their coming to Pepper Plantation."

Polly stopped a waiter and ordered a glass of Cristal. In a moment a cold and effervescing flute was placed before her. She took a long sip. "Years ago, I had a fan who would do absolutely anything for me. He was happy picking up my laundry and staying in the house when I had to be away for extended periods. I was his idol, of course. Or so I thought. He turned out to be Eve Harrington's more aggressive and devious evil fraternal twin. He thought that if he insinuated himself into my life, I'd offer him a role on my show, or one of my TV specials. I truly believe that he would have gone so far as to knock off Kate Jackson if I'd asked him too. Don't think I didn't consider that after she sucked all the fun out of the atmosphere the week she guest-starred on my show. What if these two wannabes knocked off someone for Sharon?"

"Namely . . . ?"

"Karen Richards."

Randy nodded. "Far-fetched, but nothing surprises me anymore," he said.

"Perhaps they thought that I was getting too close to the truth about who bashed in Karen's pretty skull and came after me." Polly set her champagne flute down on the table. "I'm probably looking at the murderer and am too close to see him."

Chapter 24

After a fulfilling night in the arms of her police detective lover, Polly returned to Pepper Plantation in a cheerful disposition. She bathed, applied new eyelashes, and dressed for the day and the first full-cast rehearsal of *Mame*.

Polly skipped down The Scarlett O'Hara Memorial Staircase and waltzed into the kitchen, where she found Tim draining his mug of coffee and trying to focus on *Doonesbury* in the *L.A. Times*. Placenta was standing at the center island watching the *ABC Morning News Money Report*. By now, Polly's sleepovers were no longer an exciting novelty, and they didn't look up when she sat down with a loud and happy sigh.

"Good morning to you too," Polly said. "Never mind. My ego is strong enough today not to require your undivided awareness of my presence. Just know that Polly Pepper is alive and well and having a passionate midlife Carnival cruise."

"If this is your midlife, I guess you're planning to stick around until you're about a hundred and ten," Tim said.

"Pooh!" Polly playfully jeered. "Scoff all you like at my extracurricular activities. You're just envious because I have a beau and you don't." Polly took a sip the virgin Bloody Mary that had been waiting for her. "As I see it, yesterday we were almost the twenty-first-century version of the Manson murder victims, complete with worldwide front page headlines and gruesome photos in the *National Peeper*. But thanks to those two thugs, the incident has made me much more aware of how tenuous life is. Perhaps *your* libido can wait. Mine can't."

Tim sighed. "You're right, of course, I am jealous. Not counting Randy, I haven't had a sleepover since . . . I can't remember."

Polly took another sip from her BM. "You're such a baby for a man who's supposed to be somewhere in age between Neil Patrick Harris and David Hyde Pierce. As I don't reveal my own age, I've forgotten yours. But I know that you're old enough to be playing house in the cottage behind the garden shed. What the heck are you waiting for? As Mame says, 'Live! Life is a banquet and most poor sons of bitches are starving to death!' In the looks department you're pretty much the eighth wonder of the world. Don't end up like those gardens in Babylon—a withered myth."

Placenta took a seat beside Polly and began eating her bowl of Heart Smart breakfast cereal flakes. Polly reached out and touched the back of her hand to Placenta's lacerated cheek. "Oh, my poor Placenta. I'm so sorry that you endured the brunt of those trolls' viciousness. At least they're now in a hospital jail cell. I hope that when they're strong enough to bathe themselves they both drop their soaps in the communal showers beside someone named Tito or Big Bow Wow."

Placenta milked her minor injury for all that she thought she might be able to get away with. "I'm suffering from post-traumatic stress disorder. Don't expect me to work."

Polly shook her head. "When have I ever expected that?

Frankly, none of us has time for a breakdown. We've got a ton to do. I want this murder investigation wrapped up, pronto."

Now sufficiently infused with caffeine, Tim put down his mug. "How many times are you going to tell your new man that you're *not* involved with his case, then the moment his back is turned, you end up in hot water?"

Polly shrugged. "I'll handle Randy. By the way, I had a brilliant idea last night while playing 'Red Light, Green Light.'"

"Light what?" Placenta put her hands over her ears. "I don't want to know!"

"Something that Randy made up especially for me," Polly said. "I think. I hope. Traffic citations, scandals, and bribes, oh my! Ha!" Polly sniggered, then blushed as she recalled intimate moments with Randy. "Let's just say that I'm on the verge of being sentenced to perform community service."

"Is that what you young-uns call it today?" Tim smirked.

"Speaking of being sentenced," Polly added, "Sharon won't be. I've figured everything out."

Tim stopped midgulp of his second mug of coffee.

Placenta missed what the news anchor said after "The governor fought rumors about his alleged affair with singer/songwriter . . ."

Polly backtracked. "Not exactly everything. But enough to remember what dear old Uncle Alfred Hitchcock said to me about finding murderers. . . ."

Polly was enthusiastic about getting to the Galaxy Theatre for her first full-cast rehearsal of *Mame*. While Tim stayed home to supervise the installation of the backyard tent for Monday night's party, and to personally interview and handpick the catering staff, Placenta drove Polly to the theater.

They arrived ahead of the other members of the company. While Polly had the stage all to herself, she walked through the scenes and dance steps. She was now comfortable with the choreography, and the famous Lawrence and Lee dialogue came tumbling back to her. For the first time since agreeing to reprise her role as Mame, Polly was at ease with the part and with herself. "That felt worthy of a Tony Award!" she exclaimed to Placenta, who was seated in the third row of the auditorium. "I feel like a million. Not even gruesome ol' Gerold can bring me down from my high."

"It's still early," a voice called from the back of the auditorium. It was Gerold Goss. "So glad that the reports from Tanya were inflated. I sorta liked what I just saw."

Polly curtsied. "Old leather breasts ratted on me, eh? I suppose you know that Tanya drastically altered Onna White's original choreography. That's got to be against union rules. Still, I've practiced until my feet are worn away up to my ankles!"

Other members of the company now dribbled into the theater, and Gerold ascended the steps to the stage to begin conducting his rehearsal. Mag Ryan wandered in with Stewart Long, the company's adult Patrick Dennis. What appeared to be an intimate conversation between them abruptly came to a halt when they both caught the eye of Gerold, who was taking inventory of their behavior and body language.

Charlotte Bunch arrived next with a loud clacking of heels on the wooden stage. The moment she saw Polly, and for the benefit of all others present, she called out in a voice that imitated Charles Gibson on his nightly news broadcast, "A lesson to be learned. If you break into Pepper Plantation, the mistress of the manor will shatter your vertebrae!" Charlotte switched to what was considered her real voice. "I heard all about the excitement," she said, drawing as much attention to herself as possible. "Drugged-out skinheads crashed her gates and Polly single-handedly defended her castle and sent the pervs up the river via the Cedars Sinai emergency room! Howard Stern was practically peeing in his pants about it this morning. He thought it was too funny. He usually has such mean things to say about you."

Polly waved away Charlotte's absurd scenario about the intruders to Pepper Plantation. "They were hardly skinheads," she said. "My experience with the underworld yesterday was definitely traumatic, like the time I was on *Celebrity Jeopardy!* Who knew that P. Diddy could tell the difference between a .44 magnum, and *The Magna Carta*? Or that Jessica Simpson would know the name of the house the president lives in? But the show must go on. I've always been a trouper, so here I am to honor my commitment to the theater and to all of you!"

Soon Gerold was playing his role of bombastic director and ordering his cast and the stage manager around as though he was the alpha pack leader and the talent merely obedient dogs. "We don't have the luxury of time!" Gerold bellowed. "We've got to run through the entire production before noon. Our freaking orchestra costs a fortune! You've all had plenty of time to learn your lines, so you'd better be off book. I'm not your prompter! Now git. And remember your cues!"

As the cast disbursed into the wings, Mag frantically reviewed her Gloria Upson dialogue in the script.

Charlotte was annoying everyone with her tongue-twister vocal exercise: "Red leather, yellow leather. Red leather, yellow leather." With each set of "Red leather, yellow leathers" she switched voices from Tallulah Bankhead to Jay Leno to Joan Rivers to Homer Simpson.

Emily Hutcherson sidled up to Polly. "I know that you've done this show gads of times. As a matter of fact, I caught your performance at the Ogunquit Playhouse about a decade ago. When we get to our 'Bosom Buddies' number, try not to step on my laughs."

Polly concealed her resentment that a second-rate actress and a third-rate Vera Charles would accuse her of purposely stealing a scene. "Don't worry about getting laughs. I caught your off-off-Melrose musical production of *The Man with the Golden Arm*. Honey, when you were onstage the Laugh-O-Meter went berserk. I remember the *Daily Variety* review. 'Ms. Hutcherson's notes are so sharp that she punctures the score.'"

Emily looked as though she'd just been slapped with a lawsuit and she walked away.

Chapter 25

The weekend was a blur for Polly. She and the cast spent twelve hours a day rehearsing on Saturday and Sunday in preparation for the following Friday night's opening of *Mame*. They were practically living at the theater. They returned to their homes only for a few hours of sleep and fresh clothes before coming back for more intimidation from Gerold.

Meanwhile, back at the Plantation, Tim was working equally hard to create a memorable party for his mother and her cast. When a project was marinating in Tim's creative juices, his initial idea invariably morphed into a far more grand design. This time a simple drinks party together with a mini–Polly Pepper film festival featuring a screening of her low-budget horror classic *It Ate Kowalski* had turned into a major Hollywood A-List bash.

His new party theme: extinct equatorial civilizations. It was one he'd been thinking of creating long before Mel Gibson's bloodbath film. Tim knew that it wouldn't outdo his biggest hits, but then nothing could compete with his *Brigadoon* event. That circus featured the Loch Ness Monster in the swimming pool. Or as Buddy Hackett had said at the time, "Frances Farmer's in the pool getting shock therapy!" Polly never dared ask what amphibious creature Tim found for that awe-inspiring evening of laughs and fears, but whatever it was, she knew that Beverly Hills Prada princesses still gasped with glee when they tried to figure out what may have been lurking in the dark water.

For tonight's affair the mansion was being transformed into a tropical rain forest complete with waterfalls, lush flora dusted with glitter, live parrots and monkeys, and caterers dressed only in loincloths and sarongs (hence Tim's preoccupation with the audition process for specific cater waiters). The affair was shaping up to include not only the cast of Polly's stage musical, but also many of his mother's celebrity friends. From Alan Alda to Stephanie Zimbalist, the guests on Tim's list were eager to attend another party at the famed Pepper Plantation.

Tim was confident that he would hit his usual home run (and that Polly would accept all the credit), but he was concerned about his mother's part of the bargain. Would Polly strike out when she ultimately pointed her accusing finger at whoever she decided was Karen's murderer? It was a question that worried Tim until late Monday morning when he passed his mother on The Scarlett O'Hara Memorial Staircase. She was going up as he was going down. As they moved past each other, Polly said, "Will I be pleased with the shindig?"

"Do I ever disappoint?" Tim boasted. "Have the spiders arrived?"

"Placenta's keeping them in the laundry room," Polly said, continuing to ascend the stairs. "What about that panther by the front entrance? You know I don't like to see animals caged, dear."

"He'll be off leash and out and about soon," Tim said as he reached the bottom step.

"I hope he's vegetarian, and well fed," Polly called out. "No Celebrity Tartar this evening, please, and thank you."

"Oh, by the way," Tim called up to his mother, "Sharon, Charlotte, Jamie, Gerold, Mag, Emily, or Hiroaki? Who have you decided knocked off Karen? You promised a major surprise."

Polly rested against the banister and looked down at Tim, giving him a "Ye of little faith" look. "All indications suggest—"

A frenzied Placenta, who had appeared next to Tim, interrupted Polly's response. "Pick up the phone," Placenta said to Polly. "It's a matter of life and death. Or so they say."

"Who's 'they' when we're so busy and up to our buns in humidifiers and poison darts?" Polly huffed.

"They wouldn't identify themselves, but insisted that they had to speak to Polly Pepper."

Polly rolled her eyes and exhaled. "Life and death, eh? Getting Charlie Sheen off prime-time television is a matter of life and death. I'll take the call in my suite." She continued unhurried down the second-floor landing toward her bedroom. When she arrived in her room, Polly closed the door behind her and went to the nightstand beside her bed. She picked up the cordless telephone and settled onto the chaise next to the bay window that overlooked her manicured garden. Polly pushed the Talk button, and in a professional no-nonsense voice said, "This is Miss Pepper. With whom am I speaking?"

"Never mind. All that matters is that Karen Richards is dead. She's not coming back. Sharon Fletcher is in custody and there's no need for you to continue looking for another killer."

The voice on the other end of the line was androgynous. It had the cultured New England accent and stammered pattern of Katharine Hepburn combined with the indolent and irritating whine of Truman Capote. Polly couldn't connect a face to the voice.

"I'm giving you a bit of friendly advice, stop nosing around," the speaker commanded. "Otherwise, the next time you receive unexpected visitors at Pepper Plantation they'll be far more competent than the slugs who called on you the other day."

"Who are—"

"I'm actually an ardent admirer of yours, which is why I'm giving you this warning. Just do your job in *Mame*. I'll be watching. Have your party tonight. I'll be enjoying the evening too. But stop digging around in places that may be hazardous to your health. You're wading into deep water. You're already over your head, and you're putting yourself, Tim, Placenta, and your Emmy in danger. Got it?"

"Now, wait a—"

Suddenly the line was disconnected. Polly looked at the phone and pushed the End button. She sat back on the chaise to collect her thoughts. The last thing she wanted to do was jeopardize the safety of her loved ones. For a fleeting instant she thought of calling Randy for help and advice. However, she instantly realized that he'd be angry and bring out the "I told you so" card.

Polly was startled out of her reverie by a knock at her door. Tim and Placenta then entered before Polly had an opportunity to invite them in. They both stood in the center of the room and stared down at her. "If that creepy voice doesn't make you leave the investigating work to Randy and his team, then you need a lobotomy," Tim said to his mother. "How many times do we have to be crime victims before you give up this quest?"

Placenta answered Polly's questioning eyes. "Extensions," she said. "You wanted a phone in every room in order to spy on us. It works both ways."

"So you heard that this phantom menace is coming to our little soirée," Polly said. "Obviously, it's someone we know. Did either of you recognize the voice? Very odd." Polly paused. "Charlotte Bunch!"

"Of course! She's always doing crazy voices!" Tim said. "She can imitate anyone!"

Placenta enthusiastically agreed. "At rehearsals I've watched her try out a dozen or more different voices for her Gooch character. She comes up with the most amazing and bizarre choices."

Polly thought aloud. "It has to be Charlotte. The caller said they would be around for the show and also would be at our party tonight."

"She—or was it he?—didn't exactly say they were coming to the party," Tim corrected. "They said they would be enjoying the evening too."

Polly grimaced. She stood up from the chaise and paced the room. "It could be anyone from the cast. They'll all be here tonight."

"I agree that it's got to be Charlotte," Tim insisted. "One of us would have recognized the voice of Gerold or Mag or anyone else in the cast. Charlotte has a million different vocal tricks in her bag."

"A good actor is also a good mimic," Polly said. "The caller could have been anyone in the company. Or perhaps . . ."

A hush fell over the room as Tim and Placenta looked at Polly, who, it appeared, had suddenly become catatonic. Polly stared into a vision that only she could see. And then she mumbled, "You said that we would have recognized the voice of anyone in the cast. What if our caller was someone who *isn't* in the cast?"

"Like Jamie," Tim said.

"Or Hiroaki," Placenta added.

"Sure. Maybe," Polly said. "But what about all the tech people working behind the scenes? They're *of* the show but not *in* the cast."

"You've attended too many performances of *The Phantom of the Opera*," Tim said.

Polly nodded. "Let your imagination run wild for a moment. Perhaps a lighting technician was high up in the fly space changing bulbs or gels and silently looked down on the whole nasty business with Karen. Maybe the rehearsal pianist was in the pit and overheard everything that was happening on the stage above him. All guesses, but nothing is out of the realm of possibility."

"It makes sense that someone who worked backstage might have been in the theater early that morning and witnessed what happened," Tim said.

Placenta shook her head. "No. The person who called is involved with the murder. He's not just a bystander or witness. It doesn't make sense that anyone else but someone actually involved with Karen's death would make threats against Polly . . . and us. Don't forget, Polly heard Gerold and Jamie talking about her at the theater."

"Heard!" Tim reminded her. "Polly didn't actually see who was talking that night. It's all circumstantial. I'm still voting for Charlotte or one of the tech guys. As a matter of fact, nothing that dude said was actually a threat, per se. It could have been a friendly forewarning from a third party."

A feeling of excitement once again filled Polly's boudoir. "We must be getting close to the truth," she said. "The thing to do is to keep an eye on each of our guests tonight and see if we recognize that voice, or if anyone does anything peculiar."

Placenta looked at Polly. "This is Hollywood. Everything that happens here is peculiar. Still, perhaps we'll find a clue during the evening. Cross your digits!"

A cacophony from dozens of simultaneous conversations intermingled with the histrionics of celebrities making grand entrances to the party was a miasma so intense that it made the panther cringe with dread in a corner by the boa constrictor pit. The guests were having a thrilling time wandering through the lush faux rain forest, dipping their glasses into lagoons of margaritas, holding martini glasses under waterfalls of gin, and refilling their champagne flutes from the breasts of hand-carved indigenous

Amazon goddesses. Visiting the tarantula terrariums and feeding bits of bananas and Duck L'Orange to the monkeys was nearly as much fun as watching white mice scurry around in a panic in the python tank, and seeing bats hang upside down in overhead netting.

As Polly, Tim, and Placenta circulated among their happy guests, they intentionally spent the majority of their time interacting with the cast and chorus of *Mame*, as well as the backstage and technical help. "Are we ready for eight shows a week?" Polly laughed as she tilted her champagne flute in a toast to Gerold Goss, who was surprisingly affable. "I confess, I thought that under your guidance, or lack thereof, the show would be as dead as our first director, but I think we can pull this off."

Gerold was cordial, even jovial, toward Polly. "I confess that you're just as charming to work with as everyone said you would be." He smiled warmly and reciprocated Polly's toast. "Why did we get off to such an unattractive start?"

"Hmmm," Polly thought for a moment. "I guess it had something to do with you wanting Kristy McNichol or some other 'used to be' for my role."

Gerold smiled and nodded. "The public wants their Polly Pepper. So do the backers. So I was stuck." He shrugged in easygoing resignation.

"We're going to be a smash in Glendale, and then reprise this brilliant show on Broadway. I can't wait for Jerry Herman to hear what you've done with his songs! 'Open a New Window' takes on new meaning when sung by the janitorial staff in the restrooms of the Super Dome during Hurricane Katrina. Mr. Herman has never seen a staging of his masterpiece quite like this one."

"Maybe he won't find out," Gerold teased, knowing that Mr. Herman was famous for insisting that *Mame* be presented exactly as it had been on Broadway in 1966. "He might find that bringing the old story of Auntie Mame to New Orleans isn't as crazy as it sounds."

"Don't expect roses from the playwrights," Polly said. "They're dead anyway but the most you can hope for is critical appreciation that Mame and her little nephew Patrick are universal archetypes. Having them now home-less and living at Tipitina's on Bourbon Street instead of a fancy brownstone in New York City works just fine." Polly thought for another moment. "I don't want to be near Mr. Herman when he hears the Dixieland arrange-ment of 'If He Walked Into My Life,' " she said to Gerold.

Just then, Mag Ryan appeared with Stewart Long, the show's adult Patrick.

Gerold blanched. Mag looked at Gerold and then at Polly and said, "To quote my character in the show, 'This is a bitchin' party!' "

Polly grimaced. "Has the dialogue changed since yester-day? I don't recall that line."

Looking at Mag, Gerold lost his earlier sense of affabil-ity. "No," he said to Polly, as if Mag wasn't in the room, "no changes. Miss Gloria Upson just can't remember her lines. This is what happens when one puts their life and ca-reer on the line to give a friend a break in the biz."

"Whose life and whose career, Karen's or yours?" Mag said. "Don't blame me for your guilty conscience."

Gerold turned red in the face and looked ready to lash out physically at his young actress girlfriend. However, he checked himself and made the excuse that he needed an-other drink. Then he turned and walked away.

When Gerold had disappeared into the crowd and rain forest, Polly surreptitiously began interrogating Mag. "Getting ahead in this crazy business is murder, don't you think so too, dear? God knows, when I was starting out I had to do things for minor roles for which I've never for-given myself. I'm not proud of the way I blazed the trail that led to this gorgeous home and my international iconic status, but we women know that getting a break is a tough row to hoe."

" 'Hoe' being the operative word?" Mag teased. "Yeah, it's much easier when we can get a man to take care of the unpleasant business," she agreed. "Like firing a star."

"Or getting rid of a director who wants to replace us."

Mag looked askance at Polly. "Karen was walking all over him. Gerold was going to let our director keep her little soap opera diva in my role. Sheesh! For some reason Karen Richards wanted an actor with more experience than me. I overheard her tell Gerold that I was wrong for the role. I've shown her!"

"If she can see through the veil of death," Polly reminded her.

"Ha! Right. She's dead. Too bad she couldn't have lived to see my opening."

Polly did a double take. "I doubt that she'd value that as much as Gerold, or Stewart, here. But nothing in the past matters because everything worked out for the best."

"Except for Karen and that Sharon girl," Mag said.

Polly feigned a small laugh. "At least Sharon's getting out of jail in time for our big night on Friday," she bluffed.

Mag looked confused. "She's going to fry in the electric chair. Gerold said so."

"Nonsense. For one thing, she's been exonerated. And for another, in energy-conservation-conscious California we give our death row inmates a lovely injection of Sleepytime tea instead of wasting twenty-four hundred volts of precious electricity."

"Sharon's going free? But that's impossible."

"Not to worry, my dear, you're our Gloria Upson! Sharon won't be wanting her old role back."

"No! I mean, how can they let a murderer out of prison before a trial?"

"Because she's as innocent as Heidi Fleiss and Martha Stewart. Just like those two symbols of female power and success, our dear Sharon has had to temporarily pay for a crime she didn't commit."

Mag forced a smile. "If Sharon and Karen's fingerprints are all over her cell phone, and their early morning rendezvous is chronicled in their phone logs, not to mention Sharon's Emmy smeared with Karen's blood and God knows what other DNA isn't enough to get her at least life in the slammer, then the police must have someone else in mind. D'ya think?"

"Indeed I do think." Polly smiled back at Mag.

"Who? Anyone we know and love?"

Polly shrugged. "Know? Yes. Love? Not so much. But I'm not supposed to say anything. Police business, you know. Plus, I'm rather in over my head right now. All I want to do is get *Mame* up and running. Then we'll see about trotting out the police lineup."

Mag turned to Stewart. "Let's go throw another mouse in the snake pit."

Chapter 26

As the guests at Pepper Plantation lined up before multiple buffet tables inside the mansion, Polly decided to take a brief respite from playing gracious hostess and give herself a self-guided tour through the tropical playground that Tim created. Stepping into the tent and onto a path of damp dark brown mulch, she inhaled the scent of warm moist air from humidifiers that were strategically placed throughout the jungle setting.

Stepping off the pathway to take what appeared to be a shortcut toward the sound of the champagne waterfall, Polly shimmied past tall leafy plants and grazed against loquats, African irises, bamboo, palms, and birds-of-paradise. Delighted to come across one of Tim's champagne filling stations, she held her glass under the bare breast of a carved stone idol that was dispensing bubbly through a puckered nipple. She took a long sip, then happily glided farther into the man-made tropical rain forest.

Soon she was immersed in a completely unique world embellished with the sound effects of nighttime in the Amazon. In the distance behind her, Polly could barely hear the raucous laughter of her guests. She recognized the high-pitched cackle of Roseanne Barr, and a familiar laugh from John Ratzenberger. She supposed that they were all raving about the party.

Nearby, Polly could hear crickets chirping and the old leopard snoring. As she moved deeper into Tim's botanical fairyland, Polly quickly became disoriented. She was actually lost on her own property. What should have been a major point of reference was her Olympic-size swimming pool, but she couldn't find it through the dense foliage. Indeed, she soon realized that Tim had covered over the pool with a wooden floor to make way for a maze of paths and lush tropical foliage that now covered most of the estate's acreage.

Polly took another long sip of her champagne and tried to reestablish her bearings. With the hidden speakers whispering wild birdcalls, soft drumbeats, and other sounds of a mystical nocturnal rain forest, she couldn't tell if the monkeys she heard were the real ones rented for the party, or recordings on a CD. When she first heard the sound of snapping twigs close by, she thought of the toothless panther on the prowl or the chimp that Tim had borrowed from Michael Jackson. But something seemed wrong. She could feel it. When it became apparent that cautious heavy feet were moving across the thick plywood that covered the pool, she felt threatened. Polly stepped back into the camouflage of thick plants.

Deciding that it would be prudent to immediately return to her guests, Polly pushed her way through the overgrowth and began heading in the opposite direction of the snapping twigs. But when she felt how close someone was behind her, she changed course. In doing so, she became even more confused about her location. The combination of low light and multiple recorded and real-life sounds surrounding her collided and made her dizzy with frustration and apprehension. If nearly every inch of ground hadn't been covered in plants, she would have been able to run. Instead, she was forced to pick her way through the nearly impenetrable wall of thick branches and leaves.

For a moment she thought that perhaps the champagne,

humidity, and sound effects had conspired to make her paranoid. She heard a voice whisper, "She's over there." Polly eased herself into a curtain of leaves and tried to remain calm. Holding her champagne flute as the only potential weapon she could think of that might help ward off an attacker, Polly drained the last of her bubbly and was posed to break the glass and use the jagged stem in self-defense.

The vibration of heavy footsteps on the mulch-covered plywood floor made Polly's heart beat faster. "She's hiding," she heard a voice say. "Don't let her get away."

Polly crouched down beside an elephant palm and willed herself to become invisible. She stayed absolutely still.

Polly closed her eyes and silently begged, "Rescue me, Randy!" When she dared open her eyes again she almost audibly gasped as two men dressed in business attire stealthily passed by her. A pungent musty scent hung in the air as the two bodies moved away from her and disappeared into the dense foliage.

Feeling a sense of relief that she had survived being discovered, Polly looked up to the canopy of bushes and silently said, "Thank you, God, for the camouflage of Chanel basic black cocktail dresses." Suddenly, she heard a voice ask, "Where is she?" Polly's heart beat triple time. When she found herself facing two more men, she put her hands over her mouth to mute her involuntary cry.

"Polly?" a familiar voice asked.

"What on earth?" Tim's voice added.

Polly looked up with relief to find Randy and Tim reaching down to assist her to a standing position. "Has anybody seen my pearl earring?" She pretended to look for something lost on the ground.

"Check your lobes. And you're wearing diamonds," Tim said. "Why aren't you circulating among your cast and friends? You're supposed to be working."

Polly was parched and desperate for a drink. "Let me get a refill and we'll talk."

As they walked back toward the naked goddess of champagne, Polly explained that she had simply wanted to get a better view of Tim's masterwork, but that two men had followed her. "I was actually a little worried. There was no escape. I have a mind to report you to the fire marshal. There aren't any alternate exits! Someone kept getting closer and closer, so I hid among the plants."

"You can thank me for that!" Tim said. "Probably just a couple of lost guests."

"No. They were definitely following me," Polly said.

Randy asked if she'd been able to get a description of the people.

"Not a physical sketch, but I can identify at least one. I'll tell you this much, they aren't from among our set, I assure you."

Tim and Randy both looked baffled. "You didn't see their faces, and yet you can pick one out of a lineup?" Tim asked.

"Not necessarily a lineup. Not if we're in separate rooms and I'm behind a one-way mirror. But I can sniff them out."

Tim looked at Randy. "You're getting not only a girlfriend, but a bloodhound too."

Polly gave her son the look she saved for whenever she was displeased with him.

He knew the look well, and backed away from making snide jokes at his mother's expense.

"One was wearing—God help me—Patchouli!" Polly snorted in disgust. "I'll find him if I have to hug every guest at the party . . . although I may skip Robin Williams, who could actually use a masking scent!"

"Let's head back to the house," Tim suggested. "We're supposed to be charming our guests into confessing to a murder."

"As if that's a surprise," Randy said in resignation.

Polly tried to lessen the effect of her continued interference with the case. "Placenta's alone with a hundred and fifty people she doesn't like," she said. "That's a recipe for disaster since we all know that she got her degree in social comportment from the Joan Rivers School for Tact."

Tim and Randy guided Polly onto a path that led to the tent's exit. They wandered past the python that was curled up on a wooden shelf, and Tim made a quick check to make sure there were still ten tarantulas in the terrarium. He only counted eight, but seeing that the lid was on tight he felt certain that a couple of the spiders were probably making love behind a rock. He made a mental note to have another look once his mother was settled inside the house, and if need be, to check all the guests' surprise goodie bags before they left.

As dinner was over, guests were once again spilling out of the house and into the tented jungle. Polly leaned into Tim and cocked her head toward two men standing by the life-size plastic alligators on the lawn. "Who're they?"

Tim looked at his mother as though she were nuts and said, "The one on the left is your agent, J.J. Norton. The one on the right is Alex Trebec."

"Alex is cute, but how did J.J. get past security?" She nodded toward another couple of men who seemed to be scrutinizing the other guests. "What about them?"

"Ted Casablanca from *E! Entertainment*. He's covering the party. The other is Isaac Mizrahi. Be especially nice. You might get a new wardrobe, at cost!"

"And those two over there?"

Tim followed Polly's gaze. "Not sure. Why don't you go over and introduce yourself?"

"They should come to me. I'm the star, in case you've forgotten." Polly sighed. "Why don't we all go over and pretend that we're ecstatic to have them in our little home?"

Hooking her arm through the crook of Randy's and Tim's, Polly led the way toward two men in dark suits, one of whom was chatting into a cell phone. As the trio approached, both men looked up and smiled. "Thanks for including us tonight," the man on the left said. "This is such an awesome house." The man on the right concluded his phone conversation and agreed that being at Pepper Plantation was something he could tell his girlfriend and parents about.

Polly had quickly switched to accessible star mode and smiled warmly. As discreetly as possible she got close enough to each to give them a sniff. "After all the work you've done for me and the show, this little gathering is the least I can do. It must be tiring for you adjusting lights and painting scenery just so that I and my amazing cast will be able to shine for a couple of hours each evening, and for a brief tick of the clock make audiences forget that they're in Glendale. You both do a wonderful job of supporting our humble efforts. I speak on behalf of the entire *Mame* cast when I say how much I appreciate your dedication and I haven't heard a single complaint from the tech crew. As the actor who plays the adult Patrick in the show says, 'You're top drawer.'"

Both men looked bewildered. A beat later, the man who had been on his cell phone said, "We're delighted to do whatever is required to make this production a huge success, Miss Pepper. If painting a flat or changing a lightbulb is the thing to do, then we'll gladly find a union guy to do the job. He reached out his hand to shake Polly's. "By the by, I'm your producer, Eric Ehrlich." Then nodding his head to the other man he said, "And this is Leonard Wood, your executive producer."

Polly was mortified. "You're both too young and handsome—not to mention straight—to be in charge of shepherding a Broadway musical to success!" she practically squealed in her trademark schoolgirl-meeting-a-pop-star voice. "Promise me that you'll make sure that we get to Broadway. We'll all take home Tony Awards for best revival of a musical. Wouldn't one of those darling trophies look lovely on your fireplace mantels? I know exactly where I'll keep mine. On my pillow!"

Eric promised that they were doing all that they could to book a New York theater, but that everything depended on how well the show played in Glendale. "You're going to be the best Mame since Morgan Brittany," Leonard Wood said. "Too bad the original Broadway production was way before my time. It would have been cool to see Jessica Fletcher in the show. I heard she was great."

Polly was temporarily perplexed. "Jessica Fletcher? I think Eric means Angela Lansbury, who played Jessica Fletcher on TV, and who starred in the original New York production of *Mame*."

"Yeah, that's the name, Lansbury," Eric said. "I always think of her as the lady on TV who couldn't open a can of soup without finding a dead body inside. Loved that show when I was a kid."

Polly continued to smile but silently thought, *We're in deep doo-doo if this twerp can't even keep his Broadway and television legends straight.*

Just then, Patrick Dempsey came to Polly's side and gave her a kiss on the cheek. "Great party, but it's getting late and I've got a long day on the set tomorrow. I'm doing Bariatric surgery on someone the size of your estate."

As Patrick left, so did many of the other guests. Each came to Polly and wished her great success on the opening of *Mame*. One by one they paid homage to the legend and kissed her cheek. However, no one smelled of Patchouli.

"See Placenta before you leave. We have a little something for you to take away," Polly said to each guest.

Polly was suddenly perturbed. "I'm not surprised that Roseanne didn't bother to thank me for a fabulous evening, but what happened to dear John Ratzenberger? He knows his social etiquette."

Tim looked at his mother. "Neither of them was here. Both RSVP'd that they couldn't make it."

Polly frowned. "Then they lied, dear. I distinctively

heard both of their voices. No one is as loud as Ms. Barr, or whatever last name she's using these days."

Tim remembered that Charlotte Bunch had been entertaining with her celebrity impersonations and suggested that what Polly had heard was simply a party game. "Is there anyone ol' Charlotte can't imitate? That woman's pure genius. She even looks like Renée Zellweger when she scrunches up her face like a hamster."

Polly looked around. "By the way, where'd the ol' hamster-girl go? She never said good night."

Tim shrugged. He looked at Placenta, who shook her head and said, "Guess she snuck out rather than have to stand in line to flatter the panties off of you."

Polly raised an eyebrow. "No doubt she's saving her praise for a lovely thank-you note." She looked around and realized that all of her guests had finally left the premises, and only the catering staff was left to clean up. Polly turned to Randy and Tim. "No patchouli. Either someone left when they couldn't murder me, or they're still on the property."

Tim looked around. "What if Polly's right, and not all the guests have left?" he said to Randy. Can you get a detail out here to check the property before we go to bed? With all those plants, I've left plenty of places for someone to hide."

Randy shook his head. "No way. I'll have a look around before I go."

"You're going?" Polly said, with more than a hint of disappointment in her voice. "I rather thought that . . . well, because you're failing to send in the SWAT team . . . you might feel a duty to . . . because you'd want to make sure I was fully protected . . . perhaps you would . . ."

Suddenly the panther roared and a horrific scream was heard from deep inside the tent.

Chapter 27

In a matter of seconds Polly, Tim, and Randy were running to the tented jungle and cautiously moving down the main path. Randy led the way with his gun drawn and his arms moving from left to right like an oscillating fan. Polly stopped and sniffed the air. "Patchouli!" she whispered and separated herself from Tim and Randy to follow the scent. "Over here," she said and cautiously inched her way through the pots of dense foliage.

Tim and Randy quickly caught up to Polly and were aware of every sound and movement in the jungle. "It's coming from over there," Polly said, pointing. Randy vigilantly moved forward with Polly and Tim bringing up the rear.

"Freeze!" Randy suddenly shouted. "Beverly Hills Police Department! Freeze or I'll blow you into South Central!"

Polly and Tim rushed to Randy's side and found one of the nearly naked and body-painted cater waiters crouched under a tall fern and the leopard circling him as though he were a potential mate. "Get him away!" the waiter cried.

Tim went over to the leopard and patted the cat's coat and scratched him under his chin. "Let's go play with Pla-

centa," he said and nudged the beast toward the path leading to the exit.

Although the scent of repulsive cologne still hung in the
air, it quickly became obvious that the cater waiter was
not the one wearing the heady aroma. Polly stood over the
young man in his loincloth. By the look of his well-cut
physique she knew that he was handpicked for the job by
Tim. "Why aren't you helping in the kitchen?" she asked
with a definite edge to her voice.

Still crouching on the ground, he looked up and said,
"A couple of guys gave me a hundred bucks to come in
here and distract you."

Polly, with hands on hips, demanded to know the names
of the guests who had paid for this charade.

"I don't know," the young man said. "But as soon as I
yelled, they ran out the back of the tent."

"There is no back to the tent," Tim insisted.

The young man, who had by now raised himself to his
feet and was brushing off mulch from his bare legs, looked
over his shoulder to the side of the tent. "There is now."

Polly, Tim, and Randy saw that the thick plastic material had been cut and was now fluttering in a light summer
evening's breeze.

"That'll cost a fortune to repair!" Tim burst into a small
tantrum. "Who the hell were these guys?"

"Again, I don't know," the waiter insisted. "But one of
'em stank of that stuff that immigrant gardeners bathe in."

Polly gave Tim and Randy an "I told you so" look. Her
expression made it clear that she wasn't imagining the men
who had pursued her. She turned to the waiter. "Give us a
description of the goons!"

"Both were wearing dark suits. I could tell that one was
a knockout in the sex-appeal department—"

"Never mind the editorializing," Polly said. "Be specific."

"As I said, one was a babe, and the other was . . . I think

he was a babe too. I mean, I think he was a she pretending to be a he."

Polly blanched. "And don't dis my transgender friends!"

The waiter looked offended. "It was the way he . . . er, she . . . moved about. Whatever the gender, the person waded through the plants like they were terrified of what they might find as they moved about the foliage. Ya know, a sissy sort of way of mincing. Plus, I got a look at the butt. It was too pear-shaped to be a guy's."

Polly frowned and looked down at her own rear end. "Did either of them say why they wanted you to cause a commotion?"

The waiter shook his head. "I figured they needed a diversion to make an escape."

"An escape from what? Why not simply leave through the front door?"

"Could be because they were stealing an Emmy Award from your trophy room," the waiter said.

Polly issued a sound equal to the scream that the waiter had made to attract their attention in the first place.

When Polly returned to the house and entered the great room, she found that indeed one less Emmy occupied her lighted glass bookshelves.

As Tim and Randy tried to comfort Polly, Placenta came into the room dragging Mag Ryan with her. "Nabbed your little Gloria Upson trying to weasel her way off of the estate with your firstborn," Placenta said, holding up an Emmy. " 'Debut season of the Polly Pepper Playhouse,' " she read from the tarnished metal plate. She then pushed Mag forward to face Polly.

Polly looked down at Mag with equal parts confusion and fury. "I thought we were friends."

Mag hung her head and looked at the carpet.

Randy stepped forward and flashed his badge. "Mag

Ryan. I'm placing you under arrest for burglary, theft, and extortion."

Stung by the thought of going to jail, Mag cried, "No! It wasn't me! I was only following orders! It was—"

"Who?" Polly interrupted. "Who told you to swipe my Emmy? There are at least two of you. Don't deny it. That cater waiter you paid off gave us a complete description."

Mag sighed. "Why do I always get stuck with the stinky roles?" She looked into Polly's eyes. "Okay. Here's the thing. This guy at the party tonight said he'd heard that I was a great actress and that he had a big part for me to play."

"He obviously had too many martinis," Polly cracked. "Who was this Neanderthal and what was the big role? Tell us everything, or sweet Polly Pepper will turn into Shirley Temple on a roid rage!"

Mag slumped onto the sofa and closed her eyes for a long moment. When she finally opened them, she also opened her mouth and began to spill her guts. "I'm not covering for anyone anymore. Not even for Gerold. You want a story?"

"I want the truth!" Polly said as she plopped herself down on the sofa with her arms folded across her chest.

"Okay. From the beginning," Mag said.

The others in the room immediately took seats on the sofa and wingback chairs, concentrating on what Mag was about to reveal.

"You already know that Karen and Gerold argued over casting changes," Mag continued. "I was glued to Gerold's side to make sure the dumb ass didn't get cold feet about letting me have the role of Gloria Upson. I've wanted that part ever since I saw the old Roz Russell movie *Auntie Mame*. It's a showstopper and I knew I could do it well. But Karen had other ideas, namely Sharon Fletcher."

Polly interrupted, "When did Sharon get to the theater that morning?"

"She arrived shortly after Charlotte and Hiroaki left. Karen had called each of them and asked that they come in extra early. She staggered their arrivals so that none of them would be embarrassed in front of each other by hearing that they were being let go. Anyway, after Charlotte and Hiroaki took their lumps and left, Sharon showed up with her Emmy and her Pollyanna smile and then got the word from Gerold that she was history. Sharon's a lot tougher than her bitch character on *It's Never Fair Weather*. She was furious with both Gerold *and* Karen. She said that Karen had no spine, and that Gerold was a big fat fully stocked walking refrigerator.

"Just as we've all heard from her statement to the police, Sharon hauled off and threw her cell phone at Gerold. She's a diva. When divas get mad, watch out. She looked as though she could kill both Karen and Gerold, and me too as a matter of fact."

Detective Archer leaned forward in his chair. "You said that the others had left by the time Sharon arrived, so there's no one to corroborate your story."

"Of course there is," Mag said. "Karen's boyfriend, Jamie, was there all along. He was there with Karen when Sharon stormed out of the theater."

Polly scratched her head and again leaned in toward Mag. "Are you one hundred percent certain that Charlotte and Hiroaki left the theater?"

Mag shrugged. "They left. I didn't follow them home. But I didn't see them again until the next day. Coming back as they did, I guess they thought that the death of the director might make a difference in their employment status. Gerold did what Karen tried to protect them from— public humiliation."

Polly stood up and walked to the wine cooler. She opened the glass door and withdrew a bottle of champagne. She uncorked it and filled a fresh glass and took a long sip. She filled the flute again and brought the bottle back to the coffee table. "What happened next?"

"Jamie said something about being late for an audition. Then he gave the janitor some money and a list of different coffees for each of the cast, and sent him over to Starbucks."

Polly suddenly snapped, "You just finished telling us that nobody else was in the theater and now you say the janitor was there!"

"I meant no one else of any importance, like from the cast," Mag said, stung by Polly's outburst. "Sure, there were a couple of other people, like the cleaning crew."

"Cleaning crew?" Polly ranted again. "Why are you telling us all this now? By the way, the cleaning people work in the late afternoon, not early morning! Why are we supposed to believe one word you're saying?"

Mag was unsettled and her face turned red. "You're making me confused! Maybe it wasn't the cleaning crew. Maybe the voices I heard belonged to the producers or the stage manger or maintenance people, or—"

"Or maybe what you heard was Charlotte or Hiroaki plotting to kill the director," Polly said. "Or maybe everything you're saying is a big fat lie and maybe you killed Karen to make absolutely sure that Gloria was your role. The possibilities are endless."

"No. I swear I didn't kill Karen!" Mag continued her desperate defense. "The voices weren't Karen's or Gerold's or Charlotte's or Hiroaki's. I know what they all sound like. I think the voices were in Spanish or they at least had a foreign accent. Anyway, they sounded weird and that's why I thought they must have been cleaning people!"

"Accents? You're suggesting that the butler did it?" Polly reached for the bottle of Krug. "I ought to clobber you with this thing and rattle some sense into that feeble brain of yours. You come to my beautiful show and steal a role that was perfectly cast and then you're invited to be a guest in my house and you steal the thing most precious to me—other than my Timmy and Placenta. And now you're flat-out telling me that you were at the scene of the crime, but you didn't see anything! I'm at my wits' end, my dear."

Mag was silent, but her body was shaking from the emotional trauma of the evening. She leaned forward and picked up someone's half-full glass of champagne and swallowed the drink. She reached for the bottle, but Polly slapped her hand away. "I need something to calm my nerves."

"And I need you to tell me who you were working with tonight."

The meager amount of champagne that Mag had swallowed was enough to embolden her. She looked at Polly defiantly. "One drink, one answer." She held out her glass.

Polly stared at the impudent actress for a long moment, silently transmitting her disdain. Then she reached for the bottle and began to slowly pour Mag's drink. "You'll play by my rules," she said and stopped pouring when the glass was filled halfway.

As Mag downed the drink, her eyes remained fixed on Polly's. "Charlotte," Mag finally said.

"Huh?" Polly said. "What's that supposed to mean? Charlotte what?"

"Charlotte Bunch's fence—Fernando—paid me to pinch your Emmy tonight. Charlotte has to take special medications for her MPD, and her SAG insurance doesn't cover the cost. Plus, she's broke."

"MPD? A new iPOD model?" Polly asked impatiently.

"Multiple personalities disorder," Tim said. "Now Charlotte's weird behavior makes sense!"

"She's channeling voices or something," Mag added.

"She's not imitating people, she becomes them?" Polly said with a groan. "Jeez, I'm in *The Twilight Zone*!"

Mag continued. "This Fernando guy—the one who recognized my major talent—sells movie star memorabilia to collectors all over the world. The only way that Charlotte can pay to keep her prescription filled is by getting him to sell off her celebrity garage sale junk. She was going to steal Sharon's Emmy, but her plan was foiled. You're the only other star she knows with a bunch of acting awards. She knew you'd miss a few, but could probably get 'em replaced."

"It *was* Charlotte who absconded with my Emmy," Polly cried. "And this Fernando character, I suspect he wears Patchouli."

"Charlotte said she knew that you suspected her of grabbing your other Emmy, the one you dropped off in West Hollywood Park. She wanted to stop hurting you. She knows what she's doing when the voices take over, but she can't control them or her actions. Charlotte didn't mean to be unkind. My raid on your fancy-schmancy mansion tonight was going to be the end of her stealing from you."

Polly and the others were dumbfounded. "This is a nightmare, or a bad *Saturday Night Live* sketch. We're supposed to be in la-la land, but all around us are murderers and thieves and crazy people who have uninvited guests dancing around in her head! Hollywood is beginning to feel like a strange world to me!"

Detective Archer finally spoke up and addressed Mag. "Take us back to the theater, the morning of the murder. When did you discover Karen and Gerold missing?"

"I basically turned around and pffft, Karen and Gerold were gone," Mag said. "I went to Gerold's office and didn't see Karen ever again."

"And when did you hear the cleaning people or whoever they were?" Archer asked.

Mag thought for a moment. She pursed her lips and knitted her brow as she tried to recall exactly where she was and what she had heard and seen. "As a matter of fact . . ." She paused. "When I walked backstage to go to the office, I heard some people arguing in the wings. I didn't think anything about it at the time. Why would I? As I said, I thought it was a cleaning crew."

"You could hear yelling over the sound of vacuums?" Archer said.

Mag tentatively shook her head. "Now that you mention it, I don't think I heard vacuuming."

Polly heaved a heavy sigh. "Well, we're back to freaking square one! You still don't have an alibi for the morning of the murder, and Jamie seems to have his own uncorroborated alibi—although he lied about getting coffee—and Charlotte's a mental case who was after my Emmys to sell for meds to control Charles Laughton or Elizabeth Montgomery, or whoever she has floating around up there. If Hiroaki left the theater before Sharon arrived . . . that leaves only Gerold and Sharon as the prime suspects!"

"Wait a minute," Tim insisted. "Mag just established that all the other suspects were at the theater that morning too. What if . . . and I'm simply concocting a hypothetical scenario . . . what if Charlotte didn't leave the theater? After all, she was desperate to get her hands on Sharon's Emmy Award. What if the voices Mag heard were actually Charlotte going through one of her episodes? What if she was backstage engaging in a conversation between Mama Rose, Ethel Merman, and Ethel Barrymore, in order to distract Karen and Gerold long enough for them to investigate the noise and for her to sneak out and abscond with the Emmy?"

Polly caught on. "Okay, it's like this. Hiroaki leaves the theater thinking his career is over. Charlotte pretends to leave, but hangs around because she needs the Emmy that she believes is coming with Sharon. Sharon has her snake pit meltdown scene when she gets canned. Mag and Jamie leave the stage for a few minutes. Charlotte, who has been hiding in the wings, lets her weird personalities escape.

Karen and Gerold go backstage to investigate her imitation of Pat Boone speaking in tongues, while she sneaks in front of the curtain to grab the statuette. The two returned just in time to catch Charlotte. She makes a run for it, but Karen stops her and retrieves the Emmy—hence her fingerprints on the statuette. Charlotte is totally embarrassed at being caught, so she flees. Or, there's a struggle with the Emmy and Karen gets clobbered to death by Charlotte."

Placenta looked at Mag and said, "If the killer was anyone other than Sharon, why wouldn't Gerold have said something to the police? Would he really cover up a heinous crime just so you could have stage time in a local musical production? Is he that much in love with you that he'd let your rival for the role rot in jail for the rest of her life?"

Mag smiled with self-satisfaction. "I'm very cuddly."

"It actually makes sense that Charlotte killed Karen," Tim said. "Everyone knows that when someone needs money to buy drugs, they'll do anything to score."

Randy spoke up. "It's time to consider Gerold as a prime suspect too. I'll have him picked up."

"Friday is opening night!" Polly said. "You can't risk my career by dragging him away from the production just yet!"

Chapter 28

Detective Archer looked at his wristwatch and then looked at Mag. "It's time I got you down to the station for booking." He stood and withdrew a pair of handcuffs from his suit coat pocket.

Polly smiled with lascivious delight. "You found them," she said, eyeing the shiny restraints and simultaneously blushing.

Mag began to cry. "Please, let me go!" She looked first to Detective Archer, then to Polly Pepper. "I can't go to jail. I have a show to do. What will Gerold say? Who will play Gloria? We don't have understudies."

Polly patted Mag's shoulder. "There are a gazillion girls out there who have played your role, hon. It won't be hard to fill your tiny shoes."

"Please, Polly! *Mame* is my big chance! It's everything I've worked for! I've had to put up with that Yeti for months, just to get this show. Don't take my dream away from me. Please?"

Polly faced Mag with her hands on her hips. "Someone took Karen's dream away, and Sharon Fletcher's too. Give us one good reason why we should ignore the fact that you're a thief and why we should bother to lift a finger to save your skinny, untalented derrière?"

Mag whimpered. "No other actress knows the new dialogue."

Polly shook her head. "Anyone professionally trained in the theater is forced to become quick studies. Learning Shakespeare in a matter of hours is de rigueur at RADA. As for you helping to find the *real* killer, you sound like O.J. after those idiots on his first jury acquitted him. What if *you* are Karen's killer? It makes sense. And to answer Placenta's earlier question, perhaps the reason that Gerold isn't contradicting everyone's presumption that Sharon murdered Karen is to protect you. You must be giving him plenty of lovin' in return."

"What do I have to do to prove that I'm innocent of everything except taking a bribe to snatch an Emmy? You got the damn thing back, so no harm, no foul," Mag said. "I'll die if I go to jail!"

Polly laughed scornfully and shook her head in mock amusement. "Life in the Big House didn't seem to hurt Leona Helmsley. Save the pity party for a jury. But with the beloved Polly Pepper appearing as a witness against you, the matrons at Folsom will be happily pulling on their latex examination gloves for a cavity search even before my testimony is over."

Mag looked appalled. "You'd use your fame to frame me?"

"I'll use whatever God gave me to see that justice is served!" Polly shot back. Then she considered what Mag had asked. Polly thought about the possibility that the young actress might be innocent. Suddenly, a heavy burden settled over her. Polly knew that she couldn't live with herself if she exploited her living legend status and later found that she had been wrong about Mag. She was suddenly at a crossroads and frustrated by her own sense of justice. Polly grabbed her head of dyed red hair and made a sound in frustration.

Mag looked at Polly. "If you help me, I'll help you. I have more access to all the possible suspects than you do."

Polly balked. "Strangers reveal their most intimate secrets to me. They consider me one of the family. After all, I was an invited guest in their living rooms every week for a dozen seasons. I can get people to flap their lips as easily as Dr. Laura makes me barf."

"Strangers and fans, yes. Your *Mame* cast, no," Mag countered. "It's too late for you and your famous charm to mine anything of value from these people. You've alienated the suspects by trying to dig into their personal lives. Gerold doesn't like you. Charlotte suspects that you know that she's the one trying to loot your treasury of showbiz awards. Jamie won't confess that his Starbucks alibi is a lie. Even Hiroaki is miffed that you placed him on a short list of possible killers. I'm already embedded with the director, er, so to speak. And everybody thinks I'm just the ingénue doing what ingénues have done forever—playing the youth card with an older man. I can be your eyes and ears. Just tell me what you need and I'll get it for you. But spare me from jail and a criminal record!"

Polly looked at Randy Archer and her eyes silently asked what to do.

"If I release Mag and she turns out to be the killer, or kills again, I'll not only be out of a job and career, but I'll be charged as an accessory to whatever crime she commits. And you will too, Polly!" Randy said. "I can't take that chance. For your sake and mine."

Polly nodded and then gave Tim the same look of helplessness.

"Randy is right, Mom," Tim said. "However, if you want my opinion, I think it's worth a chance letting Mag go back to the viper nest and seeing what she comes up with. She's also right about finding a replacement on such short notice. I know it can be done, but why throw off the rest of the cast, and risk getting lousy reviews that could stop the show from going to New York?"

"New York," Polly said wistfully. "That's all I want. Oh, and bringing Karen's killer to death row, of course." Then she looked at Placenta and raised an eyebrow.

"I, for one, am tired of criminals making plea bargains to get out of paying their full debt to society," Placenta said with conviction. "Somebody kills somebody else, and they cop a deal with prosecuting attorneys for a lesser degree of the crime. Hell, someone's dead regardless of whether you call it first-degree murder, second-degree murder, or manslaughter. Mag should be hauled off to jail immediately, if only for the crime she committed this evening."

"You never liked me, did you, Placenta?" Mag said.

"Nope," Placenta agreed. She turned to Polly. "However, what Tim says about sending her back to fetch more information makes sense."

Polly picked up her bottle of champagne and poured the last couple of fingers into her glass. She swallowed what little had been left and sat in deep contemplation for a long moment. "I suppose jail will always be there."

Detective Archer started to interrupt, but Polly silenced him with a smile that begged him to trust her.

Polly then looked at Mag. "You've got a new boyfriend."

"Excuse me?" Mag said.

"I said, Gerold's history. There's a new man in your life, and he's extremely jealous of you hanging out with all the sexy chorus boys in the company. Therefore he'll be at your side constantly, even in your dressing room."

Mag looked at Polly as though she were talking nonsense. "I'd love a new man, but Gerold would kill me . . . as well as any Mr. Right who came along."

Polly waved her finger and shook her head. She smiled evilly and said, "Not this man. Gerold wouldn't dare harm a legend's son."

It took a longer moment than Polly expected for everyone to catch on, but suddenly and in unison Tim, Placenta, and Mag knowingly exclaimed, "What? You're drunk, right?"

Polly shrugged. "You heard me. Tim is the new man in your life and he's going to be with you constantly and reporting back to me."

"Mother, you're insane!" Tim cried out.

"Totally nuts!" Mag seconded Tim's opinion. "First of all, Tim's too good looking to be straight. No one will believe for a moment that we're lovers!"

"Hell, no one believed Liza and David either, but there was enough tabloid press and canoodling in public for a few morons on the planet to think that she might be getting at least a variation on nookie."

Mag raised her hands up in protest. "You're off your rocker, old lady," she declared.

"You said yourself that it's too late to recast your role, so you're safe at least for a couple of weeks."

"Mother, you're the actor, not me," Tim cried. "I'm not equipped to play a heterosexual! What if I fall for one of the boy dancers?"

"I'm used to that, dear," Polly said, lightly patting her son on the face. "Nobody would believe that a man as handsome as you would limit yourself to just one sex. How boring and restrictive would that be!"

Mag began to hyperventilate as she considered the lose-lose situation she was in. She didn't want to go to jail, but she also couldn't risk being fired from the show by Gerold. "There's no way that I'll face Gerold's wrath by pretending to be in love with Tim. No offense," Mag added, looking at Tim.

Polly rolled her eyes. "Fine. You're probably right."

Mag and Tim both breathed a sigh of relief.

"Placenta will be your new girlfriend," Polly stated matter-of-factly.

Once again, there were simultaneous roars of incredulity, mainly from Placenta and Mag.

"I'm brilliant," Polly proclaimed. "This solves the problem of Gerold being jealous of a new man in your life.
Hell, he may even be intrigued by the idea of you and Placenta—"

Placenta barked, "They are so right. You are truly one
hellava loon, lady. Over the years, all those hot stage lights
must have fried your brain! Either that or fifty years of in-
haling champagne bubbles has destroyed your gray cells
faster than your doctor predicted. Trust me, Polly, I'll take
that job over at Whitney's place before I start dating trash
like Mag Ryan!"

Polly rejected everyone's notion that her idea was somehow preposterous, but she gave in to a compromise. "If
you're all going to be completely unimaginative, I'll do it
myself," she finally said. "I'll be Mag's new lover."

Randy chuckled, realizing that Polly would never change.
She was going to be investigating the death of Karen
Richards until she either found the killer or was killed herself. "Just promise to play safe and wear protection," he
teased.

Polly gave her man a good-natured elbow to his ribs.
"This really does solve almost all of our problems. Mag
takes a 'get out of jail' card—at least for the time being. If
Gerold has a problem with the relationship and kicks Mag
out of his house, we have plenty of rooms to spare here.
And I get to be intimate with our mole."

Suddenly Tim stood up and bellowed, "Oh, all right! I'll
be Mag's lover! I can't put the star lady in jeopardy. And
there's no way that the cast members are going to feel
comfortable telling their secrets to Mag if Polly's hanging
around. I'll just have to deal with Gerold and his temper."

Mag cried, "Good grief! What the world needs is to see
this family in a reality TV show. You're all too weird for
anyone to believe unless they've seen you in action!"

"Thank you, sweetie," Polly said to Mag. "I never wanted an average family. I told God to make me a baby boy who was special in every way, and look who I got— perfection. Then when I found Placenta stuck working for a Beverly Hills matron, I immediately rescued her. Mediocrity is for Hilary Duff, but definitely not for my Timmy and Placenta, and most certainly not for *moi*!"

Mag Ryan stood up and looked down at Polly. "Okay, I'm cool with whatever you want to do. You're keeping me out of jail, and that's all I care about at the moment. I'll do whatever you want me to do to help finger Karen's killer."

Polly faced the woman who only a short while ago had been repugnant to her. This time she smiled at Mag. "I'm relieving Timmy and Placenta and me of being your new beau. But your duty is to convince everyone in the cast, as well as your pal Jamie, and Gerold too, that I'm a harmless old icon into whose trust they can put every tasty bit of dish about everyone else they know. They must think of me as being as honorable as the Dahli Lama."

Tim grimaced. "Let's just say that Polly's a clam but that she loves to get her dish fresh from the source, not from some sleazy rag like the *National Peeper*. Perhaps that'll get our suspects to start yapping."

Chapter 29

The Galaxy Theatre was nearly eighty years old. The dressing rooms had never been modernized. All but the star's suite were the size of solitary confinement cells, and as dank as a basement laundry. Backstage, bare-bulb light fixtures hung from the ceilings on long black cords, and rodents outnumbered audiences two to one. The concrete walls had been haphazardly repainted over the years. This season's colors were two tones: battleship gray and avocado green. But naturally, Polly Pepper's dressing room was stunning.

During the Tuesday rehearsal, while the cast was on-stage all day, Tim Velcroed a large gold-sequined star onto Polly's door. While Placenta kept her eyes on Polly, Tim transformed the dressing room interior from what was Porta Potti nasty into a show-stopping glitz and glam environment for his mother's relaxation between performances. The reenvisioned space would have won raves from HGTV's Kenneth Brown, and once the rest of the *Mame* cast got over the shock and awe of seeing the potential for creating luxury out of little more than a walk-in closet, their envy was obvious. A new sense of camaraderie between Polly and the cast surfaced, if only so they could coax her into loaning Tim out for a helping hand in sprucing up their own dingy spaces.

After a grueling day of full-costume rehearsals and showing off her stylish digs, Polly welcomed Charlotte and Gerold as well as the show's Vera Charles and Beauregard into her sparkling new inner sanctum. "It's Lush Hour and we need a wee celebration for surviving this torturous day," she said as Placenta began pouring champagne. When each held a flute, Polly turned to Tim and said, "A toast to my very own fairy who sprinkled his pixie dust over a crummy coal bin and transformed it into Buckingham Palace! Or at least the *Royal* coal bin!"

Marshall Nash, who played the role of Beauregard, looked at Polly and in his affected baritone said, "My dear, these days it's a tad pejorative to call anyone a fairy." He looked at Tim and winked, hoping that he was scoring points.

"Nonsense. Tim knows precisely what I mean, don't you, sweetums?"

Tim chuckled and met Marshall's twinkling eyes. "It's a term of endearment. As long as my allowance check comes on the first day of every month, she can call me Gidget."

Polly smiled and continued admiring Tim's work and pointing out interesting details in the room. "My favorite son knows that I must have a proper place to receive Carol and Mary and Julie and Barbra and Bette and Sandy and Meryl, and all of my nearest and dearest." Polly dropped names for the sheer pleasure of watching Charlotte try to contain her resentment. "But I don't want to appear to be playing the queen," she added, to downplay her display of ostentation. "Everyone knows that I'm as down-to-earth as the minions who order McNuggets and think they're eating real fowl," she said.

"And they are. Foul, I mean," Tim quipped. Only Polly and Placenta instantly got his joke and laughed.

Polly then cleared her throat and looked at Gerold. "May I make one teensy observation about today's rehearsal?"

"Could a bullet stop you?" Gerold said.

"Only if you're my human shield," Polly deadpanned. She took a fortifying slug of champers. "This has been gnawing away at me from the start. It's about that darling boy who plays my grown-up nephew, Patrick, in the show."

"Stewart Long," Gerold said.

"Whatever. Where on earth did you find the poor thing? He couldn't get a laugh with a 'Knock-Knock' joke. I recommend remedial comedy classes, if not Henny Youngman gene replacement therapy."

Gerold scowled. "The kid auditioned, just like everybody else. Everyone who isn't a marquee name, that is."

Polly caught Charlotte smirking. "One more teensy suggestion?" Polly asked.

"No!" Gerold snapped.

"Hire Jamie Livingston to coach the boy. Jamie's as talented as he is gorgeous and he's played this role a gazillion times. As a matter of fact, I'm stunned that he wasn't cast in my production."

"Your production?"

"Jamie can help turn things around. We spoke during lunch break," Polly lied, "and he agreed to come by tomorrow."

Gerold slugged back the rest of his champagne and set his flute firmly down on the vanity makeup table. "Blast it, Polly! I'm the director! I make the decisions! The stage door guy, the one whose always asleep, whatshisname—George—has strict instructions not to let Jamie back in this theater!"

Polly was taken aback. "I'm just trying to make your already brilliant and cutting edge production better. *Mame* meets *Edward Scissorhands* in post-Katrina New Orleans will blow them away in New York. Who would mind a legend pointing out where she sees a need for a little theatrical magic?"

"I mind!" Gerold spat.

"Why can't poor Jamie return to the scene of the crime, so to speak?"

In a cold tone that perfectly imitated Gerold, Charlotte spoke up and said, "There's a good reason why Jamie didn't get the role and why he's not welcome in our theater."

Polly caught Gerold giving Charlotte a withering look.

"What could be so terrible?" Polly asked. "Unless he killed Karen."

Gerold turned ashen, but didn't say a word.

Polly bluffed a conciliatory apology. "Silly me, of course you're right. I should have remembered what Sharon said about Jamie and all that naughty stuff that went on in dressing room number seven."

Charlotte held out her glass and asked Placenta for a refill, while the two actors playing Vera and Beauregard discreetly said it was time for them to leave for dinner engagements.

"Yeah, dinner," Gerold said. "We're late." He looked at Mag. His body language made it clear that she should leave with him.

"I've got stuff to do," Mag said. "I'll catch up with you later."

Gerold looked at Charlotte and huffed, "Lay off the champagne. Go home and memorize. I'm warning you not to go up on your lines again tomorrow. We're almost to opening!"

Polly rose from her chair and tried to pretend that the abrupt change in the atmosphere had nothing to do with the answers she had tried to pry from Gerold or her bluff that she knew why Jamie was an outcast. She raised her glass to her departing guests. "Jamie will understand— considering the sordid circumstances."

Gerold turned and gave Polly a long look that made her feel as though he was an airport security agent looking for her concealed Kalashnikov. Finally he turned and left the dressing room.

When Polly closed the door she smiled at her confreres. "It's about time I lit a fire to smoke information out of them."

Tim shrugged. "They didn't really say anything."

Polly put her hands on her hips. "It's Jamie! No, I don't think he's the killer, but I do feel he definitely holds the key to solving this mystery."

Tim looked at his mother and applauded. "Not too shabby," he said. "Throwing Jamie's name at them. It was completely out of left field and pretty darn uncomfortable. Um, but now you've got to get him to squeeze a legit story from his lying lips about his murder-day whereabouts."

Polly suddenly looked troubled. "Ring him up. We need to have a chitty chat."

Tim flipped open his cell phone and scrolled through his phone directory. He selected Jamie's number and pushed the Send key. In a moment he handed the phone to his mother.

"Honey, it's Polly," she said into the phone. "Pepper, of course." Polly rolled her eyes. "Listen, dear, we're in the neighborhood and want to take you to dinner. The occasion?" She stopped to think for a moment, and then she quoted one of her famous lines from *Mame*. "As the lovely and talented Jerry Herman wrote, 'It's today!' Oh, and by the by, be a living doll. When Gerold calls you, and I have a feeling that he will, don't let on that we're having this tête-à-tête *ce soir*. He's acting funny today. But not in a ha-ha way. See you in a tick."

As Placenta tossed empty champagne bottles into the trash bin, she said, "We're in the neighborhood? See you in a tick? It'll take an hour for you to get dressed, and another hour to get from Glendale to West Hollywood!"

Polly began to remove her dressing gown. "You worry too much. We'll say that traffic was a bitch. Oh, and call Kevin at the Ivy and tell him that we're gracing his restaurant."

She looked at Mag. "Run along home to Daddy," she said. "Ask him to read you a bedtime story. Think 'Bluebeard.'"

Los Angeles may be the most superficial and blasé town on the planet, but when Polly's Rolls-Royce glided up to the curb in front of the Ivy, diners on the patio turned their heads to see who would alight from the vehicle. As Polly walked up the stone steps with her troupe following three paces behind her, she could hear the usual whispers of recognition and "Don't look nows" that still swirled around her when she was seen in public. Polly marched straight toward Kevin, her favorite waiter, and the man whom she not so secretly wanted to see Tim settle down with and start a family. Polly embraced Kevin and softly asked her usual greeting: "Anyone here I should be especially Polly Pepper to?"

As Kevin embraced Polly he whispered, "Connie Chung is in the loo. Ben and Jennifer are a few tables behind you over by the fichus. Clint is against the wall with his agent. You just missed Will and Jada. Tub-o Belushi has a reservation at nine, if you're still here."

Polly patted Kevin on the cheek and made a big public to-do about how thoughtful he was to remember her favorite champagne and to have a bottle chilling in an ice bucket next to her table. "So lovely as always!" she brayed. "The place would lack all sophistication without you, precious boy." Turning to Tim, she said, "You two haven't seen each other in ages!" She turned back to Kevin. "I insist that you come to the opening night cast party this Friday and become reacquainted. You don't have to stay for the stinky show, but we'll have fun afterward." Then Polly turned to Jamie. "Have you two met?"

Kevin and Jamie simultaneously locked eyes and reached out to shake hands. After a moment that lasted too long, Polly unglued their hands. "Enough with the howdy-dos. Now you're old chums." She exchanged a perturbed look with Tim, who sniggered uncomfortably as he pulled a chair away from the table for his mother to accept. "You sit there," Polly said to Placenta, pointing to the chair next to her. Tim, you're there." He sat opposite Placenta. "Which leaves you and me to stare into each other's eyes all night," she joked, seating Jamie opposite her. She looked up at Kevin again. "Let's start with the usual."

"A basket of calamari, coming right up," Kevin said as he began to fill champagne flutes.

After sympathetic toasts of better days to come for Jamie, and homilies about the dead still being with us, only absent from our sight because of our limited senses, Polly turned the focus of the conversation to the show. She slathered her banter with thoughts about how it was thrilling to be performing one of her all-time favorite roles again, but that the less-than-stellar cast made her nervous about the potentially harsh critical reviews. She raised her glass to Jamie. "Cheers! To what might have been, had you been given the opportunity to play in my show." She sighed and clinked the rim of her flute with his. "That's showbiz."

"That's Gerold," Jamie retorted.

"Ain't it the truth. Karen—God bless her beautiful soul— would have been very proud to see how well you performed that role."

Jamie set down his glass. "She didn't want me in the show."

A look crossed Polly's face that told Jamie that she was surprised by his revelation. "Dear me, you don't believe that. Surely you knew of her plan." Polly didn't know where her tongue was taking her.

"Plan?"

Polly sighed intolerantly. "You recently had a birthday, didn't you?" she guessed.

"Um, yeah, the same day that Karen was killed," Jamie said.

Polly couldn't believe that she'd inadvertently nailed the bull's-eye.

"And . . . ?" Polly asked as if coaxing the obvious from Jamie. "Weren't you both planning to have a quiet dinner together that night? Didn't Karen tell you that she had something special to give you as a gift?"

Jamie shook his head. "No. Karen was so wrapped up in the show I don't think she even remembered my birthday."

"Didn't remember?" Polly nearly shrieked. "Of course she remembered! Her big surprise was . . . um . . . she planned to present you with . . . a . . . er . . ." For a moment Polly was lost for words. "She bought you, or rather she wrapped up, the . . . um . . . the . . ."

"Contract," Tim said, surprising himself with his easy lie.

After an awkward moment, Polly said, "Yes! The contract. For the role of Patrick Dennis!"

Jamie looked confused, as though he were in shock. Polly too was shocked by what had leaped past her lips.

As Kevin began refilling the champagne glasses, Jamie drifted back to reality and Tim and Placenta carefully watched Polly as she blindly reeled Jamie in to her confidence.

Jamie shook his head and said, "Karen claimed that she didn't want to direct her boyfriend."

"The better to surprise you," Polly suggested.

"She said that she knew me well enough and that I'd flip out if she criticized my acting or singing. She claimed that she didn't want to jeopardize our relationship by us working together."

"She was right, of course. I let my first two bozo husbands direct sketches on my TV show. They both decided they could also direct my private life!" Returning to the subject of Jamie having a role in the show, Polly said, "Karen was planning to surprise you with that wonderful present."

Jamie once again stared off into a memory. He slowly shook his head and said, "Wow. If only I'd known sooner."

"Surprise, surprise," Polly sang, patting Jamie on the hand and still trying to stay one step ahead in her mental shell game.

Suddenly Jamie's face took on a hard look. Then he shook his head and growled, "Gerold *must* have known."

Kevin the waiter hovered by to take their dinner orders and Polly politely shooed him away. She returned her attention to Jamie and looked deep into eyes. "Of course Gerold knew. He was the artistic director."

"That slime bucket made me . . . I jumped through hoops for that role," Jamie growled. "Even though he knew it was going to be mine all along. I still had to . . ."

"Had to do what, dear?" Polly asked.

"I swear I could kill the son of a bitch!" Jamie said, ignoring Polly's question.

"We've had one too many murders on this show." Polly breathed a sigh of discomfort. "Let's maintain perspective. What did you mean about jumping through hoops for Gerold?"

"I planned to get into the show even though Karen objected. I just wanted her to see that I was good enough to be with a star like you."

Polly nodded her head as an idea occurred to her. "You don't have to lie any longer about where you really were the morning of the murder. You weren't ordering double-latte low-fat cappuccinos."

"Fess up," Placenta added.

Jamie was suddenly more alert, as if Polly had just kicked him under the table. "Of course I was . . ." He started to dismiss anything contrary to his original story. "I was at . . . Well, I was giving . . ."

"An audition?" Polly suggested, remembering what Mag had said about Jamie's plans that fateful morning.

Jamie turned bright red. He blinked rapidly as if trying to understand how Polly knew the details of his day. "Yeah, an audition."

"Euphemistically speaking," Tim said under his breath.

"Yes, dear, we know," Polly said to Jamie. She quietly sipped her champagne as Tim and Placenta exchanged dubious looks. Soon she cooed to Jamie, "Honey, you know that I'm the epitome of discretion. Everyone knows that I adore receiving dish, but I never actually sling the stuff myself. It's *un*-becoming a legend most. I haven't said a word to anyone about you and your untruth about being the java brigade. None of us have.

"However," Polly continued, "there's a beautiful girl wrongfully sitting in a jail cell who is depending on us for help and exoneration of her celebrity name. Surely, you of all people know what it's like to be used as a pawn in someone else's scheme."

"Think Gerold." Jamie's eyes began to water. He brushed away a tear that had begun to trickle down his left cheek. "I'm so ashamed of what I've done. I should never have . . ."

Tim leaned over and put his arm around Jamie's shoulder. "Hey, man, we all do what we have to do."

Jamie looked at Tim. "I doubt that Karen would have understood."

"Bumping off your own girlfriend made her certain not to complain," Placenta announced.

Jamie was stunned and whipped his head to look at Placenta. He sat up straight in his chair and the color drained from his face. "What? You think I killed Karen?" he asked. "You're not serious! Never in a gazillion years! I couldn't hurt the most important person in my life. She disappeared while I . . . we . . . I wasn't there."

Polly was baffled by Jamie's cryptic attempt at an explanation. However, after a lifetime spent in Hollywood she was no longer shocked by anything. "I'm sure that Tim is right. You didn't do anything that hasn't been done before . . . lying, cheating, killing . . ."

"Desperate times call for desperate measures," Jamie said, looking at Polly. Then he realized that what he was saying might be misinterpreted.

"That must have been an important audition for you to leave without looking for your Karen," Placenta said.

Jamie suddenly became very quiet as he remembered the day of Karen's death. "Gerold promised me the role if . . . Now you say that Karen was going to give it to me *free*— as a birthday gift. I'm a freakin' fool."

"Back to your lie," Polly said, trying to uncover his motive for keeping the truth of his whereabouts from the police.

Jamie looked at Polly. "Do I have to spell it out to you? I was *auditioning* with Gerold. If the police knew that Karen was the only one keeping me from getting the job, a role that I wanted badly, I'd be suspect number one."

As the picture became clear to Polly, she forced herself not to judge Gerold. Then she said, "The role of my handsome nephew was rightfully yours."

"I'll never forgive Gerold for going back on his word!" Jamie spat.

Kevin, with the hearing of a Doberman, decided that this was the perfect opportunity to appear at the table and to take their dinner orders.

Chapter 30

By the time Jim Belushi arrived at the Ivy, Tim was retrieving the car from the valet. Polly offered her left cheek for the corpulent TV star to peck. Although she never watched his series, deciding it was likely to be too lowbrow for her taste, Polly nevertheless lied and gushed that the last episode was a tickler. "Your writers place you in the most amusing predicaments," she guessed, trusting that he'd landed in typical network sitcom fare with an improbably gorgeous wife who puts up with her sloth of a hubby.

Soon Polly was making the rounds of several other tables. She air-kissed Megan Mullally, Bridget Fonda, and Will Ferrell, and when her social chores were over she hugged her waiter, Kevin, good-bye and then settled into the back of the Rolls. She made comments about several of the restaurant's famous clientele. "That's not a judgment," she defended her sniggering at William Shatner's crooked toupee. "It's merely an observation. Polly Pepper never says a negative word about her friends and colleagues."

Tim and Placenta ignored her. They'd heard her rationalizations too many times before.

Polly continued to make small talk until Jamie was deposited in front of his apartment building. After they bade good night to each other, and Tim had pulled away from the curb, Polly said, "News flash—that boy wasn't *auditioning* in the dressing room with Gerold!"

Tim looked in the rearview mirror and found his mother. Together with Placenta they both yelled out, "Duh! D'ya think?"

"Yes, I do '*think*'! But I *don't think* that either of you could have done half the job that I did in sweet-talking information out of that suspect. Under further questioning, I'll wager that he'll squeal like a Gitmo detainee and tell us who killed Karen."

Tim accelerated the car up LaCienega Boulevard to Sunset Boulevard. He turned left and proceeded toward Bel Air. When the monogrammed gates at Pepper Plantation parted, they drove through the entry and discovered Detective Archer's Honda Accord in the car park. He was sleeping behind the wheel. Polly knocked on the window.

Randy was groggy but managed a smile of recognition when he saw Polly.

"Why didn't you let yourself into the house?" Polly asked.

"You haven't trusted me with a key," he said. "And I didn't want to set off the security alarm."

"You couldn't stay away from me, eh?"

"That, and I've got some news about the case. I didn't want to tell you over the phone."

"I've got news for you too," Polly said and ushered Randy into the mansion.

Although it was after eleven o'clock, and the day had been long and exhausting for all of them, the prospect of more news about the murder of Karen Richards was enough to reenergize everyone. "I've had my fill of champers for the day," Polly said, surprising Tim and Placenta. "However, if Randy is having one, I'll have a teensy bit too."

Randy was bushed, but following an uncomfortable nap in his car he needed something to hydrate his cotton mouth. "A small one, please," he said to Placenta.

"Just a tad larger for me," Polly said to her maid. Then turning to Randy she said, "Show me yours and I'll show you mine." She giggled. "Your news of the case, of course! You've apprehended the killer? It's Charlotte Bunch! No, Mag Ryan! Um, Gerold Goss? I can't stand the suspense."

Randy accepted a flute from Placenta and took a long sip. He expressed his satisfaction with an uncouth "Ahhhh." Then he looked at Polly and raised his glass. "Cheers! To your instincts, which seem to be more on target than all the technology we use in the police department."

Polly, Tim, and Placenta huddled close by.

"We got a confession," Randy said.

"A confession!" Polly, Tim, and Placenta echoed in unison.

"We traced the Starbucks receipt to the barista who took Jamie's large coffee order the morning of the murder. She clearly remembered everything, and she definitely said—"

"That it was a skinny old guy in a janitor's uniform who placed the battalion-sized order," Polly interrupted. "He paid with two fifty-dollar bills. It wasn't Jamie."

Randy straightened his posture. "Jeez, the Hollywood grapevine is a heck of a lot shorter than a Google search."

"I thought you had something new!" Polly said.

Randy shrugged.

Polly took a sip of her champagne. "That's old info. But we got a confession too. From Jamie himself. He admitted that he lied about being at Starbucks. He was actually performing, er, auditioning for a role in the show."

"Does he have an alibi?" Randy asked.

"Bring Gerold Goss in for questioning. He'll cough up Jamie's alibi. It's his alibi too. They were in private discussions about Jamie getting into the show. Gerold hadn't been walking around Glendale that morning after all, and Jamie wasn't ordering double-latte cappuccinos for the cast. Can you arrest these people for being dishonest?"

Polly was as disappointed as she was tired. "Tomorrow promises to be another long day of rehearsals. At least I have one thing to look forward to. I'm getting my Emmy back Thursday evening. Mag promises that she's coaxed Charlotte into accidentally and conveniently tripping over it in West Hollywood Park. She'll play the hero by returning it to me here at the house around eight o'clock. If I didn't think she might have vital information about the murder, I'd file charges against her. But no, I have to act like Polly Pepper. I have to practically call a press conference to publicly thank Charlotte and all the weirdos in her head. I should get another Emmy just for the acting job I'll do."

"You can still get her for extortion," Randy said, almost eager to start the paperwork. "Those ransom notes are all the evidence we need."

"Nah." Polly waved away the idea. "All I really care about is that my baby comes back home safe and sound. Charlotte's a sick-o and I'm not interested in making matters worse. Plus, I think I can still squeeze more information about the murder from her."

Polly stood up to say good night, and touched Randy's cheek with the back of her hand. "You're welcome to stay. But I'm too tired for more than a quick massage."

Randy smiled. "If you insist." He stood up and took Polly's hand in his. He guided her out of the great room. "Night, everyone," he said as he departed with Polly and led her to the staircase.

Tim and Placenta were practically brain-dead from exhaustion. Still, Placenta poured another glass of Veuve into each of their flutes. She kicked off her shoes, lay back on the sofa, and rested her feet in Tim's lap. Tim reached down and put his hands around her right foot and began to squeeze and knead Placenta's sore instep and toes. She closed her eyes and moaned with satisfaction. "Honey, it's been a long time, but as I recall sex was never this good."

Tim smiled and continued rubbing Placenta's feet. Except for Placenta's muted moans the room was quiet. Tim fell into a reverie. He thought about what Jamie had to say about Gerold auditioning him for the role of Patrick Dennis, and felt bad that he had to barter for the role with the likes of Gerold. He remembered too Jamie's response to Polly's ruse about Karen being prepared to give him the role as a birthday present.

Tim filed his thoughts away and noticed Placenta had fallen asleep. When he gently touched her shoulder to awaken her, she smiled and said, "Thanks, Keanu." Tim let Placenta find her way to her room before he set the security alarm and turned off all the lights in the mansion.

He nearly stumbled with heavy-lidded eyes as he made his way to his suite. After a cursory rinse of Listerine, he flopped into bed and lay down. His pillow felt exceptionally comfortable. But he couldn't fall asleep. He couldn't stop thinking about Jamie and Gerold and Karen. Suddenly his eyes opened wide. Although it was pitch-black in his room he could clearly see the backstage area of the Galaxy Theatre and Karen's dead body. He threw off his blanket and stepped out of bed and made his way down the hall toward Polly's bedroom.

Arriving at the door, he hesitated, remembering that his mother was hosting her new boyfriend for a sleepover. Still, what he had to say couldn't wait. He tapped on the door. "Mom?" he whispered. He tapped again, this time a bit louder. "Polly! It's me, Tim. I need to speak with you."

From the other side of the door she heard voices and finally Polly said, "Come in, dear."

When Tim entered the dark room Polly said, "What's wrong, hon? Another nightmare? The one where Neil Patrick Harris leaves you for Anderson Cooper? Poor baby. I'd invite you to crawl in with me the way you did when you were a child, but three's a crowd, if you know what I mean."

Tim sighed in frustration. "Polly," he said, finding his way in the dark and sitting by her side on the mattress. "I can't sleep. It's this investigation. I was thinking about all the stuff Jamie said tonight. And what Gerold said earlier. And then I thought about Mag. Remember that she insisted that there was no one else in the theater at the time of Karen's murder? Then she retracted her statement and said that the cleaning people were there. Then you suggested that perhaps it was Charlotte whom she heard, using a foreign-sounding voice."

Polly leaned over and switched on the light by her nightstand and sat up against the bed's headboard.

Tim asked, "Who else was in the theater?"

Polly finger-brushed her hair out of her face. "Oh, hon, we've been over this so many times. The police have too." She turned to Randy, who was now wide awake and sitting up. "We talked to the entire cast, didn't we?"

"Absolutely." Randy nodded. "Everyone has an alibi, or at least they lied about having alibis."

Tim shook his head in disagreement. "Remember earlier this evening at the theater when Gerold made a big fuss about not hiring Jamie to coach Stewart Long? He said that George, the stage door guy, had been given instructions not to let Jamie into the theater."

Polly thought for a moment, trying to recall the words and context of what Gerold had said. She looked at Tim and said, "Oh my God! Innocuous George. He's always there. We skipped right over him because he's so obvious that he's not obvious." Polly turned to Randy. "What about the police, did they interview him?"

Randy shrugged, knowing that he never personally spoke to George, and had never heard one way or the other about anyone else getting a statement from him.

"The guy was usually asleep or looking at *Playboy* magazine when I signed us in," Tim said. "There's a good chance that he saw something that could be relevant to this case."

Polly was quiet for a moment as she recalled that no one, not even Sharon, ever mentioned the stage doorman. That Polly herself had failed to think about this bland old man to whom she gave a cheerful if cursory "Good morning!" each day as she sashayed past his desk, confounded her. "They all look alike to me, these old gems of theater tradition," Polly said, trying to find an excuse for her lack of attention to detail. "No matter what theater I play, there's always a George. Although they're usually asleep at their post, they somehow manage to keep up on all the backstage gossip. I'll speak to him first thing in the A.M." She patted Tim on the cheek.

Randy rolled over on his side and said, "That's my job."

Polly smiled at her son and winked good night. "We love our Doogie Howser, so go back and dream that he's my son-in-law."

Chapter 31

George, the stage doorman at the Galaxy Theatre, appeared to be as old as the theater itself. He sat behind a built-in desk next to the artists' entrance and spent his days napping and reminding the cast and crew members to sign in and out on sheets of lined paper attached to a clipboard. At the end of each day he filed away the attendance log in a manila folder and prepared a new one for the following day.

George had no real job description. Mainly he tried to prevent fans and lookie-loos from gaining access to the theater, but George was too old to even keep out troops of Girl Scouts who barged in to sell their Thin Mints. He had neither a bark nor a bite. However, because he more or less came as a package deal with the theater whenever it had changed ownership over the years, each successive management team had practically forgotten that he existed. He never complained and his pay hadn't changed in a quarter century, so they simply left him alone.

An early riser, George was at his station at 7:00 A.M. every day. When Polly and Tim and Placenta arrived the next morning at eight, he was dozing next to a half-full mug of coffee. Tim opened the door for Polly, who bounded into the building and sidled up to the desk beside the old man. She sang out in a booming voice, "Oh, what a beautiful morning! Oh, what a beautiful day . . ." Her dynamic entrance succeeded in startling George from his dream of Natalie Portman.

Polly leaned over the counter next to his desk and exclaimed, "George! I've been a naughty star. I haven't given you your present!"

George looked confused. He stared at a brightly wrapped package offered by Polly. "It's not my birthday," he grumbled. He had worked in the same job practically since the night that Lincoln was shot, and with the exception of Lee Merriweather, with whom he was secretly in love, nobody involved with any show ever paid him much attention. He was now suspicious of why the legendary Polly Pepper was making a fuss over him. He pushed a clipboard toward her and said, "Sign in."

Polly feigned regret. "I'm castigating myself for being so thoughtless. I can't believe that for the first time in my long and illustrious career I neglected to befriend the one person in the theater who always deserves the Euripides Spirit Award. The stage door man. You are the tireless keeper of keys to the dressing rooms and the jack-of-all-trades who plunges the backed-up toilets and changes the makeup mirror lightbulbs. You are the hero who keeps a bowl of milk by the door for the theater alley kitty cat. The man who makes even the lowliest chorine feel like a star when she walks through the door and you call out a cheerful greeting. I'm absolutely ashamed that we haven't become dear friends, but I intend to remedy that situation, pronto. To begin, I'd like to give you a wee little prezey."

George didn't recognize himself in Polly's description. Nevertheless, he accepted the proffered gift. "Keys? Toilets? Lightbulbs? Those are union jobs," he said.

"You can open it and thank me now, if you wish," Polly

said, eager to see the look on the old man's face when he realized that a great star was going out of her way to make him feel as important as any member of the cast.

The package was the size of a thick book and George feared that's what was beneath the wrapping. He hated to read, except for *Bra Busters* magazine. Still, he peeled away the paper with a bony finger. When he had torn the wrapping off he was happy to see that it wasn't a book after all. He didn't know exactly what it was. He stared for a long moment until Tim caught on and said, "It's the entire first season of *The Polly Pepper Playhouse* on DVD. This special edition comes with cast and guest-star interviews, as well as commentary by Carol Burnett and Elinor Donohue."

Polly clasped her hands together and gushed, "I knew that you'd love it. I was sure that a man of your years . . . er, appreciation for the business . . . would be thrilled to have your very own chapters of my early history. You can watch me on the tube long after I depart this venerable old theater."

"I've been meaning to buy a television," George said, aware that it would be impolite to say that the gift was of no use to him. Instead he pretended to be delighted by Polly's thoughtfulness. "The wife—rest her soul—always thought you would be nice."

Polly was touched by George's expression of appreciation, artificial though it was, and reached out to caress his cheek. "Thank you for all that you do for people of the theater," she said with as much earnestness as she could summon. "You and all the other stage doormen around the world may be overlooked, out of date, and out of place, but you're still the heart of every backstage."

Tim nudged his mother with his elbow. He gave her a look that said, "You're babbling!"

"What I mean, of course, is that you're as essential to

our business as the seats in the auditorium, and I for one must acknowledge how much I value whatever it is that you do."

George plopped himself back down on his chair. He was exhausted from listening to Polly, but said, "That's mighty fine, Miss Pepper."

"Polly! Your new best friend."

"Hmmm," George responded, taking a sip from his oversized mug of now cold coffee. He looked at his watch, then turned around and opened the door to the microwave oven that occupied a shelf behind him. He placed his mug inside, closed the door, and pushed the beverage reheat button. "Convenience. I don't have to leave my station whenever the joe gets cold."

Polly looked at George and at the microwave oven. Then she looked at her watch. "A mug that size must last a long time between refills."

"I make a pot at seven when I get in. With frequent nuking I can nurse this baby until eight thirty or sometimes nine," George proudly declared.

"So you never have to leave your station. Such a profound work ethic!"

"Except when I have to ... you know ... answer the call."

Polly was suddenly deflated. It was entirely possible that the reason that George hadn't previously come forward with information about the murder was that he was in the bathroom at the time of the crime. "Do you have to go often?" Polly asked.

"Are you taking a survey? I have a friend who has to go at least ten times during the night. I'm not that far along," he said.

The timer on the microwave sounded and George retrieved his coffee mug.

Polly wasn't interested in an old man's bladder habits, but she needed to know if he had been at his post the morning of Karen's death, or if the porcelain god had beckoned at the wrong time. "George," she cooed, "were you at your desk the last time that Sharon Fletcher was in the theater?"

George raised an eyebrow and looked Polly up and down. He crossed his arms over his chest and leaned back. "It's about time someone thought to ask me about that."

George leaned forward, picked up his coffee mug, and took another sip. He savored the taste and nodded his head, indicating that the temperature was just right. Then he set the mug down and rested his elbows on the desk. He looked at Polly and shook his head. "It's a damn shame about that nice director lady."

Polly was once again hopeful. "Did you see anything unusual that morning?" she asked.

"See?"

"Sharon running out crying? Charlotte Bunch hanging around, or someone coming to the theater who didn't belong here? Anything?"

"Actresses coming and going and running away with tears streaming down their pretty faces?"

"Yes!" Polly said eagerly.

"Yep. Not to mention the theater's artistic director who came in with his little girlfriend."

"So you did see something!"

"Um, actors backstage in a theater. Even crying actresses. What's so unusual about that?"

Polly heaved a heavy sigh. "Didn't you see anything unusual, George?"

"Nope." George looked into Polly's eyes. "Ask me if I *heard* anything."

Polly leaned in closer to George. "Tell me. What did you *hear*?"

George smiled. He looked over his shoulder. Polly, Tim, and Placenta followed his gaze to an ancient speaker box mounted on the wall. "One of you go out there on the stage and say something. Anything 't all. 'I think that I will never see a poem lovely as a tree.' Whatever. Go ahead. And you don't have to project to the second balcony neither."

Polly and her troupe were perplexed, but after a moment Tim volunteered to go out onto the stage and perform a soliloquy from *The Three Stooges*, or whatever came into his memory. Within a few moments, his voice was clearly audible through the speaker behind George's desk.

Polly and Placenta each gasped.

Tim returned presently and could tell by the look on his mother's face that something momentous had occurred.

Polly sang the first lines from the theme song to *The Nanny*.

"I just sang that song onstage. How did . . . The acoustics in this dump can't be that good!"

Polly pointed to the speaker box. "As for singing, don't give up your day job. If you had one."

"You heard that? Did George hear . . . ?"

Polly looked at George. "Every word?"

George nodded and smiled. He looked around the otherwise empty backstage area and looked at his watch again. "Others will be coming in any minute now. It's best if we talk later. If you want to know who killed Karen Richards, come by my house tonight after rehearsal." George scribbled his address on a piece of paper and handed it to Polly.

In that next moment, several dancers arrived. They called out, "Hello, Miss Pepper," thus interrupting George. Polly smiled but didn't take her eyes off George. "How can I stand the suspense all day? Just whisper something into my ear."

"You need to hear the backstory," George said, turning to the microwave and setting his mug inside. As he pushed the beverage reheat button he said, "The story of a person's last minutes of life deserves all the details." When he turned around he was looking into the eyes of Gerold Goss.

The cast of *Mame* did a complete wardrobe and sound test run-through before lunchtime. After an hour off they again assembled onstage and performed the show. By six o'clock, they had completed two full performances. The company was exhausted. However, Gerold announced that he was displeased with everything about the show and insisted that the cast perform one more time. "I don't care if we're here until midnight!" he shouted at a chorus boy who had dared to roll his eyes in exasperation.

Polly tried to set a good example for the rest of the cast by not complaining or showing that she too had more urgent things to do with her time. Beneath her paper smile was a woman desperate to leave the theater and to speak to George and finally solve the mystery of who murdered Karen Richards. After many stops and restarts, the company was finally through for the night. Gerold still complained, but the stage manager announced that everyone was dismissed.

"It's after ten. Let's get the hell out of here!" Polly said as she raced to her dressing room. In record time, she shed her costume, washed off her stage makeup, consumed a flute of Bollinger, and was out the door and in her car. "Step on it," she said to Tim, who quickly maneuvered the car out of the lot and onto the wide boulevard.

"I've set Magellan to George's address," he said, looking at his favorite navigation gadget. In ten minutes they were slowly driving along Conrad Street, and the automated voice in Magellan finally said, "You have reached your destination." Tim easily found a space to park by the curb, and the trio stepped out of the car and onto a concrete sidewalk, which was cracked and buckled, from the roots of enormous magnolia trees that lined the street.

"That must be it," Polly said, pointing to an old early

California bungalow-style house. "He's written that his place is in the back," she added, looking at George's note.

Tim led the way and as they walked down a driveway in which two cars were parked in tandem, they heard a dog bark from within the main house. A chain-link fence gate was open at the side of the house, and in the distance they could see a small cottage with its front porch light on.

"Watch your step," Tim cautioned as he gingerly stepped through the semidark yard. A faint light from inside the house spilled into the backyard, casting shadows over children's bicycles and toys, and rakes and hoses. Finally they reached the screen door at the guest house and looked at the number. It matched the one that George had given to Polly. "Either he's not home or he's already in bed," Tim said, looking into a dark window.

"He won't mind being woken up," Polly said as she opened the screen door. "This is too important to him and to us."

Tim tapped on the door. No response. He knocked louder. "There's no doorbell."

Polly stepped beside Tim and rapped on the door herself. "George? It's Polly. Wake up, honey. You're expecting me." She knocked again but still no one answered and no light shone from within. "Maybe he's not home yet. But he was gone by the time we left the theater."

The three stood outside in the cool night wondering what to do next.

As they were about to give up and head back to the car, a woman called out to them from the main house. "He's not there," she said, stepping from the house and making her way toward the trio. When she was finally among them she instantly recognized Polly. "Oh my God, it's you, from the television. What's your name . . . ? Give me a minute. The funny one. Darn."

Polly was horrified by the woman's lack of recall, but

rather than show her annoyance, she held out her hand and said, "Polly. Polly Pepper. How do you do?"

"You're right," the woman said. "You're Polly Pepper! I knew it." After a moment of awkward silence, she said, "If you're looking for George, the ambulance finally came. Took 'em long enough. He's gone."

Polly and Tim and Placenta were stunned. "Gone?" Polly said. "To the hospital?"

"To join his wife," the woman said.

Polly looked confused. "But his wife is . . ." Polly's reaction was that this was a horrible mistake; that she must have the wrong house and the wrong George. "How? What happened? Was he alone? Did he suffer? What was the cause?" She wanted to know everything, but the woman knew next to nothing.

"I came home from my first-aid class and saw him face-down in the yard," the woman said. "I rushed outside but there was nothing I could do. We don't learn CPR until next week."

"Did you call 911?" Polly asked, almost impatiently. "They could have saved him."

"I called, but it was ten minutes before they showed up. Anyway, I'd say he was a goner long before I even came home."

Polly reached out for Tim's and Placenta's hands. She squeezed them tight and closed her eyes. "George knew who the killer was. I'm a fool. And now I have nothing to prove my theory. We're screwed."

Chapter 32

"Blunt trauma to the head?" Polly said, speaking into the cell phone and repeating what Randy was telling her about what he'd learned of George's death. "Murder!" she immediately announced. "I don't care that he was eighty-six or that he's hardly cold and the coroner hasn't made his stupid official determination. The man lived in that house for years. He knew his way around that trash heap they call a backyard. It's highly improbable that George would have stumbled over a rake or a tricycle, even in the dark. He was a careful man. So careful, in fact, that he didn't want to tell me what he heard from backstage the morning of Karen's murder until he could do so privately. I don't need an autopsy report to tell me that someone wanted him silenced. And I think I know who."

Polly listened for another moment and then shook her head. "I'll tell you all about it in the morning. I'm utterly exhausted. We're just at the gates now. We have ten hours of rehearsal tomorrow and I need to get some sleep. Shall we say eight? Starbucks. The one across from the theater. Be more specific. Brilliant. Yes, much love to you too." She flipped the cell phone lid closed as the car rolled onto the estate grounds.

Tim looked at his mother in the rearview mirror. "It's too soon for an official cause of death. Just because he hit his head doesn't mean he didn't lose consciousness first. Stroke. Heart attack. Let's wait before we jump to any conclusions."

Polly was peeved. "Two dead people. Just like on my last film location. Sure, George was old. Of course it's always possible that he simply ran out of change for the meter. But I don't believe it. No, he had lots to live for . . . if only to tell me who murdered Karen. That alone would have kept him alive. The guy was knocked off. Be sure to get my DVD collection back tomorrow!"

"Gerold Goss?" Tim asked.

"Who else?" Polly affirmed. "He overheard our conversation this morning. He obviously realized that he hadn't covered all of his tracks. Just like the police, he had totally forgotten about George being in the theater when Karen died. He realizes that there was a witness."

Tim shook his head. "If you're right, then we could all be next in line for a toe tag." He stopped the car under the portico and looked around, suddenly paranoid.

Polly stepped out of the car. As she headed toward the front steps she said, "I'm this close to exposing the murderer. I know it! I feel it! I'm getting the same chill up my spine that I suppose Miss Marple feels when she's about to confront someone with proof that they stuffed the vicar's insufferable mother-in-law under a couple dozen Hungry Man TV dinners in the deep freezer. But even if I were one hundred percent certain, and could point my bejeweled finger at the SOB right this instant, I can't jeopardize the opening of my show! The curtain goes up in three nights. I have to have concrete evidence about who the killer is before I blow the whistle. Otherwise I'll be getting reviews for defamation of character."

Placenta punched in the security code to unlock the front door. Once the trio was safely inside the house, Polly touched Placenta's cheek with the back of her hand. "I promise not to let anything happen to my precious family. Now run along and open a bottle. We all need a glass or two to clear our heads. I'll meet you in the great room."

Tim tossed his car keys into the cloisonné bowl on the foyer table, and begged his mother for a promise. "I don't expect you to turn over this case to the police department, or to Randy in particular, but you're too young to join June Allyson at the Pearly Gates, so please don't do anything that could get you—or me—killed."

Polly pooh-poohed Tim's concern. "I'm not afraid to die. But I am afraid of never setting my heels on a Broadway stage. In other words, sweetums, my career hiney is on the line and I promise not to screw it up by dating the Grim Reaper."

"I'm feeling better already. Not," Tim said as he and his mother walked down the hallway toward the waiting champagne.

"Why am I no longer tired?" Polly said, looking at Tim and Placenta, who were both nodding off on the sofa. "I was fading fast while talking to Randy. Oh, I hope I'm not tiring of him already! I'm full of pep. Must be the champers. The good stuff makes me giddy. Now that I've got my second wind I should call up Randy and apologize for being rather distant when we spoke from the car."

"Telephoneitis," Placenta charged. "You get a little high and you want to telephone everybody. It's too late! Randy is bound to be where you should be, in bed! That's where I'm going right now."

"Me too," Tim said. "If we're getting up early enough to catch Randy at Starbucks, we should all be sound asleep now."

"Nonsense," Polly called out as Tim and Placenta began to leave the room. "An important idea came to me a wee bit ago, and I need your help."

Tim and Placenta both heaved heavy defeated sighs and

returned to their seats on the sofa. They drowsily looked up at Polly, who was pacing the floor.

"You may as well pour yourselves another round, because we need to toast my brilliant plan," Polly said as she held out her own glass for a refill. "Think back to early this morning—"

"That's now *yesterday* morning," Placenta corrected.

Polly continued. "When we arrived at the theater, George insisted that we sign in. He said that he was very meticulous about keeping track of everyone who came into the theater, and when they left. Before Gerold gets the same idea and destroys the evidence, we need to find the roster for last Tuesday."

"What 'evidence'?" Placenta complained.

Polly was deep in thought as she continued speaking. "I figure that if Gerold forgot about George in the first place, he probably forgot about absconding with the sign-in register too. First thing in the morning, we've got to get hold of that paper! Tim, while I'm onstage, go through his file cabinet and grab that page!"

"What if there's a new door man in George's place?" Tim asked.

"The guy just died. Who're they going to get so soon?"

Coffee with Randy lasted fifteen minutes. Polly was anxious to get to the theater and made no apologies for her eagerness to be on her way. "Now, don't start feeling as though I'm giving you short shrift, my dear. But I've got a show to rehearse. We open the day after tomorrow. Please be patient with me." As she and her troupe departed the café, she finger-waved to Randy, then made the universal sign for "Call me."

"You're getting tired of Randy?" Tim said to his mother.

"Of course not," Polly replied. "But some things are more important than small talk. We have a job to do and he's got to get used to the fact that I have an important career. I understand that he has to be at work all hours of the day. He must understand my situation too. Now let's get those files."

As the trio approached the stage door entrance, they noticed a mock police car in the parking space next to where they'd left the Rolls. With a bar of red, blue, and white lights on the roof, the vehicle was white with blue lettering on the front doors that announced: MAYDAY SECURITY. Polly, Tim, and Placenta looked at each other with trepidation. Then Tim opened the artists' entrance door for his mother. As she stepped inside, followed by her maid and Tim, they found two men dressed up as wannabe policemen in dark blue uniforms. One was seated in George's chair; the other was nursing a mug of coffee and straddling the side of the desk. Both looked up at the new arrivals and put on their best pseudomilitary demeanors.

"La! It's our brave soldiers for inner-city peace," Polly trilled, using her most disarming and winning smile. She looked at the one with the coffee mug. "Such attractive medals," she said, touching his badge. "Would you be a dear and get me a cuppa? No cream or sugar. I like an unadulterated punch this time of morning."

Both men looked down at Polly as if she were a criminal who should be busted and taken to jail. "Who are *you*?" the one with the coffee mug said.

"Just your average everyday international superstar legend." Polly smiled and held out her hand. "Think Madonna without the corny cone titties and African babies. You can call me Polly."

The man seated in George's chair smiled and punched his partner on the calf of his leg. With a southern accent, and as if Polly weren't present he said, "Hey, this one's famous. I recognize her. Mama's favorite star. What's her name? Ya know, the one with the red hair and the funny old TV show?"

Polly was slightly ticked off, but made certain that her smile remained frozen on her face. "Such darling boys. I'll save you the brainpower. Yes, I'm Mama's favorite star, Polly Pepper."

"Now I've got it!" the security guard said. "Carol Burnett. Yep, that's who you are. Can't wait to tell Mama that I met Carol Burnett. Can I have your autograph?"

Polly practically keeled over. Recovering with the help of Tim, who helped to steady his mother, Polly replaced her look of shock with a half smile. "I'm flattered that you'd think I was that other fabulously gifted red-haired legend. To be confused with Miss Burnett is a high honor."

The guard who had misidentified Polly said, "Shoot! I thought we had us a real live star."

Tim was by now as annoyed and as impatient as his mother. "Miss Polly Pepper *is* a star. She's the star of the musical that opens in this theater tomorrow night."

The second guard tried to make amends. "No disrespect intended. Luther Ray here meant a real star. One who's been on TV."

Placenta came to Polly's rescue. "Mr. Bubba here can rest easy," she said. "Miss Pepper is a legend directly from television. Before your time by at least a few decades."

The guard who was standing looked at Placenta and corrected her. "His name's Luther Ray. Not everyone from Texas is named Bubba."

Placenta looked at the man's name badge. "Excuse me . . . Orvine . . ." she said in a mock apology. "We're late for rehearsal, so keep an eye on the door. You never know who might drop by. Perhaps Carol Burnett. She's a dear friend."

As the trio began to move away from the doorman's desk, Luther Ray called out, "Ya gotta show identification and sign in to get to the stage area."

Tim was perturbed. "Since when does an international legend have to show ID?"

"Since this creepy old theater has become a hotbed for murders," Orvine said and pushed the sign-in roster toward Tim.

Polly was flummoxed. "Will my picture on the show's poster do? I don't generally carry . . . or need . . . any other form of identification."

"A driver's license or green card will do," Luther Ray said.

By now, members of the chorus who had been summoned for an early rehearsal were beginning to line up behind Polly. They were becoming edgy because the choreographer, Tatanya Morgan, would have a fit if they weren't in their places on time. Finally one of the fearless boy dancers turned on the guards. "Listen, you phony police academy rejects, this lady is the star of our show. She's a great big famous celebrity. If you don't have the brains to know this, then you should be working at the Budweiser plant instead of a theater. Now let her pass so we can get to rehearsal."

Luther Ray was mortified by the chorus boy's spot-on analysis of his career path. He merely nodded his head to indicate that they all could go to their dressing rooms, or any place else in the theater.

Always concerned about the impression that she left on her fans and the public alike, Polly leaned over and held out her hand again for Luther Ray to shake. "You're doing a marvelous job of keeping out the riffraff," she cooed. "I for one am grateful that you have our little acting company's best interest at heart. We'll catch up later, the three of us." She looked at Orvine. "Same to you, my dear." Then she whispered to Tim, "Stick around. Make friends with Tweedledum and Tweedledee. And get that roster!" Then she followed Placenta and the dancers to their respective dressing rooms.

After the others had disappeared down the hallway, Tim picked up the clipboard. "I'll sign in for my mother," he said as he wrote Polly's name on the seventh line. He looked at his wristwatch and jotted down the time. "I can tell that Mother adores you two. Trust me, she'll be inviting you to her mansion before the week is out."

Both Luther Ray and Orvine smiled when they heard the word *mansion*. Although neither man had heard of Pepper Plantation, they certainly knew that there were a lot of rich stars in Los Angeles, and that it was just a matter of time before they met one.

After that, Tim easily insinuated himself into their dreary lives and held court with showbiz stories that kept the guards entertained on an otherwise boring assignment. When Tim felt that he finally had their confidence, he suggested that the two go out for coffee, instead of drinking the supermarket brand that they'd made in George's coffeepot. He gave them a ten-dollar bill and told them where to find the nearest Starbucks. "I know this theater like I know my mother's mansion," he said, watching their eyes sparkle. "It's in good hands with me, so take your time. Have an apple fritter to go with the joe."

The moment that Luther Ray and Orvine closed the door behind them, Tim began rifling though the filing cabinet searching for last week's sign-in rosters. He found folders dated as far back as 1968 and marked with the names of such popular shows as *The Music Man*, *Hello, Dolly!*, *The Pajama Game*, and *The King and I*. Every once in a while he'd stop and look at names on those pages. He recognized Vince Edwards, Denholm Elliott, Judy Carne, Donna Reed, Mildred Natwick, and Paul Lynde, among many others. As hard as it was to tear himself away from all the original autographs, he had a job to do and couldn't spend his time looking at the names of dead . . . or near dead . . . actors. When Tim had exhausted all the filing cabinet drawers, he opened George's desk. There he found more recent files, and finally: *Mame*.

Tim was tempted to take the entire manila folder but realized that if the police—or the killer—decided to look for the rosters, one missing page could be considered misfiled, but an entire folder gone would be highly suspect. As he went backward in the dates, starting from last night, he carefully scrutinized the pages. But just as he arrived at Monday, July 10, he heard voices approaching from the dressing room area. He closed the drawer and sat back in the chair pretending to read a magazine.

Gerold and Charlotte entered. "Shouldn't you be with your mother?" Gerold said. He looked at Tim with suspicion. "She's crying her eyes out in her dressing room. Guess I shouldn't have compared her performance to Tammy Faye Bakker's mascara-smudged sermons."

Tim was suddenly angry. "You know, Gerold, Polly and Placenta and I have tried to be nice to you. But you're a louse. You'd get a hell of a lot more out of your performers if you treated them with respect and consideration. Polly will do anything her director tells her to do, and it always pays off with a brilliant crowd-pleasing performance. That's why she's a legend and why she's lasted so long in this business. You don't know a cross fade from a cutout or a rostrum. You don't belong in the theater. You should be hauling trash for the city."

Gerold was perspiring with anger. He looked at Tim with disdain. "Get out of my theater."

"I'm with your star, Mr. Mucky Muck. I ain't leavin'."

Gerold looked around. "Where's security? I'll have you thrown out!"

"One call from me to the producers and you'll never work in this theater again," Tim parried.

Gerold's eyes blazed as he stood looking down at Tim with contempt. He knew that as the star's son, Tim would hold sway with the producers. He was also aware that the producers were putting together next season's schedule and hadn't consulted with him about the shows they were considering. This was not a good sign. He presumed that his days as the artistic director of the Galaxy were numbered. Gerold didn't want to ruffle their feathers in case there was still a chance that he'd be asked to renew his contract. "I need a file," he finally said. He moved toward the desk and opened the drawer.

Tim sat in horror watching as Gerold pulled out the folder marked *Mame*. He wanted to grab it away from Gerold and flee the building. However, he realized that would be futile. He'd be accused of stealing theater property. Instead, Tim pretended to not care or have any idea why Gerold wanted the folder.

Gerold closed the desk drawer. He slipped the folder under his arm without bothering to look at the sheaf of papers inside. He gave Tim another withering look and began to walk away with Charlotte. Then the stage door opened and the two security guards walked in laughing and joking between themselves. Gerold yelled, "You're fired! You're supposed to be watching the door, not going in and out of it." He looked at their Starbucks cups. "We provided you with coffee. You deserted your post for no reason. You'll be hearing from your boss. Now git!"

The men were speechless. They looked at each other, and then looked at Tim.

Tim stood up from his desk and faced Gerold. "I gave them permission to take a break. They're allowed fifteen minutes every four hours. Unless you want trouble with their labor union, in addition to all the trouble you're in here at the theater, you'd better back off."

The security guards grinned at Tim's bravado and handed him a paper cup from Starbucks. "We brought one back for you," Luther Ray said.

Gerold stormed out of the backstage area. Tim presumed that he was headed for his office. Although he wanted to get to his mother's side as soon as possible, it was imperative that Tim rescue the folder from Gerold. He didn't know what to do. "That SOB just stole theater property," he said to the security men. "Important documents. Somehow I've got to get them back."

"Man, it's sorta his theater," Orvine said. "I mean, he's the director and all."

Tim looked around for the switch to the intercom system. "If we can hear from the stage, there should be a way for the stage to hear us," he said. Then, on the wall behind the Mr. Coffee machine, he found two ancient toggles. Neither was labeled. Tim flipped one and heard ambient noises coming through. He realized that was the switch to listen to the performance and any instructions that the director might want to send back to the stage doorman. The other switch was obviously for the stage doorman to make announcements to other parts of the theater. Tim looked up at the guards who were now more or less his buddies. "Do you guys see a microphone anywhere? It's probably a really old thing that looks like—"

"Like that?" Luther Ray said, pointing to a dusty green bulky instrument on the shelf next to a can of Folgers Crystals.

"You guys are the best!" Tim reached for the heavy mic. He set it on the desk and thought for a moment, not sure about what to say. "Heck, I don't even know if this works." He looked up at Orvine. "Gerold knows my voice too well. Would you please make an announcement for me? Just say, "Mr. Goss. You're needed in dressing room seven."

Orvine nodded his head. "No problemo." When Tim flipped the toggle and made a "go" signal with his index finger, Orvine spoke into the microphone and ended by adding "immediately."

Tim patted Orvine on the back. "If he comes this way and asks why he was paged, tell him that someone named Jamie is waiting for him," he said.

"What happens when he doesn't find anyone?" Luther Ray said.

"Tell him that this Jamie guy decided not to wait."

Chapter 33

Tim rushed to his mother's dressing room. "Gerold got the folder before I did," he said, panting. "He probably took it to the office."

"He made me cry!" Polly shouted. "He stopped my performance and said I danced like a duck! He's hateful! We have to get that file!"

"I've just paged him. If dressing room number seven means what I think it means, he'll be hustling down this way right now."

Polly stood up. "Follow me," she said. "Placenta, hold down the fort. And hold down Gerold if he tries to leave the dressing room area."

Polly and Tim slipped out of the star's dressing room and cautiously made their way down a dark corridor that was seldom used. It bypassed the stage doorman, and meandered behind the other dressing rooms. It ended at a stairwell. "This leads to the mezzanine," Polly said.

Polly and Tim climbed the old concrete stairs until they reached a door that said THE QUEEN'S BOX.

"This is the right level," Polly said. "But the only queens who ever sat up here—"

"Mother!"

Polly slowly opened the door and gingerly looked down the corridor to the right and then to the left. "I think it's all clear." She stepped into the open. Tim followed as they stealthily made their way down the long hall. "It's one of these doors," Polly said, confused. Then she saw the trash can that she'd tripped over the other night and remembered that it was just outside the door where she had overheard her name in conversation. "This is it," she said and put her ear to the wooden door. Then she placed her hand on the knob and slowly turned it to the left. The door opened and she peered inside the office. She was terrified. She gave the all-clear signal to Tim and he followed her as closely as a shadow.

"That's it!" Tim said in a loud whisper, pointing to the folder on the desk.

Polly rushed to the folder and opened it up. She leafed thought the top dozen sheets until she came across one dated July 10. She quickly picked it up and scanned the paper for names. "Look," she said, pointing to Charlotte Bunch. "She signed in at eight-oh-five, but didn't sign out."

Tim looked over his mother's shoulder. He pointed to Sharon Fletcher's name. "Just as George said. Sharon signed in at eight-ten, but someone else signed her out at eight twenty-five. Gerold said that he did that because she raced out of the theater in tears. But why then didn't he sign Charlotte out?"

Suddenly Polly and Tim froze. They could hear a conversation in the distance. It was Gerold's voice and he was approaching the office.

"Don't lie to me, you little weasel," Gerold said. "I was just paged to our dressing room! If you try one more stunt like that I'll see that you never work in this business again. Now stay away! Or else."

As Gerold stepped into his office he flipped his cell phone closed and went straight to his desk. As he settled himself into his chair, it made a squeaking sound as it strained to support his weight. He opened the folder and began leafing through the pages. "Where the hell . . . ?" he said aloud to himself as he got to the last page. He started from the beginning and once again looked for the July 10 roster. "Son of a bitch!" he screamed and flipped the folder into the air. He picked up his cell phone and speed-dialed Polly Pepper's number. "Let me speak with her," Gerold barked into the phone.

"Miss Polly is indisposed at the moment," Placenta said. "Shall I ask her to return your call?"

Gerold flipped his phone shut without a response. He stood up and walked out from behind his desk, stepping on the folder and scattered pages. He left the room and slammed the door closed.

In a moment, the small private bathroom door whined on old hinges as it was slowly opened. Tim peeked out and then reached behind him to take his mother's hand. They tiptoed tentatively across the room and left the office. Once in the open hallway, they raced for the stairwell and moved as quickly as possible down to the basement level. When they arrived in the backstage area, Orvine and Luther Ray stopped Tim and cautioned him about Gerold and the tantrum he'd just thrown when he couldn't find Polly.

Polly squared her shoulders, ready for a fight. She marched into her dressing room and found Placenta. Polly tried to move toward her maid but was caught off guard by Gerold, who had seated himself out of sight behind the door. "You want to play bully?" she barked at him. "Don't take your adolescent self-loathing out on me!"

Gerold stared at Polly. "Give it to me," he said in a quiet tone.

"I'll give it to you, all right," Polly snapped. "When the L.A. Times comes to interview me this afternoon, I'll tell them what a horror you've been to work with, and that if the show isn't a success Jerry Herman can blame only one person . . . the untalented Mr. Gerold Goss. Everybody knows that I'm a straight shooter. Audiences and the critics will all feel bad for me, and castigate you!"

Gerold drew in a deep breath and loudly exhaled. "Hand it over."

Every molecule of Polly's body went into acting mode. She first gave Gerold a quizzical look that said, *I don't know what you're talking about.* "Hand what over?" she asked, turning to indignation.

"Don't play games with me, Miss Pepper," Gerold said in a stern voice. "I want what belongs to the theater."

"I don't know what the hell you're talking about!"

"Perhaps he means the tea bags that you took home last night," Tim suggested, pointing to the hot plate and the basket of instant coffee packets and herbal teas.

"Hell, if that's all you want, subtract the cost from my paycheck," Polly said.

Gerold stood up in a rage. "We're not talking about tea bags! You know what I want, and if you don't hand it over I'll have security strip-search you."

Polly looked deep into Gerold's eyes. "I have never, in all my thousands of years in this business, been treated with such disrespect and condescension, even by the likes of Pearl Bailey. If you think that I have something that belongs to you or to the theater, you'd better file charges with Actors' Equity. But be prepared for a lawsuit that you and this theater will never financially survive."

Gerold turned to Tim. "I don't need permission from Actors' Equity to search *you*! Hand it over, or I'll get those two idiots out there to look in every orifice and body cavity."

Tim, too, stared at Gerold. "Okay," he said.

Gerold's demeanor instantly changed to optimistic.

Tim looked at Polly and Placenta, and then back to Gerold. "It's about time. I should have done this before."

"Good boy." Gerold smiled evilly.

Tim reached into his jeans pocket. He pulled out a folded piece of paper and looked intently at it before handing it over to Gerold. He then reached into his pocket again and pulled out his cell phone and began pushing numbers on the keypad."

Gerold yelled, "What the hell is this?"

"J.J. Norton's new private number. I haven't entered into my speed dial yet. "What are the last four digits? Oh, never mind. I remember." Then he continued dialing. "J.J. please. Polly Pepper calling."

Gerold was taken aback. "What the hell? Polly's agent? What do you think you're doing?"

"You've left us no choice," Tim said defiantly. "Your harassment of J.J.'s biggest client will have him seething and eating you as well as the stage scenery for lunch."

Gerold's face drained of color. As much of a bully as Gerold was himself, Polly's agent, J.J. Norton, was known as a pit bull. If he sank his fangs into someone's career jugular, he never let go until he'd destroyed them.

"Hold for Polly Pepper, please," he said into the phone and handed it to Polly.

"Sweetie!" she sang. "Oh, it's . . . going. However, not in any way that I ever expected." She listened for a moment. "I'm sure you're right, but I won't know until you see it and tell me how brilliant I am!" Polly laughed and looked at Gerold. "Darling," she cooed, "I am having one problem. Yes, I know that's what you're there for, which is why I'm calling. It has to do with the director."

Gerold shouted, "Forget it! I'm through! Get your butt back onstage for another run-through!" He quickly left the dressing room.

Polly returned to her call. "Sorry. No hablas Espanole! Wrong-o numero," she said and flipped the phone shut. She smiled at Tim for faking the connection to J.J. "You're too clever. Now, where can we safely stash this until we get home?" Polly retrieved the roster page—which had been folded into sixteenths—from inside her bra. She looked around for the right place to hide the document.

"Give it here," Placenta said, swiping the page from Polly's hand. "No one will think to look in a bottle of champagne." She slipped the folded paper into a Ziplock sandwich-size bag and ran her finger over the strip to seal it tight. Placenta then uncorked a half-full bottle of Dom and stuffed the bag down the neck of the container.

"Are you sure it won't get wet?" Polly begged. "That's all the evidence we've got!"

Placenta rolled her eyes. "Relax. I smuggled a bag of marijuana into my college dorm this way. Of course it was a liter of Pepsi, but the principle is the same. Now, get into your first act costume! Tim, go hang out with the security guys until Polly's ready."

Per Gerold's orders, the stage manager dismissed the company at four o'clock. Placenta helped Polly remove her makeup and to change from her stunning white faux-fur curtain-call costume into her everyday chic-but-bounce-around clothes. By the time the wardrobe lady came by to collect Polly's costumes for washing and ironing, the dressing room was deserted.

Tim guided the Rolls along the freeway and eventually got off at Sunset Boulevard for the last leg of the journey to Bel Air. When he reached the Pepper Plantation gates Tim pressed the automatic opener, and they drove down the cobbled lane. "Home at last!" Polly declared. "Let's go break open the champagne. And I don't mean a new bottle from the fridge . . . but do that too."

The trio practically raced up the two front steps. When the security system was disarmed they quickly headed to the great room. "I'll get a hammer," Placenta said as she left for the utility closet inside the garage. When she returned, Polly had uncorked the bottle and poured what remained of the champagne. "What a waste," she proclaimed as Placenta proffered her hammer and placed the bottle in a brown paper bag. Polly set the bag on the floor and lifted the hammer into the air. One blow was all that was required and the bottle shattered.

"Use gloves," Placenta said, handing Polly a pair of Hector's work gloves.

"Oh, I can feel his strong hands in here," Polly sighed, then immediately returned to her mission. She carefully opened the bag and looked inside. As Placenta had promised, the sandwich bag was waterproof, and Polly collected it with her gloved hand. "I should buy stock in the company that makes this stuff," she said, admiring the way the plastic bag locked out moisture just as the television ads promised.

Once she had shaken the plastic bag of all shards of glass, Polly removed her gloves and unsealed it. She retrieved the paper and unfolded it. Together, the three looked at the roster and tried to create a timeline for when each of the suspects had arrived and left the theater.

"I'm torn," Polly finally said. "I can't risk accusing Gerold when clearly it appears that Charlotte and Jamie were in the theater at the time of Karen's death. Gerold has an alibi with Jamie, or so they claim. Charlotte has zip."

"Jamie and Gerold supposedly didn't get together until after Karen's death," Tim reminded her. "So really neither of them has concrete alibis."

Polly turned to Tim. "Remember when Gerold came into the office and he was yelling at someone on his cell? I'll bet it was Jamie on the other end of the line. Gerold said, 'Our dressing room.' You paged him to dressing room number seven, which is where they had their 'audition.'"

Tim nodded. "I still don't understand why Jamie is banned from the theater. Unless he's like *The Man Who Knew Too Much*."

262 R. T. Jordan

"We need another conversaysheoney with Jamie," Polly sang. "Call him. Tell him that he's being feted tonight at Pepper Plantation and that you'll pick him up in an hour. I'll get to the bottom of this Gerold thing."

At eight o'clock Polly was in the great room with Tim and Placenta, and they were all doing their best to surreptitiously give Jamie a champagne buzz as quickly as possible. At the hands of the champagne masters at Pepper Plantation, Jamie never stood a chance. Soon he was as gregarious as Tom Cruise on a talk show couch. Placenta served hors d'oeuvres and pizza from Spago, and Polly made certain that his champagne flute was never empty. Finally, when Polly steered the topic around toward *Mame* and how unprofessional it was of Gerold to go back on his word after promising to cast Jamie in the show, Jamie suddenly became sullen.

"Anything the matter?" Polly asked.

Jamie shrugged his shoulders. "This show changed my life. I lost my partner and best friend. I lost a role that I've played a gazillion times. And I've been blacklisted from L.A. theater."

"Blacklisted?" Polly said.

"Gerold is punishing me. He's afraid that I'll tell—"

Suddenly the sound of the chime from the front gate startled everyone. Polly looked at Tim, who looked at Placenta, who shrugged her shoulders as if to say, "Don't look at me."

Tim went to the intercom on the wall and pushed the speaker button. "Yes?"

"We're here," an ebullient voice declared. "It's Mag and Charlotte. We've brought along a little surprise." There was excitement in her voice.

Polly clapped her hands together. "My Emmy! I completely forgot! This is the night that my little darling comes home! Let them in!" she demanded, completely forgetting about Jamie and the reason Gerold was punishing him. "Somebody meet them at the door." Placenta accepted the duty and scuttled out of the room. "Oh, how could I have been so stupid to forget this special night?" She looked at Tim and Jamie. "We all have to act completely surprised when Charlotte presents my Emmy back to me. I'm supposed to pretend that I don't know it's coming. Then I have to canonize Charlotte and offer her a reward."

Jamie looked at Polly. "Offer Charlotte a reward? She's the reason that Karen's dead. You can't canonize an accessory to murder."

Polly and Tim both looked at Jamie with stunned interest.

"If she hadn't begged Sharon Fletcher to bring in her Emmy—with plans to steal it—Karen would be alive today."

"Who struck Karen?" Polly asked, looking intently into Jamie's eyes. "You're already blacklisted. What do you have to lose by coming clean with the truth?"

Jamie was about to speak when he was interrupted by Mag and Charlotte entering the great room.

Polly was too excited to wait for the rest of Jamie's statement and walked over to the new arrivals. She bestowed a whisper of a kiss to their left cheeks. "Mag, dear. Charlotte, darling," she cooed. "You must have guessed we were having champagne tonight," she teased and ushered them into the room. "Of course you know my precious friend Jamie Livingston."

"Never thought I'd see you again," Charlotte said, coldly addressing Jamie.

"Aren't you the lucky one?" Jamie retuned the icy greeting.

Sensing that the temperature of the room had suddenly dipped to Minnesota in January, Polly immediately went into gracious hostess mode. "A glass of champers will make your spirits bubble," she said to Mag and Charlotte. "Two more, Placenta," she called out, even as her maid was uncorking another bottle.

"We were just having the most amazing conversation about the show, and about Jamie and Gerold and the murder and—"

"I wish you wouldn't," Jamie said with an awkward smile.

Polly noticed that Jamie and Charlotte had locked eyes. "At least we'll soon be able to put all of this ugliness behind us," Polly continued as she raised her glass of champagne to the others, who were already sipping their own drinks. "A toast to one of the great men of the theater. Not Ziegfeld. Not Belasko. Not even Sondheim. I'm referring to George, our very own stage doorman. He died last night, poor soul. But before he left this world, I convinced him to send a letter to the detectives working on Karen's murder case and to detail everything that he heard and saw that dreadful morning. Cheers to you, George!"

The only others who echoed Polly were Tim and Placenta. Mag, Charlotte, and Jamie stared at each other. Finally, Mag said, "I never knew the old man's name. What did dear George say in his letter?"

"From what I gathered, he had important information that detailed an altercation between Karen, Gerold, and a couple of cast members. All that he would mention to me was that there were peculiar comings and goings of certain people in the company that fateful morning. Canapés, dear?" she asked Charlotte and pointed to Placenta holding a platter.

Charlotte looked at the appetizers but shook her head. Placenta moved on to Mag, who also rejected the offering.

"That murder is old news. Sharon Fletcher will be locked away forever. But Charlotte Bunch has a great big surprise for you." Mag practically sang the sentence.

Polly presented a wide smile and said, "Gosh! I love surprises! Let me guess, you've going to Alan Thicke's estate sale on Saturday. You're having a colonoscopy. You're returning my Emmy."

Charlotte's smile instantly faded. She held out a soiled brown paper bag. "I found this while walking in the park," she said, speaking rehearsed lines. "The engraving says that it belongs to you."

Polly accepted the bag. "It's a heavy sucker." She set the bag down on the coffee table and slowly opened it and peered inside. With all the histrionics she could muster, Polly screeched, "I was right! My beautiful, long-lost first love has returned to me! How? What? Where?" She pretended to be nearly speechless.

Charlotte perked up, as if Polly's guess had been nothing more than a joke. "You should use your psychic gifts to find a good plastic surgeon for your neck," she said. "I was walking through West Hollywood Park yesterday and I literally tripped over the bag," Charlotte recounted the false story.

"It's a miracle," Placenta said, exaggerating her belief in the story. "And the irony is too much to bear. Imagine, you of all people on the planet, tripping over Polly's *stolen* Emmy."

Charlotte ignored Placenta and instead focused on Polly's obvious exhilaration. "I was appalled when I heard about you being ripped off, and I'm overwhelmed that I get to be the bearer of good news!"

By now, Jamie was sufficiently inebriated. He'd had more champagne than food and was feeling bold. He lashed out at Charlotte. "Why didn't you keep the award?" he asked. "You went through so much trouble to get it."

Charlotte made an uncomfortable laugh. "I don't have the vaguest notion of what you mean," she said.

"Did I say 'keep'?" Jamie said. "I meant sell," he corrected himself.

"You're drunk," Charlotte berated Jamie. "And you

wonder why Gerold wouldn't hire you for the role you so obviously coveted."

"It's not my intake of champagne that stopped Gerold from giving me the role that was rightfully mine," Jamie balked. "It was his way of punishing me. You ought to know that."

"God knows he punishes me daily," Polly said. "But what exactly happened between you two?"

The room was silent. "Another glass of champagne, please," Jamie said. As Placenta poured, Jamie began thinking about the events of the past two weeks. He looked at Mag and raised an eyebrow.

"What the hell?" Jamie looked at Polly. "After Karen's death I made the mistake of trying to convince him to keep his promise and give me the role of Patrick Dennis. I said that if he didn't let me have the part, I'd go to the police."

"Blackmail, eh?" Polly said.

As if manipulated by unseen strings, Polly, Tim, and Placenta all simultaneously lifted their champagne glasses to their lips and took long swallows.

"I was angry," Jamie continued. "Gerold had used me, and he wasn't keeping his part of our bargain, even after Karen, who was the only obstruction to my getting the role, had died."

"But the plan backfired," Polly guessed. "Not only did you not get the role, you were banned from the theater, and Gerold put out the word to all the other theaters in town that you were trouble."

"That's it. But I hold this bitch mainly responsible," Jamie spat, pointing to Charlotte. "She's wanted me out of the way since the day she tried to steal Sharon's Daytime Emmy Award."

"That's a lie!" Charlotte barked.

"Oh, sure it's true, sweetheart," Polly said in a soothing tone. "I know all about your desperate need for extra cash, and that you took my Emmy to buy meds. MPD must be an awful disease. Thank God you're in the theater where you're actually expected to be a weirdo. I'm not pressing charges. You deserve to bank the hours needed to requalify for your insurance."

Chapter 34

When Polly joined Tim and Placenta at the breakfast table the next morning, it was obvious that she hadn't slept well. Her eyes were puffy, her mood irritable, and her appetite nil. "New rule, number one," she finally said after drinking half of the Bloody Mary that Placenta had set before her. "No murder suspects as houseguests the night before an opening. God, how will I get through this day, let alone through tonight's performance?"

Tim was equally tired, but as the caffeine from his second mug of coffee slipped into his bloodstream he was at least able to speak, albeit in monosyllables. "'Kay," he said.

"New rule, number two," Polly added. "One career is enough. The next time I agree to do a project and one of the props is a real live corpse, don't let me get involved. If this production of *Mame* is as lousy as I'm afraid it is, it's all my fault for not giving a hundred percent of my time and talent. My attention was divided between dead people and ripped-off Emmys."

"Yep," Tim said, knowing full well that his mother would never be able to keep her nose out of anything as interesting as a murder investigation.

"New rule, number three," Polly continued. "Don't let me fall in love with anyone who doesn't call me every single day. I haven't heard from Randy in ages."

As Placenta removed frozen waffles from the toaster, she looked at Polly. "Detective Randy calls you every day!"

"But he didn't call last night to wish me sweet dreams."

"He was busy busting Britney Spears," she said.

Polly knew that she was being stupid about not speaking to Randy during the past fifteen hours. She also knew, from years of showbiz experience, that her attitude was simply a manifestation of her fear about opening night. It was natural. Polly was aware that everyone gets the jitters before facing an audience and critics who can either make or break a show. She was also adding self-condemnation to her mounting anxiety for not being able to connect the dots and arrive at someone other than Sharon to finger as Karen Richards's killer. "Lord," she prayed aloud, "if you let me get through this opening, I promise that Placenta won't invoke your name to telemarketers."

Placenta harrumphed. "No use making promises to the Lord that I don't intend to keep! Pray for something practical . . . like a living wage for your staff."

"Bigger allowance for your son and consort," Tim said, finally able to put two words together.

Polly faked a chuckle, then sang, "Some of God's greatest gifts are unanswered prayers."

Polly looked at the kitchen clock and made a sound not unlike someone despairing of having to go to school. "Why don't I retire? I'm too old for opening night jitters."

"You pretend that you can't afford to," Placenta teased. "But somehow you manage to pay for all of Tim's parties. It's the leading up to your entrance onstage that scares you."

Polly nodded. "But this time it's different. There's a killer in our midst. I won't be able to concentrate on my lines and those ridiculous new dance steps."

270 R. T. Jordan

The morning and afternoon moved by quickly and soon it was time to leave for the theater. Placenta packed the trunk of the Rolls with Polly's party gown, shoes, and jewelry, as well as her own formal wear and Tim's tuxedo. She made room for shopping bags from Tiffany and Cartier that held opening night gifts for the cast, director, and stage hands. Placenta made sure that Polly also had something for the new security guards at the stage door entrance. And then they were on their way.

For a long while there was no conversation in the car. For one thing, Polly was saving her voice for her performance. Tim and Placenta also didn't want to break Polly's concentration as she was going over lines and lyrics in her head. For another, they were all still consumed with trying to put their fingers on any piece of evidence—hearsay or otherwise—that would point to Karen Richards's murderer.

At six o'clock, Polly's Rolls-Royce glided into the parking lot behind the Galaxy Theatre. Tim eased the vehicle into the space next to the stage door that had been marked with a temporary sign that said: MISS PEPPER. "Someone in this dump has a little class," Polly growled, still feeling apprehensive about the show and her performance.

Tim said, "You two go ahead. I'll unpack the truck."

Even before opening Polly's dressing room door, she and Placenta were met with the scent of fresh flowers. When they entered the room, there was hardly a space that did not contain a colorful bouquet or green plant. Polly smiled warmly and like a honeybee that unexpectedly stumbled on a vast meadow of wildflowers, she went from arrangement to arrangement and put her nose into the petals. "Read me the cards!" she said with a little girl's excitement. "Oh, this one must be from Barbra," she said, pointing to a lavish collection of white orchids. "And I'll guess that dear Carol sent me the moonshadow carnations. Yes? Ha! I thought so!"

Placenta went around the room and picked up a card, reading it, then replacing it in its accompanying arrangement. Red roses. Sunflowers. Fruit and gourmet food baskets. There were so many expressions of her friends' love and affection. For the first time in weeks, Polly felt at peace. For the moment at least, she didn't care about killers running around the theater, or whether or not she would be able to hold the notes in the songs. She was simply happy to be the iconic Polly Pepper. She actually felt sorry for anyone who wasn't her.

When Tim arrived with her party clothes and the cast gifts, Placenta reminded Polly that she must personally deliver the opening night presents.

"Delighted!" Polly said, knowing that she'd be received as the great and generous lady that she cultivated as her persona. "We're a little early, so I'll simply leave the little prezies in their dressing rooms," Polly said. "Better get Luther Ray and his keys to escort me. Wouldn't want to be accused of breaking and entering."

While Placenta arranged the floral gifts and made room for Polly to dress and do her makeup, Tim and his mother went to the stage door desk. With gifts in hand, Polly was prepared for Luther Ray and Orvine, and both men were speechless when she presented them with colorfully wrapped boxes tied with blue ribbons and a personalized card that said *Something from moi to vous. Love, Polly Pepper.*

"The deluxe edition DVD collection of the first season of *The Polly Pepper Playhouse.*" Orvine beamed after unwrapping his gift.

"It's not Tiffany, like the bag I put it in, but how long will bling last? My show is forever."

To their credit, both men were genuinely pleased that Polly Pepper had thought to remember them on her gift list. She had them where she wanted and asked if they would open the dressing room doors in order that she might make her colleagues feel important. Tim nudged Polly as he always did when he felt that the needle on her obsequiousness meter was rising too high.

One by one Polly left a box in each dressing room. Of course, each gift was the same as Luther Ray's and Orvine's present. When she was finished with the cast, she moved on toward Gerold's office on the mezzanine level of the theater. As she and Tim walked down the carpeted corridor they stopped short of Gerold's office door when they heard his familiar booming voice cursing at someone.

Gerold's voice was loud enough to penetrate the door and echo in the corridor. "You've ruined it!" he bellowed. "She's not as stupid as she looks or pretends to be! If you don't get rid of that poor excuse for a legend, I will! Make it tonight, after the show!"

Polly and Tim looked at each other and instantly decided to retreat to the sanctuary of Polly's dressing room. They both turned around and started to retrace their steps down the hallway. But they were suddenly faced with Mag Ryan rounding the corner and stopping in her tracks. Quickly, Polly held up her bag with Gerold's present. "Just making the rounds. I sincerely hope that you like the gift I left in your room, dear."

Mag smiled. "I just opened it. Your old show was in color, and everything." Then she looked down the hall in the direction from which Polly and Tim had come. "Is Gerold not in? We were just talking."

"I don't know, dear," Polly lied. "We got halfway to his office and I realized I had the wrong gift! Imagine me giving anything less than Cartier to the show's director? Where on earth have I put my head? I'm rushing back to find the little box and the *trés* expensive bauble that I selected expressly for our dear Gerold. So, if you'll excuse us, we're on a mission to find that wee token of my sincere esteem."

Mag gave Polly a quizzical look. She then looked back down the corridor toward Gerold's office. "If that's another special DVD collection of your show, I'm sure that Gerold would love to have that too. Why don't we go and personally deliver it to him?"

Tim stepped in and said, "He has this DVD set. When it was first released his name was on the comp list. Polly made sure that every television, film, and theater producer and director in town received copies. Wanted to keep them aware that Polly's still around and ready for a job." He attempted a small chuckle.

"He sold it on eBay," Mag said, evading Tim's attempt to talk his way out of Polly having to confront Gerold.

"Then I should think he wouldn't want this one either." Polly began moving forward, but Mag stood in her way.

"Seriously, I know he'd love it," Mag said as she linked her arms in Polly's and Tim's and began guiding them back toward Gerold's office.

When they arrived at the door, Gerold was again yelling. "Yes! Tonight!" he roared. "I don't care how! Just do it!"

Mag knocked on the door and was greeted with silence. "H. Bear," she said, announcing herself with their lovers' pet name. "Honey Bear, it's me. I've brought a marvelous surprise for you."

The door opened and Gerold stood looking at Polly and Tim. "What?" he said with caution in his voice.

"Your darling star has a present for you," Mag said. "I found them walking away from your door. The sweet thing didn't want to bother you because it sounded as though you were terribly busy. As if you're ever too busy for Miss Polly Pepper."

Gerold looked at Polly with uncertainty.

"We should head back to my dressing room," Polly said. "Silly me, I left your opening night present there. It's very personal and very expensive. So let us rush back and retrieve it, pronto."

Polly attempted to leave, but Mag blocked the doorway. "You're too good to be true. You played well with Charlotte last night. You even listened to Jamie and didn't pressure him for more information. It's nice to find someone who's all ears and listens with patience. I'll bet you listened to Sharon Fletcher when she said she was innocent. You obviously believed her too."

Polly suddenly became emboldened. "Look, Mag, we've got an important show to perform in about an hour," she said in a threatening tone. "We should both be in our rooms resting our voices or going over our lines." She turned to Gerold. "As our director, it's about time you called everyone together for a preshow pep talk, in case you aren't aware of this tradition." Looking again at Mag, Polly said. "You've never gotten through a rehearsal without screwing up the Ping-Pong scene. You should definitely be rehearsing those lines!" Polly turned around and opened the door. This time, neither Mag nor Gerold tried to stop her or Tim.

By the time Polly and Tim reached the dressing room, Placenta was frantic. "It's almost half hour!" she said. "You've got to rush to get into your costume!"

"I'm screwed!" Polly said as she sat before her makeup mirror and began to apply her foundation. "Tim and I overheard Gerold plotting to kill me after the show. He's got someone else to do the dirty work. I'm just afraid that whoever the executioner is will take both of you out too. I'm sorry to have gotten you involved in this mess," she said as she started to cry.

Tim and Placenta both rushed to Polly's side. Tim said, "We don't know for sure that Gerold is planning to harm you. When he said, 'Get rid of that poor excuse for a legend,' he may have meant the car." He knew he was grasping at straws, but he was desperate to calm Polly and try to make sense of why they had landed in such trouble.

"La, if this is to be my farewell performance, then I'm going out there and giving the best damn show of my life. I'm just pissed off that I won't get to Broadway after all! I'm not going to worry about my fate. I was born an icon, and I intend to leave this planet with rave reviews." Polly turned to Tim. "I just hope that you've saved a fabulous party theme for my memorial service. I take back what I said in the past about not wanting Jayne Meadows and Nanette Fabray in attendance. I just didn't think they'd survive me. Everyone in show business should be there. The entire guest list is in my office filing cabinet. Ask Elton if I've left anyone important off."

Placenta was in the process of removing Polly's bugle-beaded party pantsuit from a dry cleaning plastic bag, when a knock on the door was followed by a voice that called out, "Half hour, Miss Pepper. And Mr. Goss wants everyone to meet at the stage door exit at five-to."

"I had to remind the no-talent SOB to give his cast a pep talk before the curtain goes up," Polly said. "He's not the most articulate slob on the planet, so I won't expect anything nearly as loquacious as a Tom Hanks acceptance speech for one of his gazillions of awards."

At five to eight, another knock on the door summoned Polly to the cast meeting with Gerold. Polly looked every inch the megawatt star that she was, but her hands were shaking. She looked at Tim and Placenta. "I'll see you both during intermission. And when the show is over, we'll dash to the party together. Please pray that our Little Patrick doesn't throw up again. He ruined my favorite dress last night."

Polly hugged her son and Placenta. Then she opened the door and slowly marched toward the group of cast members who were assembled with Gerold Goss. When she arrived the knot of performers parted to allow Polly to stand only inches from Gerold.

Chapter 35

"It was just a lot smoke up our collective hineys," Polly said to Tim and Placenta when she returned from the cast huddle with Gerold. "After two weeks of torture, Gerold is now all smiles and wishing us success and telling us how much he loves us and how proud he is to be our director. Rubbish, of course, but I applauded anyway. I'm sure every employee has to kiss up to his boss, no matter what business one is in."

Polly kissed Tim, then Placenta and opened her dressing room door. "It's showtime. Go to your seats," she said to reassure her family.

Reluctantly Tim, now dressed in his tuxedo, and Placenta, wearing a Caroline Herrera strapless dress that she found at Marshall's, agreed to leave Polly in the stage wings and join her fans in the audience. "Break a leg!" Tim said.

"Be prepared to be blown away by the one and only, the witty and charming, the star of stage, screen, and records, the icon of international icons, Miss Polly Pepper!" the star said.

Placenta blew Polly a kiss.

Within moments of Tim and Placenta being ushered to

their seats in the center of the sixth row, and before the houselights had completely dimmed, a bright spotlight hit the conductor in the musicians' pit and the famous Jerry Herman overture began. The audience erupted with applause for the familiar and favorite songs. The music, although much of it canned, further added to the expectation of the audience seeing not only one of Broadway's all-time-favorite and longest-running shows, but for the thrill of watching Polly Pepper sing and dance live onstage before them.

When the overture ended and more applause ensued, there was a hush as the curtains parted to reveal a darkened set that looked like the waterlogged French Quarter in New Orleans. The time was obviously night. Then Charlotte Bunch, wearing a shabby wool coat and scarf, and holding the hand of a little boy, walked onto the stage and began to speak her lines. With a backdrop of the Superdome in ruins, she was soon singing "St. Brigid," a song that was supposed to help keep up the spirits of the young orphan boy whom she was taking to his rich auntie Mame.

In a moment, the set changed and a raucous party was in full force with Dixieland bands and anonymous guests dancing and drinking. Then, the moment that everyone had waited for: Polly Pepper appeared at the top of a sweeping curved staircase. The audience applauded for a full minute before she was able to speak her first lines and fly down the stairs to greet her party guests. And the night was on.

Applause followed applause after every song. Laughter was raucous and inspired more laughter whenever Polly uttered a clever line or raised an eyebrow in response to a line uttered by Charlotte or Emily Hutcherson. The night definitely belonged to Polly Pepper.

Intermission arrived and Tim and Placenta made their way backstage and quoted to Polly the superlatives they'd heard from the audience. Tim intentionally omitted such gems as "For an old puss she still has balls." As well as "I told you she wasn't dead."

Polly was perspiring heavily and barely had time for a hug and a shower before she had to be dressed in a new costume and waiting in the wings. "We'll be back after the show." Tim kissed his mother on the cheek.

The second half of the show was as fulfilling as the first. When the curtain rang down, a standing ovation ensued. Polly, front and center of her cast, curtsied for the audience a dozen times before she was allowed to leave the stage. As she made her way toward her dressing room, members of the cast praised her. She smiled and offered variations on "I couldn't have done it without you." Or "You made me look good." As well as "I'm just a lucky star." When she arrived in her dressing room she closed the door behind her and quickly uncorked a bottle of Cristal that had been sent to her by Liz Smith. Polly was parched and didn't wait to fill a glass. She raised the neck of the bottle to her lips and took a long fulfilling swallow. "Praise Liz!" she said, looking up to heaven.

When Tim knocked on the door, Polly placed the bottle in the small porcelain sink, and checked herself in the mirror. Then she opened the door to receive her family and their delirious raves for her performance. "Hold off the fans while I shower and slip into my party clothes," she instructed.

While Placenta helped Polly make haste, Tim stepped outside the door to greet Polly's well-wishers and explain that they would be allowed to see the star in just a few minutes. "She won't mind me seeing her undressed," Goldie Hawn said and pushed her way past Tim and entered the dressing room. "Same for me," Doris Roberts said and followed Goldie. Although Tim tried to coral his mother's friends, they practically stampeded into the room. "You don't mind, do you, sweetie?" Bette Midler said to him. "Hi, dear," Carol Burnett added and patted Tim on the cheek as she passed by.

"Do you think I stand a chance of getting in there too?"

Tim looked up at the familiar male voice and smiled into Detective Archer's eyes. "What did you think of the show?"

"I thought Polly was amazing. I had no idea that she was so talented . . . and famous. Heck, if I'd known that she was a real star, not just someone who'd once been on television, I wouldn't have had the *cajones* to ask her out in the first place."

"Just don't treat her any different in private," Tim advised. "She needs the attention of fans who remember when she was really big, but she also wants to believe that she can be loved just for who she is . . . a star, but one who is unaffected. She lies to herself a lot."

"Nothing between us will change, because I know the real Polly Pepper," Detective Archer agreed. "I suppose there's a cast party, eh?"

"You're Polly's date," Tim said.

Just then, the door to the dressing room opened wide and the rest of the waiting throng tried to squeeze in. When this proved futile, Polly loudly suggested, "Why don't we all hug and kiss at the party. It'll be easier to hear all of your tributes of admiration, wonder, and awe when we're at the restaurant."

Everyone seemed to agree, and in a short while the room was cleared and Polly began to finish putting on her makeup. Just as she was about to suggest they run along to the party, Tim said, "Your escort awaits."

At that moment Detective Archer stepped into the dressing room. He and Polly smiled simultaneously at each other and as he stood over her, he withdrew a small box from his suit coat pocket. "It's not Tiffany," he said. "But the lady at Wal-Mart said . . . I'm kidding. It's just a little thing to say congratulations."

Polly beamed and untied the ribbon around the white box. She opened the lid and her eyes lit up.

"I said it wasn't Tiffany, but the lady who sold it to me said it was 'Tiffany inspired,' whatever that means."

Polly touched the contents of the box and picked up a beautiful sterling silver pendant in the shape of the Man in the Moon. "You're as precious as this beautiful piece of jewelry," she cooed to Randy, who then bent down to kiss Polly on the lips. "This is absolutely perfect. Did you know before seeing the show that I do a whole number on the Man in the Moon? You must be psychic. Either that or we're perfectly connected." Polly stood up and gave Randy a kiss and a tight hug. "Placenta, would you do the honors? she said, trying to unclasp the hook. When Placenta succeeded at hanging the chain around Polly's neck, everyone oohed and aahed and agreed that it was the ideal gift. "Now that I'm all decked out, let's get to the party," Polly said as she picked up the bottle of Cristal out of the sink and took one final swig.

As Polly sat in the back of the Rolls-Royce basking in her triumph she finally said, "Have you ever seen such an avante-garde production of this show? Jerry Herman probably had a stroke when he saw the choreography. But the audience seemed to adore me . . . and the show . . . so perhaps I'm just old and not able to keep in step with the times. I'm just now beginning to like Beyoncé, so you know what age group I'm in!"

"You've got a hit," Tim said from the driver's seat. "I hate to say this, but what Gerold and that choreographer creature did to freshen the show was darned smart. *Mame* needed a slap in the rear end."

Polly sighed and begged, "Pretty please, let the reviews

be raves and we get to go to New York." She looked out her window and frowned. "Where the hell are we?"

"It's called 'Burbank,'" Placenta said. "We're going to the Holiday Inn."

Polly sighed. "Be prepared to raid the trunk refrigerator if the champagne isn't at least Krug Grand Cuvée!"

As the car pulled up to the valet, Tim allowed Polly and Randy to exit first. One lone photographer stood snapping photographs, but Polly pretended that she was among dozens of paparazzi. She posed and preened and made sure that Randy was included in several shots. They all shared a laugh of indifference as they followed Polly and Randy to the elevator.

As they ascended to the rooftop of the hotel where the opening night party was in full swing, Polly winked at Tim. "Maybe Gerold was talking about his car after all."

Tim nodded and for the benefit of Randy said, "An inside joke."

Randy was suddenly on high alert. "I don't trust Gerold."

As the elevator doors opened onto the terrace, a pianist was playing songs from the Cole Porter catalog, and the place was jammed with guests. Suddenly, it seemed as though everyone had noticed Polly at the same time and the crowd erupted with wild applause. Polly curtsied as she had onstage and clasped her hands to her heart. Then, with open arms, she moved into the crowd to accept hugs and commendations from the three hundred invited guests. Tim quickly arrived at her side with a flute of champagne and she gratefully accepted the drink. When she spotted Gerold Goss standing alone under one of the dozens of outdoor heaters set up throughout the space, she moved toward him. "Cheers!" She clinked her flute against his martini glass. "I have to confess, you did a swell job of pulling this off. I'm still not wild about the guy who plays my adult nephew—"

"Stewart Long," Gerold reminded her.

"Whatever. He's still the weakest link," Polly said. Then she slipped into a melancholy reverie. "Poor Karen," she said. "I wish she were here to see my triumph."

"The show wouldn't have been the same," Gerold snapped. "For one thing, she didn't have the spine to take chances, as I did. Sure, you would have been fine if she'd directed you. But I made the show into something unique. I've breathed new life into the old warhorse. There's no way that today's Broadway audiences would accept the original staging of this musical. It's too old-fashioned. When you've got shows like *Wicked* running away with the box office, this thing had to be updated. Karen didn't have the vision for that."

Polly sighed. "Perhaps you're right about the show needing a contemporary look, but Karen would still have made this classic shine. Whoever bumped her off deprived us of the magic she would have brought to the material. And Sharon Fletcher would have been ideal as Gloria. Not that your Mag is too dreadful."

"Thanks for the rave review," Mag said as she sidled up to Gerold. "I'm thrilled that you approve so highly of me, Miss Pepper."

Polly smiled. "You're perfectly adequate, dear."

Mag looked at Gerold. "I could use another drinky. Would you mind?" She handed her wineglass to Gerold and he left to retrieve a refill.

"One for me too," Polly called after him. Then she looked at Mag. "I thought we had a little agreement, dear," she said, in a voice that was barely audible. "In exchange for your freedom—I can still press charges—you were going to point me toward Karen's killer. I guess it's too much to ask that you keep your promise."

"I haven't forgotten. I just don't know how to go about ratting out someone very special to me."

Polly was suddenly animated. "So you have information? Tell me. Now!"

"You know as well as I do. You just want a confession, don't you?"

Polly tried not to show her lack of understanding. Instead, she smiled and said, "Guess I'm not such a good actress after all, at least not to you." She looked around and said, "Where's that drink? I'm parched." Then, out of the corner of her eye, she saw Jamie Livingston. *Jeans and a tank are hardly appropriate attire for this affair*, she said to herself but pretended that she hadn't seen him. "Shall we go get our own drinks? That sloth Gerold has probably been waylaid by . . ." She looked over and indeed Gerold was in deep conversation with someone. That someone was the show's composer, Jerry Herman. Mr. Herman kept shaking his head and Polly knew that he wasn't pleased with what he'd witnessed earlier in the evening. "Let's go have a listen, shall we?" she said to Mag and began moving toward the famous composer.

When Mr. Herman saw Polly his attitude immediately changed. He opened his arms to her and kissed her cheeks.

"I've always been in love with you and your work," Polly said to Mr. Herman. "As long as I'm in your show, I promise to maintain at least the integrity of Mame Dennis. God knows I have no creative control over the rest of the production." She looked at Gerold. "We're on our way to the bar. May we get anything for either of you?"

Polly once again accepted kisses to her cheek from Herman, and led Mag by the hand toward the bar. When they each had their preferred libation, Mag asked, "Why are you dragging this whole thing out? Why not just get it over with?"

"I'm waiting for all the players to be here. Oh, and look," Polly said, pointing into the crowd. "There's dear Jamie."

Mag was surprised and nearly spilled her glass of wine. "What the hell is he doing here?"

"I suspect he's come to watch the fireworks."

When Jamie spotted Polly and Mag looking in his direction he stepped out of the crowd and came up to them. "Sorry I missed the show," he said, looking at Polly. "But thanks for the invitation to the party."

"It was important for you to be here," Polly said. "If it were not for a simple twist of Karen's fate, we'd be raising a glass to a splendid Patrick Dennis. As it is we're stuck with . . ."

Polly realized that the noise from the crowd had faded and that she was subtly being forced out of sight from the other guests. Without losing her cool, Polly sensed that she was in danger and that soon she would be on the opposite side of the rooftop party area. She tried to glean a few more facts to still unanswered questions. "Jamie, dear," she began. "Something's been gnawing at me. The other night you said that Charlotte had wanted you out of the way ever since the day that she tried to steal Sharon's Daytime Emmy Award."

"Yeah, she's a good one for holding a grudge," Jamie said as he moved more openly to steer Polly to the waist-high rooftop wall. "I knew that I saw a look in your eye the other night when Charlotte dropped by. I never would have agreed to come over myself if I'd known she would be there too. She knows too much about . . . everything."

Polly stopped in her tracks and looked Jamie in the eye. "Truth. Before you do whatever it is you plan to do with me, for the record, I'd like for you to tell me all about Karen's death."

"But lying comes so natural to me," Jamie said. "After all, I'm an actor. Why would you believe anything that I have to say now?"

"What have you got to lose?" Polly said. She then pursed her lips and swallowed hard. "Before I go to my eternal opening night, I simply want you to corroborate my own conclusions about what happened that morning. I'll begin and you follow. Yes? Good. According to the sign-in sheet that George the stage doorman kept, Sharon arrived at eight-oh-five. Over the theater's intercom system he heard . . ."

Jamie looked puzzled.

"Surely you knew about the intercom. In addition to being meticulous about keeping records of everyone who came and went through his artists' entrance door, he kept an ear open for other potential problems that might arise throughout the theater. You know that speaker next to his desk? It's the theater intercom system. It's ancient of course, but it still works." Polly chuckled. "Or maybe George was just a voyeur. In any event, he was appalled by the way Gerold treated beautiful Sharon Fletcher. He told me everything that he overheard that morning . . . if you know what I mean."

"Then why do you need me to tell you what you already know? Karen didn't have to die if—"

"If she'd cast you in the show." Polly completed Jamie's sentence. "You wouldn't have had that argument with Gerold, and you wouldn't have taken your frustration and anger out with Sharon's Emmy."

"Karen actually tried to stop the argument," Mag said. "Jamie pushed Gerold and Gerold pushed him back. That's when Jamie picked up the Emmy. It was meant for Gerold. Karen accidentally got in the way."

"I was stunned by what I'd done in a moment of rage," Jamie said. "When it was obvious that Karen was dead . . . accidental though it was . . . Gerold realized he could take over the show. And, with no one to interfere with his casting decisions, Mag could now have the role of Gloria Upson."

Polly was dumbfounded. "So you all agreed that you'd cover for each other?"

"It wasn't like a pact or conspiracy," Jamie said. "We simply didn't talk about it."

Polly looked at each of them and shook her head. "A

woman is dead and you didn't even discuss the matter. You didn't count on Charlotte being in the theater, and witnessing the whole horrible event, did you? The next mistake was not allowing her to take the Emmy that she coveted. She would have gotten rid of the evidence for you."

"I thought she was taking it *as* evidence," Jamie said. "I didn't know she would sell the Emmy."

"Charlotte had been fired just a short while earlier, then suddenly she was rehired," Polly said. "Gerold couldn't—"

Suddenly Gerold was among the trio. "If Jamie hadn't wanted a job so badly, none of us would be in this situation," he snarled.

"You can't blame Jamie completely." Polly stared him down. "You and Mag and Charlotte also wanted jobs.

"You'd never be considered for director if the unexpected death of Karen Richards hadn't occurred. And Mag would never have had the opportunity to be in the show, because Karen had already cast the perfect actress for the role—Sharon Fletcher. Charlotte made out well too. Knowing what she knew about Karen's death, I'm surprised that you didn't give her my role."

Gerold looked at Polly with sad eyes. He shook his head as if to say *I hate to do this.* "Yeah, I really wish I'd have given Charlotte or anyone else your role. If I had, we wouldn't be standing here now. I love talent. I hate to see it go to waste. But you've left us no alternative."

Then like a pack of zombies, Gerold, Jamie, and Mag huddled around Polly and forced her to start backing up. Suddenly she was stopped when her body met the side of the waist-high wall. With deep fear in her eyes, Polly tried to stall for time. "Champagne!" she said. "I need a last glass of champagne! It's not proper execution etiquette to send someone to their death without granting a final wish."

"Have my wine," Mag said. "I'll get another when this is over."

Polly looked as though she had been accused of shopping at a 99-cent store. "Dear, I'm not going to my death with some cheap Merlot on my lips!"

Gerold heaved an angry sigh and looked at Mag. "Hurry," he said.

Mag charged away, walking as swiftly as possible without breaking into a run. When she arrived at the bar, there was a line but she barged her way to the front. "A tall glass of champagne for Polly Pepper, please," she demanded. The bartender opened a fresh bottle and poured a flute almost to the brim. Mag didn't wait to say thank you. She quickly turned around, and as she did so, she bumped into Tim and spilled some of the champagne on his tuxedo. "Get out of my way."

Tim was taken aback by Mag's attitude but decided to ignore her rudeness. "Where's Polly?"

"I don't know," Mag said as she darted away.

"But I heard you say the champagne was for Polly Pepper."

"I always drop stars' names to get immediate service," Mag called back before she disappeared into a crowd of guests.

Tim shook his head and wandered over to a table where Randy was seated with Placenta. "I'm getting worried about Polly. She loves a party but she seems to have disappeared."

Randy nodded. "As a matter of fact, half the cast has disappeared. I haven't seen Gerold, Mag, or Charlotte for quite some time."

"I just ran into Mag at the bar. She was acting queer. She ordered a glass of champagne for Polly, then ran off. Last time I checked, Mag was drinking red wine." Then gazing into the throng of happy revelers, Tim pointed to Charlotte Bunch. "Let's go see what she's up to."

The trio left the table with their drinks in hand and squeezed their way through the crowd until they reached

Charlotte, who was obviously tipsy. "Feeling all right, Charlotte?" Tim asked.

"A little tired," Charlotte said, trying to speak clearly and not show that she was becoming unsteady on her feet. She kept sipping her martini to maintain the ruse that she wasn't drunk.

"Have you seen Polly?" Tim asked. "She's not mingling with her guests."

Charlotte cocked her head toward the opposite side of the rooftop. "I saw her go off with Jamie a little while ago."

"Jamie?" Tim said. "He's not here. He wasn't invited."

"Trust me, a stud in a tank top and tight-fitting jeans doesn't pass my notice, especially at a black-tie affair like this one. I'd like to see him again. Let's all go take a look," she said and they all went in search of Jamie.

"Aren't you a doll," Polly said when Mag came back with a flute of champagne, a quarter of which had splashed out of the glass as she rushed back. Polly reached out for the glass.

"Drink up," Gerold demanded. "Mag was an idiot not to think to bring back the whole bottle. It would have gone well with your body twenty stories down, and helped to convince the coroner that you were so drunk that you accidentally fell off the rooftop."

Polly sipped as slowly as possible and continued to stall for time by asking questions. "Jamie, you're too attractive to be involved in this crime. I have friends in the police department. In fact, I'm dating a detective. I can help you out of this. You killed Karen by mistake. It wasn't premeditated. I swear I can help minimize your jail time."

Jamie seemed to be weighing the offer when Gerold said, "There won't be any jail time at all, because nobody else knows that Karen died at her lover's hands. No one other than us and Charlotte, and she's a clam."

Polly let out a loud laugh. "Charlotte? A clam? Well, maybe the Charlotte that we all know and love, but what about her other personalities? They all know too! Potentially, you've got dozens and dozens of witnesses!" she said, still laughing at the absurdity of Gerold not having considered this possibility.

"Where is Charlotte anyway?" Gerold asked. "If we're going to do this, she should be just as involved. To hell with her. We can't wait. Polly, finish up your drink. Now!"

Polly continued to stall, and an angry Gerold suddenly grabbed her champagne flute. He forcefully squeezed Polly's cheeks with one hand, and poured the champagne into her mouth, as one would a child who didn't want to take medicine. "There! It's time to say good-bye!"

As Polly leaned farther and farther over the wall, she felt her feet rising off the rooftop. "Don't do this to me, please! I promise not to say a word to anyone. You don't have to have three murders on your hands. Please!"

"Three?" Gerold said.

"George."

"The autopsy proved he had a stroke."

Suddenly a voice that sounded distinctly like Karen Richards said, "You got away with killing me, but a big star is another story."

Gerold, Jamie, and Mag turned around while holding Polly with her back resting on the lip of the wall. There was no one in sight. Then the voice spoke again. "Jamie," it said, "I still love you. I know that you didn't mean to kill me. My death was an accident. But if you take another life on purpose I won't get to see you in heaven."

Jamie released Polly and fell to his knees in fear.

"Who's there!" Gerold demanded. "Show yourself."

"It's Karen, of course. I can hardly show myself when I'm dead. If anyone is really responsible for the way things turned out, it's you, Gerold. You used my death to further your own career. It was your idea to let the police presume that Sharon Fletcher killed me. All the evidence pointed toward her and you did nothing to come forward with the truth. You let her take the rap."

As Gerold and Mag tried to fathom the disembodied voice of Karen Richards, Polly could feel their bodies shaking and herself slipping slowly over the side of the building. "Help me, Karen!" Polly shouted and in less than an instant, a dozen policemen rushed to the scene with their weapons drawn. Gerold and Mag let go of Polly, who tilted over the edge of the building like a teeter-totter. A cry erupted from her throat just as she completely lost her balance and began to fall. She squeezed her eyes shut, preparing for her death.

Just as suddenly two pairs of strong hands grabbed hold of her as Tim and Randy brought Polly back to safety.

Kneeling beside Polly, Randy cradled her in his arms. "Everything's all right now. You're safe. We're here with you."

Placenta rushed over to her side and bent down. "You'll be needing this," she said, holding another glass of champagne.

Polly chuckled. "I think I've had enough champagne. I was hearing voices. Karen's voice to be precise."

Then Charlotte stepped out from around the rooftop emergency exit. "If I don't get my meds pretty soon I'm going to get tired of having a dead woman walking around using my body," she said. "How's heaven, Karen?" she asked in her own voice. "The theater was better," Karen's voice issued through Charlotte's vocal cords.

"I'll take that drink after all," Polly said to Placenta.

Chapter 36

"You've made the front page of the *L.A. Times*, the front page of the Calendar section, and the front page of the Metro section," Tim said as he raced into the great room of Pepper Plantation and passed out still-warm copies of the daily paper to Polly, Placenta, and Randy.

"They like me! They really like me!" Polly squealed as she began to read aloud the reviews of *Mame*. "'Polly Pepper offered audiences an opportunity to witness the reason why she's a star and will always be a star.'" Polly smiled. "'Even though she's reported to now be in her sixties . . .'" Polly crumpled the paper and threw it aside.

"'. . . she only gets better with age,'" Tim continued to read from his own copy. Now Polly smiled and took the paper away from Tim. As she read the review, she skipped over the names of anybody else from the cast who was mentioned. "'Charlotte Bun . . . blah, blah, blah. Mag Ry . . . blah, blah, blah. Bosom Buddy, Emily Hutch . . . blah, blah, blah. But this is Polly Pepper's show.' Damn right it is!" Polly put an exclamation point on the review.

While Tim half listened to his mother, he was reading the front page of the *Times* and the lead story about Polly's near-death experience and how she had helped to bring the killer of director Karen Richards to justice. Suddenly he moaned, "Oh no!" interrupting his mother and the others who were reading their papers. "Listen to this. 'Although it's not exactly "the crime of the century," police have arrested four suspects in the slaying of local theater director Karen Richards. The inimitable Polly Pepper, who is starring at the Galaxy Theatre in Glendale in a production of *Mame* (see section E page 1), helped police capture and arrest two males and two females, whose identities have not been confirmed. A suspect who was arrested early in the investigation has been released.' We forgot about Sharon!" Tim wailed. He looked at his watch. "It's nearly five A.M., but you've got to call her."

In a moment, Polly was on the line with Sharon Fletcher. "Darling," Polly cooed, "I never gave up on you, not for one measly second! After your ordeal in jail you need a place to readjust, a sort of halfway house so you can easily move back to reality and your own life. I'm sending Tim and the car. You're spending the next month here at Pepper Plantation."

Sharon apparently didn't object, because Polly seemed pleased with herself for making the grand gesture. Then she added, "I hope you spent your time in jail memorizing your lines in the play, because we no longer have a Gloria Upson."

Polly stopped and listened for a moment. "You could go on tonight? Seriously? You soap stars are quick studies. We'll see you shortly, my dear. Ta!"

Tim looked at his mother with sleepy eyes. "You don't expect me to run over there now, do you? I'm exhausted."

"She can wait until ten or eleven, I suppose," Polly said. "'See you shortly' could mean anything in this town."

Placenta yawned. "Life can't get much better for you, Polly. You've solved another murder case, and you've got a hit show. What are you going to do next? Go to Disneyland?"

"Hell no! That's too expensive!" Polly said. She looked at Randy and smiled. "For one thing I'm going to be a mother again."

Everyone in the room erupted with wide-eyed surprise and shrieks of horror. Polly's shoulders sagged. "You're all nuts!" she said. "I'll be a surrogate mother to Sharon! Jeez, you all jump to the wildest conclusions!"

Randy relaxed and made the sign of the cross over his chest.

Placenta said, "Hail Mary, full of grease . . ."

Tim said, "If you really want to be a mother again, that cater waiter who was paid off by Charlotte and Mag would be a good candidate for adoption. I'd love to have a baby brother."

Polly patted her son on the cheek. "He'd end up like all your other pets. You promised to take care of that box turtle, and Placenta ended up doing all the work. And remember your chinchilla phase? Who fed those little buggers and cleaned out their cages? Placenta, of course. No, dear, you're not equipped to care for cute and cuddly little things. Which is why you're still single."

Tim sighed. "If I can't have a baby brother, I may as well go to bed."

"It's that time for all of us," Polly added. "I can't wait to rest my head on Randy's furry chest . . . um, I mean, *my* soft pillow! Don't anyone wake me until it's time to go to the theater. When Sharon gets here, let her sleep too."

Placenta stood up and started to collect the newspapers. "I just want to say one thing. Cheers to Miss Polly Pepper! You were marvelous in the show, and I'm glad that you didn't end up dead. It's bad enough to be stuck in a theater in Glendale. It would have been an insult to your career to be scraped off a street in Burbank."

As the household began to drift out of the room, sunshine began to filter in through the windows. Suddenly the telephone rang. "Let 'em leave a message," Polly said in a tired voice as she continued walking wearily to the door-way. The machine beeped and J.J. Norton's voice was on the line.

"Where's my beautiful and sexy star?" he gushed. "Rise and shine, precious! You've created a buzz! I've already had calls from executives at Fox and Lifetime."

Polly and Tim and Placenta each looked at each other in a way that said, "If J.J. is calling, it can only mean that he smells money."

Polly picked up the telephone. "I didn't expect you to attend my performance, but I thought you'd at least come to the party for free eats," she said, dismissing her agent. She listened for a moment. "HBO?" she asked. "A pilot?" All eyes in the room were focused on Polly. "Money?" she finally said and smiled at his response. "At this stage in my career I'm only interested in, well, in interesting projects. I can't make a decision at this hour! Call me later." Then she hung up the phone.

In a near trance, which was a combination of exhaustion and marvel that she was apparently a hot property again, Polly wafted through the room and pulled out a bottle of Veuve from the wine cooler.

"Breakfast?" Tim asked.

Polly chose not to respond to the remark. Instead, she said, "HBO wants me to do a show. I doubt that I'm even interested."

"Not interested!" Every voice in the room vied for the highest octave.

"As usual, J.J. blew a lot of smoke up my hiney, but the bottom line, so to speak, is that television has dramatically changed."

"You're not a star unless you're on television," Placenta interrupted. "You heard those security guards."

Polly sipped her flute of champagne and pondered Placenta's remark. "It's a goddamned *reality* show! We're not the Osbornes! We're a normal everyday garden variety family with a twenty-seven-room Bel Air mansion, headed by a living legend with international celebrity friends, and a few dead bodies to my credit."

"Mom, the dead people alone will make this show a hit," Tim said. "Let's face it, the money could be great, and I could use an increase in my allowance. Heck, if I become an instant celebrity myself, by way of a reality show, I wouldn't need an allowance."

"And I could afford not to work anymore," Placenta added.

As Polly finished off her glass she once again headed for bed. "We'll see," she said. "In the meantime, this legend needs to rest." She looked at Randy. "Are you coming, dear? How would you like to have your fifteen minutes of fame as my hunky consort?"